Cappuccino in the Winter

Valerie Rose

avid press LLC
Brighton, Michigan USA

AVID PRESS, LLC
5470 Red Fox Drive
Brighton, MI 48114-9079
http://www.avidpress.com

Published by arrangement with the author
ISBN: 1-929613-08-3

For information contact Avid Press, LLC.

First Avid Press printing October 1999

Acknowledgments

First and foremost, I give praise, glory and thanks to the divine infinite spirit, the Lord, my God, who relentlessly continues to guide, strengthen and sustain me through this wild, perplexing ride we call life.

To Oscar, who was my Black knight--the promised prince, incarnate, who scooped me up and whisked me away to destinations that I had only dared to tour in the recesses of my mind. For that, the good times, the passion of yesteryear, and our beautiful daughters I will always be eternally grateful.

To Mommy's chocolate jewels, Samantha Elayne and Taylour Alexandria for your extraordinary personalities and the sheer joy that you bring to my life.

To my mother and father who gave me unconditional love, time and time again. Thank you for being wonderful, loving parents and giving me the kind of childhood that as a child I assumed everyone had, but learned as an adult that I had been truly blessed.

To my sisters and brothers, Stella, Helen, Elzie Jr. and Jerome for your loving support.

Thank you to all of my family and friends who encouraged me pursue my life's dream.

Thank you to Soul Sistas, my online internet support group: Michelle J., Alicia, Jackie T. and Jackie H., Cecilia, Karen, Michelle M., and Carmellia. Special thanks to Michelle J. and Alicia for keeping it real--you know?

Thanks to my friend, Renee, who when I told her of my intent to write a story about Black hackers, said something like... "yeah, they could be security experts." Thanks also for introducing me to the internet. Thanks also to Paula for schooling me in html and web page construction.

I would like also to extend a special thanks to literary artists, Sandra Kitt, Eboni Snoe, Jacquelin Thomas, and Linda Hudson-Smith, all of whom have set in my mind, shining examples of kindness for me to follow.

I have never met Neale Donald Walsch, but I would like to thank him for bringing to me the voice of the creator, in the form of Conversations with God.

Chapter One

"Wait a minute—what do you mean you're bringing in someone else?" Alayna said, uncrossing her legs, her mink-brown eyes wide with disbelief and betrayal.

Suddenly, the room was a cyclone and she was at the center of it. She'd been certain that Furi had called her in to tell her that the post vacated by Lars when he took the early retirement package was now hers. Finally, she'd thought, finally she was going to get the promotion that, for her, was long overdue. Now apparently she'd thought wrong.

Michael Tafuri ran his hand through his thick, gray streaked hair. His olive skin was ashen as he relayed the news.

"Bring in someone else or lose the account. That's what we were told." Furi's hooded lids fell hard and fast. "It's out of my hands, Alayna. Liberty's stockholders aren't happy. When they got wind of this last incident, they gave us an ultimatum."

"But I don't understand. Why? I found the hole and plugged it! I don't believe this. You're bringing someone else in? To do what? What are you saying, Furi? Am I being fired or what?"

Alayna moved instinctively to the window, her vision blurred with a hot salty rush. The unwelcome snow on the other side of the glass was fast and furious. It would be dark soon—ordinarily, a sure indication that winter would be coming soon. But not today. Today it was already here.

"No. Of course not. Nobody's getting fired. It's just that, well..."

Why is Furi hedging? Alayna wondered. They'd always had a good working relationship. He'd always been straight with her.

"Well, what?"

"Well, it's your qualifications," Furi spat quickly in one breath, as if that would take the sting out of it.

Alayna gasped audibly. "My qualifications? What *about* my qualifications? I helped bring Anti-Viral to record profits five years out of seven. What do you want?"

"That's just it. Your background is in virus fighting. They want to bring in someone with a background in electronic fund transfer technologies."

"I studied EFT at Berkeley. You know that as well as I do."

"They want someone with practical experience."

"How am I supposed to get practical experience if—"

"We just thought—"

"We? I thought it was they." Alayna no longer bothered to mask her irritation.

"It is they, Alayna. But frankly, my neck is on the line with this one. You know as well as I do that this isn't the first security compromise that we've had in recent months."

"I know, but—"

"Now that Liberty is the designated financial agent for USE-TAX, they're getting a lot of heat from Washington. The Federal Reserve doesn't want to take any chances."

Defiantly, she pushed back the brimming hot tears and turned to face him. Arms crossed, she leaned on one leg.

"So, let me get this straight. I've been working on this project for almost six months, and you're just going to hand it over to some bureaucrat who knows nothing about the business practices of either Excelsior or Liberty, or the government for that matter, to create a secured environment for USE-TAX?"

"No. We're just bringing someone in who has some experience in EFT fraud to balance the process. Besides he's not a bureaucrat. He's a well-respected computer security expert. I mean, this guy's credentials are impeccable. Besides we need some objectivity. He'll be able to catch things that we might miss. And . . . ."

"And what?"

"And I didn't have a choice. Washington was very specific when they said to bring in someone else."

Alayna eyed Furi carefully. "Who is it? Am I going to be reporting to this person?"

"No. Absolutely not. You both report to me. Equal responsibility, and equal authority. It's just that we can't afford another screw up."

"It wasn't a screw up, it was just a little glitch. You can't expect to get everything the first time out, Furi. You know that as well as I."

Furi nodded. "I know, but since Liberty has agreed to keep us as their security subcontractor, we have an obligation to make sure this thing flies. We're all working toward the same goal here."

Yeah, we're all one big happy family. I am not believing this. "Who is it?" she asked, again.

"Khavon Brighton of Brighton Securities—out of Minneapolis."

The name sounded familiar. She'd heard of the firm. Alayna turned back to the window. She wanted to scream. She'd thrown herself into her work to try to forget. To try to forget what had happened. *Just exactly how much drama am I supposed to tolerate in one year—one lifetime for that matter*, she wondered, glowering down at the black, slushy streets below.

The only thing she hated more than winter in Minnesota was winter in Minnesota in September. *Ridiculous. Whoever heard of a snow storm in September? Only in Minnesota*. She didn't even have time to whine and complain that it would be coming soon. How depressing. But no matter. At least *this* winter would be the last one that she'd have to endure. Warren hated winter as much as she did. After the wedding, she planned to talk to him about moving south. She'd heard Atlanta was nice. Atlanta, Charlotte . . . someplace . . . any place but here. Living here was a only constant reminder of what had happened. Besides, it wouldn't take her long to revise her resume.

Furi ran his hand through the curly waves in his thick mane.

"Listen, you know that if there was anything that I could do, I would, but the whole thing is out of my hands."

"I know," she nodded. *Whatever. I'm out.*

"I know this past year has been rough on you, with everything that's happened—"

Alayna shook her head and motioned for him to stop. "Does the team know?"

"No, not yet. I plan to make the announcement at the team meeting."

"So, when does this new expert start anyway?"

"Monday."

Alayna turned back to him. "You guys don't waste any time do you?"

"Theodore Mulcahy. Thank you for squeezing me in," an enormous man with flaming red hair greeted Khavon, stretching out his freckled hand.

"Pleasure. Please, have a seat. Would you like something to drink?"

Commissioner Mulcahy pushed his thick round glasses up over the sprinkling of freckles on the bridge of his pale nose, and gave a slight nod. "Yes, thank you. Coffee, black."

Khavon buzzed Julie with the request.

"You come highly recommended," Mulcahy said. "I understand that you're the best."

Khavon nodded, knowingly. "I am. And?"

"And I want to hire you," he said, straightening his bow tie.

"I'm sorry, but I'm not taking on any new clients right now. The internet explosion has

really—"

"I'm not looking to be one of your clients. I'm looking to be your only client," he said, his hand sliding a folded piece of paper across the cherry wood desk that separated them.

Khavon glanced down at it and then picked it up. When he read the figure, his eyes locked with Mulcahy's.

"What exactly did you have in mind?" Khavon interjected.

"USE-TAX."

Mulcahy reached for the styrofoam cup that Julie handed to

him.

"Thank you," he said, his cobalt eyes following her long, even strides to the door.

"USE-TAX?" Khavon said, feigning ignorance.

"United States Electronic Tax System. As a result of a government mandate, the US Department of Treasury is converting the government's tax collection system from paper to electronics. Because of the sheer size and complexity of this thing, the financial agent has subcontracted the computer security component out to a specialty firm, Excelsior Securities."

"I see." He recognized the name. Khavon's brows creased together. "But if the project has already been contracted out, I don't under—"

"Right. The problem is that the bank has had a couple of recent security breaches. Not big, but big enough to get us worried. The project lead is trained in EFT technology, but has no practical experience. Since your expertise is in electronic fund transfer, we want you to lead the project."

"I see. Who's the financial agent?"

"Liberty National Bank."

Khavon felt his blood rise with cramped waves of indignation, knowing that, in no uncertain terms would he accept the offer. His teeth ground his jaw into a rigid line.

"I'm afraid you've wasted your time coming all this way, Mr. Mulcahy. Although your offer is very generous, I'm really not interested."

"I worked for the FBI for twenty years before taking over the Department of Treasury. I'm well aware of your circumstances as far as Liberty is concerned, but their reputation for financial operations is number one in the country, and I only work with the best. That's why I'm here."

"I see that you've done your homework, Mr. Mulcahy, but I'm sorry—it still doesn't change my mind. I can't help you."

"I thought you might say something like that. So I came prepared."

Commissioner Mulcahy pulled from his pocket a crisp, white envelope, and presented it to Khavon.

Slightly irritated, Khavon shook his head. "I'm not interested in your money."

"No, this is not money. This little gem is why you will change your mind. This is the reason you will report to Excelsior on Monday morning."

"Look, I don't care what's in that envelope. I'm not going to change my mind. I don't take kindly to red lining. Neither does my father. Neither of us would be in business if it were up to Liberty."

Commissioner Mulcahy tossed the envelope on Khavon's desk and stood up. "There's something you need to know about me, Mr. Brighton. I never take no for an answer. If you're smart you'll open it. If you're not, open it anyway—you never know, the contents might save your life one day. It was a pleasure, Mr. Brighton. I'm sure we'll see each other again." That said, Mulcahy crossed the floor with huge strides and stooped to leave the room.

Toe jamb. That was the complaint that the featured comedian launched into for his finale. The TV was loud. Alayna's sides were tender from laughing so hard. At home alone, lounging in pink floral cotton pajamas, a tired green robe, and pink bunny slippers, she was in a comfortable space.

With a blissful grin, she devoured the last of the double fudge walnut brownie. Dark and delicious—so good, it almost made her forget that she was spending yet another Friday night at home alone. She slid her laptop towards her and then decided against it. She had all weekend to work on her resume. Right now she wasn't in the mood. Cruising the channels impatiently, looking for a good movie, she came across a late night fashion show featuring designer wedding gowns. Her thumb slowed and then stopped.

She toyed with the diamond ring encircling her finger, twisting it back and forth. It had been such a simple dream: a loving husband, children, a warm place to call home. That's all she'd wanted. It was so simple. *Why has it chosen to allude me? And why with such colorful defiance? As if my life really needs any more melodramatics.*

She turned off the TV in disgust. Time for bed. She tossed the empty popcorn bowl in the sink. She climbed the stairs, stopping in the bathroom to wash her face and brush her teeth. Gliding a wet towel over her sun-kissed skin, she leaned in closer, noticing a tiny line forming across her forehead—a cruel reminder that her thirtieth birthday was nearing. She pulled back her billowing natural hair and secured it with a scrungi.

Alayna's bedroom was no exception to the modern décor of the rest of her loft. The striking contrast of black lacquer against freshly painted marshmallow walls was one that she liked. Red silk flowers on each night stand added the splash of color the simple room needed.

Immediately upon entrance into the room, Alayna's eyes moved to the only wall-hanging in the room—a black-lacquer-trimmed movie poster: Carmen Jones. Love always ends in tragedy, she thought, somberly. Involuntarily, she gravitated to the photograph resting on her nightstand. Her eyes moist with emotion, she picked it up, running her slender brown fingers around the silver-plated frame. Donovan's chestnut eyes shined back at her through the glass, as if nothing had happened. Nothing at all.

Carefully, she positioned the picture back on to the nightstand. In that instant, she fell into a crumpled heap on the carpet next to her bed, delirious with grief and guilt.

Chapter Two

Drumming his neatly trimmed nails on the kitchen table, Khavon's eyes narrowed with contempt as they bore into the white envelope before him. The drumming stopped as he turned away abruptly. Through the gridded French doors, his gaze locked in on the black September night. Khavon stroked his mustache once, turned back to the envelope, and picked it up.

Two dog tags on a chain slid out when he opened it. He knew immediately to whom they belonged: Sergeant Strickland, Sergeant Wilroy Strickland. All at once, his mind was crowded with images . . . .

"Khavon, I don't want you to go," his mother sobbed when he announced to his parents that he was joining the Marines.

"Mom, I have to. I've caused enough trouble. I have to get away."

"But son…" his father started.

"Dad, please. I have to do this."

They begged him not to go, but he could not bear to stay. It was in the Marine Corps that Khavon received specialized training in communications intelligence. The experience was an eye-opener for Khavon. He could still remember the day that Sgt. Strickland had dropped the knowledge on him.

Khavon had finished the fifty that Sgt. Strickland had

ordered of him, and stood at attention. An intimidating, burly Black man, Sgt. Strickland took crap from no one, especially not some green newbie from the Midwest.

Arms folded across his chest, Strickland pathed a slow, deliberate circle for the second time around Private Brighton. Khavon watched as he crossed in front of him.

"I know one thing, you better get your beady eyes off of me!" Sgt. Strickland ordered.

"Yes, sir!" Khavon directed his eyesight into the distance in front of him. Through the window he could see commercial airplanes landing and taking off. Sgt. Strickland's caramelized skin gleamed from the San Diego sun that flooded in, filling the classroom. He toyed with his clean-shaven chin before speaking.

"Do you think this is some sort of game, son?"

"No, sir!"

"You better look at me when you're talking to me!"

"Yes, sir!" Khavon eyed him carefully.

"What unit is this?"

Khavon looked at him strangely.

"I thought I told you to get your beady eyes off of me. Now I said, what unit is this?"

"Marine Corps specialized training in communication intelligence, sir!"

"That's right. Now, do you think this is some sort of game?"

"No, sir!"

"Yes, you do. You think this is some sort of game, don't you son?"

"No, sir!"

Sgt. Strickland took a side seat on the desk top in front of Khavon, momentarily shutting his tiny black eyes.

"Alright then. You want to tell me just what you thought was so funny."

"Well, sir . . . ."

"At ease."

Khavon took a slightly relaxed stance and began again. "Well, sir, it's just that I'm of the opinion that access to information should be free and wide. It's a constitutional right, sir."

"Oh, I see. I see," Sgt. Strickland laughed, nodding his head. He was quiet for a moment before speaking.

"What's your name, son?"

"Brighton, sir. Private Khavon Brighton."

"Well, Private Brighton. You think you're pretty smart don't you?"

Khavon eyed him defiantly, without answering. *Yeah, as a matter of fact I do. And?*

"That's what I thought." Strickland shook his head in disgust and rose to his feet. He moved to within inches of Khavon's face. His tiny eyes squinted into Khavon's. "Do you have any idea of the kind of dangerous ramifications that even the most innocent hacking could have? A simple computer virus could put the entire country into chaotic disarray. Access to emergency services like the police, fire and ambulance is imperative. A prank like that causes lives to be lost."

Khavon stared at him with a loss for words.

"Get your beady eyes off of me!"

"Yes, sir!"

"Do you know how dependent this nation is on the US Federal Reserve's electronic funds transfer technologies? Do you realize how much money is transferred on a daily basis through the Federal Reserve?"

"No, sir."

"Billions of dollars. Billions of dollars in funds transfers from banks all over the world. And you think this is some sort of game. We are talking about the national security of the United States! Unauthorized access could have catastrophic ramifications! Foreign powers with harmful intent could, with the aid of a pepperoni-faced hacker, cause the United States to have an economic collapse. So you see, Private Brighton, this is no game. This is no game at all!"

Deeply affected by that one-sided conversation with Sgt. Strickland, Khavon decided at that moment that he wanted to fight computer crime for a living.

After a four year stint in the Marines, he retired home and pursued a degree at MIT. After graduation, he worked for a small security firm in California for a few years, before returning home to start a security firm of his own. Sergeant Strickland had been responsible for all of that and more. He had been a friend, mentor and a father when he needed a father.

Khavon stared blankly at the letter in his hand before opening it to read.

Khavon,

I hope this letter finds you doing well. I know that you have been trying to reach me. I have received your phone messages and letters, but I could not bear for you to see me this way. If my instructions have been followed correctly, my body has already changed form at the time of this reading.

Etched with sorrow, Khavon's wounded eyes turned again to the black September night. After several minutes, chest heavy, he returned to the letter.

Khavon, you have been to me like the son I never had. You know that I feel strongly about that and about you. So I know that you will understand the actions that I had to take in not responding to your attempts to contact me. This cancer has eaten me up so badly that I doubt that you would recognize me. I just couldn't take that. Prostate cancer is nothing to play with. When you turn 40, don't do what I did. It takes a strong man to overcome his fears. Be smart, as well as strong. Go see you doctor, and that's an order.

Now, the second reason for this letter: Theodore Mulcahy and me go way back. He saved my life in 'nam. I guess I must have been bragging on you a little bit too much. When I found out that Liberty was the financial agent, I knew you wouldn't do it and I told him as much. But you have to know something about Ted, he's a good guy, but he just doesn't know how to take no for an answer. They guy saved my life, I mean what was I gonna do? Don't just do it for me, do it for yourself. Take out that print out that you carry everywhere with you, read it again, and do it for yourself. I know that you will do the right thing. I know that you will continue to fight the good fight. And Khavon, have a full, happy life. Don't make the same mistake I did. Don't be afraid to live life the way it is supposed to be lived. Don't be afraid to love again.

Wilroy

Stroking his meticulously trimmed mustache, Khavon wondered if he was doing the right thing by not telling J.C. that he was taking on this assignment. If he knew, his father would be furious and it would be another thing that he would never be able to forgive him for. *But what would he do if he found out from someone else?* Khavon's long fingers massaged the back of his neck, thoughtfully. No, he would just have to make sure that his father never found out. *Besides, I have to take on the assignment. I just have to*, he thought, reaching again for his wallet and extracting from it a folded piece of paper.

Frayed at the edges, the paper was tattered and worn. He could reprint the content on a fresh, new piece of paper, but what would be the point? Besides, as far as he was concerned, its tattered condition helped to serve its purpose better—and that was to remind him that he was a Black man, a Black man in America. It paid to be mindful of that. And as a computer security specialist, he had learned that it always paid to have your defenses in place.

The creases from the folds had already begun to take a toll on the fifteen-year-old document.

For him, it had become a ritual of sorts to read through each sentence slowly, thoughtfully, taking it in once again, as he always did on the first day of a new assignment. . . .

WRDN/XY (S_1.3.4) ***
Path:
net!netherlandsz.com.erols.!ciao.computerz.c@!.readr.amiga.advocnet.warden.com
To: ravenger
From: trojan nemesis
Date: Mon, 25 June 1981 10:43:18 -0400
Subject: bombshell
Message-ID: <5klqkb$s!!!m5@drn.warden.com>
Lines: 25
NNTP-Posting-Host: wardens.net

: c'mon scott. reality check.

: i mean, sure, they may be able to slam dunk a basketball, but
: computer hackers they're not. besides u & i both know that he
: seems 2 really know his stuff. c'mon, there's no way.
: trojan nemesis
:
: > tom, i'm telling u. it was his voice. there was something in
: > his voice. last night when he dialed into the bridge,
: > i don't know i could just tell. i mean he didn't have an
: > accent or anything, but I don't know, there was some thing
: > in his voice. i'm telling u tom..........he's black.
: > ravenger
:
: never would have guessed it. it's kynda weird. but then again
: it sort of makes sense when u think about it. i mean him being
: the eclipse and all. never would have guessed it though.
: trojan nemesis
: >
: > no kidding. i guess we just have 2 be more careful next
: > time. screen. check it out.... i was up 'till 4, but i
: > finally cracked the password for AXPACKPENT
: > ravenger
:
: kewl. i guess the pentagon doesn't have it locked down as
: tight as they thought.
: trojan nemesis
: >
: > yeah, arrogant sobs. But man....they have some
: > really wild stuff out there...sort of scary.............
: > ravenger
:
: yeah, we should really be careful..... even though u and i

: are the only 2 who have access 2 this bulletin board, we
: better stick 2 r handles. i'm sure we have it locked down
: pretty tight, but u can't be 2 careful. U know how the feds r.
: let's not 4get what happened 2 avalanche last year.
: trojan nemesis

Breath caught in his throat, Khavon stared blankly at the words, reliving the memory once again. Stunned to find that the color of his skin would make a difference to the two computer hackers that had so easily befriended him in his online anonymity, Khavon stared blankly at the screen. *How could they so easily renege on the hard-won respect that they agreed that he deserved? How could that little piece of information make such a difference?*

Khavon placed the document on the table. The lesson learned had been a painful one. More than fifteen years had passed since that telling conversation had rolled off his dot matrix printer. The pain had dimmed, but had not completely dissipated. And he knew that it never would.

Carefully, he folded the yellowing paper back to form and slipped it back into a concealed compartment in his soft, Napa leather billfold. His thumb and index finger repeatedly stroked down the wavy strands of hair in his meticulously trimmed mustache. He had a feeling, a feeling that he couldn't shake, that it was going to be a very exciting day. Closing his brief case, he slid it off the table, picked up his laptop and headed toward the door.

Beads of sweat formed on his forehead, as even in his sleep, he wondered what he'd gotten himself into. "This is not enough! This is not enough!" Alik Ivanov's accented English was ringing in Trojan Nemesis' head when he woke up. At first the Russians had been satisfied with the free domain software that he supplied them with. He wasn't breaking any laws and they paid him well. He needed the money to support his drug habit. But increasingly over the years they'd become more demanding. They wanted more—military secrets, passwords. He sat up and after arranging the white powder into two thin lines with the edge of a razor blade, he lifted the glass to his nose. He inhaled the two lines of coke and lay back on the plaid couch. As the white powder began to cloud over his brain, he suddenly felt everything was going to be all right. He just needed a plan.

Today she would meet the new expert, Alayna thought resentfully. She had decided not to give them the satisfaction of leaving. No. It would be better to take the project on, even if she had to work with that Rico Suave or whatever his name was. It was worth it to prove her worth.

The sun was shining brightly. The weekend's warm temperatures had melted Friday's snow away quickly. Alayna smiled happily, as she merged her car into the freeway traffic. She turned on the radio and began unfurrowing the eight large twists that she had set the night before. Years of frustration with using chemical straighteners to manage her hair had pushed Alayna to cut it all off five years ago and let it grow naturally. As she untwisted each of the curly locks, they fell to the lower half of her high cheek bones. Periodically glancing into the rear view mirror, she combed her fingers through her thick wavy locks of hair.

She was late, but decided that she wasn't going to stress. But that was before she reached the dismal realization that it was definitely going take more than the typical half hour that she had expected to spend driving to work.

The morning traffic on 694 simply was not moving. A semi carrying lettuce had jackknifed and caused its cargo to spill all over the freeway, across four lanes. Braking slowly, she ultimately came to a stop. She peered into the rearview mirror and studied the dark, exotic eyes that stared back at her.

"Don't stress," she whispered to herself softly. "I'm not going to stress." She blinked hard and took in a deep breath.

As she waited for the traffic to clear, her mind traveled involuntarily to the dream from which the streaming morning sunlight had roused her. Misty and clouded, time after time, it was the same dream, and the same faceless man. In her dream, he had picked her up in his convertible and they had taken a quiet drive along the coast at sunset. It was so easy, so simple. *Elusive, but blissfully simple*, she thought as a voice on the radio pulled her back into the still, as of yet, unmoving reality.

"107.5 FM KJAZ, where the gentle breeze from the quiet storm is twenty-four seven. This is Ramsey Fields trying to make your Twin Cities Monday morning commute as smooth and relaxing as I possibly can. I'll be right back with an extended set after these few short messages."

The voice in the advertisement that followed was smooth and compelling over an arrayed background of sultry jazz. "KJAZ FM presents a jazz extravaganza: David Gilliam's Sax in the 90's." Alayna's eyes widened with the attentive alertness of a deer having heard a noise near by. "On Saturday, October 2nd, you are invited to spend an evening of jazz at the Riverside Auditorium with saxophonist, David Gilliam, and special guest Angela Weathers. Tickets available at Ticket Master. Don't miss this KJAZ-sponsored event."

Alayna made a mental note to remember to ask Warren if he wanted to go.

Fifty-nine minutes later, Alayna wheeled her white Mazda MX6 into the Excelsior Securities parking lot, quickly scanning the numerous rows for a hole—any hole with potential. Maybe she'd luck out and find a spot close to the door.

Alayna maneuvered past the employee entrance quickly but stopped abruptly when she spotted the self-absorbed owner of a foreign, gray convertible taking up not one—but two—parking spaces near the front end of the parking lot.

"I don't believe this," she mouthed to herself, her face a mask of irritation and disgust. *What a pompous jerk, Alayna thought, watching him for a moment. This guy is really unbelievable. Look at him trying to front.*

Khavon stepped out of his car and took a moment to admire the sun glinting across the smooth, contoured lines of his well-kept sports car. At first he was unaware that his usual practice of parking his treasure to occupy two parking spots was attracting so much attention. But then, sensing daggers piercing his back, he swiveled and registered the icy glare of the attractive woman behind the wheel. He gave the pretty lady a boyish grin and then a playful shrug of his shoulders.

Obviously irritated, she rolled her eyes into the back of her head before speeding off in a huff to the back parking lot.

"I'm sorry I'm late," Alayna said, walking into Furi's office. She was just about to ask when she could expect to meet the EFT expert when Phyllis Claypool lightly knocked on the door.

"We're finished processing Mr. Brighton."

"Khavon, come in. Come in." Furi gleamed, reaching out his hand as he walked to the door to greet him.

Her eyes fixated on the six-foot three-inch frame that stepped into her field of vision. Then her lids dropped hard and fast. *Not this guy. Does this nightmare ever end? This is a joke, right? Some kind of cruel joke. The man was like a lash in the eye, a constant irritation.*

Despite her aversion, Alayna decided he definitely was a man who commanded a presence upon entrance into a room. With strong elevated cheekbones, he was dark in complexion—very dark. His clear ebony skin was flawless. Smooth and dark, it was like semi-sweet chocolate prepared for the ripe, red strawberries of two young lovers on their first night together. His short black hair gradually faded to allow the coarse, wavy texture to hug, but only slightly brush the sides of his head.

After greeting Furi, his speckled brown eyes moved to Alayna's and spoke before he did. He laid them open on hers with a subtle, slow unveiling that made Alayna feel strangely naked. Suddenly embarrassed, she darted her eyes away—as though he might have been able to read her innermost thoughts. Satisfied with her reaction, Khavon moved the conversation to a verbal one.

"So we meet again," he smiled into her eyes when she looked up again.

The lynx-eyed glint in Khavon's eyes that had seemed to

invade her privacy seconds before had vanished.

"So we do," she conceded with a sharp edge of tedium. Her demeanor feigned bored indifference but her senses stood on end, transfixed by the sound of his voice. Bold and powerful, it resonated like the crashing waves of a deep black ocean. Yet, the intonation of each utterance conceived in the depth of his vocal cords was as smooth and rich as freshly churned butter. Yes, all of the distinct, recognizable qualities were there—that rolling baritone bass beneath the surface was unmistakable. There was a certain something in a Black man's voice, Alayna thought, that truly made his voice unique and special.

Lost in his voice, she focused in on the keen acoustical quality and wondered if it had been there at inception, or if it had been evolved . . . evolved over time from something else . . . . Imagining the possibilities, she wondered if the distinction was somehow transcendental. Was it the phantom voices of ancient, ancestral kings, she wondered, reflecting ... or the quiet echo of distant warriors or maybe even the hushed comforting whisper of the mother of man. Then again, she thought, maybe it was simply sheltered pain handed down from generation to generation. Alayna wasn't sure. All she knew was that it was there, and that right now it rendered her immobile.

"Oh, do you two know each other?" Michael asked.

"You could say that." Khavon smiled, tossing a quick wink.

Ignoring him, Alayna inhaled deeply and stated blandly, "No, we don't."

Khavon turned to Furi to clear the matter up. "I sort of ran into the lady in the parking lot, but I have not yet had the pleasure of meeting her formally," he admitted, noting the long, black lashes that lined the top of Alayna's large exotic eyes. *It should be a federal offense to have lashes that long.*

Michael introduced the two. "Khavon Brighton, Alayna Alexander."

Khavon smiled and extended his hand. "A pleasure to meet you."

Somehow she managed to peer far enough through the red blanket of anger that veiled her eyes to notice the twinkle in

Khavon's eye when he flashed his broad, easy smile.

Momentarily mesmerized, Alayna studied the smooth vertical creases that dimpled the sides of his face. Cautiously, her eyes traveled back to the warm, bright enamel that he offered so freely. His smile was like summer . . . . The stray thought had come to her from nowhere.

After a typically brutal winter in the land of ten thousand lakes, summer was always a well-received and formidable guest. Long-limbed and radiant, it was incredibly beautiful and full of life—but it could also be an alluring tease. Summer danced in with no apology and no explanation, and then made it painfully clear that it had only stopped in to show its pretty face—because it stayed in Minnesota all of five minutes and then was gone again.

Now, in the midst of fall when the foreboding threat of winter loomed like death in front of an old man, suddenly, lost in the reflection of this stranger's warm, bright smile, it was as though summer were back. All at once, the days were long again, butterflies floated in lilac-scented air, giddy children bathed in sparkling turquoise pools, and fireworks bloomed like flowers in the twilight sky. Without question, it was Alayna's favorite season of the year. Khavon had the kind of smile that made it happen all over again. Khavon had the kind of smile that made a girl want to smile back—even if she were determined not to.

Alayna was unprepared for the involuntary bodily response that his smile had elicited from her. Heart pounding, she breathed deeply. It seemed as if time were frozen in that moment, almost as if she were dreaming. She snapped out of her trance when Michael attempted to ease the tension of the moment.

"You and Alayna will have plenty of time to get to know one another."

"I'm sure we will." *Most definitely*, Khavon mused to himself. Alayna was a beautiful woman. Her obvious disdain only heightened and challenged his instincts. He had been unable to discern the true depth of her beauty from the distance that had separated them in the parking lot. The iridescent glow of her golden-brown face exuded the brilliant, radiant energy of the sun. Her thick, textured mane was sculpted as if it were the surrounding corona. He admired and was intrigued by her natural hair. The striking contrast of her dark features against her smooth, golden skin captivated his manhood.

Femme fatale, the words came to him succinctly. *Definitely, femme fatale. In the dictionary next to the words, they probably have a picture of her*, he thought wryly.

He quickly inspected her hand as she extended it, and managed to successfully conceal his monumental disappointment—it was only a confirmation of what he had already surmised. He stared at the white crystalline gemstone in the golden ring that caressed her slender brown finger.

"I'm looking forward to working with you, Alayna," Khavon offered enthusiastically.

Angry at herself for being so transfixed, Alayna flashed a feigned smile and replied sarcastically, "I'm sure it will be my pleasure."

Chapter Three

"Finance. Warren Harrington." His usual cool and composed voice sounded rushed over the telephone.

"Hey. I just got out of the meeting."

"How did everything go?" he asked.

"Well, it didn't go quite like I expected."

"Why? What happened? Didn't you get lead?" The other line on Warren's telephone beeped before she could answer.

"I'm sorry, Alayna. This is the conference call that I was expecting. I have to go."

"Oh. Okay. Well . . . we can talk about it at lunch. We're still on, aren't we?"

"Sure. I'll meet you in front of the cafe at noon."

"Oh, Warren. Real quick, before you go, I was going to get some tickets to the David Gilliam concert that I wanted to go to on the second, and . . . . "

"The second? Alayna, you must have forgotten that I'll be in DC on the second for the expo. I'm sorry, Alayna, but I really have to go."

Alayna glanced at the picture of Warren that sat prominently on her desk, after she hung up the phone. Finally, her life was going to be fulfilled and happy.

Warren Richard Harrington, III, transferred to the Twin Cities after becoming a widower at the age of thirty-one. His Bostonian upbringing and ivy league education had given him all the right connections to get into the door at Excelsior Securities, and opportunity was all that Warren needed. After several years in Boston, he relocated to Seattle, and then to Minneapolis.

"Is that your husband?" Alayna turned, slightly startled, to find Khavon standing in the doorway of her square, brown-carpeted work area, patiently waiting for her answer. The man had this uncanny ability to ask the most probing questions, somehow with no fear of offense, or reprisal. Absentmindedly she reached for the gold fountain pen that Warren had given to her for Valentine's day and began toying with it. "No, he's not. He's my fiancé," she responded coolly.

His clear brown eyes twinkled with the excitement of surprise. "Oh, so you're not married," he confirmed, smiling generously.

"Warren and I are planning to be married in June," Alayna answered defiantly.

"I see." His eyes roamed about the area before he asked, "Nervous?"

"No. What makes you think that I would be nervous about the wedding?"

"I wasn't talking about the wedding."

Alayna looked confused. "What are you talking about then?"

He gestured with a slight nod of his head, to the unmindful fidgeting that she was doing with the ink pen in her hand.

Realizing his arrogant implication, she impatiently placed the pen back into it's pen holder and closed her eyes hard.

"Was there something you needed?"

"I was just passing by and saw you sitting there, almost in a daze."

"I wasn't in a daze," Alayna corrected, curtly. "I was concentrating on a project strategy."

"I see. Listen, I was just thinking . . . a friend of mine is sending me some tickets to this great concert that's coming up at the end of the month. Would you be interested in attending with me?"

Alayna was astonished by his invitation. *Is this man tripping or what? What exactly is his problem?* She decided that she was correct in her original assessment. This man truly was an arrogant fool.

Alayna gave him a once-over, her dark eyebrows raised with much attitude. "Okay, I guess you just didn't hear me when I said that I was engaged."

"Yeah, I heard you. But does he treat you like the Nubian queen that you are?"

Taken by surprise, Alayna felt her heart stop momentarily. His voice, like deep, dark, chocolate syrup, was smooth and rich. His insightful discernment was inexplicably accurate. His words, spoken so nonchalantly, made her question if he had really said them or not. But if he did, she most definitely wanted to hear them again.

"What?" she asked in sort of a semi-mystified, bewildered fog.

"I said, does he treat you the way that you deserve to be treated?"

Alayna sat there, dumbfounded, not knowing really how to answer his pointed question. She said nothing, responding only with a blank, open stare, wondering what was coming next.

"That's what I thought," he said after a few seconds of quiet. His smirk turned into a wide grin. The man did have a killer smile. It almost made her weak in the knees. What was it about his smile? She could not put her finger on it, but there was something different about it.

"He treats me just fine," Alayna said, finally.

"Mm. Hmm," Khavon nodded skeptically. "Now, about the concert, you don't have to decide now. We'll talk later." He turned, and walked out of her cubicle—but not before Alayna took note of how the navy blue wool fabric of his tailored slacks fell so nicely down his firm backside. *I wonder if boyfriend's got some skills.*

Eleven fifty-five. It seemed as though ten hours had passed since Alayna first saw Khavon Brighton in the parking lot. A quick check of her wrist watch indicated that it was almost lunch time. She would have just enough time to stop in the ladies room before meeting Warren. It was 11:55 when the phone rang.

"Alayna, I'm sorry," Warren began, "we are going to be discussing next year's finance strategies. I need to be there."

"No, that's fine," she lied.

She hung up the phone, but the disappointment was all too familiar. The first eighteen years of her life had been torturous . . . in and out of foster homes. It was a constant reminder that life, at least for her, was full of disappointments. Frustrations and let downs were something that she had become accustomed to, even anticipated. They seemed, even at times to seek her out. But life experiences behind her, she had developed a tough shell—and she was determined that nothing could crack it.

Her never-ending search for Mr. Right had been only another in a series of broken promises and shattered dreams. It seemed to Alayna that searchinf for someone to love her was a lesson in futility, so, drained and disillusioned, she had decided that it was time to pursue a more realistic goal. If she could not have the love that people incessantly sang about, wrote about, and paraded across the big screen, she would certainly produce, direct, and star in the production. She would at least enjoy the facade. Alayna was determined to have the beautiful home and family that seemed to be so common place on the TV sitcoms that she had viewed with curious intrigue as a child.

It was four weeks after she made that decision that she met Warren.

Alayna had always thought there to be a fair amount of irony in the notion that the person who now contested the relationship the most, was the person who had brought her and Warren together in the first place. Donavan had only been dead for a few months when Sheila had first uttered Warren's name, Alayna recalled. She'd been in the bed with a bowl of over-salted popcorn watching a bootleg copy of 'The Thornbirds,' when her telephone rang.

"Hey, girl. What chu doing?"

"Hey. Nothing really. Watching some TV," Alayna answered, recognizing Sheila's excited voice over the wire.

"Girl, you need to sit down for this one."

"What?" Alayna exclaimed, her interest piqued.

"Well, you know Larry's car has been on the blink for the last few days, right?" Sheila began, hardly able to contain her news.

"Yeah. So?"

"Well, tonight the girls and I had to go and pick him up from his fraternity meeting. When we got there, he was talking to one of his frat brothers that I had never seen before." Sheila paused, briefly. "Alayna, he was fine!"

"Fine!" Alayna repeated mockingly, shaking her head.

"Fine. That's what I said, girl. Fine," Sheila giggled. "Girl, you need to meet this man. And you know I made Larry give me the 411 on the way home in the car. Of course, he complained that he didn't want to get involved in any matchmaking, but I managed to pry it out of him anyway."

"Oh, you did, did you?"

"Yes, I did."

"So what's the 411, Sheila?" Alayna said dryly, not attempting to conceal her disinterest. She had grown tired of the whole process. She was tired of looking and not finding, finding then losing.

"Well, he's a finance executive for Excelsior. He just moved here two weeks ago from Seattle. And he's a widower, no children."

"Oh."

"Alayna, could you try to keep the excitement down? You might wake the neighbors," Sheila replied. "Alayna, all you've talked about since I've known you is getting married. Now you trying to front like you don't want to be bothered?"

"Ain't nobody trying to front, Sheila. I thought that I told you that I was taking a break for a while. I'm just tired."

"Well, you better get untired. If you think these women are not going to jump on this man like white on rice, I'm sorry to tell you that you really need to check yourself. Do you really think they are going to just let this man walk around free and single until you decide that you want to stop feeling sorry for yourself? We do live in Minnesota, you know. Now I'm trying to give you a jumpstart," Sheila declared. "I don't understand you, Alayna. You know as well as I do that we only make up three percent of the population in the whole state. If you don't seize every opportunity you have, the only choice that you're going to have is to date someone out of your race." Sheila snickered, shaking her head. "I mean, I heard someone on the radio the other day say that Minneapolis is the capital of *Jungle Fever*."

Alayna had to laugh. Sheila was right about one thing. Living in Minnesota her prospects were almost nonexistent. Then, suddenly, without warning, she became serious. "Would you?"

"Would I what?"

"If you weren't married to Larry, and you were in my situation, would you date a man out of your race?"

"No."

"Why not?"

"I just like Black men. Period."

"What if he looked like Alec Baldwin?"

"If he looked like Alec Baldwin I think I'd have to think about it. But, I dunno Alayna, there's just something about a Black man. You know?"

"Yeah, I know."

"What about you?"

"Well, ten years ago, if you'd have asked me that question, the answer would have probably been no. Now, I'm not so sure. Now I say, it depends on the man. I mean, if someone is treating you nice, and is making you feel good, then hey, maybe it's not so bad. And like you said, we do live in Minnesota."

"Yeah, you're right about that," Sheila said.

"I mean, look at David and Heidi. They seem happy enough," Alayna said, referring to a couple from their church.

"Yeah, but one never knows what goes on behind closed doors. We don't know what kind of issues they're having."

"You got a point," Alayna agreed. "Well anyway, what does this guy you met look like?" Alayna asked, curiously.

"Now that's more like it. Well . . ." her voice was thoughtful, "he was fairly tall, I would say maybe six feet or so, slender build . . . . On second thought, now that I'm thinking about it, he was slightly taller than Larry. So if I had to guess, I would say he was probably more like six one, maybe six two." Her voice was thoughtful as she tried to conjure up his image in her mind. "His complexion was maybe one or two shades lighter than yours."

Alayna said nothing, her response was only to listen.

"His hair was dark and wavy. And his eyes—maybe it was just the light—but his eyes seemed to be green."

"Green?"

"It was kind of hard to tell in the dark, but yeah, I thought they were green."

"Mmph. That's unusual. I never dated anyone with green eyes."

"Never mind the color of his eyes, the man was fine."

"If you say so."

"Well?" Sheila asked after a few moments of silence had passed following her detailed description.

"Well, what?" Alayna asked, incredulously.

"Well, what do you think? I mean I know that you're generally attracted to men towards darker end of the color spectrum, but Alayna, I'm telling you—this man is gorgeous."

"I trust your judgment, Sheila. If you say he's gorgeous, then I believe you. So what's the hook up? What's the plan? 'Cause I know you got one cooked up," Alayna joked.

"And ya know that," Sheila laughed.

Alayna's and Warren's relationship in the beginning had been fresh, new and carefree. And for a while it seemed that they were the perfect couple. Both had agendas, but they complimented each other like sand and water. For Warren, Alayna was the beautiful accessory that he needed to get to the top; for Alayna, Warren was the physical link to the ever-elusive promise of a warm and loving family. She was the showpiece companion—a trophy girl—affording him political correctness. And Warren . . . Warren was a walking promissory note, that upon fulfillment would yield to her the flesh and blood that she had never known.

Each was unaware of the other's true motivations, and for that matter, neither would care. It was a wonderful arrangement for a while—devoid of love, but functional nevertheless.

Tired and preoccupied, Alayna had lost her appetite. The stressful events that had started the day haunted her consciousness. She began to grow angry at herself. The last thing that should be on her mind was Khavon Brighton and his entrancing smile . . . but she couldn't stop thinking about him—how his meticulously trimmed mustache curled irresistibly over the edges of the corners of his mouth when he flashed his easy, white smile. She knew that it was more than just his smile. The whole experience was spellbinding. It was his eyes. It was the way he looked at her when he smiled—yes, she was sure that that was it. He didn't just smile at her, he smiled into her eyes and soul, embracing her very essence.

He was not alone in his keen ability to see past the outer shell. The twinkle in Khavon's eyes only masked what was buried. There was pain behind those mysterious, chestnut eyes, and Alayna wondered about its source.

She remembered that she had promised Furi to speak with Khavon after lunch. It was becoming increasingly difficult for her to reconcile her feelings. Not only was she engaged to Warren, but her thoughts were suddenly consumed with the man who had, for all practical purposes, been handed her job.

She searched the last row in the sea of drab gray cubicles of the project-staff work area looking for Khavon's cubicle. No Khavon—but she knew that he was somewhere in the vicinity because she picked up a mild trace of the clean, masculine scent of the unique cologne she had noticed earlier.

Confused, Alayna walked toward Furi's office, past what had formerly been Lars Iverson's office. *Furi will know where he is,* she thought.

"Hi."

Alayna back-tracked to see who was addressing her. Much to her surprise, it was Khavon, seated comfortably behind Lars' rich mahogany desk with a flashy, black name plate in front of him.

Alayna's eyes rolled over to the antique tapestry hanging on the wall. *This nightmare never ends.*

Chapter Four

"Looking for me?" Khavon asked as Alayna stood on outer perimeter of the office doorway, mouth agape.

Her steps were slow and deliberate. She openly eyed the mosaic of fall colors displayed in the wooded acres in the distance before speaking. "Yes, as a matter of fact I was. Furi asked me to show you around to make sure that you were comfortable in your new surroundings. You look pretty comfortable to me. Are you comfortable, Mr. Brighton?" Her sarcasm was thick, caustic and stinging.

"Please, call me Khavon. And no, I'm not comfortable. Alayna, It's not what you think."

Alayna's anger had all the volatility of an active volcano. Hot lava surged to the top and erupted in her natural dialect. "What do you mean it's not what I think? You just walk up in here and just start taking over everything. It's only fitting, Mr. Brighton, that you should have a big office with a beautiful view."

"Alayna, I—"

She continued, ignoring his interruption. "I've have worked hard for this company for seven years and I've never had an office. You just waltz in and—"

Imploring her to listen, he stood up, outstretching the long fingers on both of his hands. "Alayna, please. Let me explain."

"I ain't trying to hear your sorry, weak explanation. There's nothing to explain," she shot back.

"Alayna, it's only temporary," he hastily interjected when she paused to take a breath.

Her eyes narrowed. She slowed and listened with graduated silence to what he was saying as he finally managed to grasp her attention.

"It's only for a week or so. I have been assigned cubicle AF3. From what I understand, because of all the downsizing they are shorthanded and won't be able to install the ethernet wiring to my work station for another week. Furi suggested that I use this office until then, since all of the wiring is still connected from the person who had just left."

She wanted to crawl into a deep, dark hole. Alayna stood staring at him.

"Furi said that he had forgotten to mention it to you this morning. We tried to catch you before lunch, but you weren't at your desk."

She said nothing. She cast her eyes down to collect her nerves, and then up again. She cleared her throat. "Khavon, I'm really sorry. I have to apologize. It's been a very long day for me." She postured her head to the side. "Needless to say, I feel like boo-boo the fool. Probably look like it too. I guess I shouldn't jump to conclusions so quickly." She fashioned a meek, one-sided, closed-mouth smile. "Um . . . Can we start over?"

He laughed, tickled by her obvious embarrassment and charmed by her unconventional vocabulary. "Alayna, please believe me when I tell you that you don't look like boo-boo," he laughed. "And I'd really like that. I mean for us to start over. My name is Khavon Brighton." He extended his large hand. His fingers were long and the nails on the top of them were neatly trimmed and did not extend beyond the tips.

"I'm Alayna Alexander."

"Pleased to meet you," they chimed in unison.

"Now, Mr. Brighton, if you're ready, I will show you around the building."

She was wearing a periwinkle blue fitted jacket with a matching above-the-knee skirt. He studied her toned legs and slender athletic frame as she walked in front of him. At five-foot-nine inches, she was tall and leggy. From her ankles, Khavon's eyes worked their way up her legs and stopped momentarily at her outfit. He couldn't help wondering what was under that pretty blue suit. She was stunning in it. But for him, it was that pretty blue skirt that held the real intrigue. It was from it that he could see that the bottom half of her hour glass was pleasingly full. It was under it that the mystery of her secret place lay waiting to be investigated. He had been unable to stop thinking about her since the moment of their meeting. She was different. He wanted to impress her. He wanted her to like him, but he was going about it his usual way—the wrong way.

Early in his young life, Khavon had learned that he need do nothing to gain the favors of the opposite sex. He was rarely given the chance. Women of all kinds pursued him like a rose-colored pipe dream. After his divorce, he had acquired and accommodated a rainbow following. But now he was bored and unchallenged by them. They were no longer what he wanted. What he wanted was Alayna, and Khavon had become accustomed to getting what he wanted.

"Please, call me Khavon," he said.

"Alright, Khavon. C'mon. Let me show you around. We share the office building with a number of different businesses." Alayna was his tour guide as they walked for more than thirty minutes. She pointed out significant points of interest, and introduced him to the various support staff. Alayna brought the tour to a close, as they neared the cafeteria. She still felt badly about the events that had transpired during the course of the day.

"Khavon, let me buy you some ice cream as a peace offering."

"You don't have to do that, Alayna."

"I know I don't, but I want to."

Alayna ordered a chocolate almond fudge cone, and Khavon had butter pecan.

"Okay, Alayna, now that you've bought me some ice cream, is it safe to say that we're okay?"

Alayna smiled. "It's all good, Khavon. It's all good." They laughed together.

"Let me in on the joke."

Alayna swiveled around. "Warren. What are you doing

here?" she said, surprise in her voice.

"I have a 3:00 meeting. I had to stop at the business library to do some last minute research." Warren glanced at Khavon. "So I guess you could say that I'm on a business errand. And you?"

Khavon stared at Warren, critiquing him, examining him. He imagined what it must be like for him to be with Alayna.

"Oh, I'm sorry. Warren this is Khavon Brighton. Khavon this is my fiancé, Warren Harrington. Khavon and I will be co-leads on the development of the new security system for USE-TAX. I was just showing him around."

They stood towering over her like two magnificent redwoods. There were several seconds of hesitation before each man extended his hand for the other to shake. They had just met, yet they acted almost as though they were mortal enemies.

"Pleasure," Khavon said.

"Likewise." Warren turned to his future wife. "Alayna, I was meaning to tell you earlier that you look absolutely lovely today, love. But why didn't you wear the French cuffed blouse that I bought for you for the Steven's dinner party last year? It would have really made the outfit more business-like."

Maybe it wouldn't have been so bad if he hadn't had a point. But he did. He always did.

"Oh, I don't know." Both heads turned in mild surprise toward Khavon. "I think the bare neck gives her a neat, uncluttered appearance. A classic well-tailored suit tends to offer a simple charm of its own. Wouldn't you agree?"

The question on the floor went unanswered, as Warren peeled his green-eyed glower from Khavon to cast it onto Alayna. But Alayna was conveniently engaged in a methodical examination of the shine on the patterned marble floor.

"Yes, well, I really should get going to my meeting," Warren nodded in Khavon's direction.

"It was nice to meet you."

"Pleasure." Khavon's response was terse, but amicable. He watched as Warren walked away. He wondered what in the world Alayna saw in him.

"So . . . ." Khavon finally said as they rode up the escalator. "That was the infamous Warren."

"Yes, that was Warren. And please, spare me the editorial remarks."

"Hey . . . I was just verifying that that was who the man was," he said, with a slow, sly smile.

She returned the smile. "Yeah, okay, Mr. Brighton."

"We were just looking for you two," Furi declared as they approached the two partners on their return. "Khavon, we were wondering if you would have any objections to us making Becky's birthday celebration a two-in-one."

"Yes, Khavon, we want to formally welcome you to the group," Becky enthusiastically chimed in, sliding her shoulder length brown hair behind her ear.

"I don't see why not. Sounds like fun. Where are we going?"

Becky moved slightly closer to Khavon and looked him in the eye. Her voice was soft, even inviting when she answered. "Kelsey's Bar and Grill. It's across the street from the mall. I frequent the place often. It's really very nice." She turned to Alayna, her voice was noticeably louder. "What about you Alayna? You are planning to be there, aren't you?" She and Furi looked at Alayna, obviously waiting for her well-thought-out and expected excuse for her inability to attend. Polite chit-chat with people with whom she had absolutely nothing in common outside of the job had always been a challenge for Alayna. Besides, as Warren's fiancée, her calendar at any given time, was pretty well saturated with hobnob commitments of all types. When it came down to fraternizing with her own co-workers, many times she would be all mingled out.

"Well, I do have class tonight at 7:00."

Furi seized the easy opportunity. "Great. We're meeting right after work at 5:00. You can stay for an hour or so and still have plenty of time before your class—unless there's some other problem that I'm not foreseeing."

Alayna had nowhere to go. She smiled weakly, conceding defeat. "Guess I'll see you at five." It was just as well. If she were going to be on the management track, she needed to be politically correct. She might as well start now.

When they had left her, all that Alayna could think of was how nice it would be to just sit in a lemon-chamomile-scented hot bubble bath and chill on some smooth jazz. She recalled that she had thought she might ask Sheila if she and Larry would be interested in going to the concert. She strolled over to Sheila's desk. It was empty, but not deserted for the day. She was in the process of leaving a note when Sheila appeared in the doorway.

"Hey." Alayna looked up at the small woman who had greeted her. She had grown to love the bubbly ball of fire that was her friend. Sheila and her family had become Alayna's surrogate family—but surrogate was not enough for Alayna. She wanted a family of her own. She longed for the life that was Sheila's. She had two adorable children, a loving husband and a beautiful new home. Sheila had managed to stay beautiful, despite the responsibilities that come along with raising and maintaining a young family. Her two little ones, born a little over two years ago, had done little to damage her petite girlish figure.

"Hey. I was just leaving you a note to stop by."

"Oh. What's up?"

"I wanted to see if you and Larry would be interested in going to a jazz concert. Warren's gonna be out of town and I really would like to go."

"What concert?"

"David Gilliam," she answered.

"Oh, I love him. Yeah, sure, I'd like to go."

"Great." Alayna clasped her hands together enthusiastically.

"Let me just check with Larry. When is it?"

"It's on the second of next month."

"Girl, we can't go."

"Why not?" Alayna asked.

"This year the Black Scholars' banquet is on the second. You know we go every year." Disappointment flashed across Alayna's face. "I'm sorry, Alayna. But we're already committed," Sheila apologized.

"Oh, please. It's not your fault. It's not a problem. Really. I'm sure I'll find someone to go to this concert with. But, dang, I've waited for more than three years for him to come to town—

and you know how it is in Minnesota. It'll be another three years before he comes back." Alayna sighed. "No. I'm going to go to this concert if I have to go by myself . . . ."

"Hey, now that's a thought. You used to do things by yourself before you met Warren, the love of your life. At least that's what you told me," she smiled teasingly.

It was no secret to Sheila that Alayna did not love Warren, even though Alayna never talked about it. She really felt that it was a mistake for her to marry him, but she knew that Alayna was on a mission. She had tried in the beginning to talk to her, but Alayna was too stubborn to listen to reason. Finally, she had resigned herself to making sarcastic quips on the subject.

"Very funny Sheila. And I did. And I will," she said accepting her challenge.

"You're right. There's no reason why I can't go to this concert alone. I don't need anyone to enjoy this concert with. It will be kind of exciting to go alone. Thanks, Sheila."

"You're very welcome. I know I shouldn't ask, but are you going to the big hoe-down that they're having over at Kelsey's?" Sheila was always better at playing the social game.

Alayna laughed. "Yeah, I'm going."

A look of surprise came over Sheila's face. "Mmph. I'm impressed," Sheila said smiling, half not believing.

"They ambushed me." The two women exchanged laughter.

"You're going aren't you?" Alayna asked.

"Can't. Parent-teacher conferences tonight."

"Great. I guess I'll just have to wing it alone."

"I guess. But I'm sure you can handle it. Hey, I didn't get a chance to talk to you. How are you doing about the announcement? You didn't exactly look happy in the meeting. I know you had to be disappointed."

"I was. And you're right, I wasn't happy about the situation at all. But I guess I'm okay with it now."

"Really? I mean I'm glad that you're okay with it, but what made you change your mind?"

"Well, I was talking to him, and I guess he doesn't seem as bad as I had thought."

"Yeah, boyfriend is kinda fine. I guess he must have whipped that Casanova charm out on you."

"Who said anything about being fine? I just said I will probably be able to work with the guy."

"Yeah, but he's still fine."

"I guess . . . I mean, you know, if you like that type."

"Oh, and what type is that Alayna?"

"Well, I mean, he's good looking and all, but he just seems kind of well . . . too slick or something . . . kind of too smooth. And cocky. Very cocky." There was silence as Sheila stared at her in disbelief.

"Oh, I bet he's smooth all right, real smooth. And I bet he could cause some serious damage too!"

Alayna stared at her in the few seconds that it took for the true gravity of the statement permeate. And then she laughed a little giggle. Sheila joined her giggle and then together they started to laugh.

"Sheila, you are sick, you know that?"

"Girl, you know I'm telling the truth."

Alayna moved toward the doorway. "Well, I know you need to get out of here to pick up the kids, so I'll see you later. We'll talk. Kiss the girls for me."

"Okay. See you later," Sheila said, as she dotted the moisture away from eyes with the crumbled tissue in her hand.

Sheila was right, she thought, as she returned to her desk. Khavon did look like he could do some serious damage.

Kelsey's was only a ten minute drive on the freeway. Alayna walked in and was adjusting her eyes to the darkness when she heard her name called. She turned to see Furi waving her over to a round table near the bar. Everyone was present except Sheila and Mark. As she walked over to greet them, Khavon stood and pulled out a stool next to him. She thanked him and took the seat. Becky was seated on the other side of Khavon.

"Alayna, I'm really glad that you could make it," Furi beamed.

"Yes, Alayna. I thought maybe you might have gotten lost," Becky joked.

"Well, no. It would have been kind of hard to get lost. I mean it's right off the freeway and it's kind of hard to miss the huge green shamrock. It kind of looms at the top of the exit ramp."

Not wishing to eat heavily before class, Alayna munched on crunchy raw vegetables while actively participating in the group's lively round table conversation. But soon the group discussion began to dwindle, as Becky and Furi began swapping boundary water camping stories.

When Ericka and Sundar started discussing the ramifications of the pending immigration legislation, Khavon turned to Alayna. "So, what class are you going to?"

"I teach a moderate impact aerobics class called Kilamanjaro Funk."

Khavon furrowed his brow in intrigue. "That's a really interesting name. What does it mean?"

Alayna tilted her head, taken aback by Khavon's level of interest. Warren had never even asked her what the name of her aerobics class was, let alone what it meant. "It's dance aerobics, accompanied by music from the motherland. Some of the music is African-American, but most originates from Eastern Africa. Tanzania, mostly."

"So how long have you been teaching it?"

"This is my first time. I'm a former student. I enjoyed the class so much that I wanted to try my hand at teaching."

"Where do you teach?"

"Frederick Douglass High School. They have a nice dance studio there."

"Really? I tutor there two nights a week. I've never seen you there," he said, reaching for the cheesy stuffed potato wedges that sat before him.

"Well, in the past the class was taught in a small studio in Minneapolis. This year they are offering the class to a broader audience through community education."

I bet this man's got all kind of skills, Alayna thought, watching the slow rhythmic motion of his mouth as he chewed the cheesy, yellow, morsels. When she spied through a forest of curly black hairs in his mustache a tiny black mole just to the right and top of the center, she bit her bottom lip and opted to change the subject.

"Khavon, I'm very impressed. It's really wonderful that you volunteer your time to tutor inner city school kids. How long have you been doing it?"

"I've been a tutor with this program for six years as I am a firm believer in giving back to the community."

"That's very noble of you, Khavon."

"Noble?" Khavon laughed. "I'm not trying to be noble, Alayna. In fact, nobility has nothing to do with it. It's just that I'm really concerned about the constantly widening gap that exists between those people who are computer literate and those people who are not, particularly when it comes to our children and their education. You and I both know that those children who are computer literate will have a decided advantage over those children who are not. I just want to do everything that I can to expose our kids to the technology so that, instead of being educationally disadvantaged, they will be on even playing ground."

"Yeah. I see your point. And you're right—there definitely is cause for concern because many times the schools that our children attend everyday do not even have adequate equipment. How are they supposed to learn anything about computers if they don't have any in the schools that they attend?"

"Exactly. See, this is what I'm saying. So I try to do what I can, you know?" Khavon said.

"Yeah, I know," Alayna replied, nodding her head. She was glimpsing a side of him of sincere dedication instead of the narcissistic arrogance and loud vanity that he'd first offered. She had, to her surprise, gained a new-found respect and admiration for the handsome gentleman sitting at her right.

Suddenly embarrassed by his attentive caramel eyes, she searched for an excuse to break loose from their intense hold. She darted her eyes away, sensing that her own lingering gaze must somehow be speaking volumes to him. It was those eyes and that smile. She had to get out. She lifted her arm to expose the black watch resting on her slender wrist. She gasped audibly, her voice and actions feigning surprise at the passage of time. "I really need to be getting out of here if I am going to get to my class on time." She wanted to run out.

"So soon?" Khavon smiled, disappointed.

"Well, I wouldn't want to be late."

"No, we wouldn't want to have that."

"You know, Khavon, I have to admit that at first, I wasn't too keen on the idea of leading the project with you—but now I'm beginning to think it's gonna work out okay."

Khavon looked at her strangely. "What are you talking about? I have sole leadership responsibility for this project."

Alayna blinked with surprise and turned in Furi's direction for support, but found he had gone to the men's room.

"Look, Khavon, you can believe that lie if you want to, but right now I have to go. I don't want to be late for my class."

She finished her tonic water and lime and then addressed the table at large. "Well, gang, it's been fun, but I'm afraid that I really need to get going to my class." She again prepared herself for the biting wind that would greet her when she opened Kelsey's large dungeon doors.

Pleasantly relieved that this not been the social chore she had thought it would be, she said her good-byes. Safely in her car, she headed due west. The blinding sunlight belied the true basement temperature, she thought as she reached for the designer sunglasses resting on her dash. She watched in awe, as twenty-five loon ducks flew overhead in a perfect V formation, heading south for the winter. Recounting the bizarre events of the day, Alayna could not ignore the anxiety which had manifested itself in a twisted nautical knot at the base of her stomach. Looking ahead, she could not help wondering if she should head south too.

Furi had better set that Khavon straight, she thought, as she slid her sunglasses over her eyes. She was co-lead and he had just better get used to it. She wondered again who had him believing that lie.

"Are you trying to tell me that you want out?" Alik said, his eyes blazing murderously into Trojan's. "Is that what this is about?"

Trojan's face grew pensive. He slowly nodded his head. "It's just that I didn't realize—"

"No. No need to explain. I understand. You want out of the KGB," he said through a thick accent, "simple enough. The choice is and has always been yours—but before you go, I have something that I think may be of interest to you."

Trojan stood rigid with terror as Alik Ivanov moved to open his desk drawer. The blood pounding in his ears subsided into an involuntary sigh of relief when Alik handed him a manila envelope.

"I understand it's been some time since you've heard from your friend Ravenger. There's a reason for that."

Eyes transfixed with horror, Trojan stared at the photograph of his friend lying in a crimson pool of blood, his neck slashed.

Ivanov ran a cavalier hand over his slick black hair. "He wanted out too."

Chapter Five

"Do you think I'm stupid?" Alayna snapped, bluntly.

Khavon looked up, surprised to see her.

"What is this?" she waved the paper that he'd dropped on her desk in his face, and then tossed it on his desk.

"I—"

"What makes you think that I'm gonna sit around doing busy work while you take the driver's seat? I don't think so. I don't know where you come from, or what you were thinking, but I'm from Chicago. I don't play that. Our mission is to develop a reliable, fail-safe security system for USE-TAX. So I would appreciate it if you would refrain from leaving anything like this on my desk again. I am co-lead on this project and you need to understand that," Alayna said curtly, and turned to leave.

"Fail-safe? Is that why they showed up on my doorstep, crying, because the system is fail-safe?" Khavon snapped back.

Oh no, he didn't. Alayna's eyes went wide with indignation and then narrowed with contempt. "Oh, now wait a minute—"

"No, you wait. I don't like messing around with my rep. If the system fails to secure the data, who do you think they are going to point to—the black man in charge or the black woman in charge?"

Alayna visibly softened a bit.

"Corporate America is less intimidated by you than me. You know that as well as I do. I have to protect my reputation. It's all I have. And the only way I can do it is if I am in control of all aspects of the project."

"Furi, this is not going to work. I can't work with him. The guy is a control freak. Just transfer me back to anti-viral, since you all just have to have Wonder Boy in there," she said, dropping a quarter into the vending machine.

"No. We need you. You haven't even given it a chance—it's only been a couple of days."

"A couple of days too long. I tried to work with him. I tried, but—"

"She's right," Khavon said, walking up from behind. "She did try, but I let my ego cloud my judgement. Please accept my apology," he said, directing his words across Furi to Alayna.

She nodded, and wordlessly turned to retrieve her coffee.

"Think we could start over?"

"This is becoming redundant," Alayna sighed.

Face etched in desperation, Trojan Nemesis lay in bed watching the ornate ceiling fan circling over head through the paneled moonlight. If only he had enough money, he could run away. He could run away to someplace they would never find him. . . some remote island somewhere in the tropics. His glassy eyes trailed the circular path of the ceiling fan once more, and then came to a weary close. If only he had enough money, he could hide. *Wait a minute*, his eyes flew open, a thought taking sudden residence in the forefront of his mind. *I have all the money in the world.* He sat upright in the paneled moonlight. "Literally, all the money in the world!"

"But the twenty-ninth is my birthday," Alayna countered, wondering what Warren's problem was.

"Oh, yeah right, I guess it is. So?" he asked, oblivious.

"It's my thirtieth birthday. I don't want to spend it with the Lindquists. I don't even like them! Besides I thought that you and I would spend my birthday together," she protested.

"We will be together, Alayna."

Alayna searched in her mind for a more palatable way of saying what she wanted to say, but she was too tired to even try, so she just said what first came into her mind. "Warren, you golfed with him practically every Sunday morning for the entire summer. I would think that you would have seen enough of him by now. You don't have to always do things for other people to get ahead."

"Alayna, just what are you trying to say?"

"Warren, I just meant that I didn't have to do anyt—"

"Yeah, and look where it's gotten you. You get to play Robin while Batman saves the day," Warren cut her off abruptly, in a manner that was uncharacteristic for him.

Alayna was silent. She craved understanding. He offered criticism and cynicism.

"Who is that guy anyway?" he asked angrily.

"He's an independent security specialist. Furi thought it would be good to have some outside influence on the project."

"So, why didn't you answer his question?"

"What question? What are you talking about?"

"He asked if you agreed that your suit was charming."

Alayna sighed. "I thought it was a rhetorical question," she answered wearily, not bothering to mask her irritation. "Look Warren, I've had a long—"

Warren cut her off mid-sentence to launch into another one of his lectures on her behavioral shortcomings. She heard him say something about respect, mutual support and setting boundaries before she drifted into a desperately needed sleep.

She did not hear the telephone signaling her that the party to whom she was speaking had terminated the phone call in a huff. The beeping signal gave way to a pleasant, female recording urging Alayna to please hang up if she would like to make another call—but the sleep that Alayna had fallen into was deep and black. She heard nothing. Alayna's eyeballs rolled violently under her lids.

Cold and frightened, she was trapped in the Minneapolis sculpture garden. She had been running from a little green leprechaun. Even as she took refuge behind the decorative animal plant sculptures and the giant cherry spoon fixture in the center of the garden, she did not feel safe. Checking behind her at every turn, she raced up the stairs and into her apartment. When she had slammed shut and double bolted the door, she peeked out the window in a state of panicked confusion looking for any sign of danger. Satisfied that she had escaped from the leprechaun and was safe from harm, she turned and rested her back against the door and desperately tried to catch her breath. She climbed the stairs in nervous relief and opened the door of her bedroom. At first she could not see the face of the man who was lying outstretched, in the buff, face down across her moonlit bed. He turned his head in her direction and slowly released an insidious grin.

"Khavon?"

It was at that moment that she had awakened in a cold sweat.

What kind of dream was that? she wondered. *And what was Khavon doing in it? Yes, he is easy to look at and defended my honor. Yes, he is in possession of a pair of lips that could potentially drive a woman to madness. And yes, brotha man does look like he has some skills. But so what? I am engaged to a wonderful man.*

She looked down at the newly purchased kicks that still caressed her feet, and realized that she had fallen asleep on Warren.

"I'm going to hear about this tomorrow," she whispered wearily.

An hour later, Alayna's wide eyes discontentedly tracked the rotation of the bleached oak blades in the ceiling fan above her head. Dawn's early light would soon be creeping in. She tried hard to force her mind to other thoughts, but invariably her focus would travel back to Khavon. *Why? Why can't I get that man out of my head?* She willed herself to think of Warren. Warren . . . Warren . . . . A perfect mate. An ideal spouse. A Godsend, really. Warren Harrington. She pondered his beautiful green eyes and wondered if their children would have them. *Yes, Warren will definitely make a fine husband. Definitely. Better than that pompous Khavon would anyway, with his silly white smile and that semi-sweet, melt in your mouth exterior . . . . Stop it. Who does he think he is anyway? Taking my parking space, then my job . . . popping up in my dream.* Alayna eyed the white, textured paint on the ceiling. She soon discovered just how temporal denial could be. Until now, she had successfully put out of her mind the physical phenomenon that had ripped through her insides when Khavon had taken her hand this afternoon.

Angry, she rolled over to her side. *Where did they find him at anyway?*

Chapter Six

It was five a.m. when Khavon's alarm clock went off. It was his normal practice to get up at five and work out for an hour to prepare himself for the day. He wondered why he hadn't bothered to reach over to save the unnecessary warning, as he had been awake since four. Unable to go back to sleep, he had stayed there on his back, his attentive eyes methodically following the slow rotation of the ceiling fan above his head.

The past hour had been filled with thoughts of the amazing woman he had encountered the day before. No one had ever caused him to have the feelings that he was having, not even his former wife.

Cassandra was a striking woman. What she lacked in height, she made up for in dark, graceful elegance. At only five-foot-five, one would think by the way that she carried herself that she was six feet tall. Conservative by nature, she could easily go unnoticed in a room if it weren't for her beauty and regal disposition. But deception comes in all forms, Khavon thought bitterly.

Alayna's beauty, on the other hand, was free and uninhibited. With those long golden legs, that feisty attitude, those dark, exotic eyes and that hair . . . that beautiful free hair. She was unafraid to embrace the natural beauty that she had been born with. He liked that in her. He found her electrifying.

One minute she was chewing him out and giving him grief, and the next she was meekly apologizing to him for a simple misunderstanding. Complicated, and real. He liked that in her. He supposed that was why she, like no other woman before her, continued to consume his every thought.

His thoughts moved to the obstacle that was standing in his way, and his anger began to rise. The man really had no idea how lucky he was. Warren didn't appreciate and treat Alayna the way that she deserved. From the behavior he had displayed the previous afternoon, it was a mystery why she was with the man at all, let alone engaged to him.

Khavon was captivated . . . yet confused and conflicted. He knew he had to find out where that money was being funneled to and who was doing it, and Alayna was not above suspect. As much as he wanted to, he could not count her out. A conflict of interest didn't even begin to describe this mess.

He lay there in the dark, mulling over the sequence of events that put him in this predicament. It seemed almost as if his life had only begun at age seven, because he remembered almost nothing before and could not forget anything after.

A tenacious youngster whose mother had taught him to read before he went to kindergarten, Khavon was a bright kid who loved his mother and idolized his father.

But after the accident, everything changed. Khavon became alienated and withdrawn. His parents tried to explain to him that they loved him and that it was a mistake and that they did not blame him—but their pleas were in vain.

Ultimately, Khavon became fascinated with computer technology and his skills quickly escalated to the point where he could tap phone lines and manipulate the telephone systems for free long-distance phone calls. His curiosity and intrigue lead him to look deeper into the telephone computer systems. He explored, roamed, and exploited the loopholes and vulnerabilities of computer systems for the challenge, pleasure and amusement of the game. And, simply, because he could.

'Hacking,' or 'phreaking' as it was dubbed—as a play on the words free, phone and hacking—became his obsession. Firmly entrenched in the underground counterculture of juvenile cyber delinquents, he quickly adopted and followed the general hacker creed: "Access to information should be free, wide and unregulated, as long as the information is not compromised in the process."

"It's sort of a code of ethics, dude," one hacker had told him. "There's nothing wrong with gaining knowledge, man. Gaining knowledge through information access is not only your liberty, but it's your right, man. As long as you don't tamper with the data, it's cool."

But strict adherence to the code of ethics was somewhat loose. Khavon, like most hackers, had an ego, and could not resist leaving evidence that he had cracked the system. It was not uncommon for him to leave a benign digital signature hidden within a system whenever he cracked into it.

Self-taught in computing, he spent endless hours in his room gaining unauthorized computer access to everything from credit card companies to the White House and the Pentagon. It had all been so simple. He wrote a simple program that generated random telephone numbers and called them in succession until he gained access to a computer system. In the process, he happened onto a telephone access number to an underground electronic bulletin board called Dungeons. Dungeons, a privately-secured, invitation-only message center, was set up and owned by a group of computer hackers.

Khavon lurked quietly in the background as the hackers, a cyberpunk gang known as the Wardens, exchanged electronic messages on hacking techniques and sites. By the content of the transmissions, Khavon knew that he was in the company of some of the best hackers in the world.

One night when he was monitoring the board, he found himself eavesdropping on a conversation about a plot to plant a computer bomb in the largest telephone system in the world. According to the electronic transmissions that he witnessed, the bomb had already been planted and was set to blow on Martin Luther King, Jr.'s birthday. When it detonated, the time bomb was programmed to send the electronic switching system into an endless loop, effectively causing the country's largest telephone system to shut down until the security managers tracked down the problem.

Two hours before the bomb was set to go off, Khavon was able to locate and diffuse the bomb. He also inserted safeguards to prevent the same type of bomb from being planted again, as well as his personal calling card: *This hack © 1981 by* ***The Eclipse.***

Later, after lurking in a chatroom one night, Khavon learned of Trojan Nemesis's deep seeded desire to avenge himself against the one who had diffused his bomb—The Eclipse. Trojan and his legion of computer vandals, saboteurs, and anarchists, set out to expose the Eclipse's identity and destroy him. They used every hacking technique that they knew to try to track the Eclipse down, but Khavon had used remote call-forwarding, altered telephone security codes, and constantly changed his alias to make himself untraceable. He was like onyx stealth. No one could trace him. No one except the FBI.

Unfortunately for Khavon, he had been so engrossed in the computer bomb affair that he was completely unaware that the FBI had been monitoring some of his other system exploits. Usually he was able to stay two steps ahead of them, but with everything that was going on, he got careless.

At the age of seventeen, authorities came to Khavon's home, confiscated all of his equipment and arrested him, charging him with computer fraud. According to authorities, Khavon was guilty of a public offense. Thanks to his well-connected father, the trial was a low profile one, but still, his mother cried when Judge Harper read the sentence.

"In this case, the incidence of loss was relatively minimal, including only theft of telephone service and telecommunications fraud. Although guilty of 'theft by browsing', you are under age. It is my opinion that these benign exploits were for mischief rather than malicious intent. I, therefore, am assessing a $2,500 fee and six months phone probation." When the judge's gavel slammed down, Khavon's heart followed suit.

Several weeks later, an electronic message left KGB headquarters and landed on the Dungeons bulletin board. Trojan was the first and last to open it.

"Seeking US industrial and military intelligence. Lucrative profits. Interested parties send e-mail to *red@commy.*"

Chapter Seven

More than ten years had passed since he'd last seen Pamela, but right now she was his only lead. When Khavon had called and said that he needed some information regarding the bank's mysterious funds loss, even though it was short notice, Pamela, a high ranking executive secretary at Liberty, agreed without hesitation to meet with him.

The morning employee influx had been streaming in and was in full force by the time the security desk called for Khavon to escort his guest into the building.

"Khavon!" Pamela squealed.

He beamed. "How are you?"

"Oh, Khavon, it's so good to see you."

They greeted each other with a warm, lingering hug that, to most anyone looking on, would appear to be that of a brother and sister. But Alayna was not most anyone. After she had shaken off all of the rainwater from her now-closed umbrella, she abruptly stopped in the middle of the concourse to see Khavon only a few feet away locked in an embrace with a beautiful young woman.

And she was beautiful . . . tall, almost as tall as Khavon, with shoulder length relaxed hair and cocoa brown skin. She was striking.

Alayna wondered if anyone could hear the shattering pieces

of her heart as it fell to the floor, and it was at that moment that she had no choice but to admit to herself that she did, in fact, have a thing for this man—a thing that she would have to get rid of, or at the very least ignore, if she were going to marry Warren and realize her life-long dream. Mortified, she hurried past the security desk up the escalator.

Khavon did not see Alayna in her secret humiliation, as his back was to her. He led Pamela into the cafe for coffee, donuts, and a reminiscent 'back in the day' jaunt, before turning the discussion to business.

"Anyway, I'm working with Excelsior on USE-TAX security. They gave me some background information, but I need to know the real deal. I need to find out what's really going on over there. Do you know what the scoop is on the heist?"

"Well, I don't know all the details, but I'll tell you what I do know. It's pretty tense over there. The employees started back-lashing against the rigid new security measures."

"What security measures?"

"Top-level executives launched an investigation into the backgrounds of all employees who were in positions of trust. If anything questionable was found, the employee was reassigned into a less vulnerable position." She paused. "Then they mandated that security policies, briefings, and codes of conduct be disseminated throughout the company. All of it came with stern warnings of serious consequences upon violation. Employee morale is really low because the atmosphere is such that they're now treated as suspected or potential criminals, rather than productive employees. And with the losses that the bank experienced, employees are concerned that the bank itself might be headed for a collapse."

Khavon nodded.

"They issued some new badges to the personnel in the electronic funds transfer room. From what I can gather, the badges now carry a radio frequency transmitter that sends a keyed signal to the receiver to open the main entrance to the EFT room automatically. Upon entrance, personnel must pass through a second level of security to gain entrance into the actual room."

"And what's that about?"

"Well, the employees are now required to insert a magnetic stripe card, punch in a security code and place their index finger on a glass slab for electronic verification by the computer security system."

"What else do you know?" Khavon asked.

"Nothing," Pam said, "except that publicly, as I'm sure you already know, the bank is denying that any of these events occurred, or that it lost any money due to hacking. Because of the strict security rumors people can guess, but only the insiders know for sure."

When the two had finished their conversation, he walked Pamela back to the security desk. Khavon grabbed her hand. "Now Pamela, you know that you are like a sister to me. If you ever need anything, anything at all, you be sure to call me, okay? "

Pamela giggled like a ten-year-old. "Khavon, I can't believe after all of these years you're still looking out for me. But I guess that's what big brothers are supposed to do. Right?"

"Right."

They hugged again and said good-bye.

It was almost 10:30 when Khavon ran into Alayna on her way to the restroom. He greeted her with a wide smile.

"Hi, Alayna."

"Mr. Brighton."

"Oh . . . we're back to that again, are we? I thought I told you to call me Khavon," he said in a slightly puzzled voice.

"Yes, that's right you did," Alayna stated, even more dryly than the first time.

"Alayna, is there something wrong?"

"No."

"Come on, Alayna. I'm sensing a little hostility here. Are you sure there's not a problem?"

Girlfriend, you have got to stop tripping, she told herself. She looked down, bowed her head, and closed her eyes hard. "I'm sorry. I guess I just had a bad morning. No, really. There's not a problem."

"That's two bad mornings in a row. You might need a vacation."

She tried to ignore his fresh masculine scent. "You might be right."

"Are you free at one o'clock? We really need to talk about the project."

Alayna reluctantly eyed his ebony shell. *I want you. I wish I could make it go away, but I can't. I want you. Stop it.*

"I have to check my calendar, but I believe that I am free," she said.

"Okay. Let's plan to meet in my office at one."

Alayna threw a questioning gaze. Her smile was barely perceptible. "*Your* office?"

"I mean, my temporary work area," he corrected himself, with a smile.

Would you please stop smiling at me? Please? "I'll see you at one," Alayna affirmed, as she headed into the ladies room.

Chapter Eight

The coiled telephone cord was twisted, it seemed, beyond repair, as Khavon swiveled his chair back and forth between the keyboard and the layers of computer printouts scattered on his desk. His pearly white teeth were bared as a yellow number two pencil found a firm resting-place between them. The telephone receiver was secured between his chin and shoulders, and his hands were busy typing.

Alayna gently cleared her throat to announce her arrival. Khavon half-twisted in her direction, waved her in and signaled her to take a seat. She watched his silent nods of acknowledgment as he absorbed the information that was being relayed to him over the telephone.

Watching Khavon while engrossed in his craft, Alayna felt almost as if the man had undergone some sort of weird metamorphosis. His demeanor was so completely different from what she had come to know thus far. His no-nonsense attitude was intense, and in sharp contrast to the crowing peacock that had strutted and grinned in her face for the past two days. Yes, it was very becoming, very attractive.

"I'm sorry to make you wait Alayna," Khavon said, hanging up the telephone, "but the person that I was talking to has an early morning flight and will be out of the country for some time. I didn't want to take the chance of holding things up indefinitely. I hope it's not a problem."

He watched her face for any sign of distress. Her dark features, despite their lack of expression, were enchanting and mystical. Her skin was smooth and rich like fresh coffee with cream. He wanted to reach out and touch, but he dared not. If she only knew how she set his loins on fire, just by walking into the room . . . . *I want her so badly that I can't even think straight. How in the world am I going to be able to see this woman everyday, work with her and not be able to touch her?* he wondered. His question went unanswered as he forced himself to concentrate on the business at hand. He had turned her off once with his usual brash approach, and he definitely didn't want to make that mistake again.

"No, no problem at all," she answered, blinking before continuing. "I understand completely."

His eyes inconspicuously fell to her toned legs as he turned his body full to face her. *What is that scent? I have to know. What is that scent? No, I don't want to turn her off again.*

"Good. Now I wanted to meet with you to go over some new developments that I've just uncovered."

"New developments?" Alayna's interest was piqued.

"Yes. I have a friend who works for Liberty. She gave me the inside scoop on the lockdown at the bank."

Alayna's mind immediately flashed back to the beautiful woman that she saw him holding in a locked embrace only a few hours ago. She forced herself to listen as Khavon ran down the details Pamela had given to him.

"This is all very interesting, Khavon, but if everything is supposed to be confidentially restricted, how did your friend get access to all of this information?" Alayna asked, furrowing her brow skeptically.

"Well, because she is the secretary for one of the top executives and because her husband just happens to be an EFT worker."

Her husband. Her husband. Her husband. The words rocked back and forth in her head. "Hmm. I see." She tried to act unaffected. "Why do you think that Liberty didn't bother to tell us any of this?" Alayna asked, baffled by the bank's motive for attempting to keep such basic information a secret. "We are trying to help them."

"Yes, we are trying to help them, but if they didn't trust their own intelligence outfit, what makes you think that they would trust us? Besides, if we are supposed to be top-notch security specialists who gather intelligence, even if a consented effort is being made to keep it away from us, we should be able to get it ourselves, right?" Khavon said, lifting his eyebrows.

"You have a point, I guess. But it just seems kind of elementary. I don't know. . . But then again, I suppose we wouldn't be as effective in discovering as many security holes and vulnerabilities than we could if we were already influenced in one particular direction," Alayna said, suddenly understanding.

"Exactly. Now if it's okay with you, I'd like to get your take on some ideas that I came up with, and then I'd like to talk about any ideas that you may have and find out how far you are on the task list that Furi asked you to draw up," Khavon said, taking charge again.

"That's fine," Alayna said, nodding affirmatively.

She watched him closely as he talked about strategies and tactics. Her eyes moved to his thick lips. *Oh, those lips.* She watched intently. His mustache could've sparked a flame from the intensity of her eyes. She wondered if his manhood was ever evident for her. She wondered what it would feel like inside of her. *Stop. Stop. Stop it!*

The waves of desire were almost unbearable. Fleeting bolts sliced incessantly through her body like the blinding white lightning flashes in a pink and orange summer thunderstorm sky. When she thought of his thick, luscious lips pressing against her own, the need for physical restraint was almost too much for Alayna. She closed her eyes hard and turned her head in futile attempts to repress the heat that she was feeling. Like an exposed lemon lying on a cardboard box at a seven-year-old's lemonade stand, her torso was squeezed, twisted and dripping. There was just something about a man who was inaccessible. *I have to get out.*

"Excuse me," Alayna interrupted. "I'm sorry." She stood up, out of breath, wavering slightly, with her hand to her head.

Khavon instinctively jumped to his feet and reached out to support her unsteady stance. "Alayna, are you okay?"

The gesture in itself was innocent and unplanned, but the physical contact was like a prong in a wall socket. For a moment their eyes met. There was a brief awkward silence and then Alayna stammered a response. "Yes. Thank you. I . . . I'll be fine. I'm just feeling a little . . . I just need a minute. I will be right back."

Alayna desperately wanted to take a shower, as her panties were soaked with the physical evidence of her deepest desires and fantasies. There was no way that she could deny it. It was carnal lust, plain and simple.

Alayna slowly and methodically washed her hands. Her mirrored image stared back at her as she wondered what to do. Khavon was staring out the window when Alayna returned.

"I'm sorry. I don't know what came over me."

"Alayna, are you alright?" Khavon inquired with concern.

"Yes, I'm fine," she nodded.

"Are you sure?"

Not really. "Yeah. Really, I'm fine," she assured him. "Now let me fill you in on the ideas that I had for the task list," she said, handing him an outline of possible task assignments.

Chapter Nine

Four weeks flew by in some ways like four days. In others, it crept by like four months. Alayna wasn't used to the added stress that working with Khavon inevitably had created for her. Khavon hadn't made any more overt advances towards her, but between seeing him every day, dealing with Warren, the job, and now her fast-approaching thirtieth birthday, Alayna was really beginning to feel the pressure.

A mixture of fear, dread and powerlessness engulfed her as she realized that the days in which she could honestly state that she was in her twenties were numbered. In six days she would be thirty years old. She had not yet reached her goal, but it was near—practically in hand. But the problem was that where she had once been aggressive and determined, she was now wary and ambivalent. And Khavon Brighton was the reason.

She was so thankful that tonight was aerobics. She really needed it. It was a welcome release. She could at least relieve some of the stress.

"I think that the two of you should go to the conference," Furi said, handing envelopes containing copies of the announcement and the note to each of them.

Alayna and Khavon exchanged glances. "When is the conference?" Khavon asked.

"February. But we need to start preparing for the meeting now," Furi replied.

"Well," Khavon said, turning to Alayna, "I guess we're going to Amsterdam."

The three of them spent the next thirty minutes discussing the preliminaries. Alayna had never traveled outside of the United States before. It was an opportunity of a lifetime, and she could hardly contain her excitement. The clock on the wall indicated that she had only twenty-five minutes before class. She had better stop daydreaming, she told herself, and get moving.

The parking lot was full by the time Alayna rolled up on Douglass High. There was a little spot on Sheridan Avenue, a quiet residential street north of the school.

When she had started the class four weeks ago, it was still daylight when she would arrive and dash into the building, even when she was late. But now it was dark—extremely dark. She looked around. There were lots of houses around, and she didn't have far to walk, so she pushed caution aside and squeezed into the tiny spot.

Several students were already stretching and warming up in the large mirrored dance studio when Alayna walked in lugging the huge black boom box and her multicolored gym bag.

"Hi," Alayna said enthusiastically to the partial class of waiting students. "Are you guys ready to work?"

"Yeah." The response from the waiting students and those that slowly trickled in ranged from nil to mediocre at best. "Well, you might not be ready to work, but I certainly am." For Alayna it was a welcome release.

She took the tape out of her bag and placed it into the cassette player, carefully checking it for position and volume. The class was dressed in everything from colorful leotards to sweatpants and t-shirts. Alayna's outfit was trendy enough to make a fashion statement, but appropriate for the tough workout that she was planning to give to the class. The pearl gray metallic tank that she wore was fashioned with a black zippered front and was cropped to expose her firm abdominal muscles. Adding a fun contrast was the matching wide vertical stripe casting down either side of the leg on her ankle slit black leggings. When she had seen them in the store on display with the outfit, she had also been unable to resist the high performance platinum kicks that now energized her feet.

Turning her attention to the class, Alayna began instruction.

"Before we begin, I'd like to make some announcements."

The class, reflecting the Nordic culture of Minnesota more than a cultural thirst of an ethnic group, quieted down and gave Alayna their full attention.

"I won't be here during the week of February 2nd, but I've asked someone else to fill in for me."

Alayna did not waste any time after she had made the announcements.

"As usual, we'll start off with a slow warm up and gradually build up to the core part of the workout," she said, bending down to start the tape.

The breathless, sultry sounds of the Brazilian songstress wafted through the studio like an azure Caribbean mist. Alayna inhaled and closed her eyes momentarily, absorbing the music as it reverberated through her senses. The freedom of release was instantaneous and welcome. Suddenly she was miles away from the stresses of her life. She was miles away from Warren, the project, and most of all from Khavon.

"Inhale deeply and exhale," she said, starting instruction.

Day in and day out, despite her desperate attempts to block him out, Khavon continued to consume her thoughts. But now, she had been displaced, via a salty ocean wave, to a different time and place—and she had no intentions of returning until she achieved the healing that her body and mind had come to crave.

The warm up, about twenty minutes in length, got their heart rates up high enough to safely move into the aerobics section of the workout.

As the beat picked up, Alayna became more and more energetic, and less and less aware of the crowd of onlookers that had assembled at the main entrance watching what was more like a ceremonial African dance or some kind of sacred rite than an aerobic workout routine.

The rhythm was smooth and the drumbeat intoxicated her like a drug. She swayed her hips from side to side, bobbing her head to the insistent beat of the drum.

"Imagine that your torso is a corkscrew, and you are opening an old bottle of wine!" Alayna screamed to the class over the music, rotating her hips in a circular motion.

"One, two, three, jump! One, two, three, jump!" she commanded, springing high into the air again and again from the maple hard wood floor.

Alayna let the music take hold of her and the Djembe percussion set her psyche free to seek and unearth the hidden secrets of the ones who came before her. In less than a moment, Alayna opened the sealed book of her lost kindred. Chapters that had previously been closed were now laid open for all to see. Completely immersed in her transcendental journey, she did not notice the latest spectator to join the growing crowd of onlookers.

Khavon stood outside the door watching. "She's unbelievable," he mumbled to himself.

Teaching the children how to surf the internet was a satisfying high, yet at the same time he had never known the hands on the clock to move so slowly. It was Monday night and he longed for the end of his session so he could find Alayna. Ever since she had told him at Kelsey's that she was an aerobics instructor at Douglass, the thought of viewing her full endowments squeezed into a tiny leotard would not leave his mind. He had been obsessed with the notion. Finally, he would be allowed to focus the lens on what he knew she was hiding that first day under that pretty blue skirt.

Now at last, he stood, watching Alayna like a blind man having just gained sight. Only the notion that he'd conjured up in his mind was somehow out of sync with what he was actually seeing.

Alayna had in no way disappointed him. Physically, she was everything he had envisioned, and more. But the aura that surrounded her, the energy that she emitted, produced a far different picture. It was as though he were witnessing a celestial event.

Alayna moved among the stars, her hips delicately circled the path around them like the planets around the sun. Her natural and fluid movements were so utterly and completely erotic, yet devoid of vulgarity. Each body part took its position as she aligned herself with the stars.

Suddenly Khavon was standing there in the midst of nothing but space, time, and Alayna. Unbeknownst to her, he had taken the passenger seat on her intergalactic trip, and for him it was a refreshing detour. Although he started out on the dusty road of lust, he now found himself en route to amour.

He drank in her every move like it was fine wine, savoring every sip. Watching her, he knew in his heart that he had to confront her about his feelings. Working with her these past few weeks had been both heaven and hell. He couldn't wait to see her every day and longed desperately to be deep inside her at night. Yet, not being able to tell her how he felt, not being able to take her in his arms, and kiss her full, pouty, inviting lips, had been nothing less than torture. It was no longer a question of *if*, but instead, a question of *when*.

The situation was a very delicate one that had the potential of blowing up in his face. He knew that by talking to her he could put the project at a decided disadvantage by creating an awkward work environment for them both. Or even worse, it could cause Alayna to shut him out completely and he could lose her forever. And the project—the project would basically be dead in the water. But he had made up his mind, and it was going to happen—but he also knew he had to take his time. He had to wait for the conditions to be right.

It wasn't until Alayna had led the class into the cool down portion of the routine that she began to come down from her metaphysical high. There were only a few minutes left in class when she glanced over and saw Khavon standing two heads over the rest of the crowd, smiling at her.

Alayna had just finished answering a student's question after class, and had returned to a squatting position, when Khavon sauntered up to her.

"Hello," Khavon smiled down at her, briefcase in tow.

"Hi," Alayna puffed, looking up, but continuing to gather her belongings. "What are you doing here? I thought you tutored on Tuesdays." Alayna was flushed, and slightly embarrassed for reasons of which she was unsure. Still catching her breath, she wiped her brow.

"I do tutor on Tuesdays, but the program administrator asked if I could substitute tonight because they were expecting to be short on tutors, and I didn't have any other commitments."

"I see," Alayna said, standing up and tossing her bag over her shoulder. "That was nice of you."

"I'm just that kind of guy, you know?" Khavon shrugged and smiled. "Alayna, you're really good out there," he said after a short pause. "Did you have formal training?" He eyed her damp and well-toned forearms.

"No, not really," she hunched her shoulders and smiled shyly, noticing for the first time the chestnut flecks in his eyes.

"Really? You could've fooled me," he teased. "Well, I guess it must just be in your blood."

All at once, her smile flattened horizontally like a disrupted house of cards. "Yeah. I guess so," she agreed, in almost a whisper.

"Did I say something wrong?"

Alayna shook her head to the contrary and quickly came back to life. "Listen, I'm glad you stopped to watch, but I really have to be going," she said, trying to escape the sinking feeling in her stomach.

"Can I walk you to your car?" he asked without hesitation.

"No. That's really not necessary," she said, reaching but not outpacing his zealous lunge for her heavy boom box.

"I insist."

Alayna's first inclination had been to decline his offer, but she thought better, remembering where she had parked. "Thanks."

"No problem," he said, gripping the handle of the electronic device between his long slender fingers.

"Where are you parked?"

"I'm on the other side of the building. We can just walk through here," Alayna said, pointing to the open doorway leading up the stairs.

"How was your tutoring session?"

"Oh, it went really well," he said. "We spent most of the time surfing the net. The kids were really excited. For most of them it was their first exposure to what they had been seeing and hearing so much of on TV. Once they got the basics down, they just took off on their own and started exploring all the hot web sites."

"That's really great. I wish that we would've had such an easy access to information back when we were in school," Alayna said, earnestly.

"Yeah, me too," Khavon concurred.

"Do you teach computer skills in every session?" Alayna asked.

"Probably half the time I spend teaching computer skills. The other half I spend on various topics in business, like resume writing, interviewing. Last week, I brought in some of my old coins and talked about global trade. Alayna, do you mind if I ask you something?" Khavon changed the subject, the crisp night air greeting their faces.

Alayna peered over at him suspiciously before replying. "You can ask, but that doesn't necessarily mean that you'll get an answer."

"Fair enough. Alayna, I was just wondering . . . and maybe it's none of my business, just let me know if I'm overstepping my bounds, but . . . um . . . you seemed a little distressed back there. I mean, it seemed like something that I said might have caused you to be upset. And if that's the case, I apologize—but it would help if you would tell me what I said, because I didn't mean to upset you like that and I wouldn't want to do it again."

Her pace slowed to a momentary curbside stop before slowly stepping into and crossing the street.

"I never knew my parents. Almost all of my childhood was spent in and out of state care."

"Mm. Sounds rough. Must have been pretty hard on you."

"It was," Alayna agreed.

Khavon furrowed his brow. "But Alayna, I'm not sure I understand," he started, clouds of confusion still obstructed his vision. "What—"

"What did you say to trigger my reaction?" Alayna cut him

off. Khavon nodded. "Well, when you said that it must be in my blood, I guess you kind of hit a raw nerve because I honestly don't know what or who is in my blood. And all that I could say in response to your comment is that maybe it is and maybe it's not," she confessed, making no attempt to meet his eyes.

"Alayna . . . I'm sorry. I had no idea," Khavon apologized, finally grasping the significance of his words.

"I know you didn't. It's not a big deal, really."

"So, what happened to your parents?" Khavon asked.

"My parents were teenagers when I was conceived. They were curious and, well, I guess you could say I was sort of an accident. Back then, as I'm sure you can imagine, if a woman gave birth out of wedlock, she would have been severely stigmatized. So they married to give me a name. Unfortunately, the two of them didn't get to spend a lot of time together because my father was drafted and killed by friendly fire in Vietnam," Alayna said.

"How do you know all of this?" Khavon shook his head

"Research. Research on the agency's computers. It took a while, but eventually I was able to track down the records of my adoption. Anyway, after my mother saw the Marine standing at her door in his dress blues, she knew what the deal was. She freaked and went into an early labor. From what I understand, after I was born, she was so consumed with grief that she made the decision to give me up for adoption. According to the statements in the records that I found, more than eight weeks went by before she says the grief that she'd been consumed with since the day that she'd handed me over to strangers became unbearable. She tried to get me back, but there was a waiting period and her parental rights had been severed very soon after the expiration. Plus, she had signed legal documents forfeiting her right to contest the adoption. She tried to reverse her decision, but the family that adopted me was relentless and fought her to the bitter end. I guess she just couldn't handle it, so she decided to end it all. I was three by the time child welfare figured out that I was being abused. I spent most of my life shuffling in and out of foster care homes and child care institutions."

"Alayna, I don't know what to say."

"There's nothing to say." Alayna looked down, wondering

what had caused her to be so open with this man. "Oh, you can just put that in here," she said, finally, turning the key and popping open the hood of her trunk. He obliged her request without words. "Thank you," she said, dropping in her gym bag and returning the hood to it's original position.

"No problem."

They stood in the awkward silence, facing each other under a black and white Milky Way sky. Khavon's watching eyes shined in the darkness of the clear night, daring her even the slightest movement. He was a black panther, and she was a doe, blinded by the glaring lights, sensing danger, yet immobilized by confusion and fear. Loyalty and desire raged war within her like good and evil throughout the universe. She wanted to run. . . anywhere, but it was much too late for that. Khavon's hypnotic gaze dropped down and fixated on the involuntary parting of her lips. It was in that same moment that the sexual tension became a gravitational pull. His mouth covered hers, and their lips melted together into an apprehensive, yet unstoppable kiss.

As they reveled and savored in the release and relief of finally surrendering to their mutual passions, he pulled her closer to him and one kiss turned into several short, sweet, kisses full of longing, need, and sweet release. The crisp evening air was in sharp contrast to the heat between them. Alayna abruptly withdrew, as if suddenly waking from a trance.

"Khavon . . . " she whispered, pushing him away and putting her hand to her mouth. The pain of guilt swept over her and became evident in her eyes.

"I can't," was all that she whispered before she turned and walked around him, unlocked the door, and slid in behind the wheel of her car. She rolled down the window, "Thank you for walking me to my car."

"Alayna—" Khavon started.

But Alayna closed her eyes tightly, and shook her head, imploring him not to continue. *It would be better if nothing was said . . . nothing at all.* He reluctantly stepped back, giving her space to maneuver. Alayna pulled away in a hurry, leaving Khavon standing in the cold, staring into her dust.

Chapter Ten

Why? Why me? Why now? The questions raced through her mind toward a non-existent exit. *Why did Khavon have to come into my life now?* It's not as if he didn't have enough time. She had spent all of her twenties believing and chasing the elusive fairy tale . . . waiting for Prince Charming to scoop her up and whisk her away.

She had spent more than ten years of her life searching and waiting for Mr. Right. Where was he then? That was the time to drive up and take her parking space. *Not now.* Not now, when she had grown too exhausted to continue with the facade, when she'd already decided that part of the fairy tale was better than no fairy tale at all.

Why did he have to wait to show up at the late show, popcorn in hand when the movie was almost over? Why now? Why now, when I am going to marry Warren … when I am finally going to be happy? She stared inquisitively at the flickering blue and orange flames rendered from the lazy fire in the gas fireplace, as if waiting for them to deliver some insightful wisdom.

Her unbroken gaze gradually converged on the half empty glass of Canai that rested on the matte black coffee table in front of her. She took a sip. Light and fruity, it was in sharp contrast to her current state of mind. The sun was just barely beginning to peek over the now pink and blue pastel horizon. Curled up on the black futon that had been carefully positioned directly across from the breakfast nook, she realized that she had squandered the night away reflecting on Khavon, Warren and her predicament.

All of that time wasted, and what did she come up with? Nothing, really. Khavon may be fine, she decided. And he may possess lips that could potentially drive a woman to madness. And he may even have succeeded in confusing her in a vulnerable moment, but none of that really mattered. What mattered was that she was still going to marry Warren, and that was that. *Simple enough*, she thought. Only one small problem, one tiny caveat: she was in love . . . and it wasn't with her fiancé. She let out a heavy sigh.

She was going to drive herself crazy, she decided, if she continued to try to make sense of it all. She might as well go into work. At least that would take her mind off of things. In the quiet of the early morning no one would be around to break her concentration. She could get some real work done, she thought, fluffing and replacing the bold African print pillows on the futon. That database she'd found yesterday had some real promise. She had been really close to tracking a lead. It would be interesting to see what the scan process that she'd left running the night before had come up with.

She hadn't liked leaving her machine on, but the process was so lengthy that she had really had no choice.

The office was quiet, just as she had anticipated. She heard only the keyboard chattering of some other die-hard insomniac feverishly typing away in the distance. The closer that she got to her desk, the louder the typing became. Her footsteps grew progressively softer as the sound grew louder and closer.

"I know this is not coming from my workstation," she silently mouthed, her face questioning the audacity in invading her privacy.

Alayna stood for a few moments quietly taking in the scene before speaking. Various incidents flooded her mind. She had remembered having a vague sense that her things had been gone through. Then the incidents flooded her mind in one fell swoop ... misplaced, missing and reappearing documents . . . shuffled papers . . . books, documents and writing utensils strangely out of place ... and most of all her computer on in the morning when she'd known she'd turned it off the night before. It was just a general uneasiness that things didn't seem to be in exactly the same place that she'd left them the night before. Now she knew why.

His back was to her when she finally spoke. "What are you doing?" The peaking inflection that initiated the question was pointed, clear.

Khavon turned in surprise, his face reflecting his impatience with such an untimely and unanticipated problem. "Alayna . . . I was just—"

"You were just what?" Alayna demanded, barely able to contain her anger. "This is my workstation."

"Look Alayna, I don't have time for this right now," he said, swiveling his chair to face the monitor again.

"What do you mean you don't have time for this? Obviously, you didn't hear what I said. This is my workstation."

Precious moments were slipping away like grains of sand in hourglass, and he was not about to waste them on a detailed rationale or apology for his current predicament. Khavon stoically fixed his clear brown eyes on hers.

"Alayna," he said forcefully, "I'm not trying to debate this with you. You obviously didn't hear me the first time, so I will say it again. I said, I don't have time for this. Now when I finish doing what I need to do, I'll explain it to you, but not right now. You're just going to have to trust me on this." With those clear and concise comments, he turned back to the screen and started typing furiously again.

Alayna, slightly taken aback by his commanding state and out of character tone, gave no reply and quietly lowered herself into the guest seat in her cubicle. She watched in disquieted silence as the blinking phosphorescent light sporadically raced across the screen and loudly beeped in angry protest at Khavon's last command.

"I don't believe this!" Slamming his fist on the desk, he immediately checked his watch for the time.

"Did you scan the boot drive for any known viruses?" Alayna asked, realizing finally that something was terribly wrong.

"That was the first thing I did," Khavon said.

Everything that he tried didn't work. Alayna's computer and all of her work . . . their research was five minutes away from being completely destroyed . . . forever. He could see that the bomb had even gained access to backup files. It would take months to restore the information, research and programming. Not to mention the embarrassment. They were supposed to be security experts, for crying out loud.

This is unreal. He sat staring blankly at the computer screen. He had tried everything! Everything! There seemed to be some sort of pattern, but it was like his own security system didn't recognize him . . . didn't know who he was . . . unless . . . of course, that was it. That had to be it! And in one moment of clarity, it was as though he had discovered the mystery of life. The bomb had not only fooled the computer into thinking that it was a friend, but by gaining access with Khavon's access ID and password, it had managed to make the computer believe that it was him. And now . . . instead of the author . . . the architect . . . the creator . . . now . . . he—he was the intruder.

There was no time to waste. "Alayna, quick, I need you to go to the wire room to temporarily switch the Ethernet wires from your workstation to that vacant workstation in aisle K. It's in the same row as mine so the number would be K4. It won't be long before it gets back on track, but the confusion will give me enough time to try to get in the back door. Here's the IP address," he said, handing her a small piece of paper.

"Khavon, do you know how many wires are in there?" Alayna asked, not waiting for a response. "I wouldn't know where to begin. I'm not hardware, I'm software. My knowledge on multiple network wire connections is limited." There was no time to waste. Reaching into his pocket, he pulled out two small keys and hastily, but carefully, gave her instruction.

"Okay. Take these keys. The larger one is to my file cabinet. The smaller key is for the bottom drawer. Pull out the drawer, push all the junk aside. Way in the back you will see several books. One of which is entitled, *Assyro-Babylonian Mythology: Ancient Myths and Legends*. Open this book to page 591. Inside the book, you will find a square cavity that contains a disk labeled Junebug. Bring it to me!"

She turned to leave the cubicle, then she heard him ask

what she hoped against, but knew that he would.

"Alayna, I need your access code for the wire room."

"What do you mean? Don't you have one?"

"Alayna, let's not play games. You know that access is restricted to Excelsior employees, and you know that I'm not an employee."

"Khavon, I'm sorry but I'm not at liberty to give that to you."

"Alayna, look, you said you didn't know hardware. We have less than five minutes before all of our work, research and tons of data is going to be sucked into an electronic black hole. We don't have time to play games," Khavon snapped, annoyed at the lack of trust, inquisition and waste of time. Closing her eyes hard, Alayna gave him the code and dashed off.

Her task was simple enough. Alayna waded through the power cords, mouse attachments, modems, and paper weights until she spotted a pile of hard- and soft-back books. The subject matter ran the gamut, and was as intense as the moment. Her eyes carefully scanned over the titles. *Lucy: Mother of the Earth*, *Inside the Vietnam War: The abandonment of POWs* , *Swahili, in 10 minutes a day*, *Racism in America: Today, Yesterday and Tomorrow*, *The Lost City of Timbuktu*, *How to Hack the Hackers: An Insider's Guide to Security Experts' Loop Holes*, *The Egyptian Civilization and the Untold Theft*, *Behind the Scenes on Wall Street*, *Dr. King: The Conspiracy to Hide the Conspiracy*, and strangely out of place, *Monarch Butterflies in the Mountain Sanctuaries of Mexico*. She dug through the pile and finally, lying on the floor of the deep metal drawer among several other books in the pile, she spotted a fairly thick green and black book with its front cover face down. She knew that it was it, even before she saw the red encased lettering emblazoned across the front.

"Got it!" she exclaimed to Khavon over the partition.

Frustrated with his inability to disengage the bomb and plagued with a series of taunting messages, Khavon was nearing the end of his rope. He was just finishing up when he was prompted with yet another message. He watched in personal horror that only he could know as the bold neon letters moved across the screen.

"HOW DOES IT FEEL TO BE ME? HOW DOES IT FEEL TO BE YOU? TWO MINUTES TO BOOM TIME." Again the screen went blank.

He was just about to shut down and reboot, when Alayna raced in with the disk.

"Thanks." Khavon grabbed it, turned the machine off and placed it in the floppy drive. "I hope this works, Alayna, cause if it doesn't we can kiss the project and our careers goodbye," Khavon said. As he and flipped the power switch to the 'on' position, it elicited a fear in Alayna that she didn't know that she had.

The screen came to life, flashing a colorful array of lights. And then without warning the screen went blank for thirty seconds. "Come on, baby . . . you know it's me. You know it's me!" Khavon said, intensely, balling his fists.

The waiting was unbearable. A flash of green embraced the screen, followed by a red lightning bolt. There was an eerie silence. And the screen went blank again, but this time it was for only a few seconds.

"PLEASE ENTER THE PASSWORD." Khavon typed in the password as instructed. Alayna and Khavon watched in silence as the computer debated on which Khavon it was going to believe.

"ALL INTRUDERS HAVE BEEN LOCKED OUT. KHAVON WHERE HAVE YOU BEEN? THE BACK DOOR IS OPEN. YOUR WORKSTATION IS NOW SECURE. ALL INTRUDERS HAVE BEEN LOCKED OUT."

"Yes!" Khavon heaved a huge sigh of relief. It was like fresh air to a gulping, drowning swimmer. He entered a few commands to assess the amount of damage.

"Now can you tell me what's going on?" Alayna asked, impatiently, her heart racing.

Khavon stroked his mustache quietly, trying to understand how someone had obtained access to his access code, the worry wrinkles in his face evident as he turned and stood up to answer her question. He casually looked around over the partitions before speaking.

"Okay, Alayna. Why don't we grab a conference room." It

was meant to be a declaration, not a question, but Alayna answered it anyway.

"Why do we need to get a conference room?" she asked.

"Trust me, we need a conference room. There are several conference rooms on One. I think it would be wise for us to use one of them." Alayna conceded, and followed his lead.

Somehow Alayna knew that the silence they walked in was the calm before the storm. She took a seat as Khavon closed the door and walked over to the window and began to give her the details.

Even in the midst of crisis, Khavon could not help but notice the delicate scent of her perfume wafting through the air, reminding him of the warmth of their skin touching and the passionate kiss they had shared only hours before. He wanted to push it out of his mind to get on with business. Realizing that it was an impossible task, he started the explanation in spite of his emotions. "I'm sure that you've already figured out by now that your PC had a bomb on it."

Alayna sat quietly, not responding, only listening as he continued. "It was set to go off at exactly six hours from when it was triggered. The bomb had gained access to all of our backup files as well."

"Go on." How could they have gotten so close without her knowing about it? How had they managed to bypass her security? She listened intently as Khavon continued.

Khavon focused in on Alayna. "You must have left your machine running last night before you left."

"Well, yes," Alayna said, finally. "I was searching a massive database and was doing some analysis on the data. I knew that it was going to be time consuming, so I decided to let some of it run overnight so that I could have a look at it in the morning. I felt like I was really on the verge of something."

"Well, apparently someone else knew that you were on the verge of something big, because whatever you were working on is lost for good."

"But how did—"

"How did I know?" Khavon finished her question for her.

"Alayna, I take my work very seriously. I have activity monitors on every project team workstation. A little after midnight, one of the monitors started beeping. The monitors started detecting erratic behavior on your workstation . . . memory problems . . . strange disruptions . . . virus-like activity. To make a long story short, I came in, found the bomb and had been working on diffusing it ever since."

"But all my defenses . . . . You know as well as I do—" She stopped. "You know as well as I do that I have legions of passwords, security and monitors on my machine."

Visibly fatigued, Khavon rubbed his eyes. "Well, that's the part that is bothering me. My gut is telling me that this is an inside job because my ID was the one that was logged in as the intruder."

"Your ID?"

"Yes, somehow, some way, someone gained access to my ID and was doing all of the damage under the pretense of being me."

"Who would do something like that?" Alayna asked quietly.

"I don't know, but I think that it would be in our best interest to keep this incident between us . . . on the down-low . . . you know," Khavon said, looking into her eyes without blinking. Alayna eyed him suspiciously. "Well, what do we do now?"

"Well, you have that meeting with Commissioner Mulcahy from the Treasury Department on Wednesday right?" Alayna nodded in affirmation.

"Okay. Find out everything that you can about the rumored plans to include another financial agent. Maybe someone is trying to sabotage Liberty to get them out of the way so that they could have an exclusive contract."

"Could be."

"It's just a thought. Are you going alone?"

"No, Sheila and Ericka are coming along too. I spoke to him yesterday, and told him that I would be bringing in some of my people."

"Well don't mention any of this to them or to Mulcahy," Khavon instructed.

"Why not?"

"Just don't," Khavon snapped, impatiently.

Alayna's eyes went wide.

"I'm sorry. It's been a long night. Just don't say anything."

"Okay. But I still can't figure out how all of my security was bypassed," Alayna mumbled, in disbelief.

"I don't know. I have a lot of experience in computer bombs, and I had never seen anything like this one before. But it looks like whatever you were working on was hot. Because from what I can tell, it looks like you must have run across an id or something that tripped a logical mechanism that triggered the bomb to set off. There was a six hour lead time."

"But why would they wait six hours to detonate the bomb?"

"Apparently whoever we're dealing with has an ego. They wanted to taunt us. I didn't mention it before, but periodically some pretty taunting messages would roll across the screen."

"Messages? What kind of messages? What did they say?" Alayna asked, her curiosity peaked.

He rolled off some of the threats that he had seen come across the screen and then paused. "Alayna, we need to get that information back and rerun your process. It's the only way we can find this person."

"I can't believe my security was breached. I had everything in there, power-on passwords, monitors, everything," Alayna repeated

Khavon was quick to respond. "Yeah, whoever this is is no dummy. Alayna, this is not your fault. We're dealing with a real pro. We have to find out which wire you tripped. If we find that out, we will find out who the culprit is, or a least find a clue. We have to get that information back."

"I'll get right on it," she stated, standing up to leave the room.

While relaying the details, Khavon had tried to ignore the slight hesitation of her dark lashes as they lowered and fell to meet their counterparts when she blinked. He tried to ignore the erotic formation of her raspberry-stained lips when she spoke, her soft fragrance in the air, the ever-so-slight swell of breast peeking from beneath her jacketed outfit, her delicately slender fingers . . . but the man in him was not about to let him ignore anything.

His emotions were running high. The events of the last few hours had left him high-strung and in need of release. He knew that it was not the best time, but it was as if he were a welling volcano about to erupt. As she turned to leave the room, the backside of her knee suddenly caught his eye and set him off. The words, like molten lava came spewing out, stopping her in her tracks.

"Alayna, are you feeling this too?" she heard him ask. She pretended not to hear. The silence that permeated the room was long and uncomfortable, loud even. Khavon's clenched jaw was beginning to ache. Alayna stood, head down, frozen, with her back to him. Then he repeated his question. "Alayna, are you feeling this too?"

Still she gave him no response.

"I know you hear me," he thundered, losing control of his temper. "Answer me!"

Alayna blinked a long, tight, anxious blink. Slowly she turned, voice shaking, and said softly, "Khavon, I don't need all this drama. You know what my situation is." Her eyes welled with moistness. Then with clear determination and renewed energy, she said, "Do you have any idea how long I have planned for this? I have planned for this all of my life. At this point in my life, I had planned to be married with two children. Instead I am standing here with you discussing the possibility of throwing that all away for a few weeks, probably days of . . . of . . . ." Her breathing was irregular, but not quite audible. Her eyes darted across the corded mesh carpet, searching in futility for the right words.

"Look, I'm not about to shoot down all of my plans on a sexual whim for a few nights of carnal pleasure."

"This isn't about sex," he insisted, indignantly.

She shot him a cynical glare that went through him like an arctic blast.

He raised his hands o fend off the ensuing attack.

"I just mean that something is going on here between us, and we just can't keep trying to deny it." He paused momentarily.

"Alayna, what are you afraid of?" His voice was soft.

Alayna closed her eyes hard.

"What do you expect me to do? I can't just get up and leave. I'm talking about a lifetime here." The octave of her voice raised two levels. "Why are you doing this, Khavon?"

"Doing what?" His eyes grew wide. "Do you think this is some sort of game? Do you think that I'm running some kind of game on you? I have no control over these emotions and neither do you. You don't love him." He paused momentarily, and then stated in a almost a whisper, "Alayna, you can't look at me the way that you do and tell me that you love him."

She shook her head quizzically. "Love? What does love have to do with anything?"

Khavon was incredulous. "Love has everything to do with everything. Why would you want to marry a man that you don't love?"

Her eyes went wide. "You just don't get it, do you Khavon?" She threw her hands up with exasperation, willing him to understand. "It's not that difficult. Which part don't you understand?" Alayna's eyes squinted with intensity under her crinkling brow, questioning with disbelief his inability to comprehend. "I want a stable and secure lifestyle. I want a future. I want family vacations. I want dance recitals, birthday parties, bedtime stories, and the first day of school. I want the white picket fence." She paused, and lowered her voice. "*Warren,*" she paused, glaring at him, "*Warren* can give that to me." Despite her hushed, barely audible voice, the implication was loud and clear, almost deafening.

"Alayna . . . you know what's going on here between us. This feeling is too strong, too intense for it to be just me. You *know* how I feel." His passion filled voice turned subdued. "You know how I feel because you're feeling it too."

She gazed out the window, a far away look on her face. She could see St. Paul's jagged skyline in the hazy, gray distance into which she stared. No, she didn't know how he felt. She didn't know anything—only that he didn't say what she wanted him to say. He didn't say he would marry her and give her the sweet, chocolate babies that she so desperately wanted. He didn't say he would build her a beautiful two-story in the suburbs with a vegetable garden in back. He didn't say that the two of them would grow old together and never be apart. No, he made no commitment at all. And she knew that he never would. She closed her eyes and labored in a long, exasperated, hopeless sigh. "That's what I thought," she finally said, shaking her head. She turned back to meet his nut-brown eyes. With clear determination she stated, "Khavon, I'm going to marry Warren."

She was not going to throw her future away only to serve as Khavon's next conquest.

"Alayna don't leave—" Khavon pleaded as she closed the mahogany-paneled door behind her.

She stood at the other side, her delicate, white knuckled hand still clinging tightly to the door knob, eyes tightly closed, heart pounding, trying to gain composure. Too much was happening too fast. She had to get out. She needed some space, some time . . . some time to think.

After retrieving her coat from her desk, she left a hastily scribbled note on Furi's desk. She was headed towards the back stairs when a voice came from behind her.

"Hello, Alayna."

"Mark! What are you doing here?" Alayna asked, surprise in her voice. "I mean, you usually don't get in until nine." She continued, not really giving him a chance to answer. "It's pretty early for a late bird like you isn't it?"

His eyes were wide. "Yeah, well, I couldn't sleep, so I came into work. That's not against the rules is it?"

"No, of course not. I just—"

"What are you doing here so early?"

She stared back into his icy blue eyes. "Just working. I won't be in the rest of the day. I have some business I need to take care of."

"Oh, okay. Well, I will let Furi know."

"Thanks, but I already left him a note."

"Okay. We'll see you tomorrow then."

"See you." She waved goodbye and headed toward the complex exit.

Chapter Eleven

Alayna found herself to be one of only two people sitting in the black darkness of the movie theater watching the end of the credits roll. She emerged from the darkness into popcorn-saturated air, not having a clue as to what the movie was about. The only detail that she could recall was that much of the movie was set in Las Vegas and that the guy got the girl in the end. Her mind was consumed with her own personal problems. Between Khavon's kiss, his confrontation, and the hacker that had cracked all of her security, there was no room for anything else.

Maybe if she went home and soaked in a nice long hot bath, everything would somehow sort itself out. She knew that it was wishful thinking, but she hoped against hope that all of her troubles would just swirl down the drain along with her bath water—not likely, but a relaxing bath sounded inviting nevertheless.

Submerged in a cascade of fluffy white bubbles, Alayna leaned back in the tub and tried to free her mind from her worries, at least for a little while. She sighed, closing her eyes and letting the lemon-scented effervescence waft through her senses. She slid deeper into the hot steamy water. The soothing heat was relaxing, and soon the damp citrus air turned floral, coaxing her once again into her favorite dream.

It was Warren's voice on the answering machine that eventually roused Alayna from her recurring fantasy. "Alayna . . . Alayna? Where are you? I've been trying to reach you all day. I really hope that you didn't forget that you were supposed to drive me to the airport tonight. Call me when you get in. I'll wait until six, if I don't see or hear from you by then, I guess I'll just have to make other arrangements." She heard the phone click and then the machine began to beep.

Alayna made no attempt to catch the phone. She barely had time to dry off and get dressed if she was going to get over to Warren's by six. If Warren had to make other arrangements, she knew that she would never hear the end of it.

"There's no need for you to park. I'll barely have enough time to check in. I'm sure they're already boarding." Warren snapped, as Alayna turned into the airport.

"Warren, I said I was sorry." Alayna said, fatigued and exasperated with the unceasing lectures, reprimands, and sarcastic innuendoes.

"Well, Alayna, if you would just try to stay focused, this type of thing wouldn't happen. I have to go," he said, planting a fleeting peck on her cheek.

"Have a good flight," she called after him when he got out of the car.

"Don't forget about dinner with the Lindquists," he called back, handing his bags to the sky cap as he hurried to the door.

"Alayna, girl, what's wrong with you?" Sheila asked in a tone that was mixed with concern and a small amount of annoyance.

Alayna had hoped against hope that her erratic mood swings here of late had gone unnoticed by those close to her.

"What are you talking about?" she asked under the transparent guise of curiosity.

"Alayna, c'mon, you know exactly what I'm talking about. You been tripping for the last five weeks. Hmm. Five weeks. Let's see. Isn't that about the same time that boyfriend joined the project team?" Sheila tested the water. Alayna shot her a brief but icy glare before stepping on the gas. "Okay. Okay. I'm sorry. But, Alayna, honey, c'mon—do you really think that the way the two of you look at each other, that people weren't going to notice?" Alayna stared straight ahead, giving no answer. "Alayna are you even listening to me?" Sheila demanded as they turned into Excelsior's parking lot.

Alayna parked the car and inhaled deeply. "Okay, Sheila," she said wearily, shutting off the engine. "Since you insist on talking about this, go ahead."

"I was simply saying that you think that you're playing it safe, but what you don't realize is that playing it safe is no fun. I mean I know that the stakes are high and you're risking a lot, but what you have to gain is priceless."

"And just what is that Sheila?" Alayna asked in a lackluster monotone.

"Love. Alayna, love." Alayna rolled her eyes back in her head. *Not you too!* "Alayna, life isn't about being safe, it's about taking chances. It's about making the right decisions and taking control."

"That's exactly what I am doing, taking control. My biological time clock is ticking and I'm taking control," Alayna quipped.

Alayna's refusal to listen to her admonition pushed Sheila to take another approach. "What about Warren?" she asked with a tone of desperation.

"Warren? Yeah, what about Warren?" Alayna shot back a defiant accusing glare. "Or have you forgotten that you were the one who insisted that Warren was the perfect guy for me? 'Alayna, remember we're in Minneapolis. Don't be a fool, Alayna. Don't let him slip through your fingers, Alayna. Alayna, he's the perfect guy for you,' " Alayna mimicked. "What about all of that, Sheila? And now it's Khavon. How many perfect guys for me do I have to go through before I get to the one I'm supposed to keep?"

"Alayna, stop tripping. You know that's not what I mean. What I'm trying to say is that even if you don't think that you deserve to have true love, don't you think Warren does?"

"What?" Alayna turned for only the second time in their conversation to look Sheila directly in the eyes.

Realizing that she'd struck a chord, Sheila laid it out with no frills. "Alayna, just because you have decided to live your life devoid of love and happiness for the sake of your selfish goals, is it really fair to sentence Warren to a life like that?" The truth of Sheila's words sliced through her like a free wielding machete.

Alayna sat staring silently at her, wishing, searching for a logical comeback, but none was forthcoming. Considering all of the angles had not been an option for her because for Alayna, there had been no other angles. In all of her agonizing, she had not even once considered Warren's feelings. Not really. She had only looked at the situation from her own perspective.

"Alayna, are you okay?" Sheila asked, mildly concerned. "I'm sorry to put it to you like that, but—"

"Yeah . . . ah, yeah." Alayna said, slowly turning back to the windshield. "I just have a lot of thinking to do."

"I hope I didn't upset you too much. But you know me, I just had to say my piece." Sheila said after a long silence.

"No, Sheila you didn't upset me. Really. I just—um . . . ." her voice trailed off slowly, and she paused briefly before reaching out to hug her best friend.

"Thanks. You're a good friend."

"Girl, you know we got it like that. You're my girl!"

"Well, well, well. Look at what the north wind just blew in," Cassandra said as she sauntered past the security guard, taking a seat in from of the three-inch-thick safety glass that separated them.

The dingy-green, standard-issue uniform that she wore was clean and neatly pressed. Khavon stared at the white label resting on her ample bosom. Even though it had been more than ten years since she'd been convicted, it was still hard for him to believe that she was inmate #346274-437. Cassandra had been at the Women's Federal Correctional Facility at Shakopee for more than eight years.

"Hello, Cassandra," he said simply, directing his voice to the metal speaker embedded in the glass wall.

"Mmph. And all dressed up. Sharp as a tack, as Daddy would say. If I didn't know better, I'd say you just got out of church or something."

"As a matter of fact, I did," Khavon said, nodding his head.

Her eyes bucked in response. "You were never exactly the church going kind, if I recall correctly."

"People can change, Cass."

"Sure, some people can, but not you Khavon. Not you." She

stared at him stoically but he gave no response. "So, tell me Khavon, what is it? What have I done to be graced with, no, to deserve your wonderful, eloquent presence after—what has it been? Let me see ... one, two, three . . . ." She started counting on her fingers, "Eight years? Tell me, Khavon, to what do I owe this special treat?"

Her proper voice was the same as he'd remembered it. He didn't know why he had expected anything different. Perhaps it was the less-than-delicate exterior that took him by surprise. She had not aged well, and her standard-issue uniform was a long way from the soft, feminine cashmere sweaters that he'd remembered her wearing. But he'd been happy to hear that she'd finished her degree. He was about to answer when Mary, who was strolling leisurely up to them on her way back from her own visit, stopped in her tracks and spoke to her cellmate.

"Cass! I know this ain't the fine specimen that you let slip though yo' fingers. Get away from you!" she said, her Nordic blue eyes riveted on the man in the navy blue jacket, wide starched lapel and striped red tie. Cassandra looked up and back.

"Well, ain't you gon' introduce me?" Mary asked. Cassandra rolled her eyes in her head, ignored Mary, and kept talking.

"So, Khavon—"

"Forget it. I'll introduce myself. I'm Mary. Mary Olsen."

"Hello. Khavon Brighton." Khavon nodded his head through the window.

"She's a good woman." Mary nodded her head at Cassandra. "Believe me, I know." Her voice was seductive and insinuating.

The guard came up from behind Mary and pushed her in the back with his nightstick. "What do you think this is, a night club? Move along."

"All right, all right. You don't have to get nasty about it."

"Just move it along."

"See you later." Mary laughed, provocatively, heeding the guard's instruction.

"What is she in for?" Khavon wanted to know, tilting his head in the direction of the frail young woman.

"Murder. Her husband beat her one too many times. The last time he damn near killed her. She shot and killed him before he finished the job."

"That's self-defense."

"Tell that to the judge. But you're right. She doesn't look like a criminal—and she's not. But pushed to extremes, anybody is capable of anything," Cassandra said, reading Khavon's thoughts, as she had often done while they were married.

"I guess you're right," Khavon said, agreeing.

"Take me for example. It took a bunch of steel bars and all the time in the world for me to finish my degree."

"That's great, Cass," Khavon said, sincerely. "It really is, and I hear that you're up for parole next year."

Cassandra stared at him coldly. "Anyway, since when do you give a damned about what happens to me?" Khavon was silent.

"Khavon, why are you here? The last time I saw you, I was being dragged away in handcuffs."

"Look, Cass, I know it's been a long time, but I didn't come here to fight."

"Then why did you come here, Khavon?"

"I came because—because I guess I just realized that sometimes things just happen and that you don't always have control over them. I came because I wanted—needed to get some closure."

"Closure?" Cassandra laughed.

"Yeah, closure. I've needed some closure for a long time and if I'm not mistaken I think that you do, too."

"Khavon, you must be out of your damned mind. No. Closure is not what you need now and it's not what I needed then. What I needed was for you to listen. What I needed was to be able to explain the situation to you so that you would understand."

Khavon could feel the heated pain of the memory begin to rise and capsize his insides. The memories flooded into his head….

"What's going on?" Khavon had asked the officer, dropping his grocery bag, rushing in, leaping up the stairs.

Another officer approached him when he reached the top. "Do you know this woman, sir?" Khavon looked over at Cassandra who was half-naked and shaking.

"Yes, she's my wife," Khavon said slowly, confused and frightened by her blood-splattered night-shirt.

"I didn't do it, Khavon . . . I didn't do it!!! Steve and I, we had a pact—we had a pact," Cassandra kept repeating in between hysterical sobs. Her hair was all over her face.

"Cass, what are you talking about? What's going on?" Khavon asked, trying to come to her aid.

"I'm sorry, sir. You have to stay back."

"Wait a minute. What are you doing? That's my wife! Where are you taking my wife?" Khavon shouted at the officer handcuffing Cassandra, lunging toward the bedroom door.

"I'm sorry, sir, but you can't go in there," the young officer said, blocking the doorway.

"That's my bedroom!" Khavon said, pushing him aside so that he could enter. He was able to see Steven, half-naked sprawled across the white, blood-soaked sheets that covered his bed before they pulled him away.

"I'm sorry sir, but how well do you know the victim?" the chief investigator had asked Khavon a few minutes later at the bottom of the stairs.

Khavon stared at him, blankly. His head was spinning. *The victim. The victim.* "He was my friend. My best friend." Khavon stammered slowly, disbelievingly, staring into the space between them.

"Mr. Brighton, why don't you have a seat?" Khavon just stood there, speechless.

"Do you have any idea why your wife would want to kill her lover?" *Lover?* Khavon looked up at the officer, incredulous.

"What? What are you talking about?"

"Your wife . . . apparently she was having an affair with the deceased and shot him. One of the tenants called the police. We found her covered in blood, shaking uncontrollably with the gun in her hands, his blood all over her clothes."

Now, back in the present, Khavon put his hand to his head, the memories overcoming him. "There were so many lies, Cass. I guess I was just too hurt and betrayed to do anything else." He paused. "Cass, you told me that you were clean. And I believed you. If you needed more help, you should've just told me—you could've talked to me—you should have trusted me, you didn't have to—

Cass, he was my best friend!" Khavon exclaimed finally, shaking his head.

"Khavon, I didn't sleep with him."

"You didn't," Khavon quipped, unsympathetically, bracing himself for a new set of lies.

"No. I didn't. It was the drug. The drug slept with him, not me. And it was the drug that killed him, not me. The drug had control over me, over the both of us. We were desperate and hopeless. We were both out of it. And then Steve had an idea about a suicide pact. And I agreed to it. But when he . . . when he pulled the trigger and I saw him, I just got scared and freaked out." She covered her face, the memory of the last moments with Steve overcoming her.

"Why did you come here Khavon!?!" She shouted, suddenly. "Why?"

"I know you didn't do it. And I know you need some help to prove it. And so . . . ."

"What? I haven't needed you for eight years, and I don't need you now." She stopped abruptly. "And Khavon, you don't have to worry about the legal fees. Obviously it didn't do much good, but I plan to pay you back in full."

She turned to leave and turned back again as if she'd forgotten something and said coldly before leaving the room, "Goodbye, Khavon." She paused, briefly. "And I hope you get your closure."

Chapter Twelve

Alayna was just about to take a bite out of her shaved smoked turkey sandwich when she heard the creaking sound of her cubical door swinging in.

"I really don't want to interrupt your lunch, but if you have some time this afternoon, I'd like to speak to you about the break-in the other day." More than professional, his voice was cold and distant.

He knew he had chosen an inopportune moment to confront Alayna, but he had no other way to deal with his feelings. He had never felt like this before, not with Cassandra, not with anyone. Over time, he had grown to love Cassandra—but the feeling was nothing like what he was feeling right now. It could not compare to the passion and the need that Alayna continued to summon from deep within him . . . . *But why wouldn't she talk to me? Why did she have to walk away from me like that when, for the first time in my life, I had put my ripe heart on the table? Why did she have to squash it? Why did she have to reject me in my most vulnerable moment?* It was time for him to chill for a while, as his ego couldn't take much more rejection. It was usually he who dealt out the jones like they were cards at a poker game, not the other way around.

"What break-in?" Becky asked, coming up behind him.

"Someone broke into my car yesterday." Alayna lied coolly, before Khavon had a chance to come up with his own story.

"You're kidding. What happened?" Becky asked, pushing up her glasses, now completely infused in the conversation.

"Yesterday morning when I walked out to my car," Alayna continued to improvise, "I noticed that the window seemed unusually clear. And when I looked down, there was scattered broken glass at my feet."

"Geez. Did they take anything?"

"They took my cell phone, a pair of prescription sun glasses, and some tapes. That's all that I had in there."

"Wow. Did you report it to the police?" asked Becky.

"Yeah, but they said that the chances of recovering any of the items are slim. Khavon has promised to give me some tips on some additional security measures, didn't you, Khavon?"

He was quick to pick up the story, "Yes, yes, I did, but as I said before, I don't want to interrupt your lunch. I'll stop by later this afternoon, if that's okay." He was impressed with Alayna's quick-witted ability to maintain the vital confidentiality that he had requested of her.

"Later this afternoon is fine," Alayna agreed

It was unusual for Khavon to be late. Alayna had known him for only a few months, but she knew that it was out of character for him. He might be a swaggering playboy, a cocky computer guru, a pompous, self-righteous job-thief—even a pretentious parking spot hog—but if there was one thing that Khavon Brighton was not, it was late. But it was just as well, she thought. It would give her some time to gather her thoughts on what she was going to say.

Forty-five minutes earlier, he had stopped by and asked her to meet him in a half hour in conference room one to discuss the recent security compromise. The exchange was short and to the point. But Khavon definitely was not his normal toothy self. He hadn't been since he had confronted her that day in the conference room. He had been cold and distant and to her surprise it was driving her crazy. She couldn't stand the thought of him being angry with her. The tension was unbearable and was effecting her well-being.

Suddenly, she decided that she needed to apologize, or at least clear the air a little bit. Khavon was upset with her for walking out on him like that. She could have at least talked to him about the situation. She didn't have to ignore their feelings, pretend that they didn't exist. There was no use trying to run away from it. It was real. She knew it, and he knew it. She was going to have to deal with it. It might not be pleasant, but she was going to have to deal with it. The least she could've done was to behave like an adult, instead of running away like a child.

But the big hand on the clock over her head was now tipping past twelve. It was a quarter past. She certainly wanted to clear the air, but she was getting tired of waiting.

She was just about to get up and leave when Khavon strode in.

"I was just about to leave," Alayna announced in a voice that was clearly irritated.

He had purposely asked her to meet him in a half an hour to see how long she would wait. She was playing games, he had decided, and it was time that she got a dose of her own medicine. Where did she get off walking away from him like that, acting like the attraction was all in his head?

Her predictable annoyance in response to his late arrival was both expected and anticipated by him. And he, having calculated her reaction, was enjoying every bit of it.

"That's an option that is still open to you, should you deem it necessary, Alayna," Khavon said, apathetically.

Alayna jerked back instinctively, slightly startled by his gruff manner. "What's your problem?" she asked, trying unsuccessfully to tone down the irritation. She again took a seat.

His voice had a cynical edge. "Problem? I don't have a problem," he replied, seemingly unruffled by her obviously agitated state.

"Okay, look, Khavon, I'm glad you asked me to meet you," Alayna began.

"Oh?" Khavon folded his arms across his chest, his own behavior now mimicking that of a small child.

"Yes. I—ah . . . ." Alayna said. "I just wanted to say that I'm sorry for walking out on you the other day. It was really childish and I'm sorry. I've been thinking a lot about what you said, and it took me some time to admit it, but there's a lot of truth to it. And I'd be lying to myself if I said anything different," she admitted, her gaze darting from his eyes, to the window, and back to the floor again.

Khavon did not take his eyes off of Alayna as he lowered himself into a seat. "And?" he asked, now visibly softening.

"And, I think I just need some time to sort some things out."

"Some things, like what?" Khavon wanted to know.

"Like what my priorities are. Like what's important to me. Like Warren. Or did you forget that I planned to be married in a few months?" Alayna reminded him.

"No, I didn't forget," Khavon answered simply.

"I mean, Warren is really a wonderful person," Alayna said, as if trying to convince herself.

"I guess. I mean, if you like that type," Khavon said evenly.

"And I don't want to hurt him, or anyone else for that matter."

"Do you love him?"

"Love is an extreme."

"That wasn't the question. Do you love him?"

"Warren is the ideal man for me. We have our ups and downs, but we have a certain rapport with each other," Alayna rambled, trying to explain.

"This is not rocket science, Alayna," Khavon said, trying hard to be patient. "Either you love the man or you don't. Now which is it?"

"You are beginning to sound like Sheila," Alayna complained.

"You still haven't answered my question."

Alayna inhaled deeply and contemplated the question for several moments. "Look, Khavon, I don't want to hurt anyone."

Clearly frustrated, Khavon shut his eyes hard, and raised his voice slightly. "Okay, Alayna, I'm going to ask you one more time. Do you love the man or not?"

Alayna's eyes went wide before she turned away to the window. She was quiet for a time before answering. "No, I guess I'm finally coming to realize that I don't."

Relief and triumph replaced Khavon's anger. "Well, if you don't love him . . . I mean if you're not in love with him, what's the problem?"

Shaking her head, Alayna again looked away. In her mind's eye, she could see the shiny golden ring dangling on the far edge of a tender new branch. She was still too afraid to loosen her grip from the trunk of the tree. She had already entrusted the weight of her future in Warren.

"Like I told you before, there's other issues that I need to consider before I do anything that I might end up regretting," Alayna said.

"Well, I tell you what," Khavon began, "if you did want to hurt him, the best way to go about doing it would be to marry him under the pretense of being in love with him, when you're not even close."

Alayna was silent.

"What I'm trying to say is that you should never, ever, under any circumstances, marry someone that you are not in love with. Believe me, I know."

"You do?" she asked, suspecting that he had said more than he had intended.

"I do. I've done it, and I don't recommend it. And that's all I have to say on the matter." His smooth voice was clearly marked with pain and suffering.

Alayna wanted desperately to hear more about his wife and their relationship, but Khavon had made it clear that he didn't want to talk about it.

"So, what are you saying, Alayna?" Khavon asked, finally, breaking a long silence.

"I'm saying that I am acknowledging that there is a situation here," she conceded. "But I don't know what I'm going to do about it yet. And I don't know when I will know."

"I hear what you're saying. And I understand. Acknowledgment is all I wanted . . . for now anyway. I'm glad we talked," Khavon said.

"So am I," Alayna confessed.

"Now about the security issues I wanted to talk to you about," Khavon sighed, heavily. "I'm beginning to wonder if this is an inside job . . . ."

Chapter Thirteen

As he slowly and evenly curled the heavy weight in his hand to meet his biceps, the elation that he felt from Alayna's concession was almost enough to make him forget . . . almost but not enough. If only the pain of remembering could be washed away with the drenching rain waters that splashed against his window pane. But no, it seemed that the haunting clouds of yesterday were unintimidated by the western winds to move east. The painful memories preferred instead to hover overhead like a never ending storm over a sandy seashore. How many years must pass, he wondered, before the pain of betrayal would leave him? But closing his eyes, his mind would afford him no real freedom, only short, shackled reprieves.

Cassandra had sounded so scared when she had come to him. "I can't go home to my father pregnant and unmarried. Khavon, I don't know what he'll do. I don't know what I'm going to do. I've ruined the family name. You don't know my father, he will disown me. He was very strict with us, growing up. We weren't allowed to do anything. He was always ranting and raving about the evils of the world and how none of his girls better come home pregnant," she rambled, sobbing hysterically.

"Sh. Sh." Khavon consoled, trying to calm her down. "You don't have to worry. I want to bring our child up the right way," he had told her, rubbing her back as she cried in his arms.

The wedding had been beautiful and the union promising, despite the fact that it was not one bound in love.

Ignoring the consequences of taking no responsibility was common convention in the 80's. In hindsight, he thought cynically to himself, he should've followed the convention.

He was never going to get married again, he reminded himself as the painful memories began to renew themselves in his mind. "No. Never again," he snarled in disgust. Who was he trying to fool? And he had no right, he scolded himself, to lead Alayna into thinking anything different. She had told him in no uncertain terms what she wanted, what was important to her, and he knew he was not in the position to give it to her. "Love or no love," he mumbled to himself. He closed his eyes in torment over the dilemma. How could he have listened wordlessly while she toyed with the idea of giving up her dream—a dream that he could not help her realize?

"An inside job . . . . An inside job . . . ." The words were like a throbbing migraine inside Alayna's head. Alayna was stunned when Khavon had announced his suspicions. "You mean you think it was somebody at Excelsior?" she had asked, not really believing what he was saying.

"That's what inside job means, Alayna."

"I know what it means, but I mean who?"

He had no idea and neither did she. Alayna had to admit, it was strange how the culprit had known so much about Khavon. But an inside job? Shaking her head, she pushed the hangers back and forth across the rack, looking for something to wear.

The start of the show was only an hour and a half away, and she hadn't even showered yet. In the beginning, she had been looking so forward to the concert, but with everything that had been going on. . . And now, with this business about the heist being an inside job, Alayna was too distracted to think about anything else.

She finally settled on faded blue jeans, a sleeveless black body suit, a mid-thigh black riding blazer and black mules. A thin gold chain and matching hoop earrings accessorized her outfit. She wanted to be casual, yet eye-catching. And she was—she was striking. Her jet black hair was carefully twisted from the nape of her neck into a textured French roll. Two curls fell down casually on either side to frame her golden face

Alayna had only been in her seat for fifteen minutes when the house lights flickered to a flame level, and the people began to rise and head for the rest rooms and the cash wet bars in the rear hallways. Alayna thought a drink would help her get her emotions under control.

"Hello. What can I get for the lovely lady?" the bartender said, grinning devilishly.

"Hi. Yes, can I get a white zinfandel, please?"

"Your wish is my command." He winked.

She laughed. He had to be twice her age. "Thank you."

"You are quite welcome, my dear."

She turned to leave, but before she made it all the way around she heard her name.

"Alayna, hey." Alayna turned to see Khavon's perfect frame parting the crowd to catch up with her. He was wearing a long-sleeved black ribbed turtleneck, and black ash jeans. Molding his skull and crowning the top half of his forehead was a black crocheted koofi.

"Hey, you." He greeted her again, slightly out of breath from trying to catch up to her. "Hey. I didn't know that you were planning to come to the concert." Khavon looked around scoping a bit before inquiring, "Where's Warren?"

"Warren, unfortunately, is out of town," Alayna answered matter of factly.

"Oh, I see." Khavon smiled, wickedly. "Well, who did you come with?"

"I didn't come with anyone. Am I required to have an escort to be in attendance at a public event?" Alayna joked.

"Well, no, I just thought . . . . Never mind. Where are you sitting?"

"Section Z."

"Z, huh?"

"Yeah, I know. I'm trying not to get a nosebleed. Besides, it was all they had left," winced Alayna. "I was lucky to get that."

Khavon smiled a sneaky smile.

"What's so funny?"

"Well," Khavon began, "I just happen to be sitting in the 7th row on the floor."

"And?" Alayna pretended to be bored and uninterested.

"And my date canceled on me at the last minute."

"And?"

"And, I just happen to have an empty seat next to me."

"And?"

"And, I just happen to be alone."

"And?" Alayna was enjoying the game.

"And, well I wouldn't want you to get a nosebleed . . . . Would you like to join me? We could enjoy the concert together."

She laughed. "Well, I—"

"Come on, there's no harm in two people sitting next two each other at a public event, is there?"

"Well, I suppose not." Alayna tried to conceal her excitement.

Khavon gently guided Alayna in the small of her back. She tried to ignore the electricity generated at his slightest touch.

He remained no less than a perfect gentleman throughout the remainder of the concert. They sat quietly with a few moments of awkward silence. And then Khavon said, "Alayna , you know I—" Just then, the lights overhead began to dim. The darkness fell over the concert hall like a slow thick layer of black fog.

"What?" Alayna's brown eyes were inquisitive.

"Nothing. It's starting up again." Khavon yelled over the music.

"Minneapolis!" The crowd was screaming. "Minneapolis, are you ready?! Are you ready?!" the emcee shouted at the crowd as it went wild. "Minneapolis/St. Paul, here he is, in the flesh! Mr. D-A-V-I-D G-I-L-L-I-A-M!"

"Oh, yeah! It's on now!" Alayna screamed.

Khavon laughed, surprised at Alayna's excitement. The flashing spotlights from the stage gave Alayna's face a warm inviting glow, but it was outdone by her thick, red lips, which seemed to invite him to taste.

"Well, I guess now you know," smiled Alayna, as flash of the bass player's guitar reflected in her eyes. Khavon gave her a warm smile back. Slightly embarrassed, Alayna blushed, and turned back to the show.

Together they jammed to the groove. The sax was profusely seductive, pleading. It was the kind of jazz that called for the sun at your back, a wine cooler in hand and the Caribbean at your feet, Alayna thought, bobbing her head to the music.

"David Gilliam has such a distinctive sound, don't you think? It's so . . . so . . . ."

"Sexy?" Khavon helped her out.

"Yeah," Alayna realized.

"Yeah, I know what you mean. It's smooth, but somehow raw at the same time."

"Yeah. The sax is just a sexy instrument," Alayna commented, amazed at the level of comfort she felt at Khavon's side. She couldn't tell if it was the sizzling jazz or Khavon that was melting away her inhibitions.

Khavon wanted to touch her. He wanted to just hold her hand and tell her how he felt. His hands came together in applause instead.

When the applause died down, the two of them sat in disquieted silence, their eyes transfixed, as the stage was transformed into the cosmos, and David did a cover of Norman Conner's '*You Are My Starship*.' As an encore, both artists came on stage and jammed together for twenty minutes. It was amazing, a jazz fan's utopia.

"That was wild!" Alayna squealed excitedly to Khavon when the concert ended.

"Yeah, that was spazzed!" Taking her by surprise, he grabbed her hand. "C'mon. I want you to meet someone."

Two hours later, as they exited the auditorium and the night air hit their faces, Alayna caught herself wondering what it would be like to be Khavon's lover. What would it be like, she wondered, instead of going home alone, to be going home with him? The man had skills. She could tell just by the way he walked. *Stop it.*

"Wow. That was fun. I've never been backstage before. And I can't believe how nice he was," Alayna said.

"Yeah, a little too nice if you ask me," Khavon smirked.

Alayna laughed. "I didn't ask. Besides, he was just being friendly. Anyway, you're the one who wanted me to meet him. He's your friend."

"So he is."

"So how'd you two come to be friends?"

Khavon quietly looked away, took in a deep breath, and turned to answer her question. "About a million years ago, a very good friend of mine started up a band called The Minneapolis Sound. I'm sure you've heard of them."

"Yeah, I have some of their albums."

"Well, not long after the group got started, it lost its lead sax. And as you probably already know, it was a launching pad for David's solo career."

"So which one of the guys is your friend?"

"You wouldn't know him," Khavon closed his eyes hard. "He left the group just before they went large."

"Mmph. That's too bad."

"Yeah. Nice out tonight, huh?" Khavon changed the subject abruptly.

"Yes, really nice. Thanks again for inviting me to sit with you, and for taking me backstage. I had a lot of fun."

Khavon smiled generously. "You're very welcome, Ms. Alexander," he said, noticing how her eyes sparkled in the moonlight. "I'll walk you to your car."

"My car's right in the front parking lot. There are still plenty of people around. I'll be fine, Khavon." Registering his disapproval, she smiled, "Really." Alayna half turned into the direction of the parking lot. "Well, we'll see you later."

Khavon hurried to her side to catch up to her. "Are you sure you'll be okay? Let me walk you. I insist. At least to the entry way."

"Khavon, really, it's not necessary, I'm right across the street. See you. Thanks again."

"My pleasure, Ms. Alexander," he smiled.

She gingerly nodded her head with a smile, "Bye."

He smiled goodbye, but Khavon couldn't help but notice the grace and femininity of her sway as she walked away. Quick of thought, he called after her, "Alayna, there's a coffee house right up the street a little way. Would you like to stop in for a little while?"

Alayna turned and walked toward him again. "Khavon, I don't know. I—"

"Does your engagement mean you are forbidden to engage in conversation with people?" Khavon cut her off. "I'm not asking you to go home with me. I just wouldn't mind sitting down and sharing a cup of coffee with you. We could celebrate our first breakthrough on the project. Or just get to know one another a little better." Alayna gave him a funny look. "As colleagues, I mean."

She looked with squinted eyes and saw only sincerity staring back at her. "Okay, Khavon. I don't see any harm in that."

The moon was high and full, and the dark night clouds raced across the sky as if in a hurry to some unknown destination. The crisp air sounded of bold fall leaves crinkling underneath their feet as they walked. She could hear the occasional jingle of Khavon's keys in his pocket.

"It sure is a beautiful night," observed Alayna as she and Khavon slowly strolled along the dimly lit, tree-lined street.

"Yes, it really is. I really love the early fall weather. Everyday it's usually just about 75 degrees. Not too hot, not too cold. Just nice." Khavon added.

"Yes, this is nice. But I must admit that I do have a passion for the summer. The days are hot and so are the nights. The hotter the better, as far as I am concerned."

"That's interesting. Why is that?"

"I don't know. It's just so bright and sunny everyday. It just seems to put everything and everyone in a happier disposition. I think I'm one of those people you've probably seen on TV, who are affected by the sunlight. I forgot what it's called."

"Solar Affected Disorder."

"Yes, that's it." Alayna was glad that he had remembered because she know she would have been trying to think of what it was called all night long.

"It seems that I have so much more energy, and am so much happier in the spring and summer. Do you think that's weird?"

"No, not really. But I do find it odd that you picked a place like Minnesota to live in."

"Yeah. Well, I guess that is kind of curious, given my predisposition, huh? My masochistic nature, I guess."

He lifted a brow. "Your nature sounds intriguing."

"I didn't mean it like that. I just meant enduring Minnesota's winters, year after year, has been torture and I don't know why I still stay here."

Khavon laughed. "Alayna, you have the wrong attitude."

Alayna looked at him strangely, "What do you mean?"

"I just mean living in Minnesota most of my life has given me a certain appreciation for Mother Nature. There are a lot of fun things to do in Minnesota in the winter time."

"Like what? Curling?" Alayna laughed.

"Well, I've never tried curling, but I hear it's a lot of fun."

Alayna laughed.

"Don't laugh. That's just one example. Have you ever been to the Winter Carnival or the Holidazzle parade? And there's always skiing. There's lots of things to do. You just have to be willing to put on a couple of extra layers."

Alayna looked at him like he was crazy. "Yeah, right."

"Okay, Alayna, why do you stay here then?" Khavon asked.

"I told you, I don't know. I came here in the beginning because the opportunity with Excelsior was one that I didn't want to pass up. I knew that some of the best technical minds in the country could be found at Excelsior Securities. Besides, jobs were very scarce back when I graduated."

"Where are you from?"

"Chicago, originally. Then Berkeley. I never really planned to stay here more than five years."

"How long have you been here?" Khavon asked.

"Seven."

"That's a long time."

The tick-tock of her internal clock was splitting her ears. "Yeah, I know."

"You must really like it here."

"Believe it or not, I do. Minnesota is very clean and green. It might sound silly to some people, but it's important to me. There's also a lot of opportunity here. Plus, Minneapolis is kind of a small version of a big city. And I like that. Some people call it the Mini Apple—but I suppose you know that since you've lived here most of your life."

"Mm-hm."

"And that's really unusual," Alayna continued.

"What?"

"Most of the Black people in Minnesota migrated here from somewhere else. You must like it here, too. I mean, since you're still here."

"I do. But I will probably eventually move somewhere near the ocean. I love the ocean."

"So do I," mused Alayna.

"So tell me, Ms. Alexander, how did you get interested in the computer security business?"

"Well, I wasn't really. Not at first. I just got tired of getting the run-around from the social workers at the agency when I would ask them about the adoption process or about my parents. I started tapping into their computers to get the 411. When I graduated from high school, I got a scholarship to UC-Berkeley, and enrolled in the computer science program there. I was working at the University's academic computer center when I stumbled onto a virus that had infected the University's computer systems and was deliberately damaging the University's files by overwriting them with replicas of itself and then hiding within the system. 'Bohemian.' Ever heard of it?"

"Yeah. Vicious."

"No kidding. It took me a while, but eventually I isolated it and developed an antidote for it. It was around that time that Excelsior launched its anti-viral software division to combat the threat of massive data loss. When I got my degree, I came on board and started developing antidotes and killing computer viruses for them—but after six years, I was ready for a change. That's how I ended up in wire transfer."

"Well, here we are, Java City." Khavon opened the door and guided Alayna in front of him. They studied the menu as they stood in line. "Well, what do you think?" Khavon asked.

"The Cappuccino Americano looks good. Decaf." Khavon looked surprised. "The caffeine keeps me up at night."

"That may not necessarily be a liability," Khavon said with a sly smile.

"Khavon . . . I thought you said we—"

"I was just joking."

"What are you going to have?"

"Cappuccino sounds good, but I think I need a little kick in mine."

Alayna could not help but notice that the young blonde woman behind the counter could not break her gaze from Khavon.

"Looks like you have an admirer," Alayna nodded her head in the direction of the young girl.

The girl gave Khavon a wide smile when they came to the front of the line. "May I take your order, sir?"

Alayna stepped in front of Khavon and interjected, "Yes, the gentleman will have a double Cappuccino Americano, regular. And I will have the same, decaf." Alayna's face was expressionless. Both the girl and Khavon were slightly taken aback.

"Yes, ma'am. Anything else?"

"No. That's it." Alayna chastised herself privately. *Why did I do that? Why should I care? I am engaged to another man. Why should I care if some young girl couldn't take her eyes off of Khavon?*

"For here or to go?"

"For here."

"That will be $5.89, please." Alayna was reaching for her purse.

Khavon rolled his eyes. "What are you doing?"

"I was just going to pay for—"

"Alayna, please." Khavon pulled out a twenty-dollar bill and handed it to the girl.

"Thank you."

"It's nothing. My pleasure, really."

Alayna spied the last seat over at the large picture window

facing Washington Avenue. "Let's sit by the window so we can people-watch."

"Sounds good to me." They walked over. Khavon sat the coffees on the black lacquer tabletop and pulled out Alayna's chair.

"Thank you." Alayna took her seat. It was nice to be treated like a lady for a change.

There was an awkward moment of silence after Khavon sat down. Alayna leaned back into the high-backed metal chair and studied the eclectic art on the wall before finally breaking the ice. "This is really a nice place. I've never been in here. I've driven past before, but have never been inside."

"I thought you might like it."

Through the front glass, Khavon eyed the backpack-laden student approaching from the opposite direction. "I guess you really knew what you were talking about when you said that it would a good spot to people watch."

"What do you m—" Alayna started to ask, her eyes catching and slowly following the young teenager with pink and orange spiked hair trod by their window, one combat boot plodding in front of the other.

"Variety is the spice of life."

Khavon laughed. "You know," he said, "in some coffee shops in Europe, you have to pay a surcharge for ring side seats like these."

"You're kidding." *He's so worldly. I like that in him.*

Khavon shook his head, swallowing a hot sip. "No. I'm not."

"You mean, there's a charge to sit in a window seat?" Alayna asked, incredulously.

"No joke. And in some places," Khavon continued, "the coffee is so strong that they had to put marijuana on the menu just to tame the jolt."

"I take it that you're speaking from experience."

"With the European coffee houses or the marijuana?"

"Both," Alayna stated flatly.

"I don't do drugs, Alayna, and yes, I've traveled abroad and stopped in a few coffee houses along the way."

"Sounds exciting. Tell me more." She liked being with someone she could learn something from.

"I was stationed in Rota, Spain, for two years when I was in the Marine Corps."

"Really?"

"Yeah. I toured for two and a half months after I was discharged."

"Sounds exciting." Alayna shook her head. "Here you've lived part of your life in a completely different country, and I've only made it to the U.S. coast. If it hadn't been for school, I probably wouldn't have even gone that far," Alayna remarked in awe. "I can't imagine. What was it like?"

"Well, the architecture of course, is much older than ours, ancient even, in some cases. Many of the streets are paved in cobblestone. Lots of museums and stuff. I don't know, it's just different over there. The culture is different."

"What do you mean? How so?"

"Well, for one thing, race is less of an issue over there. It's not that racism doesn't exist, it's just that it's not ingrained in the culture like it is here. And it's, well . . . ." Khavon hedged.

"What? Tell me."

"It's a lot less inhibited over there," he studied her closely before continuing. "Americans are so uptight about things. Like sex for example." He stopped momentarily, directing his brown eyes into hers. "In Europe, topless beaches are commonplace. And . . . ."

Alayna sat listening in child like innocence, as Khavon carried her with him through his memories from Spain, to Italy, to France, Switzerland, Germany, Austria and Africa. She listened with the intrigue of a child on the first day of kindergarten. Her pulse had raced with excitement as Khavon's words painted her blank canvas with the vivid, awe-inspiring imagery of the world she had yet to see. At his invitation she climbed into the beautiful Old World painting that was his memory. Stroked and dabbed with unforgettable keepsakes of his experience abroad, the retrospective collage pushed the open cracked window of her closed view of the world to let the breeze of knowledge flow in.

Alayna had been the eager tourist, and Khavon the gracious tour guide. They jet-setted on the wings Khavon's memories, from the clean, clear, swan-filled lakes of Zurich, to the rolling green hills of Dusseldorf. Together they toured the ancient ruins of Rome, steered a wobbly gondola through the meandering canals of Venice, and crowded St. Marques Square in costume for the Carnivale. They dodged the soiled streets of Paris to climb the Eiffel Tower. They even drank from the rivers of fresh fruit Sangria flowing through the night clubs of Spain. From charming java houses on every corner to the majesty of Florence, their spontaneous odyssey had been for Alayna, awe-inspiring.

But it was the pure, unabashed emotion that Khavon had emitted when he spoke of setting foot for the first time on the welcoming African shores of Mombasa that impassioned Alayna the most.

She realized at that moment that the ancestral void that she carried with her like an incurable ailment was not one that she shared alone. It was one that was shared not only by Khavon, but in fact, by many, many, other Americans who know nothing of their lineage, only that they had descended from the great continent of Africa.

Chapter Fourteen

"Happy birthday!" Sheila squealed excitedly from behind Alayna, as she opened her cubicle door.

"Thank you," Alayna reached over, giving her good friend a hug.

"Girl, you didn't have to do all of this," Alayna gestured an open hand to the huge elaborate display of ornate balloons and streamers that took up temporary residence in her cubicle.

"I know your birthday isn't until tomorrow, but I wanted to do something special for you at work," Sheila explained gleefully. "But really, you didn't have to go through so much trouble … and these . . . ." Alayna said, reaching over to inhale the delicate fragrance emanating from the bouquet of lilacs displayed prominently on her desk.

"Where in the world did you find these this time of year?"

"I didn't. They were sitting on your desk when I came in this morning to decorate your cube," Sheila reported, raising her brow suggestively.

Alayna shifted her gaze from Sheila to the desk searching for the card.

"And there's no card, cause you know I looked." Alayna rolled her eyes disapprovingly.

"Well. . . ." Sheila said, shrugging her shoulders guiltily. "It's not like you don't know who they're from anyway."

"And who might that be?" Alayna's tone was sarcastic. Sheila refused reply and pursed her lips together tightly instead.

"How do you know they're not from Warren?" Alayna asked, knowing the answer.

Khavon interrupted before she could answer. "Happy birthday, Alayna," his voice was a smooth and rich as the cappuccino that they'd shared the night before.

He had been true to his promise—a gentleman in every sense of the word. He never once touched her, or even made the slightest advance towards her. She knew that he was giving her the kind of space that she needed to have if she was going to objectively assess her life and her priorities. After Khavon had walked her to her car and she'd driven home, she'd lain awake in her bed trying to do just that. But in between, she reviewed snapshot after snapshot of the overseas jaunt that she and Khavon had spontaneously taken together.

"Thank you," Alayna said, her biological time clock gonging now.

Sheila turned to Alayna. "Well, birthday girl, I need to get back to my desk. I'm expecting a call. And Khavon, I'm still working on those notes that you gave me this morning, but I should have them on your desk by noon," she said, rushing past him.

"That's fine." Khavon nodded appreciatively.

"Well, I just wanted to stop in to say happy birthday. We'll see ya later, okay?"

"Okay, and thanks again."

Sheila waved her hand and made her way to her desk.

"Were you in on all of this too?" Alayna asked Khavon coyly, referring again to the elaborate birthday decorations display.

"Well no, not exactly. But I did think that you might like the flowers."

"So it was you?" Alayna feigned surprise.

Khavon smiled affirmatively.

Alayna thought of Sheila, who if she were still there would utter a wordless 'I told you so.' "Why didn't you leave a card?"

"Well, you know how nosy folks around here can get. I just thought it would be better this way."

"Yeah, I guess you're right."

"Well, I should be going too. I just stopped over to wish you a happy birthday."

"Thanks for the flowers, Khavon. They're beautiful. It was really very sweet of you." She smiled a smile that was like that of a child on Christmas morning. Khavon turned and lifted his head slightly to acknowledge her statement.

"You're very welcome, Ms. Alexander, and I hope your day is well . . . ." She liked how he always called her Ms. Alexander.

Warren knocked his knee against the dashboard, as he slid hastily into the passenger seat of her curbside car. "Damn it!" he swore loudly.

Alayna thought it to be mildly amusing, but she didn't dare laugh. It was best, she decided, not to aggravate the situation as she was already fifteen minutes late. "Warren, are you okay?" Her voice filled with theatrical concern.

"I'm fine, but you need to get yourself a real car, instead of this toy one," he snapped, rubbing his knee cap through his pant leg. He kissed her on the cheek. "You're late," he pronounced as the sting in his knee faded.

"Yeah, I know. I'm sorry, but for some reason traffic was really heavy. How was your trip?" Alayna asked cheerily, attempting to change the subject, pulling into the airport arrivals traffic flow.

"It was fairly interesting."

"Oh? How so?"

"I'll tell you later, but right now, since we're running late we need to get home and get dressed. The Lindquists are expecting us at seven. You didn't forget did you?"

No, I didn't forget. After all birthdays do only come around once a year. It's your sorry memory that is apparently weak, frail, and in need of repair, she thought bitterly to herself. Audibly, she chose to take the high road. "No, Warren, I didn't forget," she answered simply.

"What the hell are you people doing out there?" Mulcahy's voice boomed through the telephone receiver into Michael Tafuri's ear. Ted Mulcahy was a big, warm, fuzzy, teddy bear when things were going well. But he was also the type of person that would chew a person's head off down to his waist when they weren't, particularly when the buck had no place else to go. And unfortunately for Michael Tafuri, he was the one with the capital in hand.

The telephone had rung just as he was stepping out of his office door, leaving for the day. Having already received the bad news from Jim Lundgren at Liberty, he had debated for a few seconds on whether or not to answer the telephone. Clearly, he had made the wrong decision, he thought to himself, as Mulcahy continued to light into him.

"Do you people think this is some sort of game?" he screamed through the phone. "This is a mandate from the White House! We are talking about six million companies across the country. Do you know how much money that is?"

"Yes, sir," Furi said, holding the receiver a careful distance from his ear.

"That's more than a trillion dollars in federal income taxes! We can't afford to have every pepperoni-faced computer hacker in America, or the world for that matter, breaking into this system every time they decide that they need some extra pocket change!"

"Yes, sir. My people are working—"

"Your people better be working on it. This is the fourth and last time. It's only because I have some friendly ties over at Excelsior that I've decided to give you people one last chance, but you should know that I already have another financial agent lined up if you people can't get your act together out there. Are we perfectly clear, Tafuri?" Mulcahy said, clenching his teeth.

"Yes. Sir. Perfectly clear, sir."

"Good. Now, that said, I want to meet with your top people on this, personally, to get a clearer picture of what's going on and what you people are doing out there. Do you think you can manage that, Tafuri?"

"Mm-hmm. Yes, sir. No problem."

Mulcahy paged angrily through his date book. "I'm looking at Thursday. I have a briefing with the Secretary of State at nine, but I should have enough time to catch a flight and get out there by 2:30 that afternoon."

"That's fine, sir."

"I'll have my secretary make the necessary travel arrangements."

"Sounds good, sir. We'll be expect—" *Click.* The receiver went dead in Michael Tafuri's hand.

Hexed! It was like Alayna had him under some sort of spell or something. This morning, he recalled, he had returned to the house three different times for items that he'd simply forgotten. He'd just spent the last hour trying to retrieve his keys from inside of his locked car.

"I've lost my mind. That's what it is. I have truly lost my mind," Khavon mumbled miserably to himself as he flicked on the light switch.

He was glad to be home. He was tired. It had been a long day. A strange melancholy suddenly swept over him. *Why does life have to be so difficult?* Back in the day, things were so much simpler—not problem-free by any means, but so much simpler. He needed curative treatment, he decided. Nothing like a healthy dose of P-funk.

After consuming a hasty meal of fettuccini alfredo, Khavon made his way to the basement.

Upon making his selection, he stared disbelievingly at the year on the outside cover of Norman Conner's recording. More than twenty years had passed . . . twenty, since he had first purchased the album and feel in love with the cut, *You Are My Starship*. He shook his head. *I can't believe it's been twenty years. They don't even make albums anymore,* he thought grimly. "And this, this is an antique." Khavon smiled, running his hand over his stereo. It was ironic, he thought. He was the owner of his own high-tech computer security firm, yet still getting his groove on with an ancient, though still functioning, turntable. Sure, he had high-tech CD's and all, but still he liked his turntable—he was sort of retro-minded when it came to music. He flipped the twelve-inch disk over and carefully placed the needle at the edge of the recording. He listened to the sound of the static as the needle made its way to the beginning of the song.

Suddenly in a flash, he was back there. Rota, Spain, 1977. It seemed as though it were just yesterday. For Khavon, it had been a fresh new beginning. The carefree life of the service had been a welcome reprieve. He was lucky, he thought, to have been stationed in Rota. Rota was a place, he recalled, where the sting of his reality could be drenched in ruby red sangria, and the hurt of yesterday melted away in the midnight kisses of timid young Spanish girls. He had needed Rota. *Maybe it wasn't luck,* he second-guessed. *Maybe it was fate.* "Man, those were the days back then. Those were the days . . . ." Khavon let his head fall back nostalgically. Youth taken for granted, no responsibilities, beautiful dark-haired locals.

Through the window, Khavon studied the night sky and the luminous globe that guarded it. He sang along quietly, the haunting lyrics striking a resonant chord deep within him. The words, uttered with passion and pain, were meant for Alayna.

Before the night was over, Khavon had listened to dozens of favorites from his past. But not even a '70s revival could make him forget the stupid thing that he had done.

He was definitely in no position to give Alayna what she wanted—and he knew exactly what she wanted, and who could give it to her. So why couldn't he just sit back quietly and allow her a chance to achieve her dream? The worst thing that he could have done was to give the woman flowers on her birthday, but when he had seen her browsing the lilac web page and she'd commented that it was her favorite flower, he couldn't resist. In fact, he couldn't resist anything when it came to Alayna.

He wanted nothing more in life than to give her anything and everything, but in reality he knew he could not give her the one thing, the only thing, that she so desperately wanted most. How could he after what he'd been through? No, he'd promised himself that he would never marry again. And he didn't know which was worse—living with the certain knowledge that he never, ever, broke his promises, or knowing that right now, at this very moment, she was in all probability with that grinch, Warren.

Chapter Fifteen

"Marilyn, did Paul say when he thought he might be able to break free?" Warren asked, returning to his seat on the couch.

"Yes, he did. He said that he would try to be here by 6:30, but he also said that if he wasn't here by that time we should start dinner without him." She checked the tight-fitting diamond-studded watch on her plump wrist for the time. It's almost seven. I think maybe we'll just do that," Marilyn said, leading them into the dining room.

"Warren, why didn't you tell us that Alayna didn't eat red meat?" Marilyn wanted to know, reaching to remove the plate of bloody steak from Alayna's place setting.

"I guess I just didn't think about it," Warren said, slicing his beef into bite size pieces.

"Really, the potato and this salad are fine," Alayna said, reaching to refill her now-empty plate.

"Alayna, I'm so sorry. I didn't really prepare anything else."

"Don't worry about it. I wasn't even hungry," Alayna lied. *It's not your fault—Warren should have told you.* "I'm fine—really."

Marilyn's cherry-colored face had settled to its normal porcelain color by the time Paul strolled in.

"I'm sorry I'm late," Paul apologized, taking the head seat across from Marilyn at the dinner table.

"Well, it's about time you got here—we were beginning to wonder if you were coming at all," Marilyn said.

"I am sorry, but it was unavoidable," he apologized again.

"Alayna, how've you been? It's nice to see you again."

"I'm well, and yourself?"

"Good. Good." He smiled, eyeing Alayna's chest through her caramel cardigan.

Paul turned his attention to his other guest. "Well, Warren, you old dog, I understand that congratulations are in order. I told you that if you stick with me, you are going to go far."

Alayna stared curiously at the both of them.

"Yeah, I appreciate the good word that you put in for me, Paul. I really do."

"You better," Paul said, implying unmistakable indebtedness.

What are they talking about? Alayna wondered, curiously. Warren hadn't mentioned anything about a promotion.

"You know, Mulcahy and I go way back," Paul started, gulping down another swallow of red wine. *Mulcahy?*

"I met him at a fund raiser in 1976. His connections in Washington run far and deep, even into Excelsior, as you were so fortunate to find out. You know, that's beautiful country out there. I was born in Virginia, and that's where Marilyn and I met. In fact, it was at that same fundraiser, wasn't it Marilyn?" Paul asked jovially, reaching for his glass.

"Yes, dear," Marilyn answered tersely, clearly annoyed and embarrassed by his overzealous drinking.

Washington? Excelsior? What? I know that this man didn't lose his mind. Alayna's head was spinning. She knew that Warren was ambitious, but this was inconceivable. *I know this man didn't lose his mind.* There was no way that this man, calling himself her fiancé, would have the audacity to accept a job in Washington without first speaking to her about it. *Uh-Uh*. Alayna eyed Warren curiously, but, much to her dismay, he refused to meet her questioning gaze. Frustrated, she speared a cherry tomato and continued to listen.

"Alayna, you are just going to love it out there," Paul said, enthusiastically. The speared tomato fell to her plate, clinking loudly on the black lacquer plate sitting before her.

"I'm sorry," Alayna apologized for the mishap. She was fuming. He wouldn't disrespect her like that. He just wouldn't. There was some kind of reasonable explanation, she assured herself, rationally.

"You must be so thrilled," Marilyn added, excited by the news.

"Thrilled doesn't begin to describe what I'm feeling right now." Alayna said dryly, cutting an icy glare over to Warren, who still refused to meet her piercing eyes.

Alayna stared angrily out the window as they drove in a dead, chilly silence. The ride to Alayna's apartment complex was a long one. Both of them were glad when it ended. Warren pulled up in front of the building, wishing that he had taken the time to tell her. He wished that he knew what to say. But mostly, he wished that he was somewhere else other than where he was . . . anywhere else. Instead, Warren toyed uneasily with the steering wheel, dreading and anticipating the volcanic eruption that was sure to come from his right. He waited for the molten lava. He waited, but none was forthcoming.

"How could you do that, Warren?" Alayna finally said, coolly. "How could you make decisions about my life, without so much as even mentioning to me that you were even thinking of leaving the cities . . . without even discussing with me . . . ."

"Alayna, I was going to tell you—" Warren started.

"When?" Alayna cut him off. "When were you going to tell me? When were you going to tell me, Warren? When? In the taxi? At the airport? On the plane? When, Warren?" Her demeanor was calm as she rested the tips of her fingers on the center of her forehead. She was careful to maintain a collected composure, realizing that no productive communication could take place otherwise. She wanted so desperately to clearly understand his motives.

"Alayna, what I did, I did for us. The opportunity suddenly came up and I thought it would be a good thing. It was meant to be a good thing, Alayna, a good thing for us."

"But you see, Warren, that's the problem. That's the problem. You thought. . . You thought it would be a good thing for us, but you never bothered to discuss it with me, your supposed fiancée." She paused briefly. "Warren, don't you understand?

Picking up and starting fresh could very well have been a good thing for us, but that's something that we should have decided together."

"Okay, look, I'm sorry. I apologize." His voice was patronizing. "I should've discussed it with you. But Alayna, I'll be the Assistant to the Vice President of Finance. It won't be long before I'm Vice President. Wealth and affluence will be ours for the taking. I did this for us," Warren insisted, brushing a stray curl behind Alayna's ear.

"No, Warren. Uh-uh." Alayna said, pushing his hand away. "Why you trying to front?"

"Front? What are you talking about, front?"

"Don't try to play me. You did this for your own selfish purposes, and now you're trying to seek absolution by telling me that you did it for us. No. You did this for you and nobody else. Let's not play games."

"Okay, Alayna," he said, shrugging back into his seat in frustration. "Yeah. I admit it. I want what I want. But don't you want it too?" he asked sincerely. "Wealth, affluence, power. Alayna, don't you think that it would be exciting to move to Washington and try something different and new?"

"What I want is to be with someone who wants to be with me. Believe it or not, it's that simple." She paused. "I don't know, Warren. Maybe it would've been a good thing," Alayna said reflectively, looking into the distance, "but I guess I'll never know now, cause I'm not going anywhere." The ensuing silence, even more so than on the ride from the Lindquists, was long and uncomfortable for them both. "Anyway . . . what I want is irrelevant at this point. What's more important is how you just completely disrespected me and never even gave it a second thought," Alayna said, turning in the direction of the apartment building across the street. She fixed her gaze on it, not really seeing it.

"What does that mean, Alayna?"

"I'm not exactly sure what it means, Warren. But I know one thing—I'm not going anywhere," Alayna repeated adamantly.

"Mmph. I see." Warren gave a hard, slow blink. "Well, I'm not going to turn down the opportunity of a lifetime," Warren countered slowly.

"Mmph. I see. Well, I guess that answers your question," Alayna said, opening the car door.

I guess it does, Warren thought.

"Good night, Warren."

"Good night." She closed the car door and did not look back.

"Where is she?" Khavon grumbled impatiently as he placed the telephone receiver back in its cradle. He paced up and down the massive Oriental rug that centered the room. His office was quiet except for the occasional beep of his computer running the new software he'd hastily designed.

It had been more than two hours since Furi had first called with the bad news . . .

"Khavon?"

"Yeah, this is Khavon. Who is this?" Khavon asked, furrowing his thick brows curiously, not quite able to place Furi's voice.

"This is Furi. I've tried to reach Alayna, but I wasn't able to get in contact with her." The words had been simple enough but, even more than the aberrant phone call, they had been a troubling forewarning—like the flash of lightning before the rumble of thunder. He prepared himself for the worst. The fond memories of his polyester, bell-bottomed youth faded into a black hole. With controlled alarm, he asked the question that needed to be asked. "What happened?"

Furi answered, "This afternoon I received a phone call from Jim Lundgren over at Liberty. The inter-office settlement account in the government banking division was raided by wire three days ago."

"That's impossible," Khavon had first reacted when Furi relayed the official word he'd received from Liberty.

"Tell that to Jim. They had a $1,000,000 suspense item for three long days. Apparently, it's not impossible." His tone was no-nonsense, angry. "The money was transferred to two numbered accounts at the Union Bank of Zurich."

Khavon said nothing, giving Furi only the benefit of the sound of his even breathing on the other end of the line.

"The primary auditor in internal controls was on vacation and her back-up was out sick for the last two days. She says that when she got back, she started sifting through the audit trail reports on her desk and she ran across a 'red flag' report."

Red flag report? What red flag report? "A 'red flag' report?" Khavon asked.

"Yes. She says it indicated that the financial characteristics of the transaction were irregular and should be further investigated for possible wire fraud. She looked into it a little deeper and discovered that the suspense item hadn't been cleared. Then she reported it to the bank regulators."

This can't be happening. Khavon's mind was racing. The team had made countless visits to the wire transfer room—interviewing terminal operators and clerks, introducing deterrent policies, and making recommendations for better controls. He and Alayna had led the team in a labor-intensive effort to install the most sophisticated password and encryption process he'd ever designed. What puzzled him most was how someone had gotten past the extra tier of security that he had secretly installed as a last minute safeguard. He was the only one who knew about it. How had they managed to penetrate his defenses? And why hadn't his computers sounded an alarm?

"And the money?" Khavon asked cautiously, swallowing hard. "What happened to the money?"

"Luckily, we were able to recover it. After the auditor reported it, they reconciled with Union Zurich and the transfer was reversed." Closing his eyes hard, Khavon heaved a huge sigh of relief. "Now, what I want to know is how Liberty ended up with a $1,000,000 uncleared suspense item that went unchecked for three days, when the system was supposed to have already been secured by us."

"Listen, Furi—"

"No," he cut him off, "you listen. You were hired to do a job, and you apparently didn't do it. Now we could lose the biggest contract we have. And if that isn't bad enough, we had to be informed about the security infraction by our clients because we didn't even have a clue. Now, I need to know what's going on."

"First of all, let me just say that I'm not exactly sure what happened, but I take full responsibility for it."

"You don't have a choice, Khavon. You were specifically requested by the powers that be for this job because of your security expertise and track record." Furi's voice was anxious. "I'll be straight with you. These guys are all over me. I need some answers, Khavon. I need to know what you plan to do about it so I can get these people off my back."

He could not believe his own ears. He had designed and installed his most sophisticated piece of security software to date, and now Furi was telling him that someone had cracked all of the codes—and the only thing that had derailed their embezzlement plan was some "red flag" report that he didn't even know about.

"Well, I'm sorry, but at the moment, I don't have any answers to give you. I honestly don't know how this could have happened, except to say that when people are determined to break into a system, they search and search until they find a security loop-hole. And you know as well as I, no matter how well you try to secure a system, there will always be security loop-holes. Nothing is absolutely air-tight. We covered all the bases, and then some, but unfortunately this time it wasn't enough. We are not necessarily dealing with young kids anymore. The recent popularity of the internet is making things increasingly more difficult to secure. You know that as well as I do, Furi."

"Yeah, I know that. But at this point it doesn't matter. If you don't have any answers right now, you'd better come up with some by the end of the week."

"Why? What are you talking about?" Khavon asked.

"About forty-five minutes after I talked to Lundgren, I got a call from Ted Mulcahy. He is coming to Minneapolis on Thursday to meet personally with me, you, and Alayna about this incident. Let's just say he wasn't happy."

"Hello." Khavon's greeting was anxious, as he hoped against hope that the voice on the other end was the only one he wanted to hear at the moment.

"Hey, lover."

His voice rapidly changed from anxious to tired when he recognized the voice of Crystal Cummings, a woman that he casually dated from time to time. He really didn't want to be bothered tonight.

"Hi, Crystal. How are you?"

"Great. How are *you*?" she asked.

"I'm fine. Why do you say it like that?"

"Well, it's been forever and a day since the last time I've seen or talked to you. I miss you."

"I've just been really busy. You know how it is."

"Mmph. Yeah, I know how it is. I've been really busy myself. What do you have up for tonight?"

"Nothing, really. I'm just sitting around listening to some music."

"That sounds great. Would you like some company?"

"Well, no," Khavon said quickly. "I'm kind of tired. I think I'm going to be turning in soon."

"That'll work too."

"No, not tonight, Crystal. Maybe some other time," Khavon offered stiffly.

"Oh . . . ." Crystal said slowly. "Okay, yeah, some other time then," she said, trying unsuccessfully to mask her disappointment.

Khavon hung up the phone, only to pick it back up and redial the same seven digits that he had been dialing repeatedly since Furi had called. The vacant ringing was loud in his ear.

"She's probably with that fool!" he spat, slamming the telephone down. He knelt down in front of the albums that were strewn across the floor and began to refile them.

Alayna heard rubber burn as Warren's Mercedes pulled away. She didn't bother to look back. Tired, drained, and deflated, she opened the glass door of the apartment vestibule. All she wanted to do was eat that raspberry Bavarian chocolate torte in the refrigerator that was calling her name, and just lay down. Exhausted, she collapsed onto the black leather couch and kicked her heels off. Feeling like the wind had been knocked out of her, she wanted simply to just close off the rest of the world. If she were going to be miserable, she just wanted to process it in peace, without interruption. The first order of attack was that blamed telephone. It had been ringing off the hook when she'd left. She spied it sitting on the desk next to her, ever-so-gently lifted the receiver from its cradle, and dropped it on the unexpectant carpet. "That should do it." It was such a simplistic solution, she smiled, pleased with herself.

The lavender bouquet that Khavon had given her was prominently centered on her coffee table. Its scent wafted through her senses before she drifted off to sleep.

"I'm open, man!" The sound of Khavon's frustrated voice was directed at Warren who was posted up at the top of the key. The guttural hubbub of masculine grunts and the squeaky cadence of twenty rubber soles clamoring across the gymnasium in St. Paul's athletic club permeated the open air.

Both of them regulars for Saturday morning b-ball, there had always been a healthy rivalry between the two men—even a subtle hostility that suggested a competition for more than the game. But today was definitely different. The hostility was brazen and unabashed. Clutching the ball in the palms of his hands, Warren assessed the team's positioning. He turned to Khavon, delivered him an accusing, icy glare, and deliberately tossed the ball to another shirt, infuriating his teammate. It was obvious to Khavon and everyone else that Warren was freezing him out of the game.

"What's up with that, man? I was wide open." Khavon gestured angrily with open palms, running back up the court after the brick that was thrown up was rebounded by the opposing team.

"I guess I just didn't see you," Warren lied apathetically.

"Whatever, man." Khavon waved him off. Warren continued to freeze him out of the game, but Khavon's answer was hardly what Warren had expected.

"Over here, man," Larry yelled, gesturing for Khavon to

throw him the ball. Khavon tossed the ball instead to Warren, who was not expecting it and subsequently lost the ball to an opposing teammate.

Again and again, to the eventual dismay and open protests of his other teammates, Khavon bulleted the ball to Warren.

"Man, what are you doing?" Reggie wanted to know when Khavon's last pass hurled through the air, catching only the tips of Warren's fingers, before it went out of bounds.

"Look, I don't know who this woman is, but we are going to lose this game if you and Warren don't stop tripping," Reggie angrily explained, having pulled Khavon aside to put him in check.

"Woman!" Khavon exclaimed, still fuming. "Who said anything about a woman?"

"C'mon, man. Who you think you foolin'? Brothas don't be tripping like this unless there's some woman involved." Khavon closed his eyes hard, and turned away. "Now, you and Warren obviously have some business to take care of, but this ain't the place to do it."

And he was right. All of this was out of character for him. He wasn't sure if it was the stress from work or Alayna. It was almost as if she had him under her spell or something. This morning he had locked his keys in his car again, something he never, ever did. Still infused with anger, he looked Reggie in the eye. Grudgingly acquiescing with an almost imperceptible nod, he trudged over to the bench where Warren was sitting. Warren, rattled and incensed, let Khavon speak first.

"Look, we have a situation here."

"Oh, and what is that?"

"It's really very simple. We could continue to protect our egos by playing the way that we have been and let those guys over there think that we can't play," Khavon nodded toward the team on the opposite side of the gym, "or we could put them in their cocky places."

Warren looked down and then gave Khavon an affirmative nod of the head.

"Good game, man." Khavon patted Warren on the back when the game was over, before heading to the showers.

He has no idea who he's messing with, Warren thought as he watched Khavon disappear through the doors of the locker room. *No idea at all.*

First Donovan, now Warren. Alayna was beginning to wonder if she was destined to be alone. She stood motionless in the shower, the thick, hazy fog of steam enveloping her shapely form. She reassessed her life as the streaming cascade flowed evenly over her tired, drained body. The water was hot, but that was the way that she liked it. It didn't matter whether she was being drenched with the force of thousands of heated beads of water spewing from the head of her shower, or immersed in a foaming hot bubble bath. Alayna craved the heated, wet comfort like it was a drug and she an addict. But this morning, having woken up to a dismal Saturday morning with no blanket, no sun and no man, Alayna did not luxuriate in the soothing warmth. Instead, for more than twenty minutes she focused her blank, open stare upon a pearly white tile, near the upper right corner of the shower. Perhaps she had been drawn to it somehow, she thought cynically to herself. Blank and devoid of life, it somehow symbolized her life and state of mind, she thought wryly, noticing a tiny hairline crack progressing diagonally from the lower right hand corner up to its counterpart. Except for the pearly white color, they were two of a kind, both giving the appearance of a solid exterior, but on closer inspection, falling apart at the seams.

Why can't my life be more like Sheila's? Alayna was jealous. She hated it, but she couldn't help the way she felt. She wished it would go away and leave her alone, but it wouldn't. Maybe she was being too hard on herself. Envious. Yes, that was a better word for the way she felt, she decided. Sheila had everything. Everything . . . a wonderful husband, a beautiful home, two precious children and a rewarding career. How could she possibly want more? What did she have to complain about? Alayna would always wonder. *I mean, sure, Larry has his faults, but who doesn't?* A small part of her, a very tiny part of her, had trouble feeling sorry for herself.

A slight drop in the water temperature, although barely perceptible, caused Alayna to cease her pondering and realize that it wouldn't be long before the streaming warmth would turn to cool indifference. She dipped her face into the raining flux and felt a deluge of water rush into it, rinsing away her salty tear tracks. The flood of water ran through the length of her hair, and continued down her backside. When she had shampooed and conditioned the steaming, springy ringlets that made up her mane, she reached for and wrapped her dripping hair in the downy towel sitting on the edge of the tub. Wrapping her body in the white terry cloth robe that Sheila had given to her for Christmas, she headed for the kitchen.

Chapter Sixteen

Desperate for a quick pick-me-up, Alayna reached in the refrigerator for the last remaining piece of Bavarian raspberry torte. Before she could take a bite, she heard the doorbell ring. Through the tiny bulbed peep hole she could see that it was Jhazmyne, her five-year-old, pig-tailed neighbor from across the hall.

Alayna had fallen in love with Jhazmyne the first time she'd laid eyes on her. It was the first day she'd moved in. Eyes wide with intrigue, the child was standing at the top of the stairs as she carried in her last box.

Pleasantly surprised, Alayna had smiled. "Well, hello there."

"Hi," she adjusted her glasses and shoved her tiny hands back into her overalls. She couldn't have been more than three, Alayna thought.

"What's your name?"

"Jhazmyne."

"My name is Alayna. I'm going to be your new neighbor."

The young girl studied her closely. "You're too big to have your hair in afro puffs," she commented.

Alayna laughed out loud. "These are called twists, sweetie, and big people can wear them too." She eyed the hallway expectantly. "Sweetie, where's your mommy?"

That day had sparked the beginning of a special relationship between the two. After Jhazmyne followed her into her apartment, Alayna learned that they were sort of kindred souls. The youngest of seven foster care children living in the apartment down the hall,

Jhazmyne, although not physically abused, was being unloved, ignored, neglected. Over time, it became clear that her foster care parents were more concerned with the monthly check in their mailbox than the children in their household. She thought of reporting them, but what would she say? What could she say? They weren't actually harming her physically, and apathy wasn't exactly a federal offense. And what was the alternative? She didn't want Jhazmyne to return to the dreary institutions that she had spent much of her childhood in. She had considered adopting her herself, but the horror stories of history probes into the private lives of single parents had scared her off. Besides, she felt Jhazmyne deserved more, so she didn't pursue it. Lately though, she had been rethinking her decision.

"Hey, Jhaz." Alayna swung the door open. With no reply, the little girl marched through the door, past Alayna, taking up residence at her kitchen table. She was obviously upset. Alayna crinkled her brow. Curious, she rubbed the towel through her damp mane, closed the door and followed her into the kitchen.

Eyes welled with tears, Jhazmyne was staring angrily into the glass tabletop when she walked in.

"Jhaz, what's the matter?" Alayna reached over to console her, tugging gently at her chin until their eyes once again met. "What is it honey?" she asked again softly.

"Where were you?"

"What?"

"Where were you? I fell asleep waiting for you to come home last night!"

Alayna was perplexed. "Jhaz, I—"

"I was afraid," Jhazmyne whimpered before she could answer.

"Afraid of what, sweetie?"

"I was afraid that you weren't coming back," Jhazmyne blurted out between heaving sobs.

"Oh, Jhaz . . . ." Alayna sighed quietly, running her hand gently down the side of Jhazmyne's trembling face. "Jhaz, what would make you think a thing like that?"

"Well, you wouldn't answer your doorbell, and I hadn't seen you in a whole week, and . . . ."

Emotion welling up again, Jhazmyne tried to continue, but Alayna swept her up into her arms, the girl's little legs wrapping around her waist. She planted an emotional kiss on her cheek. "Jhaz, I don't want you to worry about anything. Don't you know that I'm not going anywhere, unless you come with me?" She planted another kiss. "Okay?"

"Okay." Jhazmyne smiled, exposing the recent evacuation of her two front teeth.

Alayna shook her head disapprovingly at the young girl. "You know me better than that, Jhaz. You should know that I wouldn't leave you. I'm staying right here, and I'm not leaving for anything or anyone." Her voice trailed off at the end.

After the misunderstanding had been cleared up, Alayna noticed a colorful catalog that she didn't recognize lying on her kitchen table. "Hey what's this?" She shifted Jhazmyne's modest but solid weight to her left side, and picked the colorful leaflet from the table.

"Well," Jhazmyne said, her mood now more relaxed, "the teacher said that we're spose to bring home candy so that we can buy another computer because the old one stopped working. And I was looking for you to see if you wanted to buy some."

Horror stricken, Alayna felt her insides twist into a tight knot. "Jhazmyne, you mean to tell me that your school only has one computer?"

"No," Jhazmyne answered quickly.

Alayna heaved a heavy sigh of relief.

"We have two computers, but the one in the library doesn't work anymore." Alayna stared at her disbelievingly.

She didn't know why she'd been surprised. Oak Avenue Elementary was a dilapidated public school, eight blocks north of their downtown apartment, where students of color made up the ninety percent majority. Recent downtown renovations had commissioned the planting of rows of beautiful green trees surrounding the downtown area. The trees stretched into the city for about four blocks, not quite making it to the school.

Alayna was all too familiar with the drab, gray slab of concrete that made up the school. Aside from driving past the gated institution everyday on her way to work, she, a registered independent, had cast her vote there in the last election. *How in the world can a child be expected to develop a passion for learning, and ultimately to succeed, in a dismal, dreary environment like this?* she'd wondered when she'd walked in. A product of similar public schools herself, she was living proof that it does happen. *But why do they have to make it so hard?* she wondered.

When she regained her composure, she again questioned Jhazmyne in a gentle, probing manner. "Honey, your school only has two computers?"

"Mm-hmm. But both of them are broke."

"Broken."

"Both of them are broken, and that's why Mrs. Burnette said we were spose to sell this candy."

"Oh, I see."

"And you know what?"

"What, sweetie?"

"Whoever sells the most gets a prize." Jhazmyne beamed.

"Really?"

"Mm-hmm. Want to buy some?"

"Sure, hun. How much do they cost?"

"A dollar."

"Okay, I'll take ten. Have you sold any yet?"

"Nope. But today I'm going to go up to some of the other floors," Jhazmyne piped out happily.

"You know, sweetie, I really don't like the idea of you running around this apartment building all by yourself. Remember when I talked to you about strangers?" Jhazmyne nodded her head silently. "Well, do you understand why I don't feel good about it?" Jhazmyne nodded her head again slowly, disappointed.

"But Alayna, I want to win the prize," Jhazmyne protested.

"Well, I'd like to go with you, but, sweetie, today is not a good day," Alayna said. "But, tell you what. Now that I'm thinking about it, lots of people bring candy to my job to sell for their kids.

If you want, I could take your candy to work with me to sell for you. Would you like that?"

"Yeah," Jhazmyne answered, still a little perplexed.

"What is it, sweetie?"

"Well, will I still get to keep the prize, if I sell the most?"

"Well, I don't see why not. People sell candy at work for their kids all the time, but I will call the school on Monday just to make sure, okay?" Alayna tugged gently at Jhazmyne's chin.

"Okay." Jhazmyne beamed. "What time is it?"

"Ten after eleven," Alayna answered glancing at the aqua blue digits on the microwave.

"Eleven! Power Riders are on! I have to go," Jhazmyne screamed, bolting to the door.

"See ya later, Jhaz," Alayna called after her.

"See ya," Jhazmyne chimed back from the hallway. Alayna closed the door behind her and returned to the kitchen. Shaking her head, she decided that she would talk to Furi on Monday about a company donation.

Eyeing the cappuccino machine on the counter, she decided that a hot cup of coffee would go well with her breakfast snack. She filled the carafe with cold water and slid it back onto the drip plate. After she'd measured the espresso and placed it into the filter basket, she noticed out of the corner of her eye Jhaz's beloved rag doll, LuLu, lying on the floor under the table. With a soft, brown pillow face and pigtails woven of black yarn, LuLu, on a quick glance, could easily be mistaken for Jhazmyne, particularly when she was propped in a chair. Stained and coming apart at the seams in some places, LuLu was Jhazmyne's favorite of all of her dolls. Jhazmyne had many dolls, new and old, but LuLu was her favorite. She carried her with her practically everywhere she went.

"Jhaz is going to come looking for you, little lady," Alayna said, bending down to pick the brown doll up. The words had barely escaped her lips when the doorbell rang again.

"This chile can't be without this thing for five minutes," Alayna laughed. The Power Riders must have paused for a commercial, she surmised.

"That was quick!" Alayna exclaimed, swinging open the

door, her eyes already fixed on what would be the little girl's height. They collided instead with the bottom half of two faded blue tree trunks. Her curiosity quickly climbed upward, momentarily lingering at his mouth as the words on his lips were just being formed.

"Hello, Alayna."

Her visual inquisition continued its ascent, reaching the summit level at his clear brown eyes. Lulu slipped through her fingers to the floor, as she confirmed the recognition that her ears had already discerned.

Chapter Seventeen

"Khavon, what are you doing here?" Alayna exclaimed, her voice thick with surprise as she bent over to rescue LuLu from the mesh carpeted floor. Her brown eyes crinkled with genuine curiosity.

Comfortably dressed in faded, worn jeans, high-top athletics, a bulky, white fleece sweatshirt, and a red canvas baseball cap, Khavon's features were in stark contrast to his relaxed attire. Jaw clinched into a rigid line, body tense and stiff, Khavon was visibly upset.

"What is it?" Alayna asked, mildly alarmed, her brows crinkling with curiosity.

He peered into Alayna's wide eyes. "Can I come in?" His face was noticeably devoid of even the slightest trace of his signature smile.

Nodding her head, she stepped aside, clearing the way for his entry. "Have a seat." Alayna pulled a chair out from underneath her kitchen table.

"What's going on? You look tired. I was just making some coffee, would you like some?" Alayna asked, after Khavon pulled his chair up to the kitchen table.

He nodded and then confirmed her observation. "I am tired. I think I have the right to be. I've been up all night calling you. Are you all right?"

"I'm fine. Why? Calling me? For what?" She asked with surprise and shock, turning from the cappuccino machine. She hoped this wasn't some kind of male ego trip.

"Aside from being worried that you were in trouble, I needed to talk to you."

"Trouble? Why would you think I was in trouble?" She inquired curiously, adjusting her robe closer to her. Suddenly she was painfully, dreadfully aware that her hair was all over her head, her face was ashy, and except for the terry robe that she wore, she had no clothes on. She made the decision in that moment that whatever Khavon had to say would just have to wait for five minutes. She was not going to be prancing around in front of this man looking haggish and scary.

She shook some cinnamon on the top of the steamed milk foam, and set the coffee cup on the place mat in front of Khavon.

"I'll be right back," Alayna said, excusing herself with no explanation. Khavon looked up at her, strangely. "Make yourself at home. I'll be right back."

She knew it was going to be bad. When she looked into the mirror, she found that her predictions had, unfortunately, proved fairly accurate. Her hair was in every direction, as she had made no attempts to set it. Her face, although clean, appeared a bit dry. She grabbed the bottle of moisturizer resting on the edge of the white pedestal sink, and slathered it over the entire surface of her receptive face. With her index finger, she slid some tinted lip-gloss over her lips. "That's better." Her face did look one hundred percent better. But it was not really her face that was causing the problem. It was her hair. She had not been expecting company, and had she not thought it to be Jhazmyne at the door she would have conveniently not opened it.

"Khavon, could you get that? I'll be down in a minute," Alayna yelled down the stairs when she heard the ringing doorbell.

"Sure, no problem." Khavon lowered his cup to the table and made his way to the door.

"This is a lost cause," she mumbled with disgust, running her hand over the springy coils that made up her mane. She was almost ready to give up hope when in the mirror image, out of the corner of her eye, she spotted something.

"Well, hello," Khavon said, pleasantly surprised.

"Who are you?" Jhazmyne inquired curiously, when she looked up at Khavon.

"I'm a friend of Alayna's," he said simply, answering her question. "My name is Khavon. What's your name?"

"Khavon? What kind of name is that?" Jhazmyne asked, crinkling up her nose, taking the liberty to enter before it was offered.

Khavon laughed, slightly taken aback by her grownup manner. "What do you mean?" he asked.

"Well, I don't know. I guess I never heard of anyone named Khavon. The boys in my class have names like John, Nicholas, and Michael, but there is nobody in my class named Khavon."

"I see." Khavon smiled generously. "Well, I guess I'm not exactly sure what kind of name it is, but my mother told me that that name just came to her when I was born."

Jhazmyne stared at him blankly. "Your mommy told you?" she asked in amazement.

"Yes, she did. One day after she had tucked me in and had finished reading my bedtime story, I asked her and that's what she told me," Khavon explained.

Jhazmyne's mouth was wide open. "You live with your real mommy and she tucks you in and reads stories to you?"

"Well I don't live with her anymore, but when I was a little one like you, I did. And yes, she read me stories. Sweetie, what's your name?"

"Jhazmyne."

"Jhazmyne, doesn't your mommy read you stories?"

"I see you two have met," Alayna interjected before Jhazmyne could answer, making her descent down the stairs. "Jhazmyne is my neighbor. She lives with the foster family across the hall," she quickly disclosed for Khavon's benefit, as well as Jhazmyne's.

"Oh, I see," Khavon understood immediately and changed the subject. "I like your hair."

Alayna entered the room wearing an oversized white t-shirt and black leggings, her head banded in the lengthwise-folded mud cloth sash that she had worn as a cummerbund the day before to accent her suit. She had run some gel through her hair to give it the pretense of a textured set. It wasn't her best, but it wasn't half bad for five minutes.

Alayna turned to Jhazmyne. "I knew you'd be back for LuLu," she said.

"Who's LuLu?" Khavon asked, looking around curiously for the another warm body.

"This is LuLu," Jhazmyne said, dashing over to retrieve her old friend. "LuLu, this is Khavon. I know, he has a funny name," she said to the doll.

"Hello, Lulu," Khavon said, taking the doll's hand.

"She's kind of shy," Jhazmyne explained the doll's mute silence.

"Know wh-a-t?" Jhazmyne asked Khavon.

"What?"

"Alayna's going to take my candy to her work so that I can win the prize."

"Jhazmyne's school is doing a fund raiser to buy computers," Alayna explained.

"Oh, that's very nice of her. Do you like computers, Jhazmyne?" Khavon asked.

"I don't know," she answered.

"Jhazmyne was just telling me that her school has no working computers," Alayna added.

Crinkling his brow, Khavon blinked a disbelieving blink. "What? Are you serious?"

"I'm very serious."

Khavon turned to Jhazmyne and took her tiny hand in his. "Sweetie, what school do you go to?"

"Oak Avenue Elementary. Know wh-a-t?"

"What sweetie?"

"I have a glow-in-the-dark Power Riders ring."

"You do?" Khavon exclaimed with exaggerated excitement.

"Yup. Alayna gave it to me. Want to see it?" she asked, reaching into her pocket.

"Yes, of course I do."

"See?" Jhazmyne pulled out a pink plastic band with a tiny picture of the only female in the adolescent crime fighting trio.

"Whoa! This is really cool!" Khavon said, examining the tiny plastic ring. Jhazmyne smiled proudly. "When I was a kid, I had a glow-in-the-dark Batman ring."

"Batman!" Jhazmyne said. "Batman is weak!" Alayna covered her giggle with her hand.

"Oh, I see," Khavon replied, having to laugh himself.

"Are you going to buy some candy or what?" Jhazmyne wanted to know.

"Well, that depends. What kind do you have? I don't just eat any kind of candy, you know," Khavon said playfully.

"Well, you can get a delicious chocolate bar, or some yummy chocolate covered raisins. You can get some, some . . . well, I can't remember what else, but it's really delicious," Jhazmyne finished, her voice trailing off.

"Really delicious, huh?"

"Yes. Very delicious."

"Is this the catalog?" Khavon asked, leafing through the pages of the brochure that had been resting on the table.

Jhazmyne nodded her head. "Yup. And you know what?"

"What?"

"The candy bars are only one dollar."

"Wow, that does sound like a good deal. Wouldn't you say Alayna?" Khavon asked, continuing with his play acting.

"Mm-hmm. Sounds like a great deal," Alayna concurred.

"Okay. Count me in," Khavon said, listing his name as the number two entry on the catalog order form.

"Jhaz, what do we say?" Alayna reminded her.

"Thank you."

"You're very welcome. And I hope that you do win the prize."

"I hope so, too."

Just then, Alayna opened the door to yet another unexpected arrival.

"Hi, Isaiah. Did you come for Jhaz?"

Isaiah barely stepped into the apartment. "Yeah." He eyed the kitchen where Jhazmyne sat at the table charming Khavon. "Jhaz," he raised his voice a level and directed it into the kitchen. "Harriet told me to come and get you because you have to come and help the rest of us clean up."

Isaiah, a few years older than Jhazmyne, was the youngest boy in Mrs. Harriet's foster care household. At age nine, he had only joined the family across the hall a few months earlier. Quiet by nature, Isaiah seemed to be the perfect counterpart for Jhazmyne. The two of them were as different from one another as two children could be. Jhazmyne was outgoing, trusting, and full of curiosity and idealism. Isaiah, on the other hand, was watchful, reserved, and tended to accept the status quo. Alayna guessed that he must have experienced a lot of pain in his young life. She could see that the pain and bitterness kept him locked and chained like a prisoner, just as it had done to her so many years before. But Alayna was not the only one to recognize the pain and internal suffering. Khavon picked up on it right away. He picked up on it right away because it was easy for him to recognize. He'd seen it before—many times before, in the mirror.

"Khavon, this is Isaiah. Isaiah, this is Khavon," Alayna said, introducing the two.

"Hey, man, what's up?" Khavon smiled, walking over to extend his hand, trying to be friendly. Isaiah returned Khavon's warm greeting with a simple "hello" that was devoid of any kind of detectable emotion.

"Isaiah, you don't have to be rude," Alayna said when Isaiah left Khavon's hand hanging in the air. Isaiah cut Alayna an icy glare and transferred it over to Khavon. Grudgingly, he shook his hand.

"Jhazmyne was just telling me that you're really into video games. Maybe we can all go to the arcade sometime," Khavon suggested, retrieving his hand and shoving it into his pocket.

"C'mon, Jhaz, it's time to go." Isaiah turned promptly to face the doorway, ignoring Khavon's suggestion.

"Kenny, don't you want to go to the arcade?" Jhazmyne pleaded.

"Kenny?" Khavon asked, momentarily thrown off guard. "I thought your name was Isaiah."

Isaiah turned around slowly. "Kenneth is my middle name. Jhazmyne likes to call me by my middle name because my given name is hard for her to pronounce. Is that okay with you?" Isaiah turned back to the doorway.

"Isaiah!" Alayna objected.

"It's okay, Alayna."

"No, it's not."

"No, really. It's okay. Back in my hacking days, my attitude wasn't exactly saccharin sweet either."

Isaiah inhaled deeply as if to control his rising anger, and angrily grabbed the doorknob for a dramatic exit, when the words that Khavon had said reached the depth of his consciousness. He turned slowly, steadily, and looked Khavon straight in the eye and asked in a slow, measured, disbelieving tone.

"You used to be a hacker?" His apathetic eyes lit up with thinly veiled intrigue and wonder. They reflected what seemed to Khavon to be a fleeting glimmer of respect and admiration. Clearly his interest was piqued, and Khavon knew it. In response, Khavon disclosed what he knew the boy so badly wanted to know, but, in the name of angry pride, refused to ask.

"Eric," Khavon said, simply. "Eric Eclipse."

His eyes went wide and the apathy in his glare was quickly replaced, first with recognition and then with awe. Eric Eclipse . . . the avenging Robin Hood of cyberspace . . . sure, he'd heard many stories about "The Eclipse," but to come face to face with him was too much. The Eclipse, as he was known, was legendary in cyberspace and among all of Isaiah's friends. Internationally renowned and highly regarded among good and bad hackers alike, Eric Eclipse was a legend.

"You're Eric Eclipse?" Isaiah involuntarily asked, opening up like a spring flower in the warm, shining sun. The question had jumped out of his mouth before he'd known it. But he couldn't help it—he'd heard the stories of The Eclipse and the wild exploits of the nation's telephone communications systems, and even the White House and Pentagon. He'd read about how he had incurred the wrath of the infamous Wardens, and about how mastering the art of cracking expensive computer games that no one else could had put him on the map in the underground hacker community. But it was the bitter and undying vow of vengeance that he had incurred as a result of dismantling what was to be the Wardens' single most defining act of anarchy that had made him internationally renown. Now, here he was, standing face to face with him. He couldn't believe it!

"Did you really download Donald Dunn's credit information and then call him to harass him about his daughter?"

"You called Donald Dunn?" Alayna asked, surprised to learn that Khavon was a hacker.

"Yeah, well I just felt that a self-avowed Klu Klux Klan member had no business running for president," Khavon answered plainly.

"What did you say? What did he say?" Alayna asked, astonished.

"Well, what I said really doesn't matter. The truth of the matter is that I shouldn't have done it. Any of it. Everyone has the right to his privacy regardless of their views."

"You have a point," Alayna said.

Khavon continued to peel away the layers that surrounded Isaiah like a well-trained chef would an onion. "I was Eric Eclipse, but I'm not anymore. I stopped being Eric Eclipse more than fifteen years ago."

"Why?" Isaiah wanted to know.

"Well, because I found out that computer hacking can be very hazardous to your health."

"Hazardous to your health? What do you mean?" Isaiah asked with great interest, copping a seat on Alayna's black leather couch.

"I mean, hacking is very dangerous business. If the wrong information gets into the wrong hands, the results could be well . . . disastrous."

Fascinated, Isaiah chatted with Khavon for fifteen minutes or so before he remembered the primary reason for his visit.

"I gotta go," Isaiah said, "but I'd like to talk to you again sometime."

"Sure. Listen, here's my card. Give me a call when you want to get together."

"Okay. Thanks," Isaiah said, accepting the card. "Jhaz, c'mon we gotta go," Isaiah called into the kitchen where she and Alayna sat. "You know how Ms. Harriet is."

Jhazmyne dutifully got up and grabbed LuLu.

"I have to go home now. It was very nice to meet you," Jhazmyne said to Khavon.

"Well, it was very nice to meet you too, Jhaz. I'm sure we'll see each other again."

"Why? Are you going to marry Alayna?" she asked pointedly, and then started to giggle. Alayna and Khavon shot each other an unexpected glance.

"C'mon Jhaz," Isaiah said, taking Khavon off the hook. "Let's go." Alayna closed the door behind them.

Khavon's disposition had completely changed from the one he had first presented her with at the front door. His demeanor was now loose and relaxed, Alayna noticed. Jhazmyne had that kind of effect on people, she surmised.

"She's a sweet girl," Khavon said.

"Yeah, she is. Bright, too. Both of them."

"Yeah, Isaiah is a really smart kid. He just needs some guidance . . . somebody to show him that they care. If not, he could easily end up wasting his potential, or worse, finding it and then using it non-productively."

"Yeah. It seems like you broke some ice when you told him that you used to be a hacker, though."

"Yeah, he seems to be really interested in computers."

"I have to tell you, I'm impressed. He has never said more than three words at a time to me."

"Well, I guess life sometimes has a tendency to harden these kids. Especially young boys. You just have to find their interest and kind of sneak in through the backdoor while they're not looking."

Alayna laughed. "Yeah, I guess so. That reminds me—how

did you get in here anyway? The security in this building is pretty tight."

Khavon laughed. "It's called social engineering, Alayna. If you tell people what they want to hear, they will let you do anything."

"Oh, I see," Alayna said. An awkward silence passed as the communication reduced to only the meeting of their eyes. Alayna prayed desperately for something intelligent to say. "I like your sweatshirt," she said finally, noticing the red emblazoned emblem on the front for the first time.

"Thanks. Are you a fan of the Monarchs?"

"Well, I guess you could say that. A friend of mine was obsessed with collecting Negro Baseball League memorabilia. The Kansas City Monarchs were his favorite."

"He must have quite a collection."

"Actually, he passed away about a year ago."

"Oh . . . um . . . I'm sorry."

She'd thought that she'd gotten over Donovan's death, but the pain was still there. It was still there, and it could erupt into something she didn't want to deal with right now, so she changed the subject. Besides, the mystery had lasted long enough. Curiosity was beginning to get the best of her.

"So, Khavon, what's going on that you had to come all the way over here,"—*unannounced*—"to talk to me about?" She watched as the mask of worry and discontentment returned to cover his benign features. Like Isaiah, he had almost forgotten the reason for his visit.

"Do you think maybe I could have another cup of coffee?"

"Sure." They both retreated to the kitchen. After Alayna had refreshed his cup, he took a sip.

"Alayna, this cappuccino is delicious."

"Thanks."

"No, really. It's really good. I've haven't tasted any quite like it. What's your recipe?"

"It's a secret."

"Mmph. What do I have to do to you to have the secret revealed?"

"You have to tell me what's going on. Then I might give you a break." She smiled a sly smile as she refreshed her own cup, leaned back against the counter, and waited.

Khavon laughed a short laugh before his features turned serious again.

"Alayna, Furi got a call from Jim Lundgren yesterday," Khavon started. The weight of Khavon's next words were heavy on her even before they were uttered. Shrugging, Alayna impatiently cued him to elaborate. "Four days ago, more than $1,000,000 was wired from an internal settlement account to two separate accounts at the International Bank of Zurich." Instinctively covering her mouth with her hand, Alayna slowly sat down to the kitchen table, preparing herself for the worst. "The transaction," Khavon continued, "went unchecked as an uncleared suspense item until yesterday, when a computer operator noticed the uncleared suspense item on some report that she'd received."

"What report?"

"Something called a 'red flag' report. I'm not sure where it came from, but that's where she saw the discrepancy."

Looking up, she placed her coffee cup on the table. "What?" she asked, disbelievingly.

"A 'red flag' report. It was the only stop gap. I haven't checked it out yet, but . . . ." Alayna's eyes sparkled with amazement. Khavon looked up and saw the expression on her face.

"Do you know something that I don't know?"

"Khavon, I put that report in as a last minute security precaution, after we launched the mock cyber-attack," she said in amazement. "I didn't mention it to anyone because, in comparison to all of the other electronic tracking and security safeguards that we had in place, it seemed so simplistic and archaic."

"Humph. Well, that last minute simplistic and archaic safeguard just may have been the only thing that saved our–"

Alayna cut him off. "The money. What happened to the money?"

"Well, it's a good thing you put that in, because after the auditor reported it to Jim, the banks were able to reconcile and did get the money back."

"What about the system? What about the alarms, the firewalls, and the user authentication we put in? What about the encryption algorithms and all of the other security we put it? What happened?"

"Whoever it was found an alternate route into the system."

"An alternate route? I don't understand. What alternate route?"

"They found an alternate route. I was able to track it and plug the hole, but I don't know. Still, I have a bad feeling about this. Something is not right."

"What's not right? You fixed the problem, right?"

"I plugged the hole, but I don't know."

"What?"

"I just have the feeling . . . well . . . I just have the feeling that something else is going on here."

"Something else? What do you mean something else? Something else like what? What do you mean?"

"Listen, Alayna, you weren't the only one who took a safety precaution. I put in a last minute safeguard too."

"Oh?" Alayna asked curiously, waiting for the answer he was about to give.

"Yeah. Um . . . I've been doing this for a long time, Alayna, and in addition to a backdoor to bypass security, I generally put in a final layer of hidden, intuitive security."

"What?" Alayna interrupted, confused.

"I put in an extra final layer of security that can only be bypassed if the user can be positively identified, either through the embedded passwords that we set up for the computer operators, our security front-end, or through the backdoor that I put in."

"You put in a backdoor?"

He put his hand up. "I know it goes against policy, but I have always put in a backdoor and I have never had a problem. I am the only one who knows the code words for the two alternative methods. In other words, whoever is responsible for this had to be somebody at either Liberty or Excelsior. Whoever it was had access to inside information . . . inside knowledge of procedures, instructions, and codes . . . ." He paused briefly before continuing. "Either that or it had to be me." His eyes raised and focused on hers. An icy cold chill raced down her spine. "At first I thought it was the internet, but now I know differently. Only a few select people know this information."

"Well, did you check the log? What did the log say?" she asked, moving her eyes quickly away from his to the opaque glass tabletop.

"Yeah, I checked the log, and the pattern is the same as last time."

"What do you mean?"

"They came in through a backdoor. There was a list of stolen access codes to cellular telephones, which you know as well as I do we can't possibly trace, and just between me and you, the other log patterns make it clear that whoever it was that broke in was impersonating me and fooled the system into thinking it was dealing with a friend."

"What about the limits on access denials and authorization failures? Didn't they kick in?" she asked, slowly.

"The limits were never exceeded. In fact, they never even came close. Whoever did this systematically bypassed the security layers, using the backdoor and a select number of passwords. What puzzles me, though, is that each of the passwords that were used had some type of personal connection to me."

Alayna stared at him disbelievingly. "What? What do you mean?"

"Well, for the backdoor password, I generally put in a name concatenated with a latchkey that only I know."

"Well, what name did you use?"

"Kenny."

"Who is Kenny?"

"Kenny is . . . was my brother."

"Was?"

"He died twenty-eight years ago."

"Oh . . . I'm sorry. You must have been very close to him." Alayna covered his hand with hers.

"I was, but that was twenty-eight years ago. Right now I need to concern myself with finding out who's doing this."

"Well, how many password attempts were made?" Alayna asked.

"Ten. Here they are," Khavon said, handing her a folded document that he took from his back pocket. Alayna took the sheet of paper and began reading aloud from the list.

"KennySep0162Liberty...Apr0760KennyExcelsiorzxz9099 ...Libertyzxz9099KennyJul3067...KennyJuly3067... zxz9099KennyJuly3067...KennyAug1259Excelsiorzxz9009. Khavon, I don't understand. What are all these different dates?"

Khavon looked down. "August 12, 1959 is the day I was born. My brother's birthday was on September 1, 1962."

"What about this one in July?" Alayna asked.

"July 30th was the day my brother died," Khavon answered.

"Mmph. I see." She was quiet for a moment. "But Khavon, I don't understand . . . . Why would you use a password that could easily be guessed by virtually anyone?"

"You don't understand, Alayna. I have been using these backdoors for years, with similar password composites. I have never had a problem before. I've never had a problem because no one even knows the backdoor is there, let alone how to get to it and what the password would be once it is found. I have put a backdoor in every security system that I have ever worked on. Since I change the password in each one, I have to have a simple base to build on so I can remember what the password is. In addition to that, as you can see, the password attempts not only include personal information to me, but also our project security code. No one has ever cracked it before because I use different combinations and keys. I just don't understand what happened this time," he said, shaking his head.

"Well, what's the password now?"

"There is no password. I closed the backdoor."

"I have to tell you something. Tuesday night I left my machine on again. I had a function to attend and I was in such a hurry, I just forgot. I wonder if that had anything to do with this," Alayna said.

"I don't know."

"I'm not believing this. I can't believe this is happening."

"Oh, you haven't heard the good part," Khavon said.

"You mean there's more?"

Khavon nodded imperceptibly. "Furi said that Mulcahy was not happy about this whole incident. He's flying in on Thursday to meet with us, to put us on notice personally that one more screw up and we lose the account. He wants a full account with explanation and future strategy."

"Great." Alayna paused. "Listen, Khavon . . . as of this moment everything is under control right? You shut off the backdoor and plugged any open holes, right?"

"Ah . . . yeah, everything is under control for now."

"Look, this is all just too much right now. I have some other things going on right now, and it's all just happening at a really bad time for me. So . . . I don't mean to be rude or anything, but I just kind of . . . well, kind of need to be alone."

"Sure. No problem. I understand. I just stopped by to make sure that you were okay." When Alayna looked at him strangely, he corrected himself. "I mean, to let you know what was up at Liberty."

"Well, thanks. And we can talk about the strategy meeting on Monday, okay?"

"Sounds good. And listen, if you need to talk, here's my number," he said, handing her a napkin that he'd just written on. "Don't worry Alayna. Everything's going to be okay. We're going to get through this, and we're going to catch whoever is doing this."

"Thanks, Khavon," she said.

"I'll let myself out." Khavon grabbed his coat from the couch, and extended one last offering before closing the door. "Now remember if you need to talk . . . ."

"Thanks, Khavon. We'll see you Monday." When the door, closed she felt like her world was crashing down around her.

Chapter Eighteen

This isn't going to be fun, Alayna thought wryly when Furi entered the conference room, slamming the door behind him. Alayna glanced over at Khavon. Seemingly unaffected, he never flinched.

"Okay, it's real simple, folks. I want to know what happened, why it happened, and whether or not the problem has been fixed. And somebody in this room better have some answers for me, or let's just say that I'm not exactly going to be a happy camper."

She had been correct in her original assessment, Alayna decided. This definitely was a side of Furi that she had not seen before. Having seen it, though, she could easily make do without it, she thought to herself.

"We have more than ten thousand banks transacting their debit and deposit turnovers through Liberty," Khavon started.

"I know that, Khavon. Tell me something I don't know, like why this happened in the first place," Furi angrily spouted, his temper barely contained.

Khavon looked over at Alayna, who was already looking at him. "Look, Furi. I know that you're catching a lot of heat on this thing, but screaming at us and biting off our heads every time we say two words is not helping the situation any," he said calmly.

Furi glared angrily at Khavon, who dispensed an earnest, unblinking return.

Breaking the steady eye contact between the two men, Furi turned to Alayna to discern her reaction. Then he dropped his gaze to the table, and raised it again to meet Khavon's unwavering brown-eyed challenge.

"You're right," he said, after a short pause, haphazardly placing his middle finger on his temple. "I'm sorry. You're right. I have been taking a lot of heat on this, but I guess that's why I get paid the big bucks. Now what did you find out?"

"As I was saying, we have over ten thousand banks transacting through Liberty. On a daily basis, the debits and deposit turnovers from these transactions, on average, add up to more than twenty-four billion dollars. On Tuesday, .1 percent of that turnover came through on a single EFT. A tenth of a percent of that, or twenty-four million, was intercepted by the perpetrator and distributed across several thousand bank patron accounts. The money went virtually unnoticed by bank patrons, EFT participants, and the bank itself because, as you know, twenty-four million is only one tenth of a percent of the total deposits for the bank. The distribution was wide enough that very little was deposited into each account. On Wednesday, the funds that had been spread across the bank patron accounts were recalled and, in effect, amassed into one transfer. That one transfer ultimately ended up in the two accounts in Switzerland."

"And the distribution among so many patrons made tracing the culprit virtually impossible," Alayna added.

"Are you sure that you've plugged all the holes?" Furi asked.

"I plugged this leak and all of the leaks like it, but there's no guarantee that a new one won't spout," Khavon answered.

"Do you have any ideas about who may have done this?" Furi asked, directing the question at the both of them. Khavon and Alayna exchanged a knowing glance.

"Um . . . well . . . ." Alayna started, but was quickly cut off by Khavon.

"No. No, we don't. But like I said, we have closed off the hole that they came through so that they can't enter through it again."

Alayna stared at Khavon, wondering why he had elected not to tell Furi what he had told her.

"Well, I suggest you two get to work on it, because when Mulcahy gets here he's going to want some answers."

"What time is he getting in?" Alayna asked.

"His plane is scheduled to get in at about 3:30, and his schedule is really, really tight. He asked to meet somewhere near the airport because he's flying back out right after the meeting. He has some other commitments in Washington, so we agreed to meet at the Bloomington office. Then he won't have to worry about the commute to and from the airport," Furi explained.

"Is Jim going to be there?" Alayna asked.

"No. Jim has a conflict. Besides, he has made it very clear to me and to Mulcahy that the onus is on us. He is, however, expecting a full report, which I promised to give him. In the meantime, I expect that the two of you will work together to pull this presentation together," Furi said, getting to his feet.

"I'm counting on you two to get this situation under control. Do we understand each other?" he asked, standing in the doorway.

Khavon and Alayna nodded a synchronized nod, after which Furi made his exit.

"Are you okay?" Alayna seemed to be in a fog.

"What?"

"I said, are you okay?" Khavon repeated.

"I'm fine. How are you holding up?"

"Believe me, I've been better, but I'm all right," he answered.

Khavon stepped in towards her and cupped her hand in his, his satiny brown eyes locking with hers. Alayna felt a warm comforting sensation fall through the length of her body.

Only inches away, his caramel eyes released their hold on hers and involuntarily fell to her ample raspberry-wine-tinged lips. Her eyes followed suit and fixed themselves on the neatly trimmed mustache that bordered the rims of his supple, inviting mouth. She watched his lips part with anticipation. Weak in the knees, she yielded to the moment. Their lips met in the center of the space that had separated them only moments before. Like a plug in a socket, electricity raced through them both and they forgot where they were. Warm liquid pleasure raced alongside the electricity, tingling through Alayna's body, as his mouth gently searched hers. Khavon couldn't remember ever wanting a woman so badly. His mind wouldn't let him forget it, and neither would his body. Definitely not his body.

"Ah . . . Alayna," he whispered, bringing her closer to him. His words were low and sweet, as he held her face adjacent to his. "Girl, what are you doing to me? What are you doing to me?"

"Khavon . . . ." she whispered back, yielding to him like never before.

"I love the way you say my—" A light tap on the door abruptly unlocked their spontaneous embrace.

"We have a nine o'clock in here," Sundar whispered through the crack in the door. Alayna nervously smoothed back her slightly disheveled hair.

"We'll be right out," Khavon said, nodding his head and massaging the back of his neck.

"Khavon . . . this is dangerous." Alayna said simply when the door closed. Her heart beating erratically, her eyes were dark with concern. "We're supposed to be running a project here. We're supposed to be trying to find out who is doing this. It's not as if we don't already have enough on our hands."

"I know," Khavon said, shoving his hands in his pockets.

"They're waiting outside. We'd better go." Alayna slid her notepad off the table as Khavon gently guided her to the door by the small of her back.

"It's all yours," Khavon told Sundar as he and Alayna vacated the conference room.

"Hi, Khavon." The enthusiastic voice came from behind them as they stepped into the hallway. They turned to find Becky and Ericka approaching them from the rear.

"Hello, Alayna. Hi, Khavon," Ericka said, extending the only greeting to Alayna.

"Hi," Alayna and Khavon said together.

"We heard about the suspense item," Becky said loudly watching intently for Khavon's reaction.

Khavon was incredulous. "Wh—" he started and then lowered his voice, his blood pressure rising. "What?"

"We heard about the transmission, and I just don't know what could have gone wrong," Becky answered, looking intently at him.

Khavon turned to Alayna, questioning her with his eyes.

"Don't look at me. I haven't discussed this with anyone but you and Furi," Alayna stated, emphatically rejecting the ensuing blame. Khavon turned back to Becky, squinting his eyes with question.

"No, it wasn't Alayna. Melissa, the computer operator who was reviewing the 'red flag' report, is a friend of mine. She called me over the weekend because she knew that I had worked on the project . . . um . . . . Is something wrong?" she asked, taking note of Khavon's clenched jaw.

"That information was confidential and was not to be disseminated to the rest of the team until Alayna and I deemed it necessary to do so."

Becky's face was red with embarrassment. "Oh . . . " she said, shrugging her shoulders sheepishly. "I'm sorry. She told me that she felt comfortable in telling me since she knew that I was on the project team."

"I see," Khavon said, shutting his eyes hard. "Who else did your friend tell about this little incident?"

"No one, as far as I know."

"Well, I have some things that I need to attend to. Alayna, I'll get back with you on that other issue." He walked away leaving the three women standing there.

"Oops. I'm sorry," Becky said.

Alayna glared at her and shook her head. "I need to get back to my desk," she said, turning into the direction of her cubicle.

"Alayna," Ericka said, "do you want to stop over at Mark's desk? He brought in rolls today."

"Mark? I thought Mark was on vacation," Alayna said, with mild confusion.

"He changed his plans."

"Oh. Well, thanks, but no. I'm trying to watch what I eat."

"Oh, okay. Well, we'll see you later then."

"Yeah, see ya." Alayna waved.

Alayna didn't see Khavon again until the next day. When she walked over to his desk, he was riffling through a mountain of paper, searching for something. He seemed to her to be too busy to talk, but she decided to say what she had to say anyway.

He turned slightly, noticing a quiet presence.

"Alayna. Hi. I was going to stop by later this morning. I thought we might continue our conversation from yesterday over lunch," he said, quietly, careful to attract as little attention as possible, gesturing with his hands for her to sit.

Alayna sat down softly in the guest chair alongside of his desk and sighed heavily. Her voice was low when she spoke. "Listen. That's kind of what I wanted to talk to you about. Do you think maybe we could wait until after Thursday's meeting to continue our discussion?" Her features pleaded wordlessly with him for understanding. Closing her eyes, she ran the palm of her hand over the wavy crimps in her hair and stopped at the crux of the chignon into which she had hastily pinned them. "I just have too much stuff going on right now. I just can't seem to think straight."

Khavon's jaw became rigid again. Bowing his head, he massaged the tips of his fingers into the center of his forehead and down to his temples. His eyes closed as he continue the massage. "Alayna, I'm trying to understand, but—" He turned, surveying the doorway for potential eavesdroppers. He lowered his voice to a level that was one notch lower than before. His words were blistering with bitterness and contempt when he spat them out at her. "There's always going to be some excuse isn't there, Alayna?" Standing up, he gave her no opportunity to answer. The nonverbal cue to vacate his work area was clear and unmistakable, but, in his anger, he wanted to leave no room for doubt. "I have some research to do in the library."

"But Khavon . . . I—" Alayna began, looking up at him from her seat, ignoring his nonverbal message.

Shaking his head, he cut her off short. "Alayna, unless you have some objection, I think it would be better if we worked on the presentation separately. I'll take the infiltration and patches, and you can take future strategies and direction."

Her brows folded together in confusion and denial. "But Khavon, it's more complicated than—"

"This is a rough cut on what I thought should be included in the presentation. If you could review it and get it back to me, return it to me with any changes you may have by noon tomorrow, we can start to finalize the approval process and begin preparing our slides," he cut her off, lifting a small stack of papers off his desk.

She was confused and somewhat intimidated. Her pretty brown eyes glassed with salty, moist emotion. Her eyelids, like two weak dams on the Mississippi at the end of flood season were just barely holding the water at bay.

"Okay, I'll get this back to you," she managed to squeak out before Khavon walked in front of her and completely outside the door.

"If I'm not at my desk, just drop it in my chair," he said, as he walked away from her.

He's tripping, she thought. *Why is he tripping?* Alayna stood there in the middle of his cubicle holding the paper that he had shoved at her, wondering what had gone wrong. *What kind of a person*, she asked herself, *could manipulate emotions so well?* He changed his personality from one day to the next. Just yesterday he was so consumed with passion that he could hardly breathe. Today he was cold, aloof, rude and disaffected.

Just when she was beginning to melt, he had to go and prove her underlying suspicions to be right. He was a playboy after all. A playboy looking for his next conquest. A hound ready to pounce. Fortunately, she had managed to wait him out.

What kind of a person could manipulate emotions like that? He had to be a good actor, she surmised. His kisses had been so tender and genuine, his words so honest and heartfelt. But then again, for a gamester like Khavon, acting was a necessary skill. She had fought long and hard against the nagging suspicion that he was only a player seeking a challenge . . . a playboy out to score. But he had been so nice . . . so charming . . . and so attentive . . . so irresistible . . . and so fine . . . ooh, so fine. She sighed wishfully. Yes, Khavon was a smooth operator, all right. She was devastated. She had been fast approaching the gate to release her tightly held inhibitions. She had been nearing the point of yielding to her base. No man had ever captivated her senses like he had. No man had ever ignited the fires like Khavon had, but all she had now was a consolation prize. All she had now was the satisfaction that she'd been right all along . . . . She'd outlasted him. More than furious, she was devastated, and she knew she would not be taken in again.

"She's tripping," Khavon mumbled under his breath. *Why is she tripping?* He was not going to waste his breath anymore. It was clear that she had a different agenda. *How can she continuously ignore the heat between us? How can she continue to deny the passion?*

It was just one excuse after the other. He had opened up to her. He had been fair and honest. *Why can't she do the same? I'm just not going to do it anymore*, he told himself. He had no choice. It was called self-preservation. Yes, it would be better if their relationship remained a business one. He had no choice.

But it's more easily said than done, he thought honestly. It was almost as if she had him under some kind of spell or something. "What is she doing to me?" he muttered woefully to himself. He had to leave her alone if he was going to maintain his sanity. It was going to be strictly business from now on. He didn't know how he would do it, and it was going to be a challenge . . . a challenge that he had no choice but to undertake.

That afternoon, over the carpeted partition wall that they shared, she heard every keyboard click, and every page rustle, but they worked the rest of the day without seeing each other.

"Yeah, I heard this morning on the news it's supposed to be something like ten inches. I just—Alayna! What are you doing?" Sheila screamed when she turned and saw the scarlet drops of blood pooling on the countertop. Alayna looked down just as another drop of blood rolled down the side of the Granny Smith apple that she had been absentmindedly slicing into bite-sized wedges. The paring knife had pierced her thumb, leaving a pretty nasty gash. Staring into space, she had been so engrossed in her thoughts about Khavon that she had not even noticed the pain until Sheila's scream brought her crashing back into reality. Letting out an ear-piercing shriek, Alayna raced to the water faucet.

"Sheila, look in the bathroom cabinet and get a bandage," she called out, running the cold water over her now-throbbing finger.

The stress was really beginning to take a toll on her, she thought, watching the water-diluted blood rinse down the drain.

"Girl, what chu trying to do, kill yourself?" Sheila laughed nervously, wrapping the flexible foam bandage carefully around Alayna's self-inflicted injury.

"I didn't even notice. Girl, my mind," Alayna said, raising her eyes to the top and shaking her head, "was just somewhere else. I didn't even feel it. But believe me, killing myself is the last thing on my mind. Not an option."

Sheila was thoughtful for a moment before speaking. "Alayna, listen to me. This is not healthy." She held onto Alayna's hand.

"What chu talkin' about?" Alayna wanted to know.

"You know what I'm talking about. You know exactly what I'm talking about. Something's up with you and I sense it's more than Donovan or the break up with Warren. Now, I'm your friend. I know you."

"But—"

"I know you're used to flying solo when it comes to your personal problems, but Alayna, it seems like whatever it is, it's really got you rattled."

"Sheila . . . ." Alayna sighed, as if she were a teenager being lectured to by her mother.

"No, I'm serious. I know we didn't get a chance to talk on Saturday, and I don't know what changed your mind since then, but you need to talk to somebody—if not me, then somebody else. Alayna, you don't have to go through this alone. Now, I'm here to listen, so why don't you just go ahead and tell me what's going on."

"Listen, I really appreciate your concern. Really, I do. But I'm fine. Really."

Sheila cocked her head to the side, pursed her lips together, and folded her arms across her chest in disbelief.

"I mean . . . . Well, what I mean is that I'm as fine as someone who just lost two fiancés in the space of a year and a half can be expected to be.

"Alayna . . . ."

"Really, Sheila, I'm fine."

"Okay. Can't say that I didn't try," Sheila said, separating the layers of wooden window blinds to peer outside at the weather. The snow was coming down in force. "Girl, let me get up outta here before it starts getting really bad. I was gonna stop by Maple's Kitchen and get some smoked turkey wings so I wouldn't have to cook, but I think I better be trying to get home. Call me if you want to talk, okay?" she said, giving Alayna a warm hug.

"Okay. You be careful. You know how crazy people can be in this kind of weather."

"Okay. See ya."

"See ya." Alayna waved, closing the door.

Chapter Nineteen

Why do I live in Minnesota? Why do I live in Minnesota? Alayna chided herself, as her unruly car slid out of control, slamming into a snow-encased street embankment. She had only a few more blocks to go before finally making it to the office, but Mother Nature had once again made the morning commute nothing short of a death trap.

The freezing rain that had been coming down so generously the night before had left a thick sheet of ice as its mark. While she slept, the cities were blanketed with a thirty inch covering of snow that topped the ice.

Her hands still trembling from the collision, Alayna maneuvered her car out from the stop sign that she'd cautiously tried to stop for, and checked the intersection for oncoming cars. Like a snail, she crept along the remaining four blocks to the corporate center, with the sound of fresh new Minnesota snow crushing beneath her tires. Exhausted by the time she finally got to her destination, her face was frigid and pained from the blustering cold wind.

"Enough of the white stuff for ya?" Frank, the security guard grinned, watching Alayna dust the snow from her coat and hair.

"Do you believe this? I know we live in Minnesota, but this

is unreal. I mean thirty inches in one night?" Alayna complained, removing her hat.

"Yeah, it's kind of crazy, especially since they said we were only going to get five ta six inches."

"They sure did, didn't they?" Alayna agreed, recalling.

"Yeah, and then when I turned on the news this morning, it was like they predicted thirty inches all the time. Now they say we could get as nine to ten inches more," he said. Alayna glared at him like he'd just called her a name, and closed her eyes hard.

"You're kidding, right?"

"Nope. I wish I were."

"Ten more?" Alayna threw her hand open in confusion, creasing her brow. "How in the world could we go from six to forty?" she wanted to know.

"I think they said something about a shift in the winds."

"Great."

"You have a good day, now."

"Thanks, Frank. We'll see you later." Alayna pulled the camel hair scarf that protected her chest down from around her neck.

As she climbed the stairs, her mind fixated on the meeting with Mulcahy and the commute to Bloomington that she would have to make in the afternoon. She was not looking forward to the drive, particularly after having seen literally dozens of cars in ditches along the freeway this morning. Reaching the top of the flight, she stopped and stared unbelievingly out the window at the chaotic white shower from the sky. Mammoth snow crystals darted through the air, each trying to outpace the other in a frantic race to the already frozen ground below. Watching the torrential ivory shower that rained relentlessly from the pregnant clouds above, it occurred to Alayna that life was very much like the weather . . . stormy, chaotic and unpredictable. And so was Khavon, running around and making women fall in love with him like it was sport. Well, he wasn't going to get her, no matter how hard he tried.

"Quite a downpour, isn't it?" a familiar voice commented from behind her.

Startled, she turned around quickly, her heart quickening,

fearing her thoughts had been aloud. "Khavon. I didn't hear you come up."

"I'm sorry, I didn't mean to startle you," he said, standing between her and the door.

"No. It's okay. Really. I just . . . I guess I must have just been lost in thought." Her eyes moved quickly away from his.

"Oh? What were you thinking about?" Khavon's eyes lit up with curiosity.

"About the presentation," she lied. "I have a couple of more slides that I need to add."

"Well, I guess I'll get out of your way then," he said, moving aside and opening the door to let her pass through. "We need to get out there at least a couple of hours before the meeting to make sure that the equipment is set up properly," he said, walking behind her as she entered the work area, his voice noticeably devoid of emotion.

"Mm-hmm," Alayna nodded. "I was planning to leave around two o'clock."

"So was I. You can ride with me if you like," he offered. Alayna looked at him long and hard. His facial features lacked the usual flirtation. There was no suggestion in his eyes, only a practical proposal for a carpool. She wasn't sure if she was happy about that or not.

"Thanks, but I think I'll be okay."

"Okay, suit yourself. I'll see you this afternoon then," he said, rounding the corner to his desk.

Alayna sat at her desk, her mind struggling to focus on the simple task of completing her last two slides for the presentation. Over and over, her thoughts invariably strayed to Khavon and the abrupt change in his personality.

Was it possible that I was mistaken about Khavon? she wondered. *Maybe he isn't a playboy. Maybe he was genuinely angry at me for pushing him away so many times. Maybe I pushed him to the end of his rope.* She didn't know. But what she did know was that his solemn manner had caught her way off guard. She hadn't realized how accustomed she had grown to the constant barrage of flirtatious innuendoes and comical remarks. She hadn't realized how much she'd taken for granted his relentless pursuit of her affections. She hadn't realized how much she'd miss the laughter that he had evoked in her everyday since the day she'd met him. She hadn't realized a lot of things . . . . But still, she refused to let him win. She would just have to find a way to get over it.

"You made it!" Furi rejoiced, clasping his hands together. Alayna swiveled her chair around to face the door. The repetitive clicking in the adjoining cubical abruptly came to a stop.

Furi entered her workspace.

"I almost got killed trying to get in here this morning, but yeah, I made it," Alayna said.

"What happened? Did you get into an accident?"

"No, I just slid into a snow embankment. I was a lot better off than some."

"Yeah, I know. The commute was pretty rough this morning. The roads were treacherous. Are you okay?" Furi asked.

"Yeah, I'm fine. But now the challenge is getting out to Bloomington," Alayna said.

"You're welcome to ride with me, if you like."

"Thanks, but no. I think I'll be okay. By the time I get ready to head out that way, the plows will probably have the highways pretty clear. That is, if it ever stops snowing."

"Right. Is everything in order for Mulcahy?" Furi asked.

"Yeah, we're gonna get out of here early to set up. Are you sure he's still coming out? I mean, with the weather and everything?"

"Well, I spoke with him this morning and he's still planning to come out," Furi said.

Alayna was pensive. "I'm really surprised they haven't closed the airport."

"I am, too, but as of fifteen minutes ago, it was still open. We need to be ready in either case."

"Well, let me know if anything changes," Alayna said, as Furi headed out the door.

"Yeah, I'll keep you posted," Furi said over his shoulder.

Alayna closed her eyes tightly, yawning a wide open-mouthed yawn, covering the open cavity with the palm of her hand. Somewhere along the line, she was going to have to find the time to get some badly needed rest.

As she finished up her last slide, it occurred to her that maybe some hot coffee would help the situation. As she headed into the cafeteria, her mind fixated again on Khavon. As she swung open the door of her cubicle to exit, she all but ran into Mark, who was coming from the direction of the main aisle.

"Oh. Excuse me. I'm sorry. I shouldn't have leaped out like that," Alayna immediately apologized.

"No problem, Alayna. How are you?"

"I'm okay, I guess, except for the arctic blast we seem to be in."

"Yeah, I've been tracking it on the internet, and it's going to get worse before it gets better."

"Great. And I have to drive all the way out to Bloomington, and then all the way back home again."

"Oh, yeah. I forgot. Today's the big meeting."

"Yeah, I really can't believe he's still coming in, and he's scheduled to fly out right after the meeting for some other commitment."

"Yeah, and that Amsterdam flight is the last international—" Mark stopped abruptly, his muted words cut short. His pensive blue eyes immediately darted to hers.

"Amsterdam? Where did you hear that Mulcahy was going to Amsterdam?" Alayna wanted to know.

"Furi, I need to talk to you," Mark called over Alayna's shoulder to Furi, who was walking down the main aisle.

"You stay warm, Alayna," he smiled, avoiding her question.

"I was just on my way to your office," he said, passing her by to catch up with Furi.

Alayna walked over to Sheila's cube to see if she wanted to take a break and go down for some coffee.

"Sheila called in. Since they closed the schools, she decided to stay at home with the kids," Ericka informed Alayna from the cubbyhole across from Sheila's.

"Oh, yeah. I forgot the schools had a snow day today."

"Yeah, isn't it beautiful?"

"What?"

"The snow . . . isn't it beautiful?"

"Well, beautiful isn't exactly the first word that comes to my mind, Ericka," Alayna said.

"You don't think that the snow is beautiful?" Ericka asked incredulously, her voice slightly accented.

Alayna shrugged her shoulders. "Snow is snow."

"How can you say that? It is a beautiful blessed gift from above." Ericka smiled a thoughtful smile.

Alayna stood there for a moment quietly contemplating what Ericka had said. "I guess I never thought about it like that. Girl, you don't let anything get you down, do you?"

"Life is too short to walk around being depressed, unless there's a really, really good reason for it . . . especially about something so beautiful." Ericka swung her dusty blonde hair.

"That's your philosophy, huh?" Alayna asked.

"That's my philosophy," Ericka confirmed, with a wide grin.

Alayna laughed. "Listen, I was just going down for some coffee. Interested?"

"Well, I was waiting for Furi, we were going to go down together. If you wait a few minutes . . . ."

"Oh, no. You guys go ahead."

"Are you sure? We'd love to have you join us."

"Mm-hmm."

"Maybe we'll see you down there." Ericka's voice was hopeful.

"Sure. See ya later." Alayna waved.

Walking to the cafeteria, Alayna noticed that the place looked relatively empty. *A lot of people must have taken vacation today.* It definitely was a good day for it, she thought wryly. With the school closings this morning, she was sure that a lot of people had just stayed home with their kids. She'd have taken the day off herself if it weren't for that darned presentation today. She wouldn't be so drained. She wouldn't have had to tippy-toe across town, almost killing herself in the process, to get to work, and then two hours later, tippy-toe all the way out to Bloomington, only to turn around and do it all over again, she thought, wallowing in a mound of self-pity.

"Double espresso, black please," she told the woman behind the counter. If a double espresso didn't give her the caffeine punch that she needed, she didn't know what would. She hoped her body didn't go into shock from the caffeine blast, but if she didn't get something, she was going to fall over from exhaustion.

"Can I have a chocolate biscotti with that too, please?" Alayna said, handing the girl three dollars.

"Better watch out, chocolate can make you fat," the voice from behind her warned. A relatively long period of time had passed since the last time she'd heard his voice. Coffee in hand, she turned to greet him.

"Hello, Warren." Her voice rang with a strange sort of friendly apathy that surprised her. She'd thought that the first meeting after their break up would be an angry one, an awkward one at the very least. But she felt neither emotion.

"How are you?" Warren asked, his eyelids dropping momentarily.

"I'm fine. How are you?"

"Good. Good. Listen can we talk?" Warren asked gingerly.

Alayna looked at him thoughtfully. "Sure. I'll get us a table."

"You should be almost ready to head out of here pretty soon. You must be really excited," Alayna said when Warren approached the table with his coffee.

"Yeah, I guess it shows," Warren laughed. "I am getting pretty geared up."

"I mean, hobnobbing with the President and everything. Who wouldn't?" Alayna teased.

"Well, I can think of at least one person. Besides, I doubt seriously if I'll be hobnobbing with the President—or even the lowest of his staff, for that matter. But I did find out that I'll be traveling abroad, which you know is something that I've wanted for a long time. Anyway, enough about me. How are you?"

"I'm fine."

"No. I mean, really, how are you?" Warren asked again, not accepting her canned response.

Alayna eyed him. "Warren, if you were that concerned about how I was doing, why did you wait until we had a happenstance meeting to express your concerns?"

"You're absolutely right. I guess . . . I guess I just didn't have the nerve to call you up after everything that happened. Alayna, I never thought it would end like this," Warren said, bowing his head and shaking it from side to side. "I never meant to hurt you. It's just, well . . . I thought we were on the same page about things."

"I know," Alayna said, covering his hand with hers. "I'm sorry too. I thought the same thing. I guess it just took a while to figure out that we both wanted different things."

"Yeah, I guess."

"But it wasn't like it was a complete waste of time or anything. I mean, we had some good times, didn't we?"

Warren looked into her eyes. "We sure did. I'll never forget that time on Lake Calhoun, remember?" Warren asked, smiling.

Alayna rolled her eyes back in her head, and laughed aloud. "How could I forget? Yeah, that was something," Alayna agreed. "I think I can safely say that's one life experience that I'll never forget."

"Me neither. I don't know what possessed us to go out there when the wind was so high," Warren concurred, chuckling.

"Yeah, I don't know. Maybe it wouldn't have been so bad, if all those people hadn't been standing around watching us," Alayna said.

"Yeah, and I don't know which was worse—the canoe tipping over, or all those people watching us."

"Yeah, we were lucky we were near the shore."

"No kidding. But the absolute worst . . . the absolute worst," Warren said laughing, "was when that guy took our picture as we hand-carried the canoe back to the rental office, just when it had started to rain." They both laughed aloud. Alayna was laughing so hard that she hadn't felt the weight of Khavon's angry, eagle-eyed stare, nor did she notice when he abruptly stood up from the table, giving Furi and Ericka a bogus excuse for having to get back to his desk.

"Oh, Alayna," Warren said, as the laughter slowed to a stop,

"I just wanted to make everything straight between us before I left. You know?"

"Yeah, I know."

"Friends?" he asked, extending his long yellow hand to her.

"Friends," Alayna agreed, accepting his hand in hers.

Alayna glanced over and saw that the lunch crowd was beginning to trickle in. "We should probably be getting back," Alayna said, her lids falling momentarily. After a short pause, she rose from the table.

"Yeah." Warren stood up following her lead.

"Hi, Alayna." Ericka waved from the table that she and Furi were seated at. Alayna waved back.

"Alayna, I'll call you before I leave," Warren said, bidding her goodbye.

"Okay, I'll talk to you later then. And if I don't, have a safe trip and . . . and you take care of yourself."

"Will do. And you do the same," Warren said. He left the cafeteria to return to the office.

Alayna walked over to the table where Furi and Ericka were sitting. "Hi."

"Heading back up?" Furi asked.

"Yeah, I think I'm going to grab a sandwich and head on out to Bloomington."

"Well, it doesn't look like the weather's improved any," Furi said, shaking his head. "In fact, it looks like it may have even gotten worse than this morning. Are you sure you don't want to reconsider riding out there together?"

"Well . . . maybe I should. Wait a minute. Furi, don't you live in Lakesville?" Alayna asked, recalling last year's group picnic.

"Yeah, but I'd hate for you to . . . ."

"Oh, no. That's too much. You'd have to bring me all the way back over here to pick up my car, and then drive all the way back out there again. No. Really. I mean, thanks, but no. That's just too much. I'll be fine, really. I'll just have to take my time, that's all. Besides I'm sure that the freeways are clear by now. I'll just have to get an early start." Alayna checked her watch. It was a quarter after eleven. "I think I'm gonna grab a bite and get ready to head on out that way."

"Okay, Alayna. Remember, if you change your mind, I won't be heading out till close to three."

"Thanks, Furi. I'll see ya later. Ericka, have a nice weekend, if I don't see you."

"You too, Alayna. Be safe."

Chapter Twenty

From the conference room window, Khavon watched as the airplanes struggled to take off and land. He wondered why they were still flying in such treacherous weather. And the weather was treacherous. Treacherous and tumultuous, just like his marriage.

Khavon had promised himself that he would never marry again. Marriage had failed miserably at keeping its promise for a lifetime of love and happiness—not only for him, but for countless people around him as well. He had watched too many people over the years profess their undying love for one another in a gratuitous ceremony, only to watch them fall into a hateful bitter divorce only a few, short years later. In some cases, months. No. No, not again. *What is it about marriage?* he wondered. It had a way of changing things. It had a way of bringing out the worst in people. It somehow had the ability to turn what used to be two good friends into two monsters.

Khavon brought his distant gaze into focus, converging on the steady, constant flux of traffic that, despite the hazardous weather conditions, continued streaming into the parking ramps of the Mall of America. What was it, Khavon wondered, that continued to draw people to the mega-mall, even in the middle of a snowstorm? He had lived in Bloomington for close to six months now, yet he had only driven past the mammoth shopping complex.

"Mr. Brighton," a pale, heavy-set woman with red-orange hair neatly tucked into a bun called from behind him. "Here are the overhead projector and power cords that you requested."

Khavon turned around with a gratuitous smile, and scanned her nametag again. "Thanks, Nancy. I hope I didn't cause you too much trouble," he said, helping her to roll the auxiliary aids in.

"No, it was no trouble at all. If there's anything else that you need, just give me a holler," she said before leaving the room.

"Thanks again. Oh, there is one more thing. Is there a coffee machine around here?"

"Sure, but it's on the blink. Ya have to go to the one on the fifth floor, across from the custodial closet."

"And where is that?" Khavon asked.

"Across from the . . . you know, I could use a good cup of java myself. I'll just take you down there."

"I'm sure I can find it."

"It's no problem. I have to drop these papers off on Three anyway."

"Great."

Khavon followed her to the escalator. When they set foot on Five on one side, Alayna was just reaching the top of Six on the other. She was in a foul mood. The slip-sloppy commute had not started off well.

After dusting what seemed to be a foot of snow off the roof of her car, she had been almost ready to go back in to see if she could still catch a ride with Furi, when her ride finally conceded with a weak start. She was already on the freeway entrance ramp when she realized that she'd left the disk containing the electronic copy of her presentation sitting on her desk. She had to backtrack to the center and retrieve it.

She'd thought that the roads would be clear by this time of the day. Instead, she found herself nervously inching by a monster snowplow, while a semi shot past her on the left, indiscriminately bulleting granules of sand at the windshield that she was trying so desperately to keep clear.

Upon entering the conference room, her eyes automatically

zeroed in on the camel hair coat that was carefully draped over one of the chairs at the table. It was Khavon's, and she wondered where he was. After removing her coat and replacing her boots with shoes, Alayna got on her knees and crawled under the presentation desk to plug in the cables from the video monitor.

"That's already been taken care of." The sound of Khavon's stiff voice startled her head into a painful bump on the underside of the desk. As the pain accelerated through the end of her nerves and registered in her brain, an unbecoming grimace masked her face, and her head immediately began to throb. Her eyes rolled into the back of her head, and her teeth clenched together as she tried desperately to temper her anger from both the painful wallop and Khavon's vaguely veiled indictment.

"I'm sorry I'm late, but in case you hadn't noticed there's a snowstorm outside. Besides, we still have more than enough time to prepare," Alayna said angrily. With fire in her eyes, she crawled from beneath the cherry wood frame to face her accuser.

"I noticed," he said coolly, glancing out the window.

"I'm so glad."

"We need to go over the logistics of the meeting," he said unaffectedly after a short pause, commandeering a chair at the table.

"Mr. Brighton, there's a phone call for you," Nancy informed him from the doorway.

"Excuse me," he told Alayna formally, before getting up from his seat.

Alayna took the opportunity to do damage assessment. She apprehensively walked over to the window. It was still snowing heavily. She wondered if it was ever going to stop. She hated the snow. And she hated the winter. When it wasn't the snowy, icy streets slipping and sliding the energy out of her, it was the wind chill freezing it out of her, she thought bitterly as she stared into the crystalline snowfall. *Why do I live in this state?* she wondered. No sun, no men. It was in total conflict with her life and what she wanted to do with it. She wanted something that she'd never had before. She wanted a family, a family of her own. She wanted unconditional love. But how was she going to find it, she wondered, in a place where the Black women seemed to out number the Black men four to one, ten to one when the woman count was expanded to include women of other races? All at once, her eyes saw past the blanket snowfall that she had intently fixed her thoughtful gaze on, and focused on the welcome red, white and blue sign across the street. "Mall of America," Alayna read aloud. *That's where I should be right now. Shopping at the Mall of America, drowning my troubles in a new rayon blend designer suit. That's where I need to be.*

Alayna turned from the window when Khavon returned to the room.

"That was Furi. He's on his way. He said Mulcahy's plane has been delayed, but he's still planning to come."

Alayna and Khavon were busying themselves preparing for the presentation and taking care of the last minute details, when Nancy tapped on the door again.

"Mr. Brighton, I'm sorry to bother you again, but there's another call for you." Khavon looked at Alayna. More than an hour had passed since Furi's last call. He should have been there by now.

"Thanks, Nancy." Khavon got up and left the room again.

"Furi, if Mulcahy called an hour and a half ago, why are you just now calling us with this?" Khavon asked.

"Because I'm stuck in traffic and my cell phone is having some problems. Phyllis has been trying to reach me, but was unable to get through. When I finally got the message, I tried to call, but then my phone went out again. I've been stuck in transit since I last called."

"That was Furi," Khavon started, upon return to the room. The news that he returned with did not surprise Alayna. "He was half way here when Phyllis called on his cell phone." Alayna watched him carefully as he spoke.

"Mulcahy's not coming. His flight was canceled. The airport finally shut down because of the storm. Furi said we should just head home. We will discuss it in the morning."

"Well, is he coming in tomorrow?" Alayna asked.

"No, he's not. He apparently had some OUS obligations."

Alayna said nothing, watching him with a curious look on her face.

"Come on, I'll walk you to your car. You can get an early start on your commute. It will be dark soon."

"Thanks, but I'll be fine."

"Suit yourself." Khavon lifted his coat from the chair, along with the rest of his belongings.

"See ya tomorrow," he said to Alayna, as she gathered her things. He was gone before she could look up and give him the cashmere scarf that he'd left lying on the floor.

Alayna was exhausted when she reached the glass exit on the ground floor. Sighing heavily, she wrapped her scarf around her face. Bracing herself, Alayna pushed the door open to the howling wind. She trudged her way to her car, the wet flakes stinging as they slapped her across the face, the white snow crushing beneath her boots. She finally reached her car, but not before slipping and falling three times. When she reached it, she dumped her belongings into the trunk as fast as she could. She brushed the new snow off all of the windows so that she could see, and jumped into the car.

Her back slammed against the seat cushion. She paused, staring in disbelief at the opaline white torrent that surrounded her and her little white car. She sat there for a few moments, listening quietly to the frozen flakes that pelted violently against her weather-beaten windshield, until her ear drums ached from the deafening cadence. She wondered again why she had chosen to live in Minnesota. It would be so nice, she thought to herself over the incessant drone of the wet shelling, if she were at home, in front of the fire, with a good book and a cup of hot cappuccino. "That would be so wonderful," she mumbled aloud. She indulged in the warm fantasy for a moment, before it froze like the sheet of ice forming on her windshield, and crashed to the ground, cracking into tiny pieces.

Slightly injured by the jagged edges of reality settling in, she angrily shoved the key into the ignition. She could at least get started on what she knew was going to be a nightmarish commute back to the city. The sooner she started, the sooner it would be over, she convinced herself.

Twisting her wrist to turn the key in the ignition, her frozen ears expected to hear the noise of her clamorous engine revving up to a start, but instead she heard nothing . . . only the sound of the torrential assault against her car.

Chapter Twenty-One

"This is not happening." That was all she had the energy to think or say. "It's all a bad dream. Any moment, I'm going to wake up," she told herself. She closed her eyes hard and tried again. "This is not happening," she shrieked, slamming her fist into the dashboard. She tried it again and again, but the ignition would make only a disturbing click when she turned the key. In an instant, she realized what the problem was. Visibility in the inclement weather had been so poor on the drive over, she'd turned on her lights, and in her rush to get inside she neglected to turn them off. That, in conjunction with the cold temperature, had zapped the last drop of energy from her tired, weak battery. It would be dark soon, Alayna thought, trying to gather her wits. Cell phone. The thought came to her in an instant. She seized her purse, grappling desperately past the lipstick and hair accessories trying to find it. She breathed a heavy sigh of relief when she found that she had not left it sitting on the counter in a frantic haste, a mistake that was not unusual for her. She pulled the bulky light of hope from her purse, but the light quickly went out as the black display on her phone told her that the battery had run out and she'd forgotten to recharge it.

Alayna was just about to get out to see if she could find someone, anyone, still left in the building that might be able to give her a boost, or to at least use the phone, when a shiny, black Lincoln navigator slowly pulled up beside her. Quickly, Alayna closed her door and locked it. Breathing heavily, she watched suspiciously as the driver of the mysterious vehicle powered the window down.

It was Khavon. "You left your lights on," he said simply, when Alayna rolled her own window down.

She was slightly irritated, but relieved. "I don't believe you. You scared me to death!" she exclaimed. "You shouldn't sneak up on people like that."

"Sorry, I didn't mean to frighten you." His voice still had a cool edge.

"You got any jumper cables in that thing?" she asked, hoping that they could revive her lifeless, silent battery. She'd been warned that she needed to get a new one, but she had kept putting it off.

"Yeah. Pop your hood, and I'll hook you up." She did as he asked, and then stepped out into the blustery cold wind to watch as he set up and closed the connection between his vehicle and hers.

His facial hair was frozen white with snow. "Get in and try to crank it up," he said, swiping the white flakes from his frozen mustache. Again, she did as he said. She positioned herself behind the wheel, turned the key and pressed her foot on the gas pedal. But again, the car was unresponsive, making only the clicking sound that she'd heard before. Khavon stood back watching, anticipating a start, but the car did nothing. He walked over to the car door.

"It's still only making a clicking sound," Alayna said.

"Let me try." Khavon got in and tried to crank the car himself, but the car did what Alayna had told him. He checked and rechecked the connections before he finally told Alayna that her battery had passed on and gone to battery heaven. Alayna stared at him blankly, the snowflakes swirling around them, wondering what she was going to do. Then it occurred to her that surrounding the mall were a variety of different hotels.

"Get your things. I only live about a half a mile away from here," Khavon said, night falling down around them.

Alayna's eyes went wide with incredulity. "I know you don't

think I'm going home with you." Her tone was thick with attitude, her lengthy lashes speckled with snowflakes.

Khavon rolled his eyes back. "Okay, Alayna. What are you going to do?" he wanted to know.

"Well, I was going to ask you if you could give me a ride to one of those hotels on the south side of the mall."

"Alayna, you're being ridiculous," Khavon said, his voice grating with irritation.

"Ridiculous? No, I'm not the one who's being ridiculous," Alayna quipped, folding her arms across her chest as the snowflakes took residence on her hat and coat. "If you think for one minute that I'm going home with you, you are crazy . . . . No, I'm not the ridiculous one," she said, raising her eyebrows.

"Alayna," Khavon said quietly, trying to squelch the rising anger that filled him, "we are in the middle of a major snowstorm. The airport over there closed an hour and a half ago, and we are across the street from the second biggest tourist attraction in the United States. Now, how many hotels do you think have vacancies left?" He was right and Alayna knew it. She stood there at first with no answer, glaring silently at him, not knowing what to do. Then, she stormed around him angrily to get her things, and waited, head bent, for him to unlock the passenger side door.

Like a lonely tourist on a train destined for anywhere but home, Alayna stared silently out the vehicle's window at the darkness as it fell down around them. As Khavon slowed down to turn, she read the green and white sign that graced the entrance of the subdivision.

Evergreen The Gateway to Your Dreams

Taking in the view, it struck Alayna as odd how Brown Deer Road had, in a few short blocks, changed from a busy, congested thoroughfare to a quiet, night-cloaked road. In truth, it had been a short trip, just as Khavon had said.

The woodland setting was straight off of a scenic Christmas card, she thought, riding past the lines of snow-covered pines. Cast against a pearly white backdrop of frosty evergreens, ice-laden branches, and crystalline snow flakes, it was beautiful landscape. She could see the brightly illuminated cottage-like homes, sparsely nestled between the heaven-bound trees, their chimneys billowing with smoke, their entrances glowing with invitation. Invading these homes with her eyes as they drove, Alayna could see the families to whom they belonged milling about, taking refuge from the storm. She could almost feel the warmth emanating from their blazing fireplaces, close-knit family bonds, and all around household love. Khavon interrupted her thoughts.

"I wasn't expecting company, so you'll have to excuse the mess," he said unaffectedly, before pulling straight ahead to the edge of the driveway to his house. Alayna turned her attention to the front of the vehicle for the first time during their wordless ride. Because it was concealed behind several trees, she was unable to see the front entrance to his house. The smoky gray color, combined with the absence of light, had made it difficult to make out the house itself.

Khavon pressed the remote garage door opener. A sort of dusky, yellow light in the ceiling illuminated the garage and its entrance.

"Is your seatbelt on?" Khavon asked Alayna.

"Yeah. Why—" But before she could finish her question, Khavon abruptly hit the gas, attempting to plow through the huge accumulation of snow in the driveway with his truck, with no success. The snowy incline was too much, even for his truck. Again and again, he backed out to get a running start, only to slip, slide, and waver back and forth in frustration, unable to surmount the slippery slope. Irritated, Khavon backed up one last time and parked the truck on the street in front of his house.

"I'm going to have to blow the driveway to get through. C'mon, I'll let you in," Khavon instructed her.

Alayna wordlessly complied, grabbing her things and trudging slowly behind Khavon through the already knee-deep snow, into the three car garage. She eyed the expensive little gray car that she'd seen him in on the first day. It was in mint condition.

"The room at the top of the stairs is yours," Khavon said without a smile, unlocking and opening the side entrance to the house, then pointing to the staircase a few feet from where she was standing.

Alayna's thickly-lashed eyes locked with his for a moment before they moved away.

"You should get out of those wet clothes before you catch cold. You'll find some dry clothes in the chest beside your bed. There's a linen closet in the bathroom next to your room. I'll be in after I finish the driveway," Khavon said coldly, before turning back to the garage. "Oh, there's some spaghetti in the fridge, in case you're hungry."

"Thanks," Alayna said begrudgingly, as he closed the door.

She removed her boots and placed them on the mud rug, and then hung her coat in the closet behind her. Except for the motion light that automatically popped on when Khavon had opened the door, the house was dark. Dark and cold. Alayna wanted to put her coat back on, but it was covered in wet snow. Shivering, Alayna slid her hands up and down her forearms, trying to create some heat from the friction. Frustrated, she hid them beneath her armpits before entering the kitchen.

The dark, noiseless house felt to Alayna like a morgue. Her eyes quickly scanned the wall for the light switch. Dimly visible from the light in the hall, she spotted it underneath what appeared to be a calendar hanging on the wall. She walked over and flipped the switch, flooding the kitchen with a wash of light. Alayna gasped audibly, taking in the breathlessly beautiful kitchen. It was as if she had turned a page in a magazine. Marshmallow walls framed the California-style cocina. Matching tiles surrounded the cooktop on the workspace island in the center of the room. She eyed the window box filled with basil, chamomile, and thyme.

Alayna stood breathing in the cold, thin air, her bones shivering. Khavon's house was like an ice box, only a shade warmer than outside. When what seemed like a bolt of ice went charging down her spine, Alayna decided that Khavon was right, she'd better get out of her wet clothes before she caught cold.

Alayna ducked her head slightly, her wide brown eyes peering up at the top of the dark staircase. She flipped the light switch on the wall, exposing a much less threatening carpeted stairwell. As she climbed the stairs, the sound of the snow blower grew slightly more distant, but she could still hear it and the others on the block.

Reaching the top of the stairs, Alayna turned and headed to the bedroom on the left, as Khavon had instructed her. The walls in the room had been painted a blue-gray hue.

Alayna walked over to the chest that Khavon had mentioned, and picked up the framed picture that sat on top of it. It was the same one she'd seen downstairs in his kitchen, secured by a magnet on his refrigerator.

Encased in an ornate, polished silver frame, was a black and white photo of two young boys dressed in checkered shirts and blue jeans, standing in front of two parked cars on the street. They stood shoulder to shoulder, their heads linked together between their arms. The boys' sizable afros and the cars in the background told Alayna that, despite its fresh appearance, the picture was a very old one.

Placing the picture back on the chest in its place, Alayna wondered who the boys were. She eyed the single rosebud displayed in a beautiful crystal vase beside it. She'd smelled its fresh, delicate fragrance as soon as she'd entered the room. Goose bumps formed on her forearms, reminding her that her purpose was to get out of her wet clothes.

Alayna slid her slender fingers over the brass plated handles of the top drawer, and proceeded to pull it open. Neatly folded inside, amid a host of other sports apparel, was a blue and green fleece sweatshirt, emblazoned with the Timberwolves' official logo. She grabbed it and the plain, gray sweatpants that were folded underneath.

Peeling off her wet stockings, she stripped down to the satiny black underwear that she was wearing.

The sweatshirt was loose and comfortable, but she was drowning in the pants. They were way too big, but they still felt better than what she'd had on, she thought, pulling them up for extra warmth over her firm, bare stomach. She folded her wet clothes into a neat pile and placed them against the wall near the vent.

She was beginning to thaw out, and the cotton felt good against her cold, damp skin, but she was still shivering, and her feet felt like two frosty ice blocks. It was then that she opted to take refuge under the multicolored quilt on the bed that had looked so inviting when she'd come in. Inside of three minutes, the constant drone of the snow blowers plowing through the mounds of snow that had accumulated outside had managed to lull her into a deep sleep.

She is such a silly girl, Khavon said to himself. *That's what she is, a silly little girl. Immature. A little girl who doesn't know what to do or how to act when a real man approaches her. Just like a little girl, she's playing games. Who does she think she is?* He could get on the phone, right now . . . right now, if he wanted to, and call any one of ten women who would, without hesitation, brave the inclement weather and find some way to make it to his house, even in the middle of this snowstorm. No, he didn't need her, he told himself over and over again to the rhythm of the smooth, sultry sax he was listening to. What did he need with a crazy person? *Talkin' 'bout she was gonna stay at a hotel. She is a crazy person.* What did she think he was going to do to her anyway?

Alayna woke to insistent hunger pangs and unfamiliar surroundings. In the paneled moonlight, she could see the shadowy outline of the rosebud in the crystal vase, but it was the shimmery, silver glint of the picture frame beside it that eventually allowed her to register her whereabouts. The photograph within the frame had been a curiosity for her, Alayna remembered. It still was.

Struggling to an upright position, she eyed the rectangular form in the darkness. It had given her such an odd feeling earlier, when she'd picked it up. For some reason, the boys in the picture had seemed so familiar to her, but she didn't know why. Swinging her legs over the side of the bed, Alayna took heed of her body's complaints and decided it was time to get something to eat. Khavon had said there was some spaghetti in the fridge. She could probably just heat that up in the microwave.

The house was much warmer than when she had first come

in, she noticed, but it was still quiet. Khavon must have turned in too, she surmised.

Wondering if it was still snowing, she separated the blinds and peered out at the black and white night. Yes, it was still snowing—and from the way it looked outside, not only had it never stopped, but it seemed to be doing overtime.

How long had she been sleeping anyway? It couldn't have been more than a couple of hours, she thought, scanning the dark room for a digital display. There was none, but there was a light switch. She remembered turning the light on when she came in, but now it was off. Khavon must have turned it off, she decided.

Pulling the loose pants up on her, she flipped the switch in her room to shed some light on the dark, quiet hallway. She was stunned when she caught sight of the clock on the hallway wall. It was a few minutes past midnight. She'd been asleep for more than six hours.

After rinsing her face and mouth in the bathroom next to her room, she headed down the stairs. When she turned on the light, it all came to her in a single word. Sanitized. That's what it was about Khavon's kitchen that had struck her in the beginning, but she hadn't been able to put her finger on it. The kitchen was beautiful, true enough, but it was a bit too perfect. It didn't look lived in. The Spanish motif was artistic and stylish and the room was bright and airy, but there were no personal trimmings, no character, no connection whatsoever to the owner. If it weren't for the photograph of the two boys between the two sports car magnets on the refrigerator, it would have no personality at all. *Odd*, she thought, zeroing in on the leftover container of spaghetti and the bottle of sangria in the fridge. It was a small amount, but enough for one. Except for the hum of the microwave, the house was quiet. A sort of dead silence, Alayna thought eerily.

When she'd finished the pasta and a second glass of the fruity, crimson liquid splashed against the back of her throat, she closed her eyes, wondering how she had managed to get herself into such a predicament. *What am I doing at this man's house?* The man treated her as if she were a child, ridiculing and criticizing her every move. Nothing she did ever seemed quite good enough for him.

There was always something wrong with it. *The man is a real egomaniac. A control freak. Where does he get off getting an attitude just because I didn't drop everything, just for the dubious honor of being in his presence for a few minutes?* If that was the reason he had his so-called attitude, she didn't like it and she didn't like him. She just wanted to go home.

A muted thud from the front part of the house jarred her thoughts. Her eyes flew open and darted at once in the direction from which the noise had come. Quietly and carefully, she placed the black stemmed wine glass down on the island countertop. Barefoot, she tiptoed quietly across the maple wood floor and into the adjoining room. Standing at a safe distance, she apprehensively peered around the corner into the next room. It was dark, but in the filtered moonlight she could see Khavon's statured form, standing in the front of the rectangular picture window that dominated his living room wall.

Quietly, she watched him as he stared out the window at the cascading snowfall in his front yard. Even though she hated winter, she had to admit to herself that the snowfall was beautiful. Against the landscape of the obscure, black night and the crystalline trees, it was more than beautiful—it was breathtaking.

He'd changed into his night clothes, she noticed. His motionless form, hands shoved into the pockets of his robe, made her wonder how long he'd been standing there. From the back, she could see the wired outline of headphones and wondered what he was listening to.

Deciding that she was invading, she turned quietly to leave.

"Well-rested, I trust?" he asked clearly, catching a vague hint of her scent in the air. His back remained to her, his head slightly turned. The sound of his voice startled her.

"For the moment," she answered turning back to his voice.

"Surprised to find yourself in one piece?" Khavon asked, removing his headphones, his voice slightly edged.

"What do you mean, one piece? What are you talking about?" Alayna asked, picking up on his thinly veiled anger.

"Well, the way you acted this afternoon, you obviously

thought I was going to do you some kind of bodily harm," he spat out angrily.

"What?" Alayna exhaled in disgust, throwing her eyes back into the top of her head. Her hand went up like one of the Supremes. "Okay. You're tripping, and I don't have time for this. I'm going back to bed," she said, turning to leave.

"Oh, and by the way, Alayna, thank you for leaving your briefcase right in the middle of the floor. I tripped and practically broke my neck," he called after her.

Alayna turned, fire in her eyes, and marched into the room where he was standing. "Khavon, why is it that you have to criticize my every move?"

"Why is it that you have to be such a baby about everything?" he snapped back.

Alayna leaned in close so there would be no mistake. "You know what?" Her voice was low, her lips tight. "Khavon Brighton, I despise you."

"Good!" he retorted angrily. "Because the feeling is mutual!"

The heated anger between them was intense as, inches away, their smoldering eyes silently burned into one another. Then, suddenly, in a simultaneous rush, there in front of a snowy moonlit backdrop, their heated glares spontaneously combusted into a passionate blaze. Their displaced anger was blackened and consumed in brilliant flames, as they impulsively succumbed to the urgent need that had been lurking beneath the surface all along.

"Alayna . . . ." Khavon whispered, finally peeling his frenzied lips from hers, his mouth resting on her cheek, still burning with intensity. "Girl . . . you just don't know what you do to me."

Loosely-tied, Khavon's heavy black robe came open, and there could be no mistake. Against her body in their locked embrace, she felt the thick, hungry urgency of his manhood.

She inhaled deeply to take in more of his wonderfully male scent. "Khavon . . . ." she sighed, as their lips came together once again. As his tongue continued its warm exploration of her mouth, gossamer winged butterflies fluttered about wildly in Alayna's abdomen, spilling the nectar of her desire into her undergarment.

Responding to her nonverbal cues, Khavon slipped his hand

under her sweatshirt and skillfully freed her breasts from their restrictive confines. Holding her close, he cupped one of her plump, fleshy mountains and began to knead it gently. Alayna tore her lips from his and gasped aloud. The sound of her uttered pleasure was almost too much for him to bear. His body screamed from within, and he wanted her more than ever.

"Alayna . . . ." he whispered in her ear. "I want to make love to you . . . . I want to make love to you right here, right now . . . in the moonlight." His voice was raw with desire. "But Alayna . . . I need to be sure that you want me as much as I want you."

Pulling her head back to face him, she answered him with a deep, wet, sensuous kiss that left no room for doubt. The union of their lips remained unbroken as Khavon shuffled out of his robe and flung it across the carpet to act as a makeshift pallet. She unbuttoned the last of the buttons on his pajama shirt as he gently laid her down. Alayna walked her fingers down his throat, over his firm, hard pecs, and down his rippled six pack. Khavon trembled involuntarily in response.

In the center of his hand, he offered to her what looked at first like a gold coin. "If you wouldn't mind, I'd like some help," he whispered.

"Where did that come from?" Alayna asked, realizing what it was.

"Oh, I had this in the pocket of my robe." Alayna looked at him questioningly. "Well . . . Alayna . . . I mean, I am a bachelor," he said, explaining. She turned away, hurt by the implication. Khavon closed his eyes hard. "Alayna . . . I'm not going to lie to you. I have had my share of women, but believe me, you are a rare enchantment that I have not been able to stop thinking about since the day I met you. And straight up, I'm not some prince, toting a white picket fence. I'm just a man who really has a thing for you." He paused. "If you haven't figured it out by now," he said slowly, with another pause. "I'm in love with you, Alayna. Please believe me when I tell you that I've never felt for anyone what I feel for you. I'm so into you, Alayna, and I would never do anything to hurt you."

Alayna looked into his satiny brown eyes and saw only sincerity. "I don't think you would, Khavon." She kissed him deeply and took the condom from his hand. She massaged the head of his throbbing vessel. Then, using a stroking motion, she spread the latex over his lengthy ridge.

"Alayna, you take my breath away," he confessed, when her body lay fully exposed to him for the very first time. She smelled so sweet. He wanted to lick, suck and sample every bit of her. He took her earlobe into his mouth, and bit her gently on the neck.

"That fragrance — what is it?" he growled, the identity of the scent having tortured him every night for months.

"Rapture," she whispered, in answer to his question.

Rapture, how appropriate, he thought. "Rapture . . . Rapture . . . ." he repeated again and again, as if it were a beautiful song.

Taking her under his nude body, he kissed her parted, ready mouth, and then proceeded to plant a torturous trail of red pepper kisses from the top of her erect nipple down the right side of her body to the bottom of her leg, where he stopped abruptly.

"I like to work my way up," he said simply, explaining. When he caught sight of her long, delicately slender foot and the tantalizing ruby red paint that decorated her toes, the fetish in him came alive and he almost lost his mind. The length of her nail bed was incredible.

"Do you know that I've sat in the middle of meetings wondering what your feet looked like?" He kissed the inside of her foot at the ankle, not waiting for a response. She was relieved, as she had none to give him. Somehow, it didn't matter, as he planted another series of kisses across the base of her foot and then on each toe. Alayna was on fire. No man had ever done that to her before.

"Please, Khavon . . . ." she whimpered breathlessly as he took her big toe into his mouth. Satisfied with her response, he retraced his path up to her dewy feminine center, and plunged his middle finger into her moistness, creating rippling waves of pleasure like she'd never felt before.

"Oh, Khavon . . . ." she whimpered again.

Ignoring the incessant dictates of his own body, he removed his finger and placed it into his mouth, as he watched her watching him. Yes, she was sweet. Very sweet. When he had sponged her down properly with his tongue, he stopped abruptly.

"Khavon . . . please . . . please . . . I can't stand it. *Please....*" When she pleaded once more and had reached the appropriate pitch, he laved her into a gushing, orgasmic waterfall. The pleasure was so intense that teardrops fell involuntarily from her eyes. When he kissed away her teardrops, he felt that he had almost sampled her completely. But not yet.

He placed his rigid rock at the mouth of her soft, flowing river, letting her gurgling cascade gently swash over it. Her body was still quivering. He continued to dabble in and out, testing the water, until neither one of them could stand it any longer. He dove in, dousing himself with Alayna's sweetness over and over again.

"Kiss me . . . ." Alayna pleaded.

He obliged, and then let her experience his full size.

"Oh . . . ."

"Alayna . . . ." he moaned. Diving in again and again, he rode the loving waves of desire into the eye of the storm. Drenched in her love, his body quaked as he climbed and finally reached the crest of a surging, white-capped wave. He caught a glimpse of a serene, tranquil clearing on the horizon, just before he capsized into a final wash of calm.

They slept peacefully in each other's arms for three hours, and then they set sail again.

As dawn's early light peeked around the heavy, wet, snow-taxed branches and began to fill the room, Khavon lay awake wondering how he had managed to lose his mind. Alayna had been exquisite. Her loving had been even sweeter than he had imagined . . . but he had been a fool to tell her he loved her. True or not. It seemed that he was an amateur after all, he told himself, because loving someone, and giving the object of your affections that privied knowledge, were two very different things . . . two very dangerous things, and two very different things. It could only lead to heartache and trouble. *How could I be such a fool?* He knew the consequences. He knew them all too well. But Alayna had simply been impossible to resist. That smooth, soft skin . . . those incredible lashes. No. Alayna's loving had been much too potent to turn away. But she had told him in no uncertain terms what she wanted, and he was not prepared to give it to her. Not then and not now. Marriage was for people who didn't know any better, he told himself. Marriage was for the naive and weak-minded.

But Alayna was so beautiful. He turned to watch her sleeping face. She looked so beautiful, so peaceful. If there ever was a woman that he would want to marry . . . *No.* He scolded himself for even thinking about it. No, he would not make that mistake again. He would not make himself miserable again. Marriage was a cruel, clever trap, with no safe escape route. No, he wouldn't do that to himself, and he would not to that to Alayna.

His head turned to the side, weighed down with the realization that he was in too deep. There was no turning back. He couldn't pull out if he wanted to—it was too late. Besides, why should he? Life was too short, and he was enjoying himself too much. Alayna had bathed him in her rapture and he wasn't ready to dry off. Not yet.

But it wasn't as simple as that anymore. It wasn't simple at all. And it wasn't the here and now he was concerned about. He knew that wouldn't be Alayna's concern either. But what to do? *I'll cross that bridge when I come to it*, he told himself finally. Ultimately, he knew he faced a dilemma like no other. He knew he could not stop seeing her, even if he wanted to, but he also knew there could be no fairytale ending.

Chapter Twenty-Two

"Mmm. That smells wonderful," Alayna said of the fresh brewed coffee filling her nostrils. Freshly showered, she hugged Khavon from behind as he stood at the stove.

"You smell wonderful," he remarked, converting her rear hug into a frontal one. Spatula in hand, he kissed her on her forehead and then deeply in the mouth.

"I hope you like French toast, sleepy head," he said, running his hand over her curly locks.

"I absolutely l-o-v-e French toast," Alayna flirted.

"Khavon," she said, peering over into the sizzling frying pan on the stove, "I know that's not what I think it is."

"What do you think it is?"

"Fried green tomatoes."

"You like them, don't you?"

"I love fried green tomatoes. How did you know that, and where in the world did you find green tomatoes, this time of year?"

"Told you. Social engineering. Tell people what they want to hear, and you can get anything you want. Now, have a seat. I'm almost done here."

"Okay. I just want to drop these in the wash, if that's alright," she said of the clothes she'd worn the day before.

"It's right around the corner there," Khavon said, pointing.

"Thanks."

When Alayna returned, she took a seat on one of the high, birch-wood stools at the counter. Elbows propped on top of the white ceramic tile top, Alayna watched his backside like it was a side show.

Dressed in a fresh, plain, white t-shirt and a pair of comfortable jeans, Khavon gave off a crisp, raw sexiness that had warnings of danger nailed to it like it was a shark-infested shoreline. The attraction was already intense, but watching him from the back as he prepared her meal only made her want him more.

"Khavon, you have a lovely home," Alayna said.

"Thanks. I like it."

"And huge. Not the typical little pleasure pad that one tends to associate with a carefree bachelor," she observed.

"I guess I just like my space. Besides, I have better things to do with my money than to give it to the government."

Alayna nodded in agreement.

"I know they're not exactly the sexiest underwear a girl could wear, but how'd they fit?" Khavon asked, referring to the red, plaid flannel boxers he'd left on the bed for her.

"Actually, they feel great. Really soft. I was really surprised that they fit me though."

"They're too small for me. My mother said they were on sale."

His mother? Funny, it had not occurred to her that Khavon might have a family. He'd told her that he was from here, but she'd never thought of him in that realm.

"Oh. Is she in the Cities?" Alayna asked.

"Yeah . . . . She and my father stay over North. I'll have to take you over there sometime. They're a feisty old couple. You'd like them," Khavon said, beaming affectionately.

"I can't believe it's still snowing. This is unbelievable," Alayna said, gazing out the window.

"Yeah. We're really getting dumped on, that's for sure."

"Anytime Excelsior closes its doors because of snow, it's got to be bad. Ah . . . Minnesota, Minnesota," Alayna groaned.

"It looks like the winds have died down quite a bit from yesterday though," Khavon observed.

"Wonderful," Alayna replied sarcastically.

"C'mon, Alayna, it's not that bad."

"Yes, it is. Is Amsterdam going to be like this?" she asked.

"I dunno. I did my touring in the summertime."

"I hope not. Geez."

"Eat and be merry," Khavon said, placing a black lacquer plate of French toast in front of her, complete with powdered sugar, green grapes and parsley for garnish.

"Oh, you're a regular chef, aren't you?" she teased.

"Well, you know . . . what can I say?" He grinned, handing her a black mug filled to the brim with hazelnut cappuccino.

"Khavon, this is wonderful," she said, crunching on one of the tomatoes.

"Thank you."

"I guess I'll just have to ask Mulcahy when he gets back," Alayna said thoughtfully, out of the blue.

"Mulcahy?" Khavon's eyes were questioning. "Ask Mulcahy about what?"

"The weather."

Khavon's face masked confusion. "The weather?"

"Yeah . . . the weather in Amsterdam."

"How would he know?"

"Cause that's where he went," Alayna said, her mouth full.

"Mulcahy went to Amsterdam?"

"Yeah. Remember that Furi mentioned he had some OUS obligations?"

"Yeah, but how do you know he went to Amsterdam?"

"Mark mentioned something about it this morning," Alayna said.

"Mark? How did he know?"

"I don't know. He just sort of mentioned it in passing."

"Mmph. That's interesting." Khavon's expression had turned serious.

"What?" Alayna asked.

"Nothing."

"No, what?"

"It's just that I didn't even know Mark knew Mulcahy, let

alone his itinerary."

"Yeah, it did strike me at the time as kind of odd, but I just let it go."

"What do you know about Mark?" Khavon asked.

"Nothing, really. I know he's native to Minnesota. He likes to travel and he hates the government."

"Hates the government?"

"Yeah, he's always railing against the government and complaining about how the government is using his tax dollars on useless programs and wasteful spending, and how if America doesn't stop sending its jobs across the border, the country is going to fail. You know . . . stuff like that."

"Wait a minute," Khavon said, stopping her. "Wait a minute . . . wait a minute. Let me get this straight. This guy hates the government, and you guys gave him the nod, put him on the security team for the automation of the government's taxation system?" Khavon's eyes were wide with incredulity.

"'You guys?' No. 'You guys' didn't do anything. Mark was already on the team when I joined. Besides you know how Mark is. He complains about everything. No one ever thought anything of it because he's always railing about something. The way I hear it, he came highly recommended from Washingt—" Alayna stopped, her eyes met Khavon's before she could finish the sentence. "Khavon, you don't think Mark has anything to do with—"

"I don't know," Khavon cut her off, his eyes pensive. "But you know that it wouldn't be the first time that an insider went bad. Typical, even." Khavon shook his head. "I don't know, I guess I just assumed everyone had been screened already. That's a mistake that I won't make again. But it's much too early to make any accusations. Let's just keep our eyes peeled and our ears to the ground."

The washer signaled its completion. "Don't worry, I'll get it," Khavon told Alayna when she started to get up.

"Okay."

Alayna turned on the television and called to Khavon from the kitchen. "Khavon! Come look at this!"

"Good morning. I'm Brad Afton," the local anchor greeted the Cities from his television news desk. "As you can see from the monitor, the top story today is the first major winter storm of the season."

"Khavon! Come and look at this!" Alayna called to him again.

With riveted eyes and open mouths, the two of them watched the incredible images that flashed across the television screen, as the WCCO news anchor recounted the cold, blustery details.

"As you probably already know, the winter storm has caused all schools and many offices to close in the Twin Cities this morning. Fifty-eight mile per hour winds, white-out conditions, three feet of snow, and near zero visibility have also forced I-94 to close. Snapped power lines have caused thousands to be without power this morning. The airport has not been open since yesterday afternoon, and as the city has slowed to a virtual standstill, the governer has declared a state of emergency."

"Do you believe this?" Alayna asked Khavon, incredulous.

"What's not to believe?"

"This weather. Look at this." Alayna pointed to the television screen. "I've seen a lot of snow in my time, but never this much at once."

A local resident digging out his car had his picture displayed across the screen.

"I mean they're talking hundreds of cases of frostbite, six-foot snow drifts, impassable roads, and look!" Alayna exclaimed.

"The winds have been so strong that bark was ripped from the trees and many flags were torn from their poles," Brad reported. "But the winds have already started to die down quite a bit, isn't that right, Dean?"

"Yes, that's right, Brad."

"When we return, Dean will have a full weather report for us."

"Yes, and I'm sure that will be a big help," Alayna replied sarcastically to the television.

"C'mon, Alayna."

"Well, that's what they are supposed to have all those supercomputers for. You would think that they could at least come close. I mean, there's a big difference between three feet of snow and a few inches, which is what they predicted."

"Alayna, the weather is too complex, too chaotic." Khavon shook his head. "You don't understand. There are hundreds of variables that go into predicting the weather."

"But—"

"No buts. Believe it or not, Alayna, the United States weather forecasting is really quite good. I mean, we could be living somewhere like Bangladesh, or someplace where a typhoon could come in and wipe out everything with no prior warnings at all. Besides, you have the wrong attitude about this whole thing." Alayna looked up as Khavon's voice became lighter. "I mean, it's not that bad out there. While you were still sleeping, I cleared the driveway and it was actually quite nice.

"Yeah, right," Alayna rolled her eyes in her head.

"No. I'm not kidding. It was. C'mon, get your boots on. Let's go outside."

"Are you crazy? I'm not going out there. It's cold out there."

"Cold is relative, Alayna. C'mon, get your gear on," Khavon said, pulling her up from the chair.

"No. It's too cold."

"C'mon. It'll be fun. I promise." He tried to pull her up by the hand. She almost yielded to his cajolery, but then she changed her mind.

"No, Khavon. I'm not a winter person. I don't want to."

"C'mon, Alayna. It'll be fun."

"No." She was adamant.

Khavon outstretched his hand for her to take. "Trust me," he directed his wide brown eyes into her own. She looked down hesitantly, and then took his hand.

She stepped out of the front door. The air against her skin felt much milder than she'd remembered it from yesterday. The sun was a hazy glow behind the cloudy sky. Alayna turned as the distant roar of an engine came into earshot.

"Now there's someone with the right attitude," Khavon said as he stepped out, commenting on the snowmobiler that zoomed down the street and swung around the cul-de-sac in front of his house.

"If you say so. What's all that stuff for?" Alayna asked quizzically, eyeing the small armful of articles that Khavon was toting.

Khavon itemized the collection. "This is a pipe. This is a carrot. These are buttons. These are psychedelic love beads. This is a tie-dyed scarf. This is an apple hat. And this, this, my dear, is an official Sly and the Family Stone afro wig."

Alayna laughed. "Official?"

"Yes, official."

"Like I said before, what's all that stuff for?"

"You and I, Ms. Alexander, are going to make the biggest, coolest, funkiest snowman this side of the Mississippi."

"W-h-a-t? Khavon, I haven't done that in years!" Alayna exclaimed.

"C'mon. It'll be fun."

"Okay."

"This looks like as good a place as any," Khavon said, pointing to the inside corner where the walkway to his front door would meet the driveway and the grass in the summertime. "We can start here." Khavon placed the props on the driveway, near the corner.

More than an hour slipped by, and Alayna was having a ball. She paused reflectively, squinting her eyes in the sunlight, as a burst of laughter came from the children playing across the street. She watched as they slid their red sled down the snowy hill again and again. Next door to them, children frolicked and romped in the snow, as their father tried out his cross-country skies in the as yet uncleared road.

The weather *was* chaotic, she thought, silently agreeing with Khavon. The news had so grimly detailed winter devastation and calamity from as far west as the Dakotas. Now, less than twenty-four hours later, it seemed to be a mild and tranquil winter wonderland.

"A penny for your thoughts," Khavon said.

"Nothing." Alayna shook her head. "Nothing at all."

"C'mon. Something was on your mind."

"It wasn't important. Really."

Khavon stared at her with an amused mixture of disappointment and disbelief. "Are you having a good time?" he asked.

She smiled, conceding. "Yes, Khavon. I'm having a good time."

"See? Told ya." They smiled at each other.

"Now, what shall we name him?" Alayna asked when they'd finished, sliding the black sunglass stems into the snowman's frozen but happy face.

"Seeing that he is wearing the official Sly and Family Stone wig and all, Sly seems like the only appropriate name."

"You know, I think you're right. Sly it is," Alayna said, eyeing the icy snowman's do.

Alayna turned as another peal of young laughter came from across the way.

"Looks like fun," Khavon said, bending down to scoop up some snow, deviously eyeing Alayna while rounding it into a perfect ball. Khavon's actions took a second to register and sink in, but when they did, Alayna's eyes went wide.

"Khavon, *no!*" she screamed, running in the opposite direction. Her pleading was to no avail, as the fluffy, white ice ball broke and fell apart in the middle of her back.

"Oh, it's on now!" She chased after him in retaliation.

"Oh, see? You are in trouble now!" Khavon warned playfully, after taking a big one in the back of the head.

As they playfully tossed fluffy white snowballs at each other, Alayna felt the crisp air in her face. She felt light, carefree, and happy, for the first time in a long time.

Khavon chased after her, and together they fell down into the snow. Khavon rolled on top of her, trapping her, leaving no means of escape.

"I told you that you were in trouble," he said.

In the cold Minnesota air, his kiss was warm and sweet. As their lips parted, they stared into each other's eyes with unspoken words. Khavon rolled over on his back and pulled his wool hat down over his ears.

"Alayna, when was the last time that you made angels in the

snow?" Khavon asked.

"Angels in the snow? I can't even remember!"

Khavon laughed. "Ms. Alexander, you definitely have to get out more."

Head in the clouds as they flapped their wings and made angels in the snow, Alayna's worries were as distant as the Milky Way. There was no cynicism or criticism, only hopeful optimism and laudatory praise. She felt no longer weary, but refreshed. Peaceful. Peaceful euphoria. She needed it . . . . She deserved it.... Everybody deserved it at some point in life.

"You see those rainbow circles there by the sun?" Khavon said, pointing to the sky.

"You mean that rainbow halo?"

"Yeah."

"Yeah, I see them."

"Those are called sun dogs."

"Sun dogs?"

"Yeah. They're caused by the sun rays reflecting off the atmospheric ice crystals."

"Khavon, can I ask you something?"

"Sure."

"Is that you in that picture that I keep seeing all over the house?" Alayna asked out of the blue.

Khavon's face grew somber. "Yes, it is."

"Well, who's the other little guy?"

"That's my little brother."

"Oh. The one who died?"

"Yes." He paused. "My little brother died in a fire twenty-eight years ago. Twenty-eight years, five months and six days ago, to be exact."

"Oh, Khavon, I'm sorry."

"I know you didn't. I was seven and I was trying out my father's cigars . . . ." His voice cracked and trailed off. He stopped short, refusing to continue.

"Oh, Khavon. Honey, it was an accident. It wasn't your fault," Alayna said, reaching out to him.

"Of course it was my fault," Khavon said, angrily breaking

away from her. "C'mon. Let's go inside. It's cold out here. Besides, it's starting to get dark."

Alayna felt dejected and was sorry she'd asked. The mood had been such a light one before she'd started to pry.

Khavon pulled his boots off, catching a fleeting glimpse of his younger brother's image on the fridge as he walked past it. "I don't know why it's always so cold in here," he complained angrily, flipping open the thermostat casing and increasing the temperature by five degrees.

"Mind if I make some coffee?" Alayna asked.

"It's a free country." Khavon flipped the wall switch and sat open-legged in front of the fireplace. Disquieted silence interrupted the coffee-making activity, and then permeated the room. Alayna felt that Khavon had taken her to the mountaintop and left her there to fend for herself. But it was her own doing, she thought. She had been just plain stupid. She should've known there was some awful story associated with that picture. It was one thing to have many pictures of the same person displayed around the house, but to have the same picture of the same person in practically every room in the house was something all together different. She should have known it was some sort of obsession. *Just how many displays does one need in his house?* she'd thought when she'd started to notice them. She stopped short, remembering the picture of Donovan in her room. That, too, had been an accident.

"I thought you might like some." Alayna handed him a cup, taking a seat next to him. Without saying thank you, he tasted the full flavor, and then turned to look over at Alayna. It seemed to her that he was loosening up.

"You do make the most wonderful cappuccino. What's in it?" he asked.

"Cocoa," she said simply.

"Yes. Cocoa. That's what it is. I couldn't place it, but yes, that's what it is," he said. Khavon's features went grave again. He paused, looking down.

"You know, I recently lost someone close to me too," she said softly. Khavon turned to face her. "My fiancé and I were planning to be married on Sweetest Day. A week before the wedding, we were coming home from the View one night. I was driving. I had had a couple of glasses of wine . . . you know. A minivan skidded on a patch of ice, broad-siding us. Donovan didn't survive. Even though it was the minivan that went out of control, I still felt like it was somehow my fault. I've never forgiven myself . . . until now. Now I realize that it was an accident. Life is just like that sometimes." Khavon eyed her intently.

"Alayna, I'm sorry. I just—I don't know what to say."

"I know. You don't have to say anything." He didn't. Instead, he turned back to the fireplace and together they sat, staring silently into the flickering red and gold flames.

But unbeknownst to Alayna, the fiery blaze was playing cruel tricks with Khavon's mind. The red-hot heat danced a gleeful dance and laughed in his face, as he watched his father open the door. He felt a monumental wave of terror and anguish consume him once again, as if he had been in the flames himself.

"I said, *get outside!*" he heard his father scream. He ran outside as his father had commanded him to. It was there that he was standing, in the street that ran in front of their house, in the arms of a neighbor, when his father had finally come out with Kenny's limp body in his arms. The look on his father's face had said it all.

Alayna moved over and pulled his head to her chest when she saw the tears streaming down his haunted face. His face enbosomed, he began to weep. He began to shed the suppressed tears of twenty-eight years of guilt and pain that had been buried deep within him. The weight came crashing down on him like a condemned building. His tears rolled down around the curve of her breast and burned deep in her soul, and she began to cry too. When he was all cried out, Alayna made quiet, tender love to him and they both fell asleep.

She was roused her from her sleep by the sweet aroma emanating from the kitchen. *Mmm. Something smells good*, she thought. Wrapping herself in the flat, white sheet that she found herself covered in, she made her way to the kitchen. Khavon sat at the head of a white-clothed, set table.

"What's this?" she asked, pleasant surprise in her voice.

"I thought you might be hungry when you woke up," Khavon said.

"Yes, as a matter of fact, I am." She stood up and reached for her clothes, the sheet still covering her naked body.

"No," Khavon declared, simply.

Alayna looked up questioning.

"It's very becoming on you," he said of the bedding material that concealed her body. "I like it."

Alayna smiled and tucked the end of the sheet under her arm. She walked over to the sink and washed her hands. "What do we have here?" she asked, eyeing the elaborate meal that Khavon had prepared for her.

"My specialty. Sautéed langostinos and Tuscany lemon angel hair pasta."

"Wow. I'm impressed—but you really shouldn't have gone to so much trouble."

"I didn't, really. I sometimes double the recipe and freeze the excess. It saves me time in the long run."

"Mmm. This is wonderful!" Alayna said, her taste buds savoring the creamy, lemon-flavored cheese sauce and the buttery baby lobsters. She parsed one of the red morsels from the pasta on her plate. "What are these?"

"Sun-dried tomatoes."

"Mmm. They're wonderful," she said, forking up another mouthful.

Having already eaten, Khavon fixed in on her, taking pleasure in the mere sight of her taking in the meal that he had prepared for her.

"So you like my outfit, huh?" Alayna asked between bites.

"Very much so. It brings out your eyes." Khavon smiled a devious smile.

"Your taste in clothing is a little bit on the bizarre side, don't you think?"

"You could say that, but it's all relative," he said, launching into a long story about how he'd won a dance contest in '78 doing the robot in lime green bell-bottoms, red stacks, and a wide-collared, floral, silk shirt. Alayna was laughing so hard that she could hardly eat.

"Yeah, I guess you're right. It is all relative." Alayna laughed.

Watching her, Khavon smiled a hint of a smile, enjoying the sound of her laughter.

"Aren't you going to have something to eat? I feel like such a pig."

"No, I want to feast on your loveliness."

Alayna smiled curiously.

"Take it off," he said simply.

"Take it off?" Alayna asked, clearly taken aback.

"Yeah, take the sheet off. I want to feast on your loveliness."

Alayna took the sheet off as he requested. Khavon's brown eyes watched her as she ate naked. She felt a little uncomfortable at first, but then she began to feel extremely feminine.

"C'mon, I have a surprise for you," he told her, taking her hand after she'd finished eating.

They ascended the steps, and Khavon lead her by the hand through his bedroom and into his bathroom. The solid white pillars on either side of the bathtub platform, and the lush green plants surrounding it, gave the room a sort of Mediterranean flavor.

"Khavon, this is beautiful, but—" Alayna stopped abruptly.

"But why all the candles after the story I told you, right?" Khavon said.

Alayna nodded her head.

"If we don't face our fears head on, we'll never move forward," he answered simply. "Don't you agree?" Alayna nodded, quietly.

Khavon tapped the water off until it had reached a suitable temperature.

"You get in," Khavon instructed her. "I'm gonna grab some towels."

"Okay."

When Khavon had left the bathroom, she took the opportunity to quickly run a finger full of toothpaste across her teeth and through her mouth.

She gasped aloud when she slipped her foot into the hot water. "Mmm. This feels wonderful," Alayna said softly, submerging herself deeper into the hot, liquid refuge.

When Khavon returned, he joined her, sliding down, resting his back against her breast. He depressed the underwater button. When the whirlpool bubbles started, she giggled and slid her fingers over the thorny green vine that encircled his forearm.

"Interesting tattoo," she said.

"It's a reminder."

"A reminder of what?" she asked.

"It's a reminder that a rose, no matter how beautiful, will always, always prick you with its thorns."

Someone must have really hurt this man, she thought to herself. She wondered who and why.

They soaked for more than an hour, drinking champagne, laughing, and talking about everything from A to Z. When they had finished bathing, they adjourned to the bedroom.

Wrapped in an oversized black cotton towel, her body still tingled from the effervescent rush of whirlpool bubbles. Besides the master bath, Khavon's bedroom was the only other room in the house that had any noticeable character. From what Alayna could see, Khavon's living style was one that stressed minimalism. All of the other rooms in the house were modest and unassuming, appearing only to serve their functions. The master suite was different. From the bedroom, one could gain some sense of who the man was—who he really was.

The design was a contemporary one with clean lines and colorful, cultural accents. A huge mahogany desk with a matching armchair took up the north wall and set off the red cinnamon flecks in the soft beige, textured paint. Matching night stands flanked either side of the massive king size bed. Intricate African masks hung from the walls. Overhead, Alayna admired the wide array of urns, vases and other pottery that proudly lined the L-shaped soffits. Her eyes traveled to the intricate works of art that came together on display in the center.

"Khavon, those carvings are beautiful."

"Thank you. They're West African. The headdresses that they're wearing are used for welcoming a good harvest."

"What about the pottery—is that from West Africa too?"

"Mostly. but that one on the end is from Spain, and the blue one in the middle is from India."

"They're beautiful, all of them," Alayna commented.

"Thank you."

Alayna stared at the symbol-bearing picture encased in the black lacquer frame hanging on the wall. "And that?" she asked, curiously.

"The looped cross in the center is the ankh, the Egyptian symbol of life. The bird and animal drawings surrounding it are Egyptian hieroglyph text. When transcribed, they spell out my name."

"Mmph. You're really into this Egyptian stuff, huh?"

"You could say that," Khavon said, giving her a peculiar smile.

Alayna cautiously turned away from him.

"Now, take the towel off. I need you face down across the bed," Khavon stated bluntly, after a light kiss on the back of her neck.

She was taken aback and a little bit apprehensive, but she followed his instructions anyway, laying her nude body across the mud cloth spread that surfaced his bed.

"I need you to close your eyes, and don't open them until I'm finished." Alayna's eyes went wide. Eyes closed? Until he's finished? *What is this man planning to do to me? Is he some kind of closet freak or what?* She eyed him apprehensively.

"Remember what I told you, Alayna. I would never hurt you," Khavon said, sensing her fear.

She was no fool. She closed her eyes, but not all the way. She didn't know what he was planning.

The room was still for what seemed to Alayna like an eternity, but she kept her eyes closed, as Khavon had requested. His voice was soft when he finally spoke.

"Alayna, have you ever heard of the Nile river?"

"Sure. It's a river somewhere in Africa."

"It's more than that, Alayna." His voice was still soft. "It's special. The Nile is the cradle of all civilization. It is the longest and only river in the world that flows from south to north. It flows 4,145 miles from Lake Victoria to the Murchsion Falls, through upper and lower Egypt, finally spilling out into the Mediterranean."

Alayna listened quietly, her eyes not quite closed, wondering what trip he was on and growing increasingly apprehensive.

Having not yet touched her, Khavon could see the anxiety building up, tensing up Alayna's body, but he continued anyway.

"The valleys and banks of the Nile are clustered with fig and date-palm trees, and water birds flock there. The Nile's annual floods gave rise to many great Nubian and Egyptian civilizations that prospered of adobe temples, palaces and lush green gardens surrounding them. And in Egypt, the women had the same legal and economic rights as the men." Alayna said nothing, only listening, as Khavon gave her no audible cue to speak.

"In Egypt, the women were queens, and the men treated them accordingly, for without the queens, there could be no kings."

Alayna involuntarily became more relaxed, closed her eyes completely and felt herself going along with him. Khavon continued.

"In the orange and purple twilight sky, the Egyptian men would take their women by the hands and lead them to the river banks. There they would bathe and cleanse themselves in the gurgling waters of the Nile. If you listen closely, you can hear the river currents running over the rocks. Listen, Alayna. If you listen closely, you can hear the water birds calling out." Khavon pressed the play button on the remote and Alayna heard the faint sound of water and birds chirping. "Do you hear them, Alayna?"

Alayna smiled comfortably. "Mm-hmm."

"When they'd finished bathing, they would retire into their adobe homes and temples overlooking the Nile."

"Do you see it, Alayna? Do you see the beautiful Nile below?"

Alayna nodded transcendentally. "Yes, Khavon, I see it."

"Then, in the heat of the African night, under the quiet echo of distant drums, the Egyptian man laid his queen down and rubbed her down with fragrant oils and incense."

Suddenly, Alayna gasped aloud, feeling a heated drop of liquid splash into the middle of her back. Her muscles were tense as she felt it roll down her back and disappear into the crescent of her flaring, soft brown hips. She felt several more drops.

"Without the queen there could be no king," she heard him say again as she finally felt Khavon's hands move across her back. When he'd finished with her back, he caressed her legs, and he massaged her feet. He massaged her body from the top of her head to the pads of her red painted toes. When he finally entered her, Alayna was on fire. His strokes were slow and methodical. Over and over again, he entered her, coaxing her into releasing her tightly held inhibitions.

"Oh, Khavon. What are you doing to me?" Alayna moaned, catching Khavon's descendent mouth over her own. As he pulled her to him, she arched her back and wrapped her legs around him.

His body ached with desire, but he continued on.

All at once, Alayna gasped aloud. She had reached both the pinnacle of her femininity and her physical peak all in one rapturous moment. The core of her essence was alive with pleasure. She screamed his name, just before her body diffused into a deep, slow, pulsating delirium of bliss.

The sound of her guttural outcry pushed him over the edge, and he lost control. Alayna was sweet, oh, so sweet . . . .

"I don't know if this is going to work," Khavon told Hank Edwards over the telephone. Hank Edwards had gained national fame after winning a wrongful death suit for a world-renowned rock star based in Minneapolis. He'd been a friend of the Brighton family for many years. In light of some newly-discovered evidence, Khavon had hired him again to help him get Cassandra's conviction overturned.

"I mean, I've been to see her several times already, and with her being up for parole in a few months, she doesn't feel the need to listen to me, or even want to, for that matter. I'm just trying to make it right—you know." Khavon's voice was tired and emotional.

"I know, man," the voice on the other end of the receiver said.

When Alayna woke up, she was in a blissful state of euphoria. She looked over, expecting to see the face of the man who was responsible for her elated state, but she was alone in the bed. She thought that she could hear the vague sound of his voice downstairs, so she slipped on his robe and started down the stairs. She stopped when she saw Khavon with his back to her, talking on the phone.

"You know how she is, man." Alayna's eyebrow creased as Khavon's voice rang in her ears.

"Yeah, I know. So, you think if I keep at her like this, eventually she's gonna break down," she heard him say before she turned and started back up the stairs.

Khavon looked over his shoulder, suddenly cognizant of her presence.

"Look, I have to go," he said.

"Mm-hmm. Okay. I'll get back with you." He hung up the phone.

"Alayna," he called up to her, "how's my sweets doing this morning?"

Tell people what they want to hear, and you can get anything you want. She turned in his direction. "I'm okay," she lied. *This was all some sort of game. How could I have been so stupid?* "I should probably be heading home soon. They've finally cleared the roads," she said sadly.

Chapter Twenty-Three

A quarter of the day had passed since Khavon had helped her to dig her car out and put the new battery in. He had asked her to call him to let him know she'd gotten home okay. When she didn't, he called her instead.

"Hi," Khavon's voice boomed, over the line.

"Hi."

"Careful—if you get any more excited to hear from me, you might spontaneously combust."

"I'm sorry. I'm just kind of tired."

"Ordinarily, I'd take that as a compliment, but you seemed kind of distant today. Are you sure there's nothing wrong?" Khavon was clearly concerned.

"I'm sure. Listen, Khavon, I was just about to wash my hair," Alayna tried to hurry off the phone.

"Oh, sure. I, uh, I'll call you later," Khavon said.

"Okay. Goodbye, Khavon."

"Bye."

Alayna hung up the phone. Up until she'd heard him talking on the phone this morning, the weekend had been wonderful. The best she'd every had. But . . . . Alayna shook her head, closing her eyes, reliving the words she heard him say. *"You know how she is*

. . . if I keep at her like this, eventually she's gonna break down." Could he have been talking about her? Was this some kind of playboy game? And what did he mean, *"eventually she's gonna break down"*? Break down for what? What was it that he wanted from her, anyway? Despite Alayna's best efforts to concentrate on other things, Khavon's true motivation had been nagging her off and on for six hours. She was just being silly, she finally resolved herself. After all, she didn't hear her name, or anyone else's for that matter. The man probably wasn't even talking about her.

A hot bath might help her to relax, she decided. She had just started towards the bathroom when she heard the doorbell ring. She looked out the peephole, but did not recognize the red-haired man waiting at the door. She wished the tenants would stop letting people piggyback in after they've opened the security door. The man eyed the hallway and then impatiently checked his watch.

Alayna eyed the man's uniform and then read the writing in the red and white oval nametag that was sewn into it. *Brad. House of Flowers.* He was holding an oblong box.

Alayna cracked the door, leaving the chain lock in place. The young man stopped his gum chewing to acknowledge her presence.

"Yeah, I got a delivery here for Ms. Alayna Alexander. Are you her?"

"Yeah."

"Ma'am, if I could just get you to sign here, please." *Ma'am. Do I look like a ma'am?* It sounded so old, like she was some kind of spinster or something. Then again, maybe it was her biological paranoia.

Alayna stuck her hand out the door, reaching for the pen and pad.

"Crazy weather, huh?" the man said, attempting to make small talk as he checked his watch again.

"Yeah. Crazy," Alayna said, signing her name, handing him the pen and pad back to him.

"You can just leave the box out there," Alayna told him.

"Sure thing, ma'am." He placed the oblong box in front of her door.

"You have a nice day, now."

"Thanks, you too."

Alayna watched him until she couldn't see him anymore. She waited until she heard the security door close before she opened the door. She picked up the box and hastily locked the door again.

She slid the card from underneath the wide, red bow-tied ribbon. Placing the box on the kitchen table, she opened the envelope and read the card inside.

Had no idea cappuccino in the winter could be so much fun. Can't wait for an encore. Khavon P.S. Alayna, you were absolutely breathtaking.

She opened the white cardboard box and stood open-mouthed as, not one, but two dozen incredibly beautiful, long-stemmed roses nestled in baby's breath and greens, stared back at her.

After that, any doubts that she may have had about Khavon's motivation began to lose color in the face of the brilliant red flowers. By the time she'd opened the cabinet door, the few pale uncertainties that still remained within her had crumbled into tiny pieces to fertilize the water in the under-utilized crystal vase that she placed them in.

So that she could enjoy their sweet aromatic scent all through the night, she carried them up to her room and placed them on her dresser. She picked up the silver-plated frame that was sitting next to it. Donovan's chestnut eyes shined back at her through the glass as if nothing had happened. Nothing at all. Carefully, she pulled open the top right-hand drawer. Her slender brown fingers traced the ornate pattern in the silver frame one last time and then she placed the picture face down underneath some clothes.

Chapter Twenty-Four

"Alayna, are you sure that you won't change your mind about Thanksgiving? Milwaukee is only a five-hour drive from here."

"Khavon, you know that I would like nothing better, but I can't renege again. I've already committed myself. If I renege this time, it will be the third time in a row that I've disappointed Sheila on Thanksgiving. This year, she's invited all of those people to her house. Khavon, I can't just not go after I promised her that I'd help her cook. If I don't keep my promise, I think this time it would be more than just a disappointment to her. This time, I think it would really put her into a serious bind. I just can't. Why don't you come to her house?" Alayna asked.

"I told you, I promised I'd drive down," Khavon explained again.

"Your Mom would understand, wouldn't she?"

"No. My mother is really funny about this family reunion stuff, which is why I've never missed one. If I didn't go this year, I'm telling you she just wouldn't understand."

"Well, you know how the holidays are. Christmas and New Year's will be here before we know it," Alayna said, optimistically. "And then, I'll be all yours."

"You'd better be," Khavon warned, teasing her.

What was it about this woman, he wondered, recalling their

conversation as he zoomed through Wisconsin, past the black and white dairy cows that were grazing in the grass fields. *What kind of spell does this woman have on me*, he asked himself. *What am I doing?* he asked himself again.

A man of his reputation introducing a woman to his family was practically a prelude to the altar—and he knew there could be no altar. Cassandra had made sure of that. Yet, something deep within him yearned for the day when Alayna would meet the most important people in his life. But what would it mean to Alayna?

Maybe she didn't want to get married, he tried to convince himself. Maybe it wasn't important to her. Right now it was good. Really good. Maybe they could keep going on like they were. *Maybe....*

He stopped himself short. Maybe he was being a fool. The charade had become even too ridiculous for him. A collision was on the horizon. Alayna had made her needs and desires painfully clear from the get-go. He knew the consequences coming in, but he had been unable to withstand Alayna's tantalizing draw. He knew that he was walking a very precarious line, and the last thing that he wanted to do was to hurt Alayna.

He couldn't be worried about tomorrow, he told himself, because as his mother always told him, tomorrow was not promised to anyone. He had to live for the moment. It was the here and now that was important, he told himself. The only thing that he wanted to do now was to be with Alayna, and that's what he was going to do. Khavon turned his attention back to the green forests aligning I-94. He wasn't going to worry about the consequences, he decided finally. He had to live for the moment.

"Alayna . . . Girl, where are you at?" Sheila remarked, when she turned around and saw Alayna staring into space while stirring a bowl of sweet potato pie filling.

Alayna woke from her trance, shaking her head. "Oh, nowhere. I just . . . . "

"That Khavon has really got you all tied and twisted, doesn't he?"

Alayna laughed. "No. He's just really nice, that's all." Her eyes sparkled with admiration when she spoke of him.

"Alayna," Sheila's voice was soft, as she moved close to Alayna, placing her hand on her shoulder, "you're in love with him, aren't you?"

Paradoxical features of blessed contentment and worried concern captured Alayna's face, as she slowly nodded her head in confirmation.

"Alayna, I'm so happy for you!" Sheila exclaimed, wrapping her arms around her. And she was. But she couldn't help notice that sinking feeling in her stomach. She couldn't help envying Alayna. Fresh, new love—it was a wonderful thing.

She and Larry had shared it once, but that had been a long time ago. Before the fire went out. Before the intensity became barren. Before Larry had decided he wanted to sleep with someone else. Sheila desperately wanted it back. The passion that they'd shared in the beginning had been so sweet, so pure and unabashed. She desperately wanted it back, but she didn't know how to get it. Neither did Larry. Too much pain had come between them.

Alayna had told Khavon that Christmas would be here before they knew it, and she was right. Time passed very quickly. It was Christmas Eve, and they found themselves at Alayna's apartment, sitting in front of the fireplace after having consumed a holiday dinner that Khavon prepared for them.

Together over candlelight, they had feasted on Cornish hens, jalapeno mustard greens, and sweet yams. And when he had found out how much she loved it, he'd made some hot water cornbread to accompany the rest of the meal.

It was snowing outside and the festive lights from Alayna's dwarfed Christmas tree flickered on and off to the soft yuletide music. Comfortably lying back into Khavon's chest, she pressed play on the remote, expecting to hear the voice of Donny Hathaway singing her favorite Christmas song. Instead, her ears came alive as Khavon started to sing.

His lips eventually left her ear to explore her neck. After leaving a trail of tantalizing kisses there, his mouth covered hers in a deep and gentle kiss that said he loved her. After running his fingers through her thick locks of hair, he kissed her on the side of her face at her temple.

"Are you nervous about tomorrow?" he asked.

"It shows, huh?"

"Well, you just seem a little quiet tonight."

"Well, yeah, I am a little bit nervous. I've been having second thoughts. Maybe we should have picked a regular day for me to meet your parents," she said.

"C'mon, sweetie. You'll be fine."

Despite his reassurances, the worried look did not leave Alayna's face.

"Okay. I was going to save this for tomorrow, but you look like you could use a pick-me-up tonight," he said, standing up to make his way to his coat pocket.

"What? What is it, Khavon?" she asked impatiently, her voice excited with surprise.

"You just wait. Close your eyes, and don't open them until I tell you to." Reclaiming his position on the floor, he instructed her to open her eyes. She did as he asked.

"What's this?" she asked crinkling her brow at the folded white piece of paper that lay in front of her.

"Read it."

She picked up the piece of paper and began to read the printed words.

If you forget to leave cookies out for Santa when he comes down the chimney, he does a b-line for the cookie jar.

Alayna smiled a confused smile. "Khavon, what is this?"

"Hey, I'm just a spectator in this," he said happily.

Still slightly confused, Alayna raised herself and made her way to the teddy bear cookie jar next to the microwave. She opened the top and looked inside. Inside she found another note.

Maybe Santa would like some milk with his cookies.

Alayna smiled, intrigued. She turned and opened the door to the refrigerator. Taped to the top rack was another note.

Sometimes Santa likes to take in a movie or two.

Alayna smiled at Khavon and moved to the video case.

And guess what . . . . Santa has a green thumb.

Alayna was having fun. Amused and intrigued, she watched Khavon's playful eyes as she crossed over him and glided over to the plant stand in the corner. From behind the broad, pointy leaves of the flourishing green fern that centered the stand, she caught a glimpse of something foreign. Eyeing Khavon, she pulled the oblong box from behind the foliage. Trimmed in gold, the black velvet box looked as if it held something very expensive.

"Merry Christmas, Alayna," he said.

Slowly she took the box into her hand and opened it.

"Khavon, it's beautiful," Alayna exclaimed when she saw the 24-inch herringbone.

"It's just what I wanted," she said. She turned and wrapped her arms around him. "Thank you."

"You are most welcome."

"Now, help me put it on."

Khavon opened the clasp and slipped the chain around Alayna's neck. "There. Beautiful, just like you."

"Now I have something for you," Alayna hopped up.

"You do, do you?"

"Yes, I do," Alayna said, disappearing into her bedroom. She was carrying a beautifully-wrapped box when she returned. Khavon promptly tore the paper off. Alayna was slightly disappointed to see that Khavon had failed to take notice of the elaborate wrapping she had specifically requested.

"Alayna, this is beautiful," Khavon remarked, pulling out the expensive multicolored designer sweater. "I just love it. Thank you, sweetie." He kissed and hugged her. "Now, how do you feel?" he asked.

"Better," she admitted.

"Good. And don't worry. My parents are going to love you."

"I hope so."

"I know so," he said, taking her by the hand and leading her to the bedroom. They made quiet holiday love and slept until morning.

"Merry Christmas, sleepy head," Khavon said when Alayna's brown eyes fluttered open slightly. He had been quietly watching her for more than a half an hour. He gave her a peck on the lips.

"Merry Christmas," she mumbled back. She could see that the sun was shining brightly through the window blinds.

"Today's the big day. C'mon, let me make you some breakfast," he said, pulling her out of bed by the hand. *He is definitely a morning person,* Alayna thought. *But they do say opposites attract . . .* . "But Khavon, I—"

"Alayna, it is a beautiful day—look." Khavon rolled up the shade in her room.

Squinting, Alayna blocked the sun rays with her hand, and turned in the opposite direction. "Khavon, why don't you go ahead and get breakfast started. I'm just gonna lay here for a minute or two. I'll be there in a little bit, okay?"

"Okay, sweetie." He lowered the shade back to its original position. *Yes, he's definitely a morning person*, Alayna thought, pulling the covers over her head and eventually drifting back to sleep.

She had been sleeping for about an hour when Khavon reentered the room with a breakfast tray of pancakes and decaf cappuccino.

"Wake up, sleepy head. It's time for breakfast," he said, rousing her from her sleep again.

After breakfast, they made love again and lounged in bed, talking about everything and nothing, but as the clock grew closer to one, Alayna found herself getting more and more nervous.

* * *

Alayna wrung her sweaty palms together, and then ran them over her forehead. She wasn't sure that she was ready to meet Khavon's parents for the first time.

Khavon moved his hand from the steering wheel and placed it on her knee. "Alayna, are you okay?" Khavon asked, noticing that that Kleenex in her hand was limp with perspiration.

She stared out the window at the Metrodome in the distance. "Yeah, sure. Why?"

"Well, I don't know. You seem kind of nervous."

"I am. A little. But I'll be okay."

"I don't know what you're worried about. I told you, they are going to love you."

Alayna eyed him closely.

"Really. Alayna, they're good people," Khavon smiled, trying not to show too much amusement.

"Okay. Okay. I'm sure I'll be fine."

"Mommy, Uncle Jooney's here," Keisha and Tosh screamed to their mother from the front living room window, spotting Khavon's black jeep pulling up in front of their grandparent's home. "And he's got a girl with him!"

"What?" Kattrina's voice was two octaves higher than normal, removing the bottle from her baby's mouth.

"Mom, did June Bug say he was gonna bring anyone with him?"

"No." Kathryn's voice was mild and sing-song, coming from the kitchen. "Why?"

"Keisha and Tosh say he just pulled up and he's got a woman with him."

"He's got a woman with him?" Her voice reflected surprise.

"Yeah, he's got a woman with him," Kattrina confirmed, now at the window herself.

Placing the pan of sage and onion corn bread dressing in the oven, Kathryn wiped her hands with the towel on the counter and joined the rest of the family at the window to see for herself. Her mouth dropped open when, through the purposely-opaque curtain panels, which allowed visibility out but not in, she spied her son—who hadn't brought a woman home in eight years—walking up the front steps hand in hand with a pretty young woman like it was nothing.

"What's all the ruckus about?" Khavon's father asked, when he entered the room. He had been in the basement at Kathryn's request, searching for some of her Christmas table accessories.

"Jooney's here, and he brought home a girl," Kathryn answered with her own amazement, turning to get her husband's reaction. But there was none. There was no time. The key turned in the lock, and the family scattered about the house, feigning preoccupation. All except Keisha and Tosh.

"Uncle Jooney! Uncle Jooney!" The two of them ran right up to him and jumped in his arms, causing him to drop the bag of gifts that he was toting.

Uncle Jooney? Alayna thought.

"Hey! Hey! Merry Christmas!"

"What did you bring for me, Uncle Jooney?" Tosh wanted to know, jumping down again to ramble through the green plastic garbage bag, whose contents had now partially spilled onto the thick beige carpet.

"Tosh, give your uncle time to take off his boots, and to introduce his guest," Kattrina instructed from across the room. Keisha was curious too, but not about the contents of the green bag.

"Who's she?" her face resolute, waiting for his explanation.

Alayna felt as if she were on display, like she was some sort of odd curiosity, or the featured attraction in a carnival side show. All eyes on the house were on her.

"This is my friend, Alayna. Alayna Alexander. And this . . . this is my feisty little niece, Keisha," he said, pinching her jaw.

"Ouch. I don't like it when you do that."

Khavon just laughed.

"Hi, Keisha."

"Hi." She turned to Khavon. "Are you going to marry her?"

"And this is Tosh," Khavon ignored her question, rubbing the locked head of his young nephew.

"Hi," Tosh said hastily, without looking up. He had located

and ripped open his gift and was busy playing with the space rocket that had been inside.

"I said, are you going to marry her?"

"And this is my baby sister, Kattrina, and her husband, Sam.

"Hi." Alayna flashed a friendly smile, which they returned.

"This is my father. And last but not least this is my lovely mother, Kathryn." He hugged her neck, and then kissed her on the cheek. "Merry Christmas, Mom."

"Merry Christmas, Son."

"Mom, this is Alayna." Alayna timidly extended her hand to the woman who had borne the boy, now man, that she loved. Kathryn put her hand over Alayna's, her nails painted pomegranate red. Without hesitation, Kathryn pulled Alayna to her chest and gave her a big welcome hug that made her feel like part of the family.

"So, how was Christmas in New York?" Alayna asked Sheila when they were finally able to catch up with one another.

Sheila wrinkled her brow over her morning coffee. "Uh-Uh. I don't think so girlfriend. Larry and I spend Christmas in New York every year. I want to hear about your holidays. Did you meet his parents?"

"Yeah."

"How'd it go?" Sheila's voice was alive with curiosity.

"Well, it went better than I thought it would. It started out kind of shaky at first. I was really nervous. And it didn't help any when I found out that the man apparently hadn't brought a woman home since his ex-wife."

Sheila's eyes went wide.

"And I still haven't figured out that story—he wasn't exactly overflowing with the 411, you know."

"Yeah," Sheila nodded.

"You're the first woman the man has brought home to his mother in . . . . How long has he been divorced?" Sheila asked.

"Eight years."

"In eight years . . . . He must be getting serious."

"I don't know, Sheila. When we were at his mom's house, his niece asked him if he was gonna marry me and he just acted like he didn't hear her."

"Mmph." Sheila took another sip of coffee.

"But the day ended up being pretty nice, once his family came out of shock."

"What about his mother? How was she?"

"Oh, she was a sweetheart. I really liked her. She had prepared a huge elaborate meal. I couldn't believe it. I'd never seen so much food in my life." Alayna took a bite out of her donut, and looked around the cafeteria. It was practically full, almost like it was lunchtime. First day back after the holidays, she guessed.

"How did he like the sweater?"

"He liked it. At least I think he liked it. Well, he said he liked it anyway."

"And?" Sheila's tone was searching.

"And what?"

"And what did he give you?"

"He gave me this gold chain." Alayna ran her fingers over the shiny gold on her neck.

"Herringbone…ooh…nice. Now, what about New Year's Eve?"

New Year's Eve . . . . Alayna had scarcely been able to think of anything else.

"He hired a limo," Alayna started, her brown eyes lit up into a sparkling glitter as she began to relive the evening over again, as she had already done a thousand times before. It was a holiday night to remember, a holiday night that she would never forget.

Alayna had been putting on a few last minute touches when she heard the buzzer go off loudly in her apartment.

Flashing what he knew was an infectious and irresistible smile, Khavon immediately started in on his excuse as soon as she'd cracked open the door to her place.

"I know. I know. I'm a little late. But¾" he started, and then stopped abruptly as Alayna opened the door fully. His words, along with his irresistible smile, had been abandoned in midair and left dangling in the hallway draft as he laid eyes on Alayna. It was as if the word elegant had been coined especially for her.

"Look at you!" Khavon's eyes were immovable. "Alayna, you look amazing."

Simply stunning in powdered champagne, Alayna stood back enjoying the rush of femininity that pumped through her veins when Khavon looked at her that way.

As he ran his wide eyes over the subtle polygon neckline and down the bodice of her silky satin gown, Alayna pretended to be unaffected, smoothing her sleek, shiny, black hair into place. Her floor-length hemline pooled behind her into a small train that trailed behind.

"Yes, you are a little bit late, but I forgive you." Hair blown straight and smoothed into a soft romantic upsweep, Alayna looked like a totally different person . . . a person Khavon hadn't seen before.

Alayna was dazzling and she knew it. She felt beautiful, sexy, regal, and sophisticated all at one time, but she was not the only beautiful one in the room.

"You clean up pretty nice, too," Alayna said, eyeing Khavon's ensemble. Decked out in a black shawl tuxedo, he looked like a prince in waiting.

Khavon swallowed hard. It was rare for him to find himself at a loss for words, but the words wouldn't come to him.

"Alayna, you look incredible," he said again, finally, still eyeing her.

"Thank you," Alayna said, running her index and middle fingers down the inside on his satin lapel and finally greeting him with a light kiss on the mouth.

"I'm all ready. Just let me grab my purse."

Khavon surveyed her from behind. Watching the sway of her hips, Khavon felt himself becoming aroused.

"You know, Alayna, we don't have to go out if you if you don't want to," Khavon started not really wanting to go himself. He would be perfectly happy with a couple of broiled lobster tails in the oven and a bottle of chilled champagne in the fridge. He'd never really liked the pomp and circumstance of it all, big parties and the like.

"Oh no, you're not getting off that easy, you promised me a glamorous night out." Alayna knew the deal. If one were going to go out to ring in the first, Kelly Price's annual New Year's Eve bash was the place to be. Invitation only, it was a formal affair held at the top of the IDS Center.

Kelly Price was "the man" in Minneapolis. A thick, stocky, power-hitting anchor for the home team, Kelly Price was a homespun hero. Well-loved in the Twin Cites by Blacks and Whites alike, Kelly was akin to a fuzzy brown teddy bear; an all-around nice guy, who could tag a baseball into the stands like no one else. Growing up on the north side of Minneapolis, Kelly had fielded a fair amount of teasing about the size of his backside, Khavon remembered, but Khavon's mother had always warned her children about teasing other people. "To be different," his mother would always say, "is to be special. And to be special is to be blessed." Khavon always remembered that, and while the other kids teased, he and Kenny had befriended the young boy.

As it turned out, his mother was right, because Kelly's backside turned out to be like Samson's long, black mane, the source of his power and strength. Although the two had remained friends over the years and Khavon was a frequent visitor to the Kelly's home, he had preferred to skip the New Year's fanfare. But this year was different. In some kind of love daze, he'd offered to take Alayna to the party.

"Wow, you really go all out when you want to, don't you?" Alayna said when she saw the shiny, long, black limo waiting outside her apartment door.

"Oh, that's not for us," Khavon said, with a stone face.

"Oh." Alayna tried not to show her disappointment.

"I'm just kidding. Of course it's for us. C'mon," he laughed.

"Khavon!" Alayna slapped his shoulder, grinning excitedly.

The chauffeur came around to open the door as Khavon

helped Alayna into the rear of the car. Once seated, Khavon poured two glasses of chilled champagne and handed one to Alayna.

"You know, you really do look incredible tonight."

"Thank you." Alayna smiled and sipped from her glass. "This is really nice, Khavon. Really . . . . But you didn't have to go to all of the trouble of getting a limo. The IDS is only four blocks away from here."

"I know, but I thought we'd ride around the city a bit before we head over there—if that's okay with you." Khavon raised his brow with question.

"Oh, that's fine." Alayna looked out and up at the stars. "It's a beautiful night for it."

"It certainly is," Khavon said quietly when she turned back to him. Looking into her eyes, he lightly caressed her soft, smooth face and kissed her deeply.

They snacked on paté on sesame wheat crackers, champagne, and sweet strawberries as they drove through the city.

Their metro tour started with the radiant Christmas lights of the City Center.

"Aren't they beautiful?" Alayna asked.

"Yes, absolutely beautiful," Khavon said, staring at her in a mesmerized daze.

They crossed Loring Park and Walker Art Center. Alayna eyed the famous colossal cherry/spoon piece in the sculpture art garden. She looked over at Khavon and he was smiling just like in the dream sequence she'd had. Only now, his smile was warm and generous, not sneaky and menacing like it had been in the dream. They drank, snacked, and drove through every major district in Minneapolis . . . Uptown, Dinkytown, Frogtown, and then through the warehouse district. They circled the capital to Summit and Grand Avenue in St. Paul. They crossed back over the Mississippi and proceeded through the chain of lakes.

When their tour of the Twin Cities was complete, Khavon pressed the button next to the window power.

"Jeff, we're ready now," Khavon instructed the driver over the intercom.

"Yes, sir, Mr. Brighton," the driver said, taking a right turn off Lyndale onto Hennipen and making his way back towards downtown Minneapolis and the IDS Center.

The tallest building in the state at 774 feet high, the IDS Center towered over the rest of the Minneapolis skyline like a proud, watchful parent. With the beautiful glass-enclosed Crystal Court at its base, the IDS Center was a Minneapolis landmark.

Through the window, Alayna could see the fifty-four piece black and white orchestra playing in the middle of Crystal Court's open plaza.

"Oh, Khavon, they're wonderful," Alayna commented, standing at the entrance of the mammoth building. Their rendition of "Meditation" was flawless.

"C'mon." Khavon took her hand, leading her to the escalator. With a much better view of the musicians below, they stood on the second floor of the two story retail center looking down into the open plaza.

Twenty minutes had passed when Khavon remarked about the time. "It's eleven-fifteen. We probably should go up now."

Khavon took Alayna's hand and led her to the elevator. They stepped in and he pressed fifty-one on the panel board.

When the door closed, Khavon wasted no time sweeping Alayna into a sensuous kiss that escalated in intensity with each of the ascending floors. The elevator stopped, and they tore their lips apart just as the door slid open.

"Jooney!" squealed a petite woman with closely cropped hair from behind the front table when they stepped out of the elevator. The woman's bright yellow face looked vaguely familiar to her, though Alayna didn't know why.

"Hello, Sasha," Khavon said. "How've you been?"

"Wonderful now! It's been a long time," she said, looking him up and down.

"Yes, it has been a long time," Khavon admitted. "So, how do you like living in Atlanta? Every so often I'll catch your segment on the news."

"I like it. It's an exciting town."

Suddenly, Khavon realized his rudeness. "Oh, I'm sorry.

Sasha, this is Alayna Alexander. Alayna, this is Sasha Price, Kelly's sister." Sasha turned to Alayna and promptly began to size her up.

"Hello," she said politely, with a forced smile.

"Hi," Alayna said quietly.

"I suppose you're looking for this." Khavon pulled out a shimmering gold envelope from his inside pocket.

"Okay, Jooney. You know you didn't have to bring that thing. Just go on in. Kelly and Gloria will be thrilled that you decided to come."

"It was really good to see you again, Sasha." Khavon smiled. Sasha smiled awkwardly, and again gave Alayna a once over before the two of them went into the reception area.

The excitement was almost too much for Alayna to stand. The night had already been much too wonderful. She felt like Cinderella making her grand entrance to the ball, only she had somehow managed to bring the Prince with her. Alayna held tight to Khavon's hand as he opened one of the festively decorated double doors.

It was a beautiful room, much more beautiful than Alayna had imagined. Greeting them was an eight foot Christmas tree, trimmed in ornamental gold.

"Oh, Khavon, isn't it beautiful?"

He was just about the answer when from the far wall near the bathroom, he noticed a tall man against the wall eyeing Alayna.

"Yeah, beautiful." He pulled her close. "Come on, let's get something to drink."

It was a dazzling setting. Dimly lit, the festively decorated room was abuzz with lively music and laughter, and the voices of high-spirited guests, formally clad in sequined evening gowns and starched black tuxedos, filled the room. The view behind them was breathtakingly spectacular. The city lights of Minneapolis and St. Paul twinkled like stars in the panoramic view through the frosted windows. Bordering the windows were lines of white linen-covered tables, blanketed with flickering candles, half-filled glasses of champagne, confetti, and colorful party favors. Sprinkled between them were the branches of pale birchwood trees that were adorned with twinkling white Christmas lights.

Pulling her along by the hand, they passed a black leather wet bar to the right. They made their way to the beautiful sterling champagne fountain that was only a few feet away. Khavon interrupted the flow of one of the golden streams with a long-stemmed crystal glass, filling it to the brim.

"Here," he said, lifting the glass to Alayna.

"Khavon, I don't think I should have any more. I'm already a little woozy."

"Hey, it's New Year's. You're supposed to be woozy."

"If I didn't know better, I'd say you were trying to get me drunk so you can take advantage of me," Alayna said playfully, taking the glass from his hand.

"Beautiful, and perceptive too. That's what I like about you, Alayna." He smiled mischievously and turned to fill his own glass.

"So, what's the story with Sandy back there?" Alayna finally asked.

"Oh, you mean Sasha," he corrected quietly.

Alayna took note, drinking down some champagne. "Okay, Sasha."

"Sasha is Kelly's sister. She's had a crush on me since the sixth grade."

"And?"

"And, I never pursued it. I never pursued it because of Kelly." He paused briefly, musing. "She never could appreciate that," he said before closing his eyes to swallow some champagne.

"Jooney!" A husky man and his apparent wife approached Khavon from across the room with open arms. Alayna recognized the man to be Kelly Price.

"Gloria kept saying it was you, man, but I didn't believe her. I had to get up close to see for myself. And then, I still thought my eyes were playing tricks on me," Kelly laughed jovially, still shaking Khavon's hand.

"Aw, man, I told you I was gonna come."

"You say that every year. And who might this lovely lady be?" Kelly asked, as Gloria and Khavon exchanged a friendly hug.

"Oh, I'm sorry. Alayna, this is Kelly and Gloria Price. This is Alayna Alexander."

The three of them exchanged hello's. An avid baseball fan, Alayna felt strange talking to the man who'd been dubbed by the media as the Home Run King. She'd seen his face so many times on the screen and in the news paper, she felt like she knew him like an old friend, yet she didn't know him at all. It was a strange feeling.

"Welcome to the party, Alayna," Kelly said.

"Thank you."

"And Happy New Year!"

"Happy New Year!" Alayna smiled.

"Girlfriend, what did you do to this man to finally get him here? We've been trying for years," Gloria grinned knowingly, grabbing her hand.

"I—wh—I didn't do anything," Alayna stumbled over the words, surprised that they were making such a big deal. "I just said I wanted to go."

Gloria and Kelly looked at each other, then at Khavon and then finally back at her. It was as if she'd just spoken in fluent Russian. The shock value in their faces was enough to make Alayna think they'd briefly considered committing her.

"Well, have you all had anything to eat yet? There's plenty of food." Gloria led them to the reception area where chefs in tall hats, white jackets, and knives in hand, waited behind a dozen or so white-clothed tables to serve them. Sliced turkey, roast beef, and scampi led off the entrees. Rumaki and shrimp cocktails led into the turkey and roast beef entrees. Roasted red potatoes and glazed carrots were next. Assorted salads and deserts lined the other half of the U-shaped reception area. Alayna and Khavon ate and drank until five minutes before the midnight hour, and then headed to the dance floor.

The crowd, dancing to the thunderous beat, their heads bedecked with silly party favors, was rowdy and loud. Alayna and Khavon stood in the midst of the feverish excitement. Despite the crowd, they remained locked in a close embrace, moving slowly to their own private song.

"Thank you, Khavon," she whispered in his ear, her coral-stained lips brushing the side of his face, driving him crazy.

"Thank you for what?"

"Thank you for bringing me here tonight."

"You don't have to thank me. I wanted to bring you here tonight."

"You did?" Alayna sounded surprised, after the way Gloria and Kelly had reacted.

"Yes, I did," he said.

"Why?"

"Because, well . . . . I don't know," he said, pausing to think for a moment. "It just does something to me to see you happy. You are happy, Alayna, aren't you?"

"Very," she said simply.

"10, 9, 8, 7, 6 . . . ." The countdown began. They were already kissing when confetti rained down on them from above and the crowd yelled, "Happy New Year!"

"Happy New Year, Alayna."

"Happy New Year, Khavon," Alayna whispered, rejoining her lips to his.

Khavon had stared at her all night long as if she were the most beautiful creature he'd ever seen, Alayna recalled.

"It was wonderful," Alayna told Sheila, conveniently leaving out how she and Khavon had danced for a while and then gone back to Khavon's and rung in the new year properly.

"Mm. Alayna, that's so romantic," Sheila admitted, as they climbed the stairs back to the office. "I wish Larry and I could be like that," she said, her voice mildly envious. "When the clock struck twelve, my man was in bed, asleep." Alayna shook her head, sympathetically. "Here comes Mr. Wonderful now," Sheila remarked as Khavon took long but quick strides toward them.

"Hello, Khavon," Sheila said.

"Hi, Sheila. How are you?"

"Fine."

"How was your holiday?"

"Good."

Feeling like a third wheel after an moment of silence, Sheila said, "Well, so much for my coffee break. Furi is expecting an updated version of the Gantt chart."

"Okay, Sheila. I'll see ya later," Alayna said, waving.

"Yeah, see ya later, Sheila," Khavon said.

"Hi." Alayna was smiling.

"Hi." Khavon's face was pensive and Alayna's smile gradually began to drop.

"What's up?" Khavon pulled her aside.

"Alayna, I checked the logs from Liberty. It seems that we have a nocturnal guest."

"What?"

"There's been some unauthorized access."

"What happened?"

"Well, nothing, really. I mean, whoever it is hasn't taken anything, but the nocturnal entries clued me in that something is going on."

"Well, what time were the entries? And what did they say?" Alayna asked, her eyes showing riveted concern.

"Whoever it was logged in between two and two-thirty in the morning, regularly, and they always logged out by 4:45."

"What do you mean, whoever it was? Weren't you able to trace the log register we put in once you found them?"

"Well, I just found them last night. Whoever it was knew what they were doing. They sidestepped all the hidden alarms, including the log register that the team put in. None of the alarms tripped either."

"But if our log didn't record anything, what log are you talking about?"

"That's what I'm trying to tell you. As a regular practice, I put in a special hidden log that I didn't tell anyone about. That is the log that recorded the intruder. And yes, I did trace them, but there was a problem, which is why I came to see you," Khavon said, looking around, lowering his voice even further.

"A problem? What kind of problem?" The level of Alayna's voice followed Khavon's lead.

"There were at least seventy-five different connections, and I went through all of them." Khavon's face was distressed.

"And?"

"And whoever it is, is using an Excelsior computer as a launching point."

Alayna said nothing, her features contemplative.

"I've checked every computer in Excelsior that I have access to and I didn't see anything unusual."

Alayna said nothing, still only staring into the floor, her brow deeply creased.

"Now, I noticed there's an unmarked door on the northeast side of the building near the water cooler."

Alayna said nothing. Khavon stared at her intensely before continuing. "I think it's being secured with magnetic stripe cards. At least, that's what I'm guessing the black security slab on the wall two doors down seems to be for. If my hunch is right, there's a computer behind that door. I haven't mentioned this to any of the others because it's hard to know who to trust around here. But Alayna, I need to find out if you have, or can get, access to that door."

Alayna's mind was racing. Khavon was right. There was a computer behind that door, and she did have access to it. But that computer was restricted to Excelsior's top security personnel, and Excelsior only. All of Excelsior's sensitive business intelligence was stored in that room. Everything was in there. Everything—from the R&D for old and new products, leading edge technology, legal defense records for past and pending law suits, detailed financial records of Excelsior's financial activities, disposition of assets, and millions in billing records. Not to mention the company's backup copies of programs and files stored on tape in case of an emergency.

Khavon was right. He had not been able to access that computer because it was the only one in the company which had no remote access. The only way someone could get into or out of that computer was to gain physical access to the computer and attach a modem—and the only way to do that was to physically penetrate the elaborate security system that had been especially designed to protect Excelsior's sensitive data records.

Khavon had been close, but not exactly right. The magnetic stripe flag was only a decoy. After an exhaustive background check, Alayna had been chosen to be the newest member of the trusted security personnel that had access to the room. As one of six authorized members of Excelsior's top security personnel, Alayna, after receiving the appropriate security training, was given a badge with a radio frequency transmitter in it.

For the computer room, the electronically-locked door opened when it received the appropriate encrypted key signal. An electronic log recorded the entrance of the key that opened the door, and initiated a ninety-minute timer. If the entrant had not vacated before the time on the timer elapsed, a silent alarm went off. All doors to the building would be electronically locked and the appropriate authorities would be called. The security business was cutthroat, and they wanted to take no chances.

Excelsior was very serious about their business intelligence. Very serious. Alayna had been placed in a high position of trust to protect that commodity because it was Excelsior's lifeblood. Now the man she loved was asking her to compromise that trust. *Could this be what he wanted all the time?* Alayna thought back to the telephone conversation she had overheard when she'd spent the night with him. She found herself wondering if everything the two of them had said and done was part of some kind of con game. Suddenly suspicious, untrusting, and most of all hurt, Alayna's dejected heart fell into a black haze.

Chapter Twenty-Five

"Alayna." Khavon's voice was edged with anger. He was losing patience with Alayna's silence. "Haven't you been listening to anything that I've been saying?"

"Khavon," she whispered finally, "do you have any idea what you're asking me to do? I could get fired or even go to jail. Besides, that computer has no connection to Liberty's computer system. It's not even accessible from a remote site."

"Yes, I know that, Alayna. But once you have access to the computer, you know as well as I do that any amateur can connect up a modem and go anywhere he wants to go. And yes, I do know what I'm asking you to do, Alayna. But you should know that I would never do anything to hurt you. I love you."

"I love you, too . . . but—"

"But what?"

"But if you really loved me, you wouldn't ask me to risk everything I have on a hunch. You wouldn't ask me to betray the company's trust."

"Alayna, I'm trying to save the company, not hurt it."

The man she loved was asking her to compromise the trust that Excelsior had bestowed on her. Her heart said, *What's mine is yours*. Give him what he wants and everything that you have. But her brain asked, *Why? Why does he really need this information? Could he be up to no good somehow? Could he be some sort of corporate spy sent to penetrate Excelsior by seducing me? Could it be that I was mistaken? Could this be what he was referring to when I overheard him talking on the phone? "She's gonna break soon."* The words replayed over and over in her head. *Have I been a fool all this time? A fool in love? Or maybe I wasn't . . . . Am I overreacting? A little paranoid, perhaps?* she thought, staring into his soft brown eyes. Alayna felt the perspiration forming on her head.

"Khavon, what exactly is it that you need from in there? Maybe I could just get it for you," she said, looking for some way, any way out. "Why don't you just let me print the log for the times in question, and then we can go from there?" she said before he could answer.

Khavon stared at her disbelievingly, seeing right through her hesitancy. "Mmph. I see trust and love don't necessarily go hand in hand. I would never betray you, Alayna. You should know that."

"Khavon . . . ."

"That's okay, Alayna. My objective is to catch this guy. And yes, I do need the logs. That's the first step, but ultimately, Alayna, I'm telling you that I will need access. The only way to catch this guy is to install my tracking software onto the hard drive."

"I could do that for you," Alayna suggested, quickly.

"No, you can't. This is my specialty software. It's very delicate. There are too many hooks and booby traps. It would take weeks to instruct you on all of the hidden features, and we don't have that kind of time. But you do what you have to do. I'll meet you at the door tonight at six." Khavon walked away quickly, leaving behind a trail of hurt and anger like it was a defensive scent.

Alayna sat at her desk the rest of the day in a trance, unable to do any work. Attempts at concentration were futile. Her brain was saturated with an unending parade of winter snapshots of her and Khavon. She could think of nothing else.

Funky snowmen and hot cappuccino, chauffeured limousines and chilled champagne . . . had it all been a clever ruse? A black web of deception that had been carefully spun to perfection in order to trap her and use her as a pawn in a dangerous game of corporate espionage?

She'd been warned in her training. "Corporate spies and vulnerable women in positions of trust." She remembered the chapter well. It came right before the one on middle-aged crisis and the balding man, and she recalled wondering how the women in her text could be so incredibly stupid. She'd told herself that she would never fall prey to such sugar-coated lies. Never in a million years. She was too smart for that. Now here she sat, a case and point textbook example.

But to Khavon's credit, she reasoned in her own defense, he had been no amateur. The man had staged a cunning seduction. Sweet-smelling flowers, flattery and freely expressed words of love. Love. The word collared her runaway suspicions and pulled them back for re-examination.

Khavon had told her that he loved her that first night that they were together. They'd made love in the paneled moonlight, Alayna recalled staring into distant space. They'd made sweet, tender, emotional love in front of a lazy fire that night. And every night since. It was real and it was honest. It was no dutiful task in a Casanova's mission. It was no intelligence gathering session. It was real. Besides, the man was a local resident who owned a home and had a family here.

Spies don't establish permanence or residence, do they? And he didn't seem to be living beyond his means. Although, he did own that expensive-looking foreign car, she mused. *But he's an entrepreneur with no immediate family to support, so that's not unusual. Besides the man served in the military and gives his time to charity. Intelligence agents don't spend their leisure time tutoring inner city kids,* Alayna reassured herself confidently. And hadn't he been through the same rigorous company investigation that she'd been through?

Then there was her most important motivation for believing in Khavon's inculpability. It was simple, but significant. She loved Khavon, and she didn't want to lose him. She didn't want to lose him or the potential promise of a future. After all, this man could be the father of her as of yet unborn children. If she didn't trust

Khavon, who could she trust? How could she marry a man if she didn't trust him?

Maybe she could just get a print-off of the log. Besides, they really needed to catch this guy, and the log would give them definitive proof. It would point the finger to the culprit. He'd have to come up with some pretty good excuses as to why he was in the security room at 2:00 a.m. It would only take a minute to print. Plus, it would buy her some time as well as verify Khavon's story about the logs.

Khavon was no spy, she told herself. She was being silly, she told herself ultimately. She would give him the accounting log and apologize.

Khavon hadn't uttered a sound since they'd spoken this morning, but Alayna could smell the scent of his cologne over the partition.

"Working late tonight, huh?" Furi startled Alayna out of her thoughts.

She looked at her watch. It was ten till six.

"Oh, I, uh . . . yeah. I just have a couple of things to take care of before I leave," she said nervously, suddenly cognizant of the reason for her keeping a late hour.

"Alayna, are you okay? You look kind of, well . . . stressed," Furi said, noticing the perspiration forming on her upper lip.

"Just a little tired." Alayna feigned a yawn. "But I'm heading out soon."

"Good. I wouldn't want any rumors to get started that I'm burning people out," Furi joked. "You get home and get some rest."

"I will."

"I'll see you tomorrow. Good night, Alayna."

"Good night, Furi."

The office was fairly quiet. Alayna could still smell Khavon's scent, but she no longer heard any typing or shuffling. *He must have gone to the computer room already,* she thought. She leisurely strolled by his cube in the next aisle. He wasn't there. She looked at her watch. It was five to the hour.

The computer room was on the far side of the floor. Khavon was waiting by the door when she arrived.

"I didn't think you were coming, but you're right on time, Ms. Alexander," Khavon said in a cold, callous business tone.

"Khavon . . . ."

"Alayna, we don't have time for chit-chat. At least not now. Not here. You need to go in and get the logs and get out. Now, here's a listing of the dates and times my computer recorded." He presented her with the folded bond paper. "Unless, of course, you've changed your mind about that now, too."

Alayna eyed him circumspectly, grabbed the listing, and pressed the red button on the transmitter to activate the key to unlock the door. Alayna slid in quickly while Khavon kept watch outside. The huge, windowless room was dark, quiet and cold. Alayna had only been in there a few times before, and always with other people.

Climate controlled, the room always felt cool, but today it felt eerily cold, almost like a morgue would feel, she imagined. Then again, maybe it was just the cold sweat rolling down her back.

She flicked the light switch on, illuminating the room. Her eyes moved past the power supply, over to the four networked computers that lived up against the thick, concrete wall on the north side of the room.

They'd moved them since the last time she'd been in there. Clutching the five and a half inch computer disk in one hand and Khavon's time logs in the other, she sat down in front of the flickering green console of the first computer in the network.

She glanced quickly over her shoulder and slid the disk in to the disk drive. *I must be crazy,* she thought, unfolding the printed document that Khavon had given to her. Alayna quickly located the electronic log directory on the computer. In it, she found all of the log files from the last five years, listed by date. She breathed a sigh of relief. She cross-checked the dates in the list with the ones on the paper that Khavon had given her, highlighting each matching entry as she went along. Alayna finally reached the last one, and instructed the computer to copy each one to her disk. She heard the disk drive whirring in response to her instruction. She took another quick look over her shoulder and wiped the sweat from her forehead. Finally, the red light went off, signaling that the copy procedure was complete. Alayna extracted the disk and headed toward the door. Her hand was on the knob to open it when she heard voices.

Khavon had barely sat down and turned the machine on in a nearby cubical, when Rico, one of the custodians, rolled his trash bin into the row that he was now sitting in.

"Hey, Rico, man, *qué pasa*?" Khavon said.

"Just trying to make a living, man, that's all. Another day, another dollar, ya know."

"Yeah man, I know what you mean," Khavon agreed.

Tall and handsome, Rico had always been a friendly sort of guy, especially towards other people of color. Over the months, he had developed a friendly office rapport with Alayna, Khavon and Sheila.

"What chu doing way over here anyway, man? I thought you worked on the other side of the floor," Rico said, rubbing his hands through the shiny, black waves on his head.

Khavon eyed the secretary's wall of certificates. "Ingrid . . . Ingrid asked me to stop in and take a look at her PC. She thinks it has a virus on it."

Rico furrowed his thick, brows together. "Hmm. That's funny. Ingrid's been gone for a week. She was going on her honeymoon."

"Yeah, she told me before she left and I'm just now getting around to it, I've been so busy. You know how it is, man."

"Yeah, man." Rico dumped the last of the trash in the large gray bin. "Well, I'm almost finished with this floor, but I still have two more floors to go. So, I'll see you later, man."

"Yeah, later, Rico."

Rico rolled the trash bin down the aisle and over to the next row. Quick about his business, he was gone inside of a few minutes. Khavon knocked on the door and Alayna slid out.

"That was close. Let's get out of here before someone sees us," Khavon said, leading her by the small of her back.

Chapter Twenty-Six

"Khavon." Alayna was sitting in the guest chair at his desk, careful to keep her voice low.

"Mm-hmm," Khavon mumbled, the bulk of his attention on the console.

"I've been doing some thinking, and I just want to say I'm sorry. It's not that I don't trust you. It's just that in the security training that we had . . . ." Alayna rambled on.

Khavon sat back in his chair, still staring at the monitor. "Alayna, I think you ought to take a look at this."

"I think that if two people really care for each other, trust is imperative. And . . . ." she continued her spiel, not listening.

Khavon turned around, his face grave with consternation.

"Alayna, I said I think you ought to take a look at this." The severity of his tone stopped her one-sided conversation.

"What? What is it?" she said, her features growing concerned.

"Take a look for yourself," Khavon said, standing up to give her his seat.

Alayna's brows came together as she rose slowly to take his place. Slightly irritated by his refusal to just tell her what was going on, Alayna turned to him with another questioning look of confusion before opening the first correlating electronic file in the chronological listing.

Speechless, Alayna stared blankly at the screen output.

Excelsior Securities Daily Log File
09/15 12:08:43 AM - 09/15 12:08:43 AM

09/15/97 12:08:43 AM AMgr: Logging daily statistics for CN=AlaynaS.Alexander/OU=US-Corporate/O=EX/C=US
09/15/97 12:08:43 AM Total scheduled runs: 20
09/15/97 12:08:43 AM Total event triggered runs: 25
09/15/97 12:08:43 AM Total errors: 0
09/15/97 12:08:43 AM Total access denials: 0
09/15/97 12:08:43 AM Total agent elapsed run time (seconds) 0
09/16/97 12:08:43 AM AMgr: Logging daily statistics for CN=AlaynaS.Alexander/OU=US-Corporate/O=EX/C=US
09/16/97 12:08:43 AM Total scheduled runs: 20
09/16/97 12:08:43 AM Total event triggered runs: 25
09/16/97 12:08:43 AM Total errors: 0
09/16/97 12:08:43 AM Total access denials: 0
09/16/97 12:08:43 AM Total agent elapsed run time (seconds)

"Wait a minute." Alayna's forehead grew frowns of confusion as she opened one file after the next. "Wait a minute. There's gotta be some mistake. I must have grabbed the wrong logs." One by one, she continued to open the files, and one by one, they revealed their electronic recording of her inexplicable access to Excelsior's main computer in the wee hours of the morning.

Stunned, Alayna turned to Khavon. "I didn't do this. Someone is trying to set me up."

Sudden terror shot through Alayna, as a vivid image flashed through her mind of her being dragged down the front stairs of Excelsior in handcuffs in front of a crowd of reporters, pointing co-workers, and a police car waiting to take her downtown. Alayna was on the verge of sliding into a hysterical fit when Khavon calmly grabbed her hands. Khavon's satiny eyes were pensive when they moved to hers.

"Alayna, tell me you didn't have anything to do with this."

"Khavon, I swear to you. I—" Her eyes started tearing, her voice cracked. "I didn't have anything to do with this." Khavon studied her carefully for several seconds. "Don't you believe me?"

He studied her exotic brown eyes and made his decision. "Yes, I do." Alayna breathed a sigh of relief. "Okay, no one knows about this except you, me, and whoever's doing this. Right now, whoever it is is still probably operating under the assumption that we don't know what's going on. We want to keep it that way. Somehow, they must have switched transmitter badges. Either that or they've figured out a way to mimic your key transmission."

"I keep my badge with me all the time," Alayna said defiantly.

"I'll tell you what, we need to check today's log. If someone did switch badges with you, they should have an entry in the log file from five minutes ago when you went in," Khavon said.

"Well, I only copied the files corresponding to the log dates that you gave me."

Khavon stared at Alayna. "Alayna, do you have any idea who would want to do something like this to you?"

"Mmph. Mmph. No." Alayna exclaimed, shaking her head. "I can't think of anything I've done that would—" She stopped abruptly, remembering.

"What?" Khavon curiously questioned.

"Well, remember how upset I was when I found out that you were going to be co-technical lead?"

"Yeah."

"Well, I wasn't the only one who had a problem with Furi's decision."

"What do you mean?"

"Well, I don't know how much background they gave you, but a few months before you came, Liberty contracted us out to do a backup system to their security system."

"Yeah, we plugged the hole in it. So?"

"So, Becky and Mark were head developers on the original project, but they had somewhat of a rivalry going on and there was a lot of conflict and bickering between the two. It was a real distraction for the team, but they managed to get the project done in spite of everything that was going on. Given the success of the project, the unspoken expectation among the team was that the next big project would go to one of them. But when Liberty came up short, we discovered that Excelsior's backup system had a hole in it.

"Needless to say, Liberty was not happy, and Furi was most definitely not happy. This all happened around the same time that Liberty found out that they had been awarded the government contract for developing the U.S. electronic tax system. I guess Liberty didn't want to take any chances, and neither did Furi. That's the only thing that I can think of that would make someone want to do this to me," Alayna said, finishing her thought.

"Well, I think that's enough, don't you?" Khavon said.

"I guess. Listen, Khavon, I've been thinking and, well, I want you to put your monitoring system in."

"Oh, you do, huh? It's amazing how quickly being framed can change a person's mind," Khavon said sarcastically.

"Khavon, please, I'm trying to apologize here. Besides I was trying to tell you this before I found out that someone was trying to set me up. I want you to know that I do trust you. And I'm sorry. I'm sorry, but at the same time, you have to understand where I was coming from. I have a certain responsibility and I'm really jeopardizing my livelihood here."

"I understand where you were coming from, Alayna," Khavon cut her off, "but you have to realize that I would never hurt you."

"I know that, Khavon."

"Now, c'mon. We have a lot of work to do."

Chapter Twenty-Seven

They sat together on the couch watching television, after having consumed a meal of spicy Szechwan shrimp and rice that Khavon had prepared for them.

"It still bothers me how someone could enter the system without us being able to trace it," Alayna said to Khavon as he massaged her foot.

"They covered their tracks by erasing it. But the one advantage that we have now is that whoever it is doesn't know we're watching. The monitoring system that I wrote has been silently watching and recording his activity for a while now."

"But Khavon, it's been more than a month," Alayna said impatiently.

"I know, Alayna, but like I told you before, his first connection is to a digital communications company. It's been kind of a slow process up to this point. And they compact the telecommunication data together and sent it to this country. I have to try to decipher all of that information. He has created so many layers that it's hard to trace him. He is jumping from network to network, and not only that, but the trail appears to go cold at each stop because he's electronically camouflaging himself at each one. Ever since I programmed my computer to page me every time an outside connection is made, I've been able to watch his activity more closely, but—" Khavon stopped short shaking his head.

"But what?" Alayna asked, picking up on the concern in Khavon's face.

"Last night I traced him to a computer network in Langley, Virginia."

"Langley, Virginia. Why does that sound familiar? Langley, Virginia."

"CIA headquarters is in Langley, Virginia," Khavon said.

Alayna's eyes went wide. "Khavon what are we getting into?"

"There's more."

"There's more?"

Khavon nodded his head. "This guy has been tapping into military computer networks all across the country . . . Navy ship yards, Air Force systems, Army missile bases, and even classified labs that do nuclear red."

Alayna stared at him incredulously. "Khavon, what we getting into?" Her voice was trembling.

"I don't know, Alayna, but it doesn't look good. Not only is he infiltrating U.S. classified networks, but I've been monitoring his keystrokes and he's searching for words like defense, stealth, top secret, SDI, classified, confidential, and nuclear. The company in Langley that I traced him to is called Volmute. Volmute is a government defense contractor who has secret contracts with the Pentagon, CIA, and NSA. Testing computers for security is their business."

Khavon's subdued eyes cut over to Alayna.

Alayna reclaimed her feet, turning her body forward on the couch to place them on the floor. "Khavon, you're scaring me. If you are trying to tell me that the person we're looking for is some kind of international spy, we need to call the NSA or FBI or somebody, because we are in way, way over our heads. This is way out of our league."

"No, Alayna. We can't do that," Khavon stated, emphatically. "We need to keep watching and tracking him to see where he's sending his information."

"Why can't the NSA or the FBI or somebody do that?"

"Because I don't know who we can trust over there. If we approach the wrong person, we could be putting both of our lives in danger."

"Khavon, what are we going to do?" Alayna sounded afraid.

"We just have to keep watching him. He's bound to make a wrong move sooner or later."

"What if he doesn't?" Alayna asked.

"Oh, he will," Khavon assured her with confidence. "He will. We just have to be patient," he said, rubbing his shoulder.

"I just want to catch this guy, Khavon." Alayna's eyes began to water as she caught her forehead in her hands.

"I know, Alayna."

Alayna was trying unsuccessfully to hold back her emotion, when a thought suddenly came to her. Her head came up from her hands.

"Khavon, I was just thinking . . . instead of waiting for him to make a wrong move, what if we helped him along?" Alayna's eyes sparkled.

"What do you mean?"

"Well, if this guy is searching for top secret military documents, what if we gave him what he's looking for?"

Khavon raised his eyebrows. "What? I don't think that would be wise. Besides, we don't have access to them if we wanted to."

"No. No. You don't understand. I mean, what if we set up a sting? We could set up a series of fake files with phony data and label it with Star Wars or Strategic Defense Initiative or something. We could come up with all kinds of crazy stuff, and he would bite, I know it."

"You know, Alayna, that's not a bad idea," Khavon said, stroking his mustache. "If we set if up right, that just might work."

"We could create a fictional user id and make the files readable only by the owner, so no one could find them except us and the hacker."

"But we have to be very careful not to be too obvious. Otherwise, he'll suspect something is funny and we'll lose him." Khavon was quiet for a moment, thinking. Finally, he turned to her.

"Alayna, you're a genius." She managed a smile through her still watery eyes.

He hugged her shoulders. "C'mon, you need to unwind." He lead her by the hand down the carpeted stairs into the lower level of his home. Alayna had been to Khavon's home many times before, but this was the first time she'd been in the basement. He'd converted the wide open space in the center into a veritable fitness center. A treadmill, a bench press, and a red and black punching bag were at the core of the room. Scattered on the floor were various weights, a jump rope, and a pair of boxing gloves. The huge exercise room was flanked by a door on either side. A spin cycle was in the corner.

"This is where I come when I need to unwind," Khavon said.

"I like to exercise, Khavon, but I'm not exactly in the mood," Alayna remarked, trying hard not to turn up her nose.

Khavon laughed an amused laugh.

"I mean, there's a time and a place for these things, you know?" she tried to explain.

He chuckled again briefly, and then looked into her caramel eyes. "Take your clothes off." His smile had disappeared.

"What?" she asked, not quite understanding.

"I said, take your clothes off."

Alayna looked at him strangely, wondering if she really had hooked up with some kind of freak or something.

"Alayna is something wrong?"

"Oh—uh—no—I just—" Alayna's heart began to beat rapidly as she followed his instruction and began to remove her clothes. When she stood fully naked in front of him, he slowly looked her up and down, taking her in inch by curvy inch. Alayna thought her heart would pop out of her chest, it was beating so rapidly.

Frightened and vulnerable, Alayna felt strangely feminine and slightly embarrassed at the same time.

When he had taken her in sufficiently with his eyes, he removed his own clothes and led her to the door on the south wall of the exercise room.

Alayna was moving slowly, partly terrified and partly intrigued. "What's in there, Khavon?" she asked nervously.

Sensing her fear like it was a scent, he answered her question.

"Don't worry, I told you I would never hurt you." He opened the door, leading her by the hand.

The surprising, clean scent of fresh cedar filled her senses, catching her by surprise. Still, Alayna's eyes were wide with nervous curiosity and fear, her legs primed for a sprint. Shaking her head, Alayna could see a stack of folded white towels, and matching robes hanging from two hooks on the wall. Grabbing two towels, Khavon handed her one and kept one for himself.

"After you," he said, gesturing to her right.

Alayna apprehensively peeked around the corner to where Khavon was gesturing.

Through the glass window in the cedar wood door, Alayna could see the hot red coals in the corner. "You have a sauna in your basement?" Alayna turned and asked incredulously.

"It's not that unusual, Alayna," Khavon answered with a chuckle.

"Really? You're the first person that I've ever met with one."

Khavon chuckled. "Well, maybe a little unusual. C'mon."

Twenty minutes later, the two of them emerged, dripping with perspiration but relaxed. Alayna caught her reflection in a pane of glass. The humidity had not been kind to her hair. Tightly curled, it had swelled into a giant afro. Her hand immediately went to her spongy head.

Khavon removed her hand, replacing it with his own. "Alayna, you look beautiful," he said, his tongue outlining her hairline. He moved down to her moist lips and they retired to the shower.

In the warm spray of water, Khavon introduced her to a bar of soap that quickly became a close and intimate friend. Properly lathered, Khavon pressed her hard against the white tiled wall and began a slow teasing grind. When the time was right, he made vertical love to her. She came explosively, setting off a chain reactive detonation in him. Afterwards, they rinsed and collapsed in Khavon's bed.

Several sporadic jerking motions coming from the opposite

side of the bed started to stir Alayna from a deep and peaceful slumber. A quick, sharp jab of his elbow into her side finally jostled her completely awake. She heard Khavon mumbling and turned toward him. He was doused in sweat and fighting with the air.

"No!" he yelled out loud, sitting straight up in bed before she could wake him.

"Khavon, honey, you're dreaming. It's just a dream," Alayna said, trying to calm and console him, stroking his back and shoulders.

Khavon threw up his hands. "No! No! It's not a dream! It's not a dream! That's what you don't understand, Alayna. It's not a dream!" He twisted away angrily, his heart still beating rapidly, his feet now planted firmly on the floor.

Alayna's hand was left hanging in midair, her features filled with confusion, and her feelings now hurt.

She wrapped her legs around his waist and caressed his back with the side of her face. "Khavon, honey, what is it? Talk to me. Please, I want to help."

"You can't help," Khavon said, plainly, shaking his head, breaking free from her leggy grip.

"How do you know I can't help?"

"Because you're not helping now!" he snapped, pacing to the window, his hand on his head.

Alayna was silent, her feelings hurt again.

Khavon turned to her, apologetically, running his fingers through his hair.

"Look. I just don't think it would do any good to talk, because I just don't think—I just don't think you would understand."

Alayna looked at him squarely. "Try me."

Khavon turned his head to the side, thinking. Finally, he acquiesced, and sat beside her on the bed.

"Alayna, I can't do this anymore. I love you too much to keep doing this Alayna."

"Doing what?"

"I feel like we're on a train with no destination."

Alayna's heart skipped a beat. "What do you mean?"

"Well, Alayna, it's just that I want to give you so much, but…."

"But what?"

"But I can never give you what you really want."

"Khavon, what are you talking about? I don't even recall us discussing what I want." *This should be interesting,* she thought.

"You're right. I never did ask you, but then again, I didn't have to. You didn't leave a whole lot of room for guessing when I first confronted you about your feelings. Any fool could see that you had marriage on the brain."

Alayna looked down, her heart sinking into the mud print pillows. "And what's wrong with marriage?" Alayna asked.

Khavon was silent at first. "Nothing is wrong with marriage, I guess." He turned to face her. "I just know that I can't do it again."

"Why not?" Alayna wanted to know.

He turned away and stood up.

"Because I'm just not into it."

Alayna shook her head disbelievingly. "Khavon, c'mon. Either we're gonna talk or we're not. People don't just wake up in a cold sweat screaming about something because they're 'just not into it.' There's gotta be more to it. There's gotta be more to it because otherwise you wouldn't be so freaked out."

Khavon's eyes grew wide. "Freaked out!" he exclaimed. "I'm not freaked! You know what?" He shook his head and closed his eyes hard. "This isn't working. Let's just talk about something else."

"No. I want to talk about what happened in your marriage."

Khavon walked over and flicked the television on.

" . . . . more blood shed in the Mideast. And on the local front thin ice on Lake Minnetonka has claimed the life of yet another snowmobiler," the young, blonde news caster continued her report. "Searchers found . . . ."

Alayna walked over, turned the TV off and stood there.

Khavon hit the power button on the remote and the TV flashed on again.

Alayna reached behind her and turned it off again.

Khavon angrily threw the remote on the floor and laid back on the bed.

"Tell me what this is about, Khavon." Alayna folded her arms across her chest. Khavon's gaze remained steadfast on the white textured ceiling paint and he refused to part his lips.

"Okay, Khavon. If this is the way you want it," Alayna said, giving up. She walked over and stood next to the brass bed. Staring at Khavon's motionless body lying across the bed, she decided to give it one last try. "Look, I don't want to get hurt either. And it's real easy to shut off from the world so that you don't. Many people choose that path and it works for them. They never get hurt. They never get hurt because they never feel anything. They walk through their lives unmoved and unaffected by anything. In the end, they die angry, lonely, and bitter people."

She waited for a response, any response from Khavon. But there was none. Alayna shook her head and then slipped into her underwear. Khavon could see her dressing from out of the corner of his eyes. He watched her button the buttons of her white cotton blouse. He loved how she looked in that plain, white shirt. He loved how her hips flared out in the stone-washed blue jeans that she generally wore with it. Alayna grabbed her purse and he watched her walk towards the door. She was just about to walk through it, when she heard his reluctant voice.

"I met Cassandra when I was a student at MIT . . . ."

Lifting her head, Alayna halted her determined stride.

"She was a beautiful girl," Khavon said, pausing for a moment. "I just wasn't in love with her." Khavon began to recount the rest of his story. She turned slowly and returned to the bed, taking a seat next to him. Alayna listened quietly, refusing to interrupt, as he recalled the painful details of his circumstantial union and the disaster that followed.

"Oh, Khavon, I had no idea," Alayna said, when he'd finished recounting it.

"I'm surprised you hadn't heard about it. It was all over the news," Khavon said, blinking away the emotion.

Alayna nodded her head. "I do vaguely remember something about the murder of a local musician. But I hardly ever watch the news. It's just too depressing."

"There's more," Khavon said, simply, convincing himself that he'd come too far not to tell the whole story.

There's more. How could there be more to this horrible story? Alayna thought as Khavon continued.

"A few months after the divorce was finalized, I started experiencing some lower abdominal pain from the stress, so I went to see Dr. Fenceroy. He's been our family practitioner for years," Khavon said, recalling grimly, as if it were yesterday . . . .

"Khavon, Khavon, it's good to see you." Dr. Fenceroy grabbed Khavon's hand and shook it vigorously. "It's been a while since you've been in."

"No offense or anything, but I try my best to stay away from you guys," Khavon said, attempting to smile. It had been a trying year.

Dr. Fenceroy laughed out loud. "So what brings you in today?"

"Well, it's just that I've been having these stomach pains. I think I may be developing an ulcer or something from all of the stress I've been under lately," Khavon had said.

Dr. Fenceroy's face grew grave. "Yes, I've been watching the news. I'm sorry, Khavon. It must be really awful for you and your family."

"Yeah, it's been really tough, especially so soon after losing the baby and all."

The doctor emphatically placed his hand on Khavon's shoulders expressing concern. "You sound like you're having second thoughts."

"Well, no. I'm not having second thoughts. Divorce was the only option. I had no choice, really."

"No, I mean second thoughts about the baby," the doctor clarified.

Khavon turned to the doctor, his face a mask of confusion. "What do you mean, second thoughts about the baby? There was nothing we could do about it. Accidents happen. I mean, after Cass fell down the stairs . . . ." The doctor looked at him strangely. Khavon stopped when he noticed the doctor's face go dark.

"I'm sorry, Khavon. I thought you knew. Cassandra told me that you'd approved, but that you were out of town on business and would be for the next few weeks. That's why I went ahead with the procedure without your signed authorization."

"What the hell are you talking about? Cass had a miscarriage."

"Khavon, I'm sorry. I thought you knew. Cassandra came to me and requested a termination. I had no reason to—" The doctor stopped. "Khavon, I'm sorry."

"I . . . I was out of town, but only for a couple of days. When I got back, Cassandra told me that she'd fallen down the stairs and lost the . . . " Khavon's voice cracked, "lost the baby."

The doctor stared at him helplessly. "I'm sorry, Khavon."

A tear fell out of the corner of Khavon's eye. Even though it had all happened years ago, the memories were all too fresh.

"Oh, Khavon. Honey, that's awful." Alayna laid down beside him, bringing his head to her chest. "Honey, I don't know what to say," she confessed, softly.

"There's nothing to say," Khavon reassured her. And he was right. There was nothing to say, at least for the moment. So she made no attempt. Instead, she silently held him close into the morning hours.

The story was awful. But eventually, Khavon would change his mind, Alayna thought. He had to. And she was going to help him. She was going to help him change his mind if it was the last thing she did.

Chapter Twenty-Eight

"Alayna, what time does your plane leave?" Sheila asked, watching Alayna tuck a few last minute items into her travel bag. Khavon had told her to pack light and adopt a student's style. "What time are you supposed to get there?"

"12:25 tomorrow afternoon."

"That's fifteen hours!" Sheila exclaimed. "Do you have a layover or something?"

Alayna shook her head. "No, it's direct and it's only a seven hour flight. You're forgetting that Amsterdam is eight hours ahead of us. When we get there, it will already be tomorrow afternoon, whereas here, it will be early in the morning—just 4:30 to be exact.

"Anyway girl, thanks for braiding my hair, because I sure didn't want to have to be bothered with it over there," Alayna said.

"Girl, it wasn't nothing. Just have some fun for me too."

"Okay, I'll try," Alayna said dryly.

"Alayna, girl, what's the matter with you? You're supposed to be excited. I know I would be. In a few hours you're going to be with your man, in a completely different country, experiencing a completely foreign culture."

"I am excited, Sheila. I guess I just have a lot on my mind." Alayna tried unsuccessfully to sound perky.

Sheila laughed and stood up from the bed. "Girl, you're my best friend, and I love you, but I guess I'll never understand you."

Alayna laughed. "What? What did I do?"

Sheila laughed and shook her head. "I gotta go."

The two friends hugged and walked together to the door.

"Have a great time, and, oh yeah, bring back some great information too." The two of them laughed.

"Bye, Sheila."

"Don't forget to send me a postcard," Sheila yelled from down the hall and then disappeared behind the corner.

I'd better hurry up, Alayna thought. Khavon would be there any minute. She threw a few extra pairs of panties in the elongated nylon travel bag that was resting on her bed. Satisfied that she hadn't forgotten anything, she zipped the bag up securely, and carried it to the front room. Keeping an eye out for Khavon, she separated the window blinds with her fingers. Her eyes searched the front and intersecting streets for his black Navigator, but it was nowhere in sight. She checked her watch, and contemplated what she would say when he did arrive.

Grabbing a tourist magazine from her carry-on bag, she took a seat on the couch and started flipping through the pages. She eyed the colorful and exciting pictures of Amsterdam in the magazine. She should be happy about going to Amsterdam—and she was, it was just that it was tempered by the conversation she'd had the night before with Khavon.

Like a summer thunderstorm in a cloudless, blue sky, the whole thing had come up quite unexpectantly, surfacing from out of nowhere. The timing had caught her off guard, yet despite the suddenness of it all, she could not truly say that it had come as a surprise. She could even go as far as to say that on some gut level, she'd actually expected it. And why shouldn't she? It was the story of her life, after all. Her life had been a temporal one, full of disappointments as long as she could remember. This was just another in a string of let downs. Another episode in the story of a little girl abandoned, who grew up to hope for the best but expect the worst. All she'd ever wanted was to be happy. It was such a simple word. It was simple, uncomplicated, and at the same time elusive, terribly elusive.

Happiness had eluded her all of her life, and now, when she'd finally managed a brief encounter, it was in danger of being snatched away from her again. After all of those years, she'd thought she'd prepared for this type of thing.

But she'd had no idea that Khavon felt so strongly about marriage and commitment. True, there was no question that commitment wasn't exactly on the top of Khavon's 'things to do' list, but for most men it never was.

In the beginning, she'd told herself that she'd convince him otherwise. But no, it had to be his decision she realized now. Still, what was she supposed to do now—turn her feelings off like they had been running out of a faucet? No. It was too late for that now. She was in love, and that was not going to change, marriage or no marriage. These few months with Khavon had been like no others in her life. He made her feel beautiful, sexy and smart. He made her heart beat and sing whenever he flashed his infectious smile. When they made love, he made her scream with a passion that only he could invoke. He made her happy, and she was not ready to give that up. She couldn't, even if she wanted to. Yes, she'd thought she'd prepared herself for this type of thing. She was wrong.

Thinking she'd heard a car pull up, she checked the window again. A car had pulled up, but it wasn't Khavon. Then she spotted the black Navigator turning the corner toward her house. She slipped her jacket over the bulky, generous sweatshirt that she was wearing. She looked down at the hiking boots that graced her feet. It wasn't exactly airport avant-garde, but Khavon had told her to dress like a student and to pack a similar wardrobe. Besides it was going to be a long flight. Grabbing her teal duffel bag and matching carry on, she locked the door and headed outside.

Khavon was just pulling up to the curb when she stepped outside. He put the car in park and jumped out to help her with her bag.

"Hi," Khavon said awkwardly, his hands lightly brushing against hers as he took the larger bag from her grip.

"Hi." Alayna's eyes met with his for a moment before hurrying away in a search of a different focus of attention. The concrete seemed as good as place as any.

"You shaved," Alayna commented, noticing his missing mustache right away. She didn't like it.

"I've been told I look younger without it. We need to fit in as much as possible. Did you want me to put that in the back, too?" Khavon gestured at the carry-on bag that she held in her other hand.

Alayna looked down. "Oh, yeah. Thanks." Alayna handed the bag to him and let herself into the waiting vehicle. The driver side door slammed simultaneously as the engine turned over.

Khavon pulled away and headed toward the freeway entrance. The silence was painfully awkward to both of their ears. They each began to speak at the same time. "About last night . . . ." They laughed at their coincidental word selection.

"Go ahead," Khavon said politely, forever the gentleman.

Alayna acknowledged and began her scripted and rehearsed monologue.

"Khavon, I appreciate you being straight up about all of this. I understand how you feel, I really do. And I can't blame you for feeling the way you do about marriage. At one time, marriage and commitment were very important to me, and they still are. But there's a difference between then and now. Back then, I wasn't in love with you. Now I am."

"Alayna . . . ."

"No. Let me finish. I also realize that tomorrow is promised to no one, and I've searched all of my life for love and now I have it. I've found what I was looking and praying for. And sometimes in life, things don't come wrapped neatly with bells and bows, the way you planned. Sure, I thought I wanted to get married and have kids, and the whole nine yards, but my life experience has taught me to be a realist. And the reality is that I love you, I'm happy, and that's all I need. And, believe it or not, I'm okay with that." Alayna turned to Khavon.

"Alayna, I love you, too." Khavon replied, without hesitation, checking his rearview mirror for cars. "And I know you well enough to know that you really believe in what you're saying, otherwise you wouldn't say it. But Alayna, you say that now, but I know eventually you'll start to resent our relationship and me," Khavon said, as soon as she'd finished. His voice trailed off. "And I couldn't stand that."

"I could never hate you, Khavon," Alayna said, quietly. "And you're right. I do really believe in what I'm saying. That's because it's true. Now it would be a different story if you had been leading me on and making promises that you couldn't keep, but you didn't do that. You've been pretty straight up with all of this from the beginning, and that's what makes the difference. Besides, there are lots of couples who choose to be together but who, for one reason or another, have decided that marriage is not a necessity, or even an option for them. I believe we fit into that category." Alayna paused, briefly. "Of course, our reason has more to do with you than me, but I am truly okay with that."

"Let me get this straight." Khavon checked his mirror again and changed into the airport exit lane. "We can just keep doing what we're doing, with no expectations?"

"Mm-hmm," Alayna agreed.

Intrigue lit up his face and then faded into a mask of confusion and doubt. "Are you sure about this, Alayna?"

"I've never been more sure about anything in all my life." She slid her hand over the inside of his thigh. Khavon felt a shiver go up his spine.

"Alright . . . you're gonna fool around and make me have an accident," Khavon laughed, feeling much better about the weight that had just been lifted from him.

"Okay, I'll leave you alone," Alayna joked.

Chapter Twenty-Nine

Wearing civilian clothes for the first time in more than eight years, Cassandra stepped out onto the snow-covered concrete steps, closed her eyes, and let the cool, crisp February air fill her lungs. The fluffy white flurries felt refreshing as they disappeared into her chocolate brown skin, but it was the sweet cherry blossom scent in the southern Virginia winds that she longed for. She was a long way from Virginia, though, and the life she'd once known with her father, her only family. After she was convicted, her father had disinherited her. Soon after, Khavon divorced her. Life as she knew it came to a screeching halt. Eventually, deep seeded resentment and fears of how she would take care of herself, if and when she got out of jail, began to consume her thoughts.

It was then that she decided to finish up her degree. That had the potential of solving one of her problems, but the other remained. She developed a relentless hatred for the man who was once her husband. Oddly, she felt that it was he who had betrayed her, instead of the other way around. Without question, it was her drug addiction that had caused her to hit rock bottom, but ultimately, she blamed Khavon for her drug addiction because he had never loved her.

Almost from the beginning, he had returned her sincere warm-hearted sentiments with simulated affections. Where she was intense and passionate, he was distant and indifferent. His actions were sedate and subtle, yet the message was ear-splittingly loud. He didn't love her. Never had and never would.

* * *

Alayna listened carefully to the flight attendant and then looked over her shoulder to count the number of seats to the closest exit. The plane was sparsely filled. She never liked flying, not really. She did it out of necessity, but she never liked it.

"You seem a little nervous," Khavon whispered, leaning over.

"Counting seats is a basic safety precaution," Alayna said, defensively.

"I know. But I'm not talking about counting seats. You just seem sort of tense."

"I don't like to fly."

Khavon covered her hand with his. "You know that I wouldn't let anything happen to you," Khavon reassured her.

"What can you do?" Alayna laughed. "You're just a helpless passenger with no control, just like me."

"Alayna, you're forever the optimist," Khavon shook his head, as the intercom began to crackle.

"Ladies and gentlemen," the pilot's voice was hoarse, but authoritative, "once again, we apologize for the delay. The wings have been de-iced, and we should be on our way in just a few moments. As you can see, there's a little bit of a queue on the runway, but it looks to be moving fairly quickly. We should be on our way in just a few minutes. Your patience is appreciated, and we would like to thank you again for choosing us." The intercom went silent.

"Now see, he's the man with the control," Alayna said. "And sometimes he doesn't even have control."

Khavon shook his head again.

The aircraft began backing away from the gate. "Alayna, relax. Everything is going to be fine." Khavon stopped the airline attendant that was making her way through the aisle. "Excuse me. Would you bring us a couple of pillows, please, and some blankets?"

"Sure. No problem. I'll be right back." She smiled.

"Thanks."

Khavon turned back to Alayna. "I used to be afraid to fly too, Alayna," Khavon admitted.

Alayna turned to him in astonishment. "I find that hard to believe."

"It's true."

"Well, you seem fine with it now." Alayna was curious.

"The only way to conquer your fear is to face it." Khavon looked her in the eye.

"What did you do?"

"Every Marine Corps recruit has to go through basic training. I was no exception. My drill instructor pushed me out of an airplane."

Alayna rolled her eyes up into her head. "Great."

Khavon chuckled deviously. "C'mon, Alayna. You're taking this much too seriously. Travel by air is the safest mode of transportation, much safer than your car," Khavon tried to reassure her.

"That may be true, but at least in your car you have some control. In an airplane you just sit and wait."

"Thank you," Khavon said, reaching for the blankets and pillows that the flight attendant returned with.

She smiled. "You're welcome."

Khavon positioned the pillows behind Alayna's head and back, and covered her lap with the two blankets.

"Thanks." Alayna felt a little bit better. "I'm glad you suggested that we leave a few days early. I think I need some rest and relaxation."

Khavon laughed. "I never heard anyone refer to Amsterdam as a place for rest and relaxation."

"What do you mean?"

"Well, Amsterdam can be kind of a wild and crazy place," Khavon said.

Alayna was about to ask another question, when her head was forced back into her seat by the acceleration of the plane. She gripped Khavon's arm so tightly that her knuckles turned white, and she promptly forgot what she was going to ask.

"A little bird told me that you were planning on leaving town," Cassandra spoke matter-of-factly into the telephone receiver. "I hope it wasn't going to be before you settled your accounts." She paused briefly. "I just came back from the bank and it seems I'm missing a deposit for few thousand dollars . . . fifty to be exact." She eyed the anonymous passersby through the thick phone booth glass.

"You're gonna get your money," the voice on the other end said.

"I know I'm gonna get my money! You don't have to tell me that! If you think that I told you all of Khavon's little secrets for nothing, you are sadly mistaken. Do the words *price tag* mean anything to you?"

A homeless man leaned on the glass. "Hey, lady! Can you spare a dollar?"

Cassandra shot him an icy glare that was so full of hatred that the man took off in the other direction.

"That's more like it. Yeah, I know where Minnehaha Falls are. I'll be there, and don't be late." Cassandra hung up the phone without another word.

Chapter Thirty

The flight was a fairly smooth one. After Khavon ordered her a couple of glasses of white wine, Alayna managed to sleep a good part of the way. They were not far from their destination when Khavon gently roused her from her sleep.

"C'mon," he said. "I want to show you something." He lead her toward the cockpit.

"Khavon, what are you doing? We can't go in there."

"Yes, we can. It's all been arranged," he said, opening the cockpit door.

Alayna's eyes grew wide as they took in the breathtakingly beautiful view of the black velvet sky above the earth. Sprinkled with twinkling white stars that seemed to make a path for them, the scene was like no other Alayna had ever seen. They stood there and watched the evening exchange hands with the dawn, via a spectrum of purple, blue, orange and yellow light. It was an awesome spectacle, Alayna recalled as they stood in line at customs.

"Khavon, how did you get the pilot to agree to let us watch the view in the cockpit? We could have been some kind of terrorists, for all they knew."

"Don't you remember what I told you Alayna?" Khavon asked rhetorically. "If you tell people what they want to hear, they'll give you anything you want."

"And what did you tell them?"

"That's not important. What's important is that if you tell people what they want to hear, they'll give you anything you want."

"I guess I'll have to remember that," Alayna said, wondering how many times he'd told her what she wanted to hear, in order to get what he wanted.

Khavon handed the customs officer his passport. "We need to go to the exchange. I believe some places take U.S. currency, but it's probably best that we convert some of our money into gulden."

"Gulden?"

"Dutch currency."

"Oh, I forgot about that. What's the exchange rate?" Alayna asked.

"Well, their monetary system is decimal, so it's very similar to ours. One U.S. dollar equals approximately two gulden," Khavon explained.

"Oh. I forgot to ask—do they speak English?"

"Sure, probably better than you and me. Their educational structure is such that they have to be fluent in at least three different languages."

"You're kidding!" Alayna was astounded.

"No, I'm not. C'mon, let's go." They picked up the bags and headed in the arrivals hall and Schiphol Plaza.

Trains were leaving Schiphol Plaza every fifteen minutes for Amsterdam. They boarded one, and twenty minutes later they were standing amidst a busy flux of people in the middle of Central Station.

"Now what?" Alayna asked, looking up at Khavon for some direction.

Khavon was studying the map of the city that he'd gotten from the tourist information center. It was then that Alayna noticed that the recorded message that had been playing over the loud speaker in different languages was now speaking in English.

"Please do not leave your bags unattended, as they may be stolen. Please keep all of your valuables in a secured location, as pick-pocketing is rampant. Please watch your belongings."

After listening to a string of warnings, Alayna gave Khavon, who was still studying the map, a consternating look. "What kind of place is this?" she asked.

Khavon looked at her. "The word uninhibited comes to

mind, maybe a little unconventional. But you'll like it. I promise. C'mon. Let's go." Khavon bent down, picked up his laptop and duffel bag, and headed toward the front doors of the train station, Alayna trudging behind.

After a string of winter wind chills well below zero, the cool forty-degree temperature felt to Alayna like a heat wave. Alayna and Khavon blended in well with the students and tourists, many of whom were heading to the left. For what reason, Alayna didn't know. They walked with the crowd past the young band that was playing out front. Alayna reached into her pocket for some change and threw it into the open guitar case.

"Don't you want to stop and listen for a moment?" Alayna asked, running to catch up with Khavon.

"No, we need to get to the hotel and get some rest and get settled first. A lot of people will be coming in for the conference." Khavon smiled a sly smile. "Believe me, there's a whole lot more to see in Amsterdam than that little band. C'mon."

A young man who was spying them overheard their conversation. "A hotel? Do you need a hotel? I know a nice one . . . . Follow me."

"No thanks, man," Khavon said. "C'mon." Khavon grabbed Alayna by the hand.

They followed the crowd across the bridge, past the sporadic line of artists, performers, florists, and sidewalk vendors.

"What river is this?" Alayna inquired about the water they were crossing over.

"It's not a river, it's a canal. Amsterdam is full of them. Later on, we can take a boat ride through them, if you want."

"Yes, I'd like that." Alayna smiled happily, squeezing his hand. She enjoyed the feel of his hand swallowing hers.

The two lovers departed from the right-bound stream of sightseers, and headed towards the narrow street to the left. The age-old architecture was so different from what Alayna was used to. Detailed and intricate, the rows of narrow houses lined the streets like soldiers.

Taking it all in, Alayna suddenly became embarrassed when

she realized that the columns of posts staked along the street had a strikingly phallic appearance.

"Khavon," Alayna stopped. "Is it just me or do these posts…?"

Khavon laughed a devious laugh, cutting her off. "I told you there was a lot to see in Amsterdam." Blushing, Alayna covered her face and shook her head.

They walked a few more blocks and turned the corner. The neighborhood became increasingly more run down with each block that they traveled. Compared to winter in Minnesota the weather was relatively mild, but still Alayna's nose was turning red.

"There! There it is!" Khavon pointed to the massive cathedral-like structure at the end of the block.

"That doesn't look like a hotel. It looks more like a church," Alayna commented.

"It is a church, or at least it was. Now the Paradiso is a theater where they hold music events and underground activities like the conference."

They stood staring at the ominous, ornate, three-story structure.

"Are we going in?" Alayna asked.

"No, I just wanted to see where it was so that we could find a hostel in the general vicinity," Khavon replied.

"A hostel?"

"Yeah. A hostel is sort of like a communal motel for students. You and I are going to stick out enough as it is. At least if we stay in a hostel, we have a better chance of blending in and establishing some credibility and trust."

Out of the corner of his eye, Khavon had been watching the approach from his left of a tall, dusty blonde-haired fellow wearing an oversized camouflaged jacket. He looked as though he'd stepped out of a 60's hippie movie.

"C'mon, Alayna." Khavon grabbed her hand.

"Hey, man, you wanna get high?"

Khavon turned to the man and answered. "No, man. We're just out for a walk."

They hurried around the corner.

"That's strange," Alayna said.

"Not really. Drugs are not illegal here, like they are in the States. As a result, they have something of a drug problem here."

"Mmph. I hear people on TV all the time claiming that the legalization of drugs will curtail addiction," Alayna commented as they walked.

"Well, I don't know about all of that, but what I do know is that this is Damrack Square," Khavon pointed to the open, square plaza to their right, "and in the summertime people from all across Holland and other places are lying around on the ground, passing around joints the size of cigars and getting high."

"You're kidding."

"No, I'm not. And if you walk anywhere near here, you will get a contact high because the smoke is so thick. So whether or not that's considered to be a problem is debatable. C'mon, we need to find a place to stay."

"Khavon we're not actually going to stay here, are we?" Alayna asked, peering around at the tiny, dingy room with her nosed turned up.

"I know it's not a four-star hotel," Khavon said, "but it's clean, and at least we have our own bathroom. Some of the other rooms have to share the one down the hall. And I've been in some real dives. Some have had standing water in the shower." Alayna looked aghast. "So believe me, there are worse places to stay in Amsterdam. Alayna, we really need to try to blend in."

"I know. You're right. I guess, you know, when you have a certain idea in your head about how something will be . . . it's kind of hard to get it out. It's really not that bad," Alayna said, looking around.

"No, it isn't. But let me see if I can make it better." Khavon pulled her into his arms and kissed the lids of her eyes ever-so-gently. He pulled her face away from him so that he could look into her dark eyes. "You have the most beautiful eyes, Alayna," he said, running his hand over her soft, braided tresses, bending down to kiss her smooth bare lips. She tasted to him like warm, sweet honey. His body responded immediately. They furiously undressed each other. It had only been a few days, but it felt as though it had been a lifetime since they'd been together. Alayna lay outstretched before him on the rickety old bed.

"You're incredible, you know that?" Khavon said, taking in the entire length of her fully nude body. Alayna smiled broadly.

"Come here, you." Khavon worked his way down the length of her neck to her breasts, taking her erect nipple in his mouth. He licked and suckled her breasts and caressed her hot spot until her body was in a creamy, erotic frenzy. Alayna guided his body to hers, and Khavon gently entered her secret place.

Pulling her leg close to him, Khavon grabbed the sole of her foot and began to pound into her at an accelerated rate.

"Oh, Khavon," Alayna moaned almost unintelligibly, feeling herself beginning to lose control. In a teasing mood, Khavon withdrew almost completely in response.

"Oh, Khavon, please, please." He kissed her deeply and plunged into her again.

Alayna came instantly and violently, on the spot, as if it had all been the realization of some sort of Alpine dream.

Reaching the mountaintop shortly after she, Khavon exploded too. Spent, he collapsed on top of her.

Alayna ran her hand over her head and kissed him on the forehead.

"Khavon, you make me so happy," she whispered in his ear.

Khavon gazed into her eyes. "Alayna, are you sure this is—"

"I'm absolutely sure," Alayna interrupted, anticipating the question before it was asked. "A marriage certificate is only a piece of paper. What's most important is love, and you've already given that to me. What more do I need?"

Still not fully convinced, Khavon kissed her, pulled her close, and went to sleep. Alayna soon followed.

Eyes still closed, Sheila rolled over and turned the alarm clock off. Seven o'clock already. She reluctantly opened the lid of her eye and let it collapse onto its partner. How could it be seven o'clock already? she wondered. It was still dark outside. She reached over to the other side of the bed and then withdrew her hand in disappointment. The cold empty spot next to her told her that Larry had decided to go into work again. She spied the time out of the corner of her eye. Seven-o-five. She'd better get up and get the girls ready for church. Yawning, she picked up the remote and powered on the TV.

"And Bob, while the police in St. Paul were looking into that homicide, police in Minneapolis are still investigating another. The authorities say that a woman found last night in Minnehaha Park has been identified as a recent release from Shakopee's women's correctional facility. Investigators are looking for a blonde man, approximately six feet tall, wearing a black leather jacket, who was seen in the area talking with the woman. The cause of death was a bullet wound to the head."

What is this world coming to? Sheila wondered. She wished she could just run away from it all. Alayna was so lucky.

Alayna and Khavon had been napping for just under two hours when an ear piercing shrill sounded from Khavon's jacket pocket waking them up. Khavon jumped out of bed and scooped up his jacket.

"What? What's going on? What is that?" Alayna asked, sleepily, rubbing her eyes.

"My beeper."

"Your beeper?"

"Yeah. Our boy is accessing our sting files."

"He is?" Alayna hopped out of bed, slipping on her robe.

"Yeah. I started thinking that maybe we had them hidden too deeply for him to find, so before we left I set up a phony id and logged it on twenty-four seven in the SDI account that we set up," Khavon said plugging in his laptop. "Then I programmed the computers at home to call me when he tried to access the files.

The two of them waited as the scratchy, high pitch of the modem connected them to the other side of the Atlantic seaboard. Their eyes were riveted on the screen, as they watched him read and copy fake memorandum and phony purchase orders. They continued to watch him rummage through tons of classified and non-classified documents, dumping one after the other.

"How's the trace going?" Alayna asked. Khavon clicked over to his tracing software. It's close, but we don't have it yet."

Khavon clicked over to check the trace again. The two of them stared at the screen and then each other.

"This can't be right," Khavon said, shaking his head.

Alayna curiously read from the screen. "DUT—Delft University of Technology? Never heard of it, have you?"

"Yeah." Khavon's face was pensive. "DUT is near the city of Rotterdam."

"Never heard of that either. Where is it?" Alayna wanted to know.

Khavon turned slowly, until their eyes locked. "Approximately forty miles from here."

Chapter Thirty-One

"What do you mean forty miles from here?" Alayna's voice was alarmed.

"I mean, whoever it is that's going through our files is here in Holland."

"But Khavon, how can that be . . . ? We were so sure it was someone inside."

"I don't know. Maybe this isn't the same guy."

"What's he doing now?" Alayna asked.

Khavon toggled over to the monitoring program again.

"He's gone. Logged out about thirty seconds ago."

"What are we gonna do now?" Alayna asked.

"There's nothing we can do except wait. I suppose we could go to Delft, but the dial-in port that I traced it to was one of hundreds. Anyone on campus could've been using it. No. I think our best bet is to wait until he tries to access our files again."

"But what if he doesn't?" Alayna's voice was concerned.

"Oh, he will. You can bet on that. It seems like this guy is into some sort of computer espionage. We had a whole slew of top secret files waiting for him to snatch up. He's only gone through probably a quarter of them. If he's really a spy, he'll be back for more. What I can't figure out is why he's here in the Netherlands." Khavon's contemplative features were mingled with confusion and intrigue. "C'mon. Get dressed. We might as well do some sightseeing," Khavon said.

"Yeah, and it's been a while since we had anything to eat," Alayna said, putting her hand to her stomach. "I'm starving."

"Where to first?" Alayna asked when they got outside.

"Well, it kind of depends on you. Like I told you before, there's lots to do in Amsterdam." Khavon tilted his head southward, toward the heart of the city.

"Let's head back towards Central Station. We can decide on the way." He cupped Alayna's hand in his. "We could go to a museum. They have sixty-two in this town. They have a cat museum, a bible museum, a sex museum..."

"You're kidding. A sex museum?" Alayna raised her eyebrows.

"Yeah. Practically anything you can think of, they have a museum for."

"Mmph."

"Or we could go to Anne Frank's house."

"That would be interesting to see, too," Alayna said, just as a savory aroma from the kiosk across the street caught her attention. Alayna read the words on the yellow canopy. "Pomme Frites."

"Dutch fries," Khavon answered her question before she could ask.

"Mm. Let's grab a snack to tide us over. I'm starved."

"Okay."

They crossed the cobblestone street and approached the vendor. Khavon asked the man for two frites and handed him three gulden.

The vendor handed them each their fries in a brown paper cup wrapped in a napkin.

"What's this?" Alayna asked the vendor when he handed her a small paper receptacle containing a creamy, white substance.

"Mayonnaise, ma'am."

"Mayonnaise?"

"Yes, ma'am."

"Do you have any ketchup?"

"You are a true American girl."

"Alayna," Khavon interrupted, "the Dutch don't eat ketchup on their fries, they eat mayonnaise. It's good. Try it."

Reluctantly, she did. "Mm. This is good," she said.

They continued to walk along the narrow cobblestone street.

"So, what else is there to do Amsterdam?" Alayna managed to ask in between bites.

"Hmm. What else is there to do in Amsterdam? Well, we said we were going to cruise the canals, and there's always the red light district. But it's a little early for that."

"What do you mean?"

"Well, it's a place where people go to experience the night life in Amsterdam. For some reason the word uninhibited comes to mind."

"Uninhibited.... Sounds like a euphemism to me." Alayna said.

"Well, you can judge for yourself tonight."

"Is that an invitation or a challenge?" Alayna teased, as the two of them strolled through the Victorian neighborhood.

"Both. But like I said, it's much too early for that now. I don't know if you'd be interested or not, but we could take in a tour of a diamond factory," Khavon said, his memory jogged by a family owned jewelry shop that they passed.

"Well, Mr. Brighton," Alayna said, tossing her empty cup into the trash, "that all sounds great, but right now my stomach is ready for some real food."

They found a quaint little place just off Kalverstraat, the city's busiest shopping street. Seated at the window at Khavon's request, they dined on fish and spinach salad. It was fun and interesting to people watch in a different country, Alayna thought, taking another sip from the most exquisite cup of cappuccino that she had ever tasted.

"So, have you decided?" Khavon asked, wiping his mouth, when they'd finished eating.

"You know, the diamond factory intrigues me for some reason. Why don't we take in a tour, then cruise the canals while it's still light, and then head over to the red light district? And then tomorrow after we register we can take in some of the museums."

Night fall had come and practically gone when they finally got back to their hotel room.

"I don't know about you, but I'm beat," Alayna mumbled taking off her shoes. She slipped off her jacket and lay back on the bed, parallel to the headboard.

"I'm just gonna rest my eyes for one minute, then I'm gonna get up and wash my face," she said, as her thickly lashed lids heavily came to a close.

Khavon came out of the bathroom and was smiling down on her, when suddenly her eyes flew open.

"I forgot, I was supposed to call Jhazmyne. I promised her I'd call when I arrived," Alayna said, pulling herself upright and reaching for the phone.

"You're obviously tired. Why don't you just wait until tomorrow, or rather later on today?" Khavon suggested.

"Well, she was pretty upset when I told her that I was leaving. She managed to convince herself that I wasn't coming back. So I promised that I would call. Besides she'll be in school by the time I wake up tomorrow."

Khavon shrugged his shoulders and got into the bed. "Good night."

"Good night," Alayna said, as she began dialing in her calling card number.

Registration for the clandestine international gathering didn't take long at all, Alayna thought, considering the number of people. Swarming with the multi-ethnic conglomeration of fiber optic fanatics, the first floor of the Paradiso had been packed when they first arrived. A cadent buzz of adventurous excitement permeated the room. Two thirty-somethings in the midst of a throng of adolescent hackers, computer vandals, virus writers, and electronic thieves, Alayna and Khavon should've stuck out like two brown thumbs; but both were in possession of some fairly good genes, and having prepared and dressed for the part, they managed to keep a relatively low profile.

As they made their way back through the crowd, Alayna and

Khavon could pick up bits and pieces of their conversations. The computer savvy exchanges ranged everywhere boastful stories of glamorized high security break-ins to the ethics of hacking.

After registration, they stopped at the Rijksmuseum. They were admiring the brilliant colors in Rembrandt's "Night Watch," when Khavon's beeper again sounded off loudly. Khavon pulled the pager from his pocket.

"Is it him again?" Alayna's eyes were wide.

"No. It's the office."

Alayna's brows creased. "The office?"

"Yeah. We need to get to a phone. They wouldn't page us way over here unless something was really wrong."

Barely breathing, Alayna stood at Khavon's side with her mouth open and her eyes riveted as Khavon slowly placed the receiver back into the handset. His face was broken.

"What? What is it?" Alayna's voice was panicked.

"Furi says that all the computers at Excelsior and Liberty are locked up, and no one can get in."

"What do you mean, locked up?" Alayna's eyes went wide.

"All of the monitors are flashing the torched image of a burning American flag, followed alternately by the lyrics to *The Star-Spangled Banner* and *America The Beautiful*. And no one can get in."

Alayna was incredulous. "All of them?"

"All of them." Khavon closed his eyes and nodded. "We need to get into the system to see what's going on." Khavon sounded worried.

They found a nearby library and made their way to the public terminals. Khavon had suggested that they may already be set up to access DAMEX, the Netherlands national network that connected computers together.

"It's sort of like TYMNET in the States," Khavon had told her. He was right. They logged in and eventually made the connection to the States.

"I can't get in!" Alayna tried to whisper, her voice panicked. The backdoor is locked!"

"I expected as much. He put in a patch to close the door. He knew we'd try to get in that way," Khavon said. "But I always put in at least two back doors—one for security emergencies, and one for me," Khavon stated confidently, as he continued to type in access to his secret entrance into the system.

Khavon continued his entry procedure and then stopped suddenly. He sat there stunned, staring wide-eyed into the side image of the wooden Trojan horse that practically took up the entire monitor screen, the words of reprisal emblazoned across its saddle. "Like a fine red wine, Wardens' revenge is aged and mellowed over time for just the right amount of sweetness."

"Khavon, what is it?" Alayna said, alarmed by the look on Khavon's face, getting up to take a look for herself.

"Khavon . . . what is this? The Wardens?" Alayna asked. "Isn't that some kind of cybergang?"

With no response, Khavon only stared blankly at the screen.

"Khavon! Snap out of it!" Alayna exclaimed.

Startled out of his apparent trance, Khavon closed his eyes and began to speak softly. "Back in the day when I was a hacker, I by happenstance discovered a plot by some hackers to detonate a computer bomb on the U.S. telephone system on Martin Luther King's birthday. When I realized the implications, I went in and diffused the bomb." Khavon was quiet for a moment. "I couldn't resist the temptation of leaving an encrypted signature. They weren't able to decode the signature, so they resorted to posting threats of retaliation on their bulletin board to whomever had done them in. Trojan was the ring leader. I don't understand how he could have traced it to me."

"I don't know, Khavon. And there are a lot of things I don't know, but what I do know is that we need to figure out something quick, because this is a diversion tactic. Something big is going down, and it's going down right now," Alayna said.

"You're right." Khavon closed his eyes, trying to think. "Using essentially the same code is . . . ." Khavon stopped midstream, his eyes opening up as he turned to the screen.

"What? What is it?" Alayna asked.

"I didn't use the same procedure this time," Khavon whispered, almost surprised himself.

"For what? Your backdoor?"

"Yes. Well, I did and I didn't."

"What's that supposed to mean?" Alayna asked, confused and frustrated.

"I used a modified version of the code," Khavon said.

"I don't understand."

"See, a couple of years ago when the internet started gaining so much popularity, it occurred to me that there could be an increased security threat, so, almost as an afterthought, I added a new piece of code to relay the opening of another backdoor in secret in case this one was ever locked up by an intruder."

Their eyes locked in excited anticipation, as the two of them leapt in front of Alayna's terminal. Khavon started typing furiously, as Alayna looked on. "This has got to work," Khavon said, pressing the Enter key.

Alayna crossed her fingers. They held their breath as the system went away for a few moments to think about it. Khavon didn't know how the new piece of code would react in the system. He'd tested it, but he knew that the real world was unpredictable. Seconds felt like minutes as they continued to watch the monitor for any sign of recognition. Alayna felt her heart jump into her throat when the system finally came alive again. Suddenly disillusioned, Alayna read the screen. "System Failure."

"No. No." Khavon's eyes lit up excitedly. "That's part of the sequence." As if there had been no system error, Khavon typed in his password just as the system had requested him to do. The system again responded with a message of system failure. Khavon ignored the error message and typed in his password again. All at once the system went blank. Ignoring the system's response, Khavon continued to knock at the door, typing in his secret password for the third and last time. "C'mon baby," Khavon mumbled. Suddenly coming to life again, the system ushered them in and escorted them directly to the main menu for Liberty's interoffice settlement accounts.

"Yeah!"

"Yes!"

Their palms connected together in an enthusiastic high five. The librarian at the desk peeped disapprovingly over her black rimmed glasses at them, and put her index finger to her lips, signaling them to keep it down.

"The first order of business is to get them back up and running," Alayna said. "Now that we're in, I can load the antidote files that I had in the system. They're immune to any viral infections. Let me drive."

"It's all yours," Khavon said, giving her the driver's seat.

"I think I've seen this one before," Alayna said. "From what you said Furi described on the phone, it sounds like a variation of the viral strain of the Liberty Bell virus. It's multi-partile, infecting both the boot records and the program files."

Alayna easily located the antidote files, made a few changes, and executed it on Liberty and Excelsior networks.

"It's taking," Alayna commented, watching the antidote replicate the cure throughout the systems.

"Good," Khavon said. "Now that you've taken care of the diversion, we need to find out what's really going on. Let's check out the incoming and outgoing transmissions first."

"I'm way ahead of you," Alayna said, returning to the main menu for interoffice settlement accounts.

"But Khavon, you and I both know that Liberty handles more than twenty billion dollars in bank transfers everyday. It's gonna take us forever to sort through all those transactions."

"We don't have a choice. It'll be days before the Federal Reserve asks for a settlement. Besides, if I know anything about this business, something will jump out at us."

They'd scanned through more than six screenfuls of what looked like normal transactions before Khavon's theory started to prove itself correct.

"Wait a minute," he stopped Alayna just before she hit the Enter key to go to the next screen. "Look at the transactions on lines seven, fourteen and twenty-one."

Alayna looked closely at the screen. "They're all for the same amount. So?"

"So they're all for $7,212, which is just a little bit less—"

"Less than the amount requiring notification of the authorities," Alayna said, suddenly understanding.

"And I saw similar transactions on the previous screens."

"And look," Alayna said, "they all have the same destination bank ID."

"Yeah. Go to the Federal Reserve ID table to see what bank that ID corresponds to. After we pinpoint the bank we can check to see if there are any outstanding uncleared suspense items." Alayna did as he said. "Check the international codes. If he's here in Holland, you can bet that he's looking to cash in at one here, too."

"There's a ten million dollar suspense item resulting from all of those transfers into a numbered account at the Central Bank of Holland. He's crazy if he thinks they're going to give him ten million dollars in cash without alerting the authorities," Alayna said.

"Yeah, but he's gotta convert the money and get the money out of the system somehow, because he knows a simple account transfer will just get electronically recovered like last time." Khavon furrowed his brow. "Let me drive," he said.

Alayna got up, letting him take her seat.

"We need to find out who that account belongs to. Maybe that will give us a clue," Khavon said.

"But Khavon, we don't have access to account information at the First Bank of Holland."

"You're right, we don't. Not yet, anyway." Khavon eyed her squarely, his eyes sparkling, before he turned his attention back to the computer. It didn't take him long to break down the security system at the De Elandstat Bank of Holland, as much of it was very similar to the one he'd replaced at Liberty.

It was locating the account number that gave him trouble. He'd searched through all the files listing personal accounts, and none of them matched the destination account in the transmissions from Liberty.

"I don't understand," Khavon said finally. "None of them match."

"Are you sure you checked all of them?" Alayna asked.

"Yeah, I'm sure. But I'm still coming up empty." Khavon was perplexed. So was Alayna.

"It has to be here," Alayna said.

"Maybe we got the wrong bank ID or the right ID and the

wrong bank," Khavon said.

"No. The bank IDs correspond to this bank. I double-checked it. Maybe we should look at commercial accounts," Alayna added, grappling for an answer.

"I guess it wouldn't hurt to take a look," Khavon said hesitantly, entering the command to bring up commercial accounts.

When he'd given the computer the command to search, he turned away from the screen, his eyes intensely bearing into thin air as if it held some invisible clue to this mystery. Suddenly, he did a double take. His mouth dropped open when the computer returned with a resounding beep and the results of it's search.

"There it is! Alayna, you're a genius!" Khavon exclaimed. "De Looier Diamond Brokerage House. Diamonds! That's it! That's how he's going to remove the money from the system," Khavon said, just as the librarian started to approach them. Catching her movement out of the corner of his eye, he glanced at the address on the screen and turned the machine off.

"C'mon, let's go."

"But, Khavon . . . ."

"Get your coat." He grabbed Alayna's hand with one hand and his own coat with the other. "We can talk outside."

Chapter Thirty-Two

"Diamonds are an excellent means of conversion," Khavon said, as they hurried across Museumplein to the brokerage house. "They're small, easily hidden, and that explains why he's in Amsterdam. It all fits together. I don't know why I didn't think of it before."

"And," Alayna added in understanding, "it's irreversible because if the brokerage house sells the diamonds to the thief, they have entered into a legitimate business transaction and will have a rightful claim to the money."

"Exactly. That's why we have to get to the brokerage house and the diamonds before he does."

They walked across the Amstel River, past the waterlooplein flea market.

"Hoof Straat is only a few blocks from here," Khavon said, as Alayna took in the colorful curiosities in the market from a distance. A slightly tarnished silver bell announced their arrival as Khavon opened the heavy oak door to the red, medieval style brick building.

A small man, with a ruddy complexion and black rimmed glasses that were too small for his face, came from the back office and greeted them.

"Good afternoon. Can I help you?"

Khavon spoke first. "Yes, I'd like to speak to managing director, please."

"I am Peter De Looier, the managing director," the man said simply. Khavon and Alayna exchanged glances.

"My name is Khavon Brighton, and this is my colleague, Alayna Alexander. We are U.S. computer security specialists working for Liberty National Bank."

"Liberty National Bank?" The man's eyebrows raised in concern.

"Do you have somewhere that we can talk?"

"Yes, of course." The man led them to an office in the back.

"We have reason to believe that this brokerage house has been targeted for the facilitation of an EFT wire transfer crime."

"What are you talking about?"

"Sir," Alayna interjected, "has anyone contacted you regarding the purchase of ten million dollars in diamonds?"

The man looked at her strangely. "Yes. I just closed the deal less than a half an hour ago."

"What do you mean you closed the deal?" Alayna asked, her eyes wide, her voice ringing with alarm.

"Alayna," Khavon said warningly.

"Well," the man started, "Friday afternoon a man came in and asked to see all the diamond gems that I had that were three to five carats in size. He said that he was looking to expand his business."

"What did the man look like?" Khavon asked.

"As I recall, he was tall, dark and well-dressed."

Confusion became evident over Alayna's and Khavon's faces.

"He told me that he wished to purchase all of them, and to expect payment via a wire transfer to our bank account on late Friday afternoon or Monday morning at the latest."

"Do you still have the diamonds?" Khavon asked, fearing the answer he already knew.

"No. The courier came here to pick them up a half an hour ago, which was odd. I figured that he must have been new at the job, because I had to explain that the diamonds had to be picked at airport customs."

"Wait a minute," Khavon said. "You mean it wasn't the same guy as before?"

"No. This guy was blonde, medium height, blue eyes."

"Thank you, sir. You've been a big help," Khavon said, standing up to leave.

"But my money—what about my money?"

"Your money is safe as far as the system is concerned. You have a rightful claim to the money." The man breathed a sigh of relief and escorted them to the front door.

"That's absolutely amazing," Alayna commented, marveling through the train window at the seemingly endless rows of early tulip blooms in the passing Dutch countryside. Her wide eyes traced the stark white blades of the revolving windmills that dotted the pink, yellow and red floral meadow.

"It is spectacular isn't it?" Khavon remarked.

"I wonder what they use them for."

"The windmills? An energy source. They used to have thousands of them in Holland, but after the advent of the steam engine, there was less of a need for them."

"But what do they use them for?"

"Grinding grain, controlling water, that sort of thing. Alayna—"

Alayna turned away from the window in response to the somber change in Khavon's tone.

"You know, I just can't get that image—"

"Tickets, please," a tall, slender man, wearing a conductor's hat interrupted.

Khavon reached into his pocket to retrieve the tickets, and handed them to the man.

"Thank you."

"You're welcome," Khavon said, and turned back to Alayna. "I just can't get that image of that burning American flag out of my mind. Something's been bothering me about it since I saw it." Alayna eyed him carefully. "Did you ever find out how Mark knew Mulcahy was going to Amsterdam?"

"No," she answered, "but I've been thinking about that too. And I've been thinking about your inside job theory and wondering why Mark was there that morning that we diffused the bomb on my PC."

"Mark was in the office?" Khavon asked, surprise in his voice.

"Yeah."

"Are you sure?"

"Of course I'm sure," Alayna said. "I saw him. I talked to him."

"Why didn't you tell me?" Khavon wanted to know.

"I don't know. I guess I just didn't really make the connection until De Looier said that the courier was a blonde man with blue eyes."

"Yeah, I think that's when it all came together for me too. Mark's our man," Khavon said.

Alayna nodded affirmatively.

"There's Schipol up ahead. You ready?"

Alayna nodded.

"Khavon, I really think we should have called the police," Alayna said when they entered the plaza at the airport.

"Alayna, I told you, if we call the police this thing could turn into some kind of international incident. We can't risk having this thing appear on the front page of the morning paper. You know as well as I that Liberty doesn't want any more bad publicity. It's not as if its image isn't already tarnished. The stock is down and some customers have already pulled their accounts, citing unsafe and unsound banking practices. Besides, if we call the police and what happens becomes public knowledge, not only are we exposing Liberty's vulnerabilities to other potential criminals, but we risk being sued."

"I know all of that, Khavon, but it's just that, well . . . we're out of our league. We don't know who Mark is working with or for. We don't have anything to protect ourselves . . . . He could have a gun," Alayna shrieked, beginning to panic.

Khavon made a quick assessment of their surroundings, and then pulled her aside into his arms.

"Look, baby, I know you're scared, but you have to trust me. I wouldn't let anyone hurt you. You believe that?"

Alayna nodded her head as Khavon wiped her tears with the pads of his thumbs.

"Good, because it's the truth. And don't worry. He's not going to have a gun because he'd never get through security with it. Besides, even if he did, he won't have time to access it. All we have to do is keep calm and execute just like we talked about on the train, okay?"

Alayna nodded again. "Okay. What if he doesn't have the diamonds with him?"

"Oh, he'll have them with him, alright. He wouldn't risk them below. Would you?"

"I guess not," Alayna admitted.

"Are you going to be okay?" Khavon asked.

"Yeah, mm-hmm. I'll be okay."

"Are you sure?"

"I'm sure."

Khavon lifted her face to his and kissed her lightly.

Schiphol Plaza was full of people. Everywhere. They were never going to find Mark in this crowd anyway, Alayna thought secretly, as they made their way to customs. How could they? The man was probably already on his way to Bimini or somewhere.

The two of them scouted the area like hawks, waiting and watching for Mark to show. He was nowhere in sight.

"Maybe we should check the departure hall," Alayna said.

"It's worth checking out, but it's a long shot. We have no idea where he's headed. Keep your eyes peeled around here, and I'm gonna take a look around in departures."

"But Khavon, what do I do if he shows up?"

"You don't do anything except keep out of sight. I won't be gone too long."

"But Khavon . . . ." Alayna shouted after him, but he was gone.

Twenty minutes went past before Khavon returned.

"Did you see anything?" Alayna asked on his approach.

"No . . . you?"

"No."

"You know, Alayna, I'm beginning to wonder if he took a train out of here in order to cover his tracks."

"Why do you think that?"

"Well, if I'm guessing right, he probably picked up the diamonds with a previously agreed upon secret access code. If he picked them up and then made a rail connection, he could travel all across Europe with no worry of customs. All he'd have to do is flash his passport."

"Well, I don't know about you, but if I'd just stolen ten million dollars, I'd be trying to get lost real quick," Alayna said.

"You have a point—but I'd also try to be as inconspicuous as I possibly could. Don't forget, he knows we're in Amsterdam."

"That's true, but that doesn't necessarily mean that he knows that we know he converted the money to diamonds, or even that we know that there's any money missing. He probably thinks we're still working on the antidote to the virus. And we probably would be if I hadn't seen a similar strain back when I was in school. That was a very mean and stubborn infection, meant to wreak havoc on the system and anyone who tried to stop it. I spent more than—"

"Wait a minute," Khavon interrupted, guiding her back behind a stone pillar with an outstretched arm. Alayna quieted immediately, as her eyes followed Khavon's line of sight.

"Look! It's Mark," Khavon said, peering from behind the pillar, into the crowd of people.

"That's him, all right," Alayna quietly agreed, feeling her adrenaline beginning to rise. They watched him cross Schiphol Plaza into Departure Hall One.

"I'd bet anything that the diamonds are in that black bag," Khavon said. "He must have picked them up earlier."

Under two pairs of very watchful eyes, after checking in, Mark proceeded to passport control.

Placing his garment bag on the floor beside him, Mark stopped briefly in front of the airport casino to read the airport monitor. It was then that Khavon turned to Alayna.

Alayna nodded. Khavon looked at her with concern.

"You're sure you're up to this?"

"Yeah. I'm okay."

"Okay. Remember, the timing has to be right, and remember what I told you," Khavon said.

They quickly made their way over to Mark. Khavon gave Alayna a slight nod of the head just before they reached him.

Disguising his voice with a heavy British accent, Khavon knocked over Mark's garment bag with his foot, while simultaneously extending an apology. A crude plan, but it was all they had, and it was enough. In an unguarded moment, Mark fell for the distraction and turned to the voice behind him. Seizing the opportunity, Alayna snatched the black bag from his unwary fingers.

Mark's reaction was swift, but not swift enough. Alayna gasped as he managed to catch the tail end of her jacket.

"Let me go!" she squealed, struggling to free herself before Khavon levered a hammer blow across Mark's upper arm.

Suddenly unrestrained, Alayna quickly started making her way through the crowd of onlookers. Her pace never slowed as she routinely watched her back for Mark's pursuit. She could see from a distance that Khavon had managed to get Mark into a tight chokehold. Clutching the bag tightly, adrenaline flowing, she was breathing hard when she turned back around, only to run smack into a six foot tall, human road block. Eyes wide with surprise, she gasped aloud. "Warren! What are you doing here?"

"I thought you were a smart girl, Alayna," Warren hissed, pulling a gun from his jacket. "Haven't you figured it out by now?" he spun around and jabbed the gun into her side, concealed from view. "You're coming with me," he said. "Do you think I invested all of this time and effort to have you and your computer geek boyfriend take my money away like it was nothing? Not a chance."

"Warren, I don't understand," Alayna said, her eyes wide with fear and confusion. "What are you talking about?"

"I told you I wanted to live the good life and that's what I'm going to do. It was the only reason I hooked up with you," he whispered cynically in her ear, as they walked out of the departure lounge.

"What?"

"Yeah. Did you think it was your charming personality or

your third-world good looks?" he sneered sarcastically. "No. You had the expertise that I needed to get to where I wanted. Unfortunately, I didn't realize that you were such an upstanding citizen until it was too late. We were a couple. So I moved on to Plan B. Mark was a lucky break. Not only was he willing and able, but we later found out that his sister was sharing a jail cell with your boyfriend's ex-wife. It was a match made in heaven, until the fool started moonlighting for the KGB. Idiot!"

Alayna stared at him incredulously out of the corner of her eye. He was like some kind of monster, not the Warren she knew and was recently planning to marry. Sure, he was a little mercenary, but . . . .

"Warren, I don't want the diamonds. Here you can have them." Alayna shoved the bag toward his hand.

"Oh, I'm taking the diamonds," he said, snatching the bag from her hand. "You don't have to worry about that. But I'm no fool. You're coming with me. A little insurance couldn't hurt at this point."

"But Warren—"

"Shut up! Just keep moving."

They were nearing the entrance for the shopping plaza when, over the screaming crowd, they heard a familiar voice of reckoning that stopped them in their tracks.

"Let her go, Warren! It's all over."

Warren turned slowly, the gun still at Alayna's side. Alayna's eyes went wide.

A cross between twisted betrayal and overwhelming shock came over Warren's features as he eyed Theodore Mulcahy and several other armed men pointing guns at him.

On edge, Khavon was at their side. "Warren, man, it's all over. Let her go."

Stunned and infuriated at the sudden realization that the man who had pretended to befriend him was actually an undercover agent with the FBI, Warren flew into a rage and jolted the trigger for the gun he was holding at Alayna's side. Alayna gave a blood-curdling scream, and fell into a crumpled heap on the floor. The diamonds scattered.

"Oh, my god! Alayna! No!" Khavon screamed leaping to Alayna's side. Khavon put Alayna's head on his lap. Warren, killed instantly, lay next to her. "Somebody get an ambulance! Alayna it's gonna be okay. It's gonna be okay," he told her, his eyes tearing as Alayna's blood continued to pool onto the floor.

Epilogue

Hands shoved into the wide, square pockets of the cashmere bathrobe that Alayna had given him for his birthday, Khavon stared blankly out the window. The sweet, comforting aroma of the cinnamon rolls rising in the oven wafted into the room, enveloping him in warmth. It was in sharp contrast to the scene on the other side of the window—a pearly white backdrop of frosty evergreens, ice-laden branches, and crystalline snow flakes. *Minnesota can be so beautiful when it wants to be.* The snowy cascade reminded him of that first weekend he'd spent together with Alayna. She had been so delicious, he recalled, lying there, naked under the paneled moonlight. It was a wonder how he'd been able to control himself. He had loved her so intensely, so deeply . . . still did.

It had been more than a year since Alayna had been shot, yet the image of her lying in a pool of blood was one that tormented and haunted him still. He was the one who had urged her to go forward with the whole thing. He had promised her that he wouldn't let anything happen to her. Many sleepless nights had followed that fateful day at Schiphol Airport, and this was one of them. But now, day was beginning to break and he could tell that the snow was starting to taper as he stood there watching the light emerge from under the layers of clouds. He wondered how he had made it through.

Out of the corner of his eye, he caught a glimpse of the painting hanging over the mantel, a southwestern depiction of the Buffalo Soldiers. Alayna had told him she thought that it would look good there. So he'd bought it. She was right. His eyes fell down to the mantle display, and the photographs that lined it. *A string of memories.* He focused in on the picture in the center. He and Alayna had stopped for cappuccino at a small coffee house just off Kalverstraat in Amsterdam. The waiter had offered to take their picture. Frozen in time, they smiled happily.

Over the scent of the rolls, the faint, haunting scent of her fragrance began once again to fill his senses. He took it in like air to a drowning man. Lost in her scent, he felt her long slender fingers slide under his arms, over his midsection and up onto his chest from behind. He closed his eyes and pleasured in the feel of her soft face cradled into his neck.

"Didn't anyone ever tell you that a girl could get into trouble sneaking up on her husband like that?" Khavon said, flirtatiously.

Alayna bit him lightly on the ear. "No, but I like the sound of it."

Her brown eyes glistening with blissful euphoria, she focused them straight ahead, taking in the winter panorama through the frosty frame of the front picture window.

"It really is beautiful, isn't it?" Alayna sighed, eyeing the frozen pines through the powdery downpour and spotting a doe on the wooded hill in the distance.

Khavon smiled a secret smile of satisfaction. *Took a while, but she finally came around.*

"Yes, it is, but not as beautiful as you."

Alayna released her grip as Khavon turned around, took her in his arms, and kissed her passionately. Then, tearing his lips from hers, he stopped momentarily. He took her face in his hands to tell her, at the beginning of this new day, what he had everyday since the shooting.

"Alayna, you are the best thing that has ever happened to me, and I will never forget that. I love you and I always will."

"I love you, too, honey." Alayna flashed her bright eyes at him. "C'mon, let's go upstairs."

They'd barely crawled under the covers when their bedroom door creaked. Their eyes darted to the doorway.

"Jhazmyne, honey what is it?" Alayna asked as she entered the room, clutching LuLu.

"There's a green monster in my room."

"Sweetheart, you must have had a bad dream again. There are no monsters in your room. We checked when we tucked you in last night, remember?" Khavon tried to reassure her.

"But there is! I saw it! Can I sleep with you?"

Alayna slid her hand off Khavon's rippled chest. "Sure, honey. C'mon."

"I'm glad you and Khavon adopted us," Jhazmyne said to Alayna, crawling into bed between them.

"I am too, sweetie. I am too."

Jhazmyne ran her hand over Alayna's now slightly bulging belly. "When your babies come out, are you sure that Isaiah and I won't have to go back to foster care?" Jhazmyne asked what had been on her mind for some time now.

"Positive. That's what adoption means," Alayna said. "Adoption means that now you have a permanent home and a permanent family."

"What does permanent mean?"

"Permanent means, always…all the time."

"Even when I'm bad?"

"Yup. Even when you're bad. And guess what?"

"What?"

"Remember that story that I read to you last night before you went to bed, where the handsome prince saved the beautiful princess and they rode away together on his white horse and lived happily ever after?"

"Yes, I remember," Jhazmyne nodded.

"Well, one day, one day when you're all grown up," Alayna said, glancing up at Khavon, whose twinkling eyes were smiling over at her, "a very nice boy with big brown eyes and an irresistible white smile will come to your house and ask you to marry him, and then you will have a family, a permanent family of your own. Isn't that right, Khavon?" Alayna asked with a coy smile.

Khavon smiled back. "That's right, Alayna. That's exactly right."

Dead Wrong

by Robert L. Iles

Sheriff Walker Whitlow must solve the murder of a beautiful young girl as he struggles to keep his job, his family, and his belief in himself.

ISBN 1-929613-15-6 $5.50 US/$7.50 Can

The Rhythm of Revenge

by Christine Spindler

D.I. Rick Terry sifts through a storm of suspicion when tap star Jessica Warner disappears. Devious secrets are revealed as Terry delves into the intimate lives of the dance troupe.

ISBN 1-929613-18-0 $5.99 US/$7.99 Can

Song of Innocence

by Margery Harkness Casares

From the moment she first sees Charles, Mignon San Marco knows he is her true love. Through the perils of the Napoleonic War, treachery, and other intrigues, they struggle to find their way together.

ISBN 1-929613-02-4 $6.50 US/$8.50 Can

Ask for these books at your local bookstore, or order them below

Mail to Avid Press, LLC 5470 Red Fox Drive Brighton MI 48114-9079, or fax to (503)210-6765

Please send me the books I have checked above.

☐ My check or money order (no CODs please) for $__________ is enclosed (please add $1.50 per order for postage and handling--Canadian residents add 7% GST). Make checks payable to Avid Press, LLC.

☐ Charge my VISA/MC

Acct#__________________ExpDate________.(please add postage and handling of $1.50 per order; Canadian residents add 7% GST).

For faster service visit our website at http://www.avidpress.com

Name:________________________________ Telephone:______________

Address:____

City, State, Zip___________________________ Email:______________